JIM MCTAGUE

Follow the Leader

This book was professionally typeset on Reedsy.
Find out more at reedsy.com

Special thanks to my dear wife Rachel for her tireless editing and to our friend and newspaper editor Lynn Hume for her feedback on early drafts of the novel.

Contents

1

True Confession

A humbled Martin Boundary knelt in a narrow wooden booth before a gauzy screen behind which sat an elderly father confessor and said "Bless me Father, for I have sinned. It has been a year since my last confession."

The penitent's broad shoulders were stooped. His shaggy, blond head was bowed. This was an uncommon posture for the cocky young man who generally stood straight as an Army officer, with shoulders squared and chiseled chin thrust forward, inviting confrontation. His huge, powerful hands, once terrible weapons in the ring, were at the moment clasped in prayer. His fierce blue eyes were filmed with tears. His deep voice quaked.

The priest was frail, thinned by old age, with frost-colored hair and milk-white hands that shook with palsy. The gauze partition gave him the appearance of an apparition.

"One year since your last confession!" The priest made a show of looking at his wrist watch. "Well, I guess I have all night, if you do. What brings you here?"

'Here' was the red-brick St. Matthew's Roman Catholic Cathedral on M Street in Washington, D.C. It was 11 a.m. on a sizzling Tuesday morning during the first week of August. The church was a few blocks from Boundary's office at the Washington Observer, the city's leading daily news operation.

Boundary cleared his throat. He looked down at his clasped hands. "I had an affair—a one-night stand. Last night. I'm married."

"Oh my, an awful betrayal," said the priest. He shook his head sadly.

"I love my wife, Father. I don't know what came over me. We had an argument. I stormed out. I went to a bar for a drink. I guess I have trouble controlling my temper."

"You guess?"

"OK, I have trouble with my temper," he snapped. "I went to the bar and drank a Templeton Rye."

"Good choice," said the priest.

"A beautiful woman sat on the bar stool next to me and she began to flirt. I enjoyed it. I played along. She looked like a movie star. But I had no intention of bang... going home with her.

"She said she knew me. Well, I didn't know her. She said she was going to give me the biggest exclusive of my career. I'm a journo. She works on the Hill for a big-wig senator. The promise of a scoop got my attention. I bought her a drink. Bought myself another. That second Templeton was a jolt—it knocked my legs right out from under me. I mean, I usually hold my liquor better than that. But all of the sudden the room started spinning in slow motion and my legs felt rubbery, like someone had landed a haymaker on my chin. You know what I mean?"

"I've never taken a haymaker on the chin, but I get your drift," said the priest.

2

"The woman offered to give me a lift home because I was in no condition to be let loose on the streets—and I accepted. I wanted to get home and lie down. That's the last thing I remember. When I woke up it was four in the morning and there I was, next to her in bed. I felt awful."

"Why, because you were hung over or because you couldn't remember screwing her?"

Boundary laughed. He could not restrain himself. He never expected such common, direct language from an old priest.

"No... because I had betrayed my wife." The quaver in his voice had become more pronounced. "I love her, and after 18 months of marriage I broke my vow. That's unbelievable. Jesus!"

"That's another sin—taking the Lord's name in vain."

"Sorry."

"Now, I'll grant you that breaking a wedding vow in 18 months is pretty fast; but it is by no means a world's record. Still, you nailed it when you called it an 'unbelievable' act."

Boundary broke down: "I know Father," he sobbed. He tried but could not stem the outpouring of emotion.

"It's a good thing Jesus came along when he did," said the priest. "He forgives you through me, by the way. This is one of His many gifts to us. We can move on and change, unburdened by our past imperfections. His is a brilliant idea. Go and sin no more. God-like, wouldn't you say? Jesus, our creator, had more than a passing knowledge of our human psychology, as well as more than a passing interest in the battle of good versus evil. Now is there anything else that you want to confess? This cannot have been your first sin all year."

Boundary shifted nervously on the kneeler, again.

"When I dressed to leave, I was angry. I asked the woman

3

how I got there and she laughed in my face. She said, 'You don't remember anything? I should write it all down for you. You were phenomenal.' Then she mentioned my wife. It turns out that they often run into one another on Capitol Hill. That's how she knew who I was. I threatened to kill her if she ever uttered a word about what happened. I really meant it."

"Good heavens, that's some temper! Have you ever killed anyone?" The priest was being facetious.

"In the boxing ring—by accident. I hit my opponent in the left temple; and he went down and never got up again. It was an amateur match, so we were both wearing head gear. But it turned out he had a brain aneurysm and the punch made it pop."

"How did you feel?"

"Like shi... crap. I gave up boxing. My heart went out of it. Seeing a guy die before my eyes like that! I work out at the bags, you know, just to stay in shape; but nothing more than that. I am learning to play golf, too, for the walking. Anything to keep me far from the fridge."

"Yet another sport that brings out the worst in a man," said the priest, with no hint of humor. "I myself have taken the Lord's name in vain on the links and have flung a club or three into the water hazard; so, I avoid golf as much as humanly possible for the sake of my immortal soul. I would focus on the speed bag, if I were you. That's only a suggestion, not part of your penance."

The priest said the words of absolution and assigned Boundary a week's worth of rosaries.

"Do you have a set of beads, young man?"

"I don't, Father."

"There's a box full of plastic rosaries by the front door of

4

the cathedral. Take one. They're a free gift from the Knights of Columbus."

The priest also advised Boundary to memorize the Ten Commandments, since he obviously had forgotten Number Seven. And he instructed him in the future to avoid bars in general and his beautiful seductress, in particular, if he was serious truly serious about saving his immortal soul.

"And maybe you should switch to light beer from Templeton Rye."

"That's a good suggestion," said Boundary.

"The afterlife is much closer than you think. You're a young man, but you really should live each day as if it were your last one. You never know. Check out your newspaper's obituary pages."

Boundary cleared his throat.

"Do you think I should tell my wife, Father?"

"Leaping lizards, no," said the priest. "Not if you want to stay married. But if the woman you sacked up with spills the beans, then in that case you've got to own up. Lying never will do. Lies are a tool of the devil and politicians. You do believe in Satan, don't you?"

"Yes."

"That's a good start," said the priest. "Most people today think the devil is a fairy tale; and they are beginning to think of God as a fairy tale as well. Pray to God for the sake of your soul. Keep forevermore true to your wife."

"I really do love her. I want our marriage to last."

However, Boundary had a gut feeling that all would not end well for him—that talk about him and the woman was going to find its way to Twyla. Gossip flowed through Washington, D.C., at the speed of light. Knowing everyone else's business was a way of life in the nation's capital. It was small-town U.S.A. writ large. You had to be plugged into the gossip circuit to be considered an insider. Gossip was currency; and spending it to bring someone down was a popular blood sport.

"I wish you the best, my son," said the priest. "So, does Jesus. He really does love you. Now go and sin no more."

Boundary blessed himself and left the cathedral, still terribly worried that Twyla would learn what he had done. He had unusual faith in his gut feelings—and they told him that the blond bombshell would destroy his marriage.

2

Murder

T he terrified woman batted her long eyelashes—her last line of defense. She was lying face up on the notorious 13th tee of the U.S. Congress Golf Club, a par five with a wicked dog-leg that traversed two ponds and ended on an elevated, kidney-shaped green 530-yards away. Only a handful of PGA pros had ever birdied there, a fact that obsessed her kidnapper but would not have interested her.

She was wrapped mummy-tight from her collarbone to her ankles in layers of gray duct tape and could not move her arms or her legs. The young woman batted her eyes like a truck-stop waitress angling for a bigger tip. She knew that her life was in danger. Her last hope was that her kidnapper would soften when he noticed her eye movements.

A strip of duct tape sealed her lips, barring her from crying out with the full force of her fear. Only her eyes could scream. The kidnapper looked down bemusedly at the frightened face, smiled malevolently, stooped over and punched a three-inch-long wooden tee through the tape that covered her lips. She jerked her head when the sharpened end of the tee pricked her upper lip.

"Hold the tee rigidly in your teeth, as though your life depended on it, because it does," he commanded.

She was a high-voltage beauty—a 25-year-old with corn-silk hair, apple cheeks, large sky-blue eyes, and full pink lips. She was five feet,ten inches of curves and bulges, all strategically placed by Mother Nature to drive men wild. She done that long enough to finance a lavish lifestyle, including a pair of deluxe residences—a Capitol Hill townhouse and a spacious, designer condo near tony Cleveland Park. Her list of conquests included several foreign ambassadors, half-a-dozen congressmen, innumerable lobbyists, two full colonels, a rear admiral, and several high-salaried athletes. Her kidnapper had paid her handsomely for blackmailing some of these persons. But he was miffed. She was seen consorting with a journalist. He had grilled her about the meeting. He had asked her if she betrayed him and his secrets.

She hadn't. She thought he might be trying to frighten her, to teach her a lesson. But she wasn't sure. She batted her eyes furiously.

Instead of arousing sympathy, the fluttering irritated the kidnapper. The eyelid movement disrupted his concentration.

"Stay perfectly still. Haven't you ever played?"

She shook her head "no."

"I said to stay still!" He added, "If you make me muff this shot, you will be sorry."

The kidnapper was trim, a rare bird in a society where obesity had become the norm. This deviation from caloric excess made him more frightening in the woman's mind. It connoted super-human determination. If the kidnapper had already decided to kill her then...oh God! She squeezed her eyes shut like a child trying to expel a goblin from a dark bedroom.

The golf course was located beside the Potomac River in Virginia, eight miles from the ivory dome of the Capital. It was 11:45 p.m. on a Wednesday in the first week of August. The course was one of the world's most exclusive play grounds. Only members of the Congress and select members of the city's elite—like powerful lobbyists and celebrity talking heads—were permitted to join the club. The initiation fee for congressmen was zero; and $1,000,000 for everyone else. A million bucks was a sizable chunk of change. Nevertheless, there was a two-year waiting list for non-congressmen.

Small wonder. Political deals worth billions of dollars were negotiated on the lush fairways. Votes on the floor of the House and the Senate often were a mere formality—the rubber-stamping agreements previously cut at the club.

A full moon illuminated the fairway with a creamy light, giving it the appearance of a movie set. A gentle westerly breeze cooled the air. Tiny tree frogs trilled from a nearby copse of crepe myrtle. A big fish splashed in a distant pond.

The kidnapper filled his lungs with the fresh evening air and then slowly exhaled, savoring it.

"What a gorgeous night," he said, gazing at the full moon. "Have you ever seen the heavens look more inviting?"

He slid a pig-skin golf glove onto his right hand. He reached into his right pocket, withdrew a new, bright-white golf ball, and carefully set it on the tee. He positioned himself parallel to the woman's head and carefully addressed the ball.

She wet her white shorts. She wondered, fearfully, if he would notice the stench through the duct tape and go into a rage.

He was lost in concentration, his eyes transfixed on the moonlit ball. He pulled the club back over his shoulder and flexed his knees.

Anticipating a blow, the frightened woman instinctively turned away her head, spilling the ball from the tee.

"Now look at what you have done," he sputtered. He smacked her hard on the cheek with his leather-gloved hand.

"Don't spoil my shot." He poked her in the ribs with the tip of his shoes.

He took another deep breath; then in order to relax himself, exhaled very softly, as if trying to bend a candle's tenuous flame without extinguishing it. When he concluded this bit of Zen, he looked back down at the terrorized woman and said softly, "Listen, this isn't all that difficult. Let's pretend that I'm William Tell and you are a gal with an apple on top of her head. You want William to make a perfect shot, don't you?"

She nodded and began to sob.

"Swallow those tears, girlie. I'm fast losing my patience. I must make a perfect shot while the moon is full. Never toy with a mad man and his obsessions." He laughed heartily at as his own cleverness.

He teed up the ball again. She was beautiful but aroused no sexual feelings in him. She was a means to an end, the total defeat of Senator Kent Cisco in the upcoming election. She also had played a dangerous game with a reporter, jeopardizing all of his political schemes. He had warned her before against freelancing. She had not listened.

The woman tensed every muscle in her body to stay perfectly still. Maybe if she cooperated, he would spare her. She closed her eyes and placed her thoughts elsewhere—on a sugary tropical beach by an azure sea.

The thin man carefully addressed the ball again. Then, with renewed determination, he brought the club back over his head and brought it down and forward with all of his force. His swing was masterful, the product of a lifetime of practice. From a distance, he looked just like one of the great players—a Woods or a Palmer.

Had not the frightened woman opened her eyes and jerked her head in the final instant, the club face would have struck the ball squarely and sent it on a low, whistling trajectory well down the middle of the fairway. Instead, he sliced the ball, tearing the tee from her lips as well, breaking her front teeth in the process. In the moonlight, he caught a glimpse of the ball veering sharply to the left. Seconds later, he heard a distant "ker-plunk." His ball had joined the fish in the water hazard.

"You never listen!" He banged the club on the ground again and again beside her head, as if he were trying to drive a spike deep into the earth. She felt the percussion running up her spine.

She responded with a flood of tears.

"Ok, let's both calm down and try this again."

He teed up another ball. The woman involuntarily swallowed the saliva that had been accumulating in her throat. The action slightly jerked her head. The ball rolled from the tee again.

The kidnapper bent over and peered directly into her frightened eyes.

"I am a patient man. One more time."

He stood up, flexed his knees, gritted his teeth, and addressed the side of her head with the wood. Then he brought the club head back over his shoulder.

"I changed my mind," he said. "I am not patient at all."

3

Call Waiting

Martin Boundary's desktop phone rang. He tried to ignore it. It was 2:00 a.m. on a Wednesday morning. The copy desk had just cleared his story for the front page of the morning edition. Ten people had been shot during a rap-music concert. Five of the victims were dead and three others were on life support.

Nailing down the facts of the story and then writing it had been exhausting. Boundary's sole desire was to go home and put his exhausted, 27-year-old bones into bed next to Twyla. He loved her more than anything—and feared he was going to lose her.

Boundary was standing by his cubicle, stretching his cramped muscles when the phone rang. After so many hours hunched over his computer keyboard, he felt like Quasimodo. The phone rang four times—and then kept ringing. Most callers hung up after four rings. Boundary looked at the phone's digital display. It was a 202-area code—Washington, D.C.

"Damn you, I've had enough," he barked at telephone. He picked it up and slammed it down. The process of reporting

12

and writing and editing his story had taken ten grueling hours. Boundary had badgered the cops, the medics, and the concert goers as he attempted to reconstruct the deadly shooting. Back at his desk, he had searched hundreds of databases for background information on the shooter and his victims. Then he painstakingly had pieced all of the disparate information into a compelling narrative. His lead was "Twenty bullets fired in five seconds a community concert by a gunman with a Glock in each hand left 5 people dead and three seriously wounded, early yesterday. Two of the victims were each killed by a single bullet to the head. They knew the shooter, a notorious drug dealer. The other victims just happened to be standing nearby, listening to the violence-strewn lyrics of the Sidewalk Kings."

Boundary considered the story his finest piece of reporting and writing in his journalistic career, until the Observer's crusty copy-desk editors got hold of it. They homogenized his masterpiece. They went at his adjectives with electronic machetes.

"We're a newspaper, not Vanity Fair," one of the copy editors had grumbled when Boundary objected to their butchery.

Another criticized his use of elongated sentences.

"You are trying our readers' attention spans," he snapped. "This is the 21st Century, not the 18th. Forget all that crap you read in college. Write short declarative sentences. Use simple words and few adjectives. Drop the modifying phrases! Pretend that words are money and that you are a miser!"

The copy desk chief asked him how he knew that the shooter was a drug dealer."

"The cops told me."

"How many cops?"

"A detective. Look, why would he lie?"

13

"Do you have any evidence that he sells drugs?" barked the editor.

Boundary admitted he did not, so the drug-dealer reference was crossed out and the word "alleged" was inserted before the words "gunman" and "shooter."

The end result was an example of what Boundary considered to be hack work. A writing algorithm easily could have produced the listless text. In a high-volume, explicative-laced rant, Boundary let the bemused gray heads on the copy desk know exactly how he felt about their "craftsmanship."

The editors, in language equally enriched with obscenities, told him to shut his trap. He was a rookie. He had lots to learn. If he wanted to write purple prose, then he should become a poet.

The defeated Boundary now wanted to walk his bruised ego out to the parking lot, mount his reproduction "Captain America" motorcycle, and speed away. But the phone began to ring again. The display showed the same number. Someone desperately wanted to reach him.

Human curiosity got the best of him. The call might be the story of a lifetime. He shouted out a four-letter word in protest of his news addiction as he lifted the receiver.

Before he could bark his last name, a strained voice inquired, "Martin?"

"Yes?"

"It's Carl—Carl DeSales. Listen, I have a scoop for you."

DeSales was a journalism professor at John Adams University, whose campus was in Foggy Bottom, not far from the White House. Boundary had not heard from DeSales in many months.

One of the capital's most recognizable persons, DeSales

was Tom-Thumb short in a metropolitan area overrun with exceptionally tall people. He drew further attention to himself for being a rare, unfiltered cigarette chain smoker.

"I'm not worried about stunting my growth," he'd quip to those who commented on his unhealthy habit.

As a fail-safe for his being mistaken for someone else, Mother Nature had given him an unusually prominent nose, which he proudly referred to it as his "de Gaulle," after the 20th-Century French general.

In journalistic circles, the mere mention of DeSales sparked controversy. He was a hero to the younger set like Boundary. The profession's gray heads, on the other hand, dismissed DeSales as a slanderer. As a magazine writer in the 1990s, De-Sales' prejudices strongly informed his reporting—something unheard of at the time. Critics dismissed his combative, self-referential style of news writing as an affront to a tradition of neutrality. Even so, his radical departure from the norm attracted a huge fan base.

"I'm very sorry if I'm interrupting you on deadline," said DeSales. "Something terrible may have happened to one of my students. I'm frantic."

"Shoot," said Boundary. He glanced at the clock on the wall and then at a small portrait of Twyla that occupied a corner of his desk. He loved her strawberry blond hair and the spray of freckles across the bridge of her nose.

"An exchange student from Holland named Cynthia Rootew-erke is missing. I suspect foul play."

"You've called the police?" Boundary asked. Boundary didn't see what this missing person case had to do with him. He wasn't a private eye.

"Of course, I have. The cops won't budge. She's not officially a missing person for 48 hours. Cynthia disappeared last night. I'm genuinely worried about her safety. So are her parents. They are asking the Dutch Embassy to intervene with the State Department."

"So, you want me to to get Chief Jackson off her big fat ass?"

Boundary had no love for the chief, Marguerite Jackson. In his opinion, she was inept, lazy, and probably corrupt.

"No. The reason I'm calling is because there's a highly explosive angle to this story. You're the only journalist I know who has the balls to handle it."

"You're making me blush, Carl," Boundary deadpanned. "What's the angle?"

"Cynthia was following a U.S. senator when she vanished."

This stirred Boundary's interest. The story could burnish his status at the politics-obsessed Observer. He flipped on a cheap Radio Shack taping system that he had rigged to his phone.

"There are 100 senators, Carl. Which one are we talking about?"

"Martin give me a minute to tell it my way, OK?"

"At least tell me why your student was following a senator," snapped Boundary. He wished that he had a cup of coffee.

"Rootewerke was taking part in a J-school right of initiation."

"Hazing?"

"Nothing of the sort. It's a useful exercise, Boundary—a hands-on introduction to our craft. Thirty-three incoming journalism students accompanied ten upperclassmen to the Capitol Rotunda for a special broadcast of Preston Ferguson's show, 'The Big Event.' The frosh were instructed by the older students to pick out one of the lawmakers and shadow him

16

or her for the remainder of the day. The assignment required some wiles because the students don't have press credentials. The savviest students just asked the lawmakers if they could tag along to get a glimpse of their busy lives."

"Then what?"

"The freshmen were instructed to rendezvous with us for dinner at The Eagle and the Lark."

Boundary knew the place. It was dark and smelled of stale beer. Interns and young congressional aids and journalists were the chief patrons. The bar had been operating since 1947. The booths, the bar, the bar stools, were all darkened oak. Boundary doubted that the bar ever had been upgraded.

"Once gathered, the freshman shared their experiences with us. The student with the most entertaining presentation receives a large, silver-colored, plastic loving cup. Everyone but Cynthia came back. She had been shadowing Senator Kent Cisco of North Carolina."

Boundary whistled. Cisco! The story was dynamite.

4

Hot Potato

Senate Majority Leader Kent Cisco was the most powerful politician on Capitol Hill. He ruled the Senate with an iron fist, backed by a solid Republican majority. Any president, regardless of party, who refused to horse-trade with Cisco accomplished zero. But the reason that Boundary had whistled owed to Cisco's explosive history. Another young woman—a member of his personal staff—had vanished nearly seven years ago under suspicious circumstances.

Cisco had been in an unusually tough re-election campaign. Susan Hastings, a 22-year-old working in his office, had told her mother during a phone call that she was going out for a run in Rock Creek Park. She never again was seen.

The police immediately assumed she had been murdered, owing to the discovery of her blood on the carpet of her Connecticut Avenue apartment. Cisco became their prime suspect after the girl's parents told DeSales that the married senator and Hastings had been lovers and that she was pregnant. Cisco had furiously denied any romantic involvement with Hastings. He claimed he was being set up by his political opponents. Nevertheless, the story DeSales wrote from the perspective of the parents created a sensation.

The city police grilled and hounded Cisco and his staff. They had searched his residence and forced him to submit to a DNA test-events that generated damaging headlines. In the meantime, posters of the plain-looking Hastings were posted around the city. There was a cash reward of $50,000 for any leads that would help solve the case.

Newspapers, magazines, cable, and bloggers shrilly chased the story for three months. DeSales, in his reports, was exceptionally aggressive, denouncing Cisco as a crazed killer. In one story, DeSales quoted "unnamed sources" who painted Cisco as a hot-tempered, foul-mouthed tyrant who frequently made unwanted sexual advances toward the women in his office.

Journalism is an echo chamber: Lesser luminaries imitated DeSales. The feeding frenzy intensified until an enterprising reporter at an audacious and obscure website called "The Daily Bugler" exposed Hasting's parents as serial filers of dubious injury lawsuits. Over the course of a decade, one or the other of them allegedly had slipped and fallen in dozens of department stores; had been sickened by food poisoning at multiple chain restaurants; had found shards of glass in food purchased at multiple national supermarkets; and had been bitten by bedbugs in top hotels. Every one of the "nuisance claims" had had settled out of court for an undisclosed amount of money.

Hastings parents threatened a $10 million libel suit against the Daily Bugler. Contemporaneously, the police announced that Cisco no longer a person of interest in Hasting's disappearance. Her doctor, they said, had examined Hastings the week prior to her disappearance and saw no signs of pregnancy.

DeSales left the Washington, D.C., bureau of his magazine in January of that year and in April reappeared as a staff reporter at an environmentalist newspaper in Berkeley, California. There, he quickly reinvented himself as the Woodward and Bernstein of the tree-hugging set, winning two consecutive Golden Root Awards and five-years later, a prestigious Sparkling Waters teaching fellowship at John Adams, where he taught environmental muckraking. Now, Cisco once again was in a tough re-election campaign election and DeSales was trotting out another missing woman.

Boundary was wary of the story because of the Cisco-DeSales nexus. The professor, for all Boundary knew, might be a serial fabricator of scandals. But then again, there was an actual missing coed.

Boundary knew that if he did not break the story then someone else would, stealing all of the glory. He was electrified until, in a darkly eureka moment, he remembered that Bernadette Kathleen Malone, his one-night stand, was Cisco's aide-de-camp. If he were to link Cisco to the disappearance of the Dutch student, then Malone might retaliate by blowing up his marriage. He was unwilling to risk this.

"I'm not sure this is a story for me. Capitol Hill is not my turf."

"Come on, Martin. This is a possible murder."

"She's gone from missing to dead? Give me a break, Carl. And how do you know for sure that she disappeared while following Cisco?"

"I've got a video clip from 'The Big Event' that shows her walking out of the rotunda right behind Cisco and his aides."

'Big Event' was Brit expat Ferguson's popular Sunday morn-

ing news program. Ferguson was a best-selling author of political gossip, a bon vivant, and an ego-maniac par excellence.
People in town hated him; yet they kissed his ass because of
his tele-power.

"A million things could have happened to her, Carl," said
Boundary. "She could have run off to Hollywood; or shacked
up with some AWOL Marine. Anyway, what the hell could
Cisco possibly tell you? How could he have known he was
being tailed by a college kid? Why in God's name would he
kill a strange woman in the middle of a re-election campaign?
None of it makes sense."

"Cisco is stone-walling me about Cynthia."

"You called him?" Boundary was incredulous.

"Of course, I called him. I have some responsibility for that
girl. All I asked for was his itinerary for the day so my students
could retrace Cynthia's steps and post flyers with her picture
along the route. Is that such a big deal? He should want to
help us find her. But instead, he screamed obscenities at me,
before hanging up."

"Was that a surprise, Carl? He probably thinks you cooked
up another disappearance to smear him. You have to admit
that the timing is highly coincidental. An election year! Can
you blame him?"

"Cisco's involved whether he likes it or not, Martin. He has
a moral obligation to help out before the trail goes cold."

"Are you sure that the girl was tailing Cisco?"

"Martin, each of the students took a photo of their target
and e-mailed it to an upperclassman. Cynthia snapped Cisco.
There's no question."

"Can you email me a copy of the picture?"

"I already did, Martin, along with a photo of Cynthia." A new email popped up on Boundary's computer screen with two jpeg files attached. He opened the first photo and there was Cisco on stage after Ferguson's Big Event taping had concluded. He looked like he was being badgered by three reporters, including the Observer's congressional correspondent, Malcolm Truitt. The other two journalists were Lenny Cooper, a chubby, 20-something blogger for a political website; and Ferguson.

The accompanying picture of Cynthia showed an unsmiling young woman with henna-colored, spiked hair, a silver nose ring, and a matching ring through her lower lip. 'She looks pretty tough,' Boundary thought.

"How about her cell phone? Have you tried calling it?"

"There's no answer."

"Tracking?"

"Her location finder is off."

"Wouldn't it be better to wait a day or two before you start screaming murder? She might show up. She doesn't look helpless to me."

"I can't chance it, Martin. It's a cruel world. If I had Cisco's itinerary, then I could send 30 students to canvass people living along the routes he traveled. But he won't do it. I called his flack, Lola Gutierrez. She won't cooperate either."

Boundary laughed. Lola had a reputation for having a short fuse. Reporters had nicknamed her "The Dragon Lady." Lola had more swear words at her command than any sailor in any navy. She also had the habit of abruptly ending a phone call when a journalist on the other end was in mid-sentence.

"It's no laughing matter. You have to understand something, Martin: Cisco is a psycho, plain and simple. He got away with murder once and thinks he can do it again. Can't you see the pattern. It's as plain as day.''

22

Boundary looked at the clock on the wall. DeSales' theory had more holes than Swiss cheese—the biggest hole being that there was no corpse. He should have told DeSales he had no interest. But then, how would it look to his editors if the girl turned up dead after he had punted the story away? He ought at least to run it by them.

"Look, Carl, there's not much I can do at this hour. It's already 3 a.m. I'll tell you what, I'll run this stuff by my editors first thing in the morning and let you know what happens."

"Just remember, Martin, Cynthia's most likely is in grave danger—if she's not dead already. Someone may have seen something. That's more than enough reason enough to get the story in the paper."

"Except that my editors are likely to argue that it's not our policy to write about missing persons until the cops officially rule that they're missing," challenged Boundary.

"Are you punting, Martin? I can give this story to Jeff Dwiggens at Bugler.com."

Boundary felt the missing-girl story slipping through his fingers. He should have let it go. But he didn't want to lose a scoop to another reporter.

"I'm not punting," Boundary replied. "But I don't have a lot of clout around here. I will go to my editors first thing tomorrow and run it by them. It's the best I can do."

"I knew I could count on you."

"You have to promise not to spill this to Dwiggens or to anyone else until I get back to you. I'm not going to stick my neck out for anything less than an exclusive."

"I'll give you until 10 a.m.," DeSales said. "Then it's Dwiggens' baby. I can't afford to wait. Rootewerke's life is at stake."

23

Boundary hung up the phone. A headline about a missing Dutch girl had visceral appeal. He looked at the clock: 3:05 a.m. He had to be back in the office by 9 a.m., but he felt compelled to do some sleuthing.

Boundary knew that Cisco lived in a townhouse on a short, narrow street somewhere behind Union Station. He wondered if the senator had walked home the previous evening or had gone somewhere to eat instead. Union Station had dozens of restaurants. If Rootewerke had disappeared inside the massive building, then that would shed an entirely different light on the story. A lot of rum characters hung out there.

Boundary decided to phone Cisco's flack, Gutierrez, to see if she knew where Cisco had gone. If he could squash the Cisco angle then he'd be able to take the story for himself. For this, however, he needed her home phone number. He had a good idea where he might find it. He strolled casually across the nearly empty newsroom toward the windows where star political reporter Malcolm Truitt's oversized workstation was located. Boundary was taking a big risk. Journo's were not allowed to rifle through the desks of their colleagues. If anyone saw, he might end up getting fired.

"Don't be an idiot," he said to himself. But he did not listen to that sage advice.

5

Cat Bungler

Boundary moved catlike into Truitt's cubicle. He slid down in the older reporter's high-backed, red leather swivel chair—an antique from a bank president's office—to become invisible behind the gray, cloth-clad partitions. There was no turning back. He sat still and listened. The only sound came from the janitor, vacuuming the carpet on the opposite side of the massive newsroom. The janitor was wearing headphones and looking down at the floor.

The three sides of Truitt's cubicle were decorated with portraits of Truitt with powerful politicians, going back decades. A youthful Truitt shook Ronald Reagan's hand in one picture and a middle-aged Truitt clapped Donald Trump on the back in another. The overall effect of the "shrine" was that a journalistic eminence grise occupied the space.

Boundary couldn't fathom why members of congress universally liked the thin, dour-faced, straw-haired reporter—but they did, showing their affection by leaking him one big story after another. The Observer's editors appreciated his worth and pampered him. His stories generated online clicks, which in turn, generated ads. Truitt was pure gold in an era of declining newspaper revenues.

"Neat as a matron's vanity table," Boundary muttered as scanned Truitt's desk top. Every scrap of paper had its proper place. Truitt had a retinue of pen holders and paper-clip bowls, paper spikes and binders, as well as an oak caddy for scissors, a stapler, and gold-embossed envelopes and writing paper. He kept a stack of new notebooks next to his phone and a leather-bound desk diary next to his computer. Stack trays loomed like miniature skyscrapers on the far end of the desk; and in the right corner stood, in stark contrast to the utilitarian skyline, a lovely oriental vase held a huge sunflower, a Martha Stewart-like touch.

Boundary was intrigued by the older journalist's extreme orderliness. His own desk was the typical newsman's ocean of clutter—a miniature land fill with paper heaps and precariously tilted piles of manila folders. An experienced geologist would have comprehended the system with each stratum of paper representing a particular news cycle. Dig down and then tunnel horizontally across Boundary's desk and one could discover exactly what he had been up to several weeks earlier. Truitt's desk, on the other hand, could have graced the pages of Architectural Digest. Boundary had to be careful before he searched for the phone number. Truitt would notice if any item was out-of-place. Boundary took a photo of the desktop with his phone's camera to make certain to leave it exactly as he had found it.

Truitt's colossus of a Rolodex especially fascinated Boundary. Without a doubt, it was the largest model of that ancient, paper-based, storage system Boundary ever had seen, reminding him of the giant Ferris wheel at the Texas State Fair.

Boundary eyed the contraption carefully before touching it.

Truitt was famously paranoid, known for lacing his private space with booby traps like a secret agent. Boundary antici-pated a snare of some sort, like the strand of hair affixed to the wheel. Careful scrutiny found no hairs; but the W's were at the apex of the Rolodex. He'd have to carefully restore it to that position after he found a card for Gutierrez. He also noticed a stray paperclip propped up against one side of the contraption's base. How unlike Truitt to countenance a stray paperclip. He photographed the clip.

Comfortable that he had spotted all of Truitt's traps, Bound-ary spun the bulky Rolodex to the 'G' listings. The wheel squeaked. The janitor switched off his vacuum. Boundary peered over the top of the cubicle at him. The man removed his head phones and cocked his ear and began to walk towards Truitt's cube. Then, he abruptly stopped, shook his head, and switched the vacuum on again. Boundary remained still as a mouse until the man moved farther away. When the coast was clear, he thumbed carefully through Truitt's index cards until he found the one he was after.

Boundary scribbled Lola's number down in his notebook and left the desk as he had found it.

He peered cautiously over the cubicle partition, glanced furtively around the newsroom and, while the janitor had his back turned, scurried back to his own cubicle. He sat down and stared at the number, debating whether to wake Lola or to wait until morning. Better to wait, he decided. Then, on impulse, he picked up the handset and dialed. "You're a damned idiot," he muttered as her phone rang.

6

Twyla's Two Cents

Boundary eased himself into bed next to Twyla. She was snoring like a saw mill at peak production. He smiled. He thought it humorous that such a tiny body could produce such a large sound.

The steel springs of the maple-frame bed, a hand-me-down from her parents, squeaked as he turned on his side. Twyla's eyelids popped open. She looked at the LCD display on the alarm clock—4 a.m.

"If I didn't know you better, Martin, I'd say that you'd been out tom-catting. Give me a big kiss."

He wrapped his arms around her passionately. He loved her more than anyone. She was smart and beautiful, with strawberry blond hair, eyes as deep green as emeralds, and that delightful spray of fine freckles across the bridge of her nose. He was afraid of losing her, because of Malone. He kissed her again and again.

"Give me another kiss," she demanded. They kissed and kissed; and it soon became apparent to a physically exhausted Martin Boundary that Twyla desired more than just kisses. Though dog tired, he mustered the energy to oblige her.

28

Afterward, she propped up her head on her elbow and asked, "What have you been up to, Martin? It's nearly wake-up time?"

He snapped on the light. He told her about Rootewerke. Twyla's eyes looked big as silver dollars when he revealed the Cisco connection.

"Wait until Big Barney gets wind of this! He's been down on Cisco recently."

Twyla was the deputy counsel for tax policy for Big Barney, the volcanic Democrat from Pennsylvania who was Speaker of the House. She met with him daily. Since revenue bills began in the House, she kept him appraised of the possible impacts of bills in various stages before several subcommittees.

Boundary knew that Big Barney would not hear the news from Twyla. The couple had a strict agreement: no information exchanged inside their home would be repeated outside of it. But Boundary had been in Washington long enough to know that no secret would hold for long. Gossip was the Capital's most valuable crypto-currency, the means to access and influence. Any gossip about a big-wig like Cisco was pure gold. Someone in the know—perhaps DeSales or one of his students or a cop on the beat—would want to cash in on the knowledge. Big Barney would be privy to the story within hours.

Boundary then told Twyla about his call to Lola, Cisco's notorious "Dragon Lady."

"You're going to take some heat, Martin," Twyla laughed. "You should at least have waited until dawn."

"I know! I know!" he said ruefully. He tried to make light of it: "I prefer Lola when she's groggy."

"Lola was a pussy cat?" asked Twyla.

"I never said that. Lola was half asleep, but still managed to tear my head off. She called me a newspaper lowlife out to make a name for myself by smearing her boss. I am paraphrasing to spare your delicate ears. That woman can out-swear our armed forces. She uttered some imaginative pairings of obscene words involving various and sundry members of my family tree, all the way back to my great granddad."

"You don't have to tell me, Martin!" said Twyla. "I've had run-ins with her. Cisco uses her as an attack dog whenever he's pissed off at someone. What a keening comes from her!" she added in a mock Irish brogue, "A shriller banshee there never was!"

Boundary told Twyla that when he politely asked Lola about Cisco's route home and the press aide screamed that the senator was entitled to a personal life.

Lola had added with menace, "How would you like your personal life poked and probed and then broadcast, Mr. Reporter?" He left this part out of his story. Lola had shaken him. Boundary wondered if Malone had spilled the beans to her.

"Lola added that DeSales was a son of a syphilitic whore who ought to be fired for turning his aspiring journalists into peeping Toms and paparazzi. She said I should write about that.

"She has a point about DeSales, Martin," said Twyla. "He is sleazy. He gives me the creeps."

"He's not that bad, just intense," said Boundary.

"The stalking game—I have to agree with Lola—it's perverse given these kids enrolled as journalism students."

Twyla suggested to Boundary that if his editors complained about his pre-dawn phone call to Lola, then he should tell them he planned to write about DeSales' weird student-

30

initiation ritual.

"That's a good strategy," he said, fluffing his pillow. Twyla was like a chess player, always thinking two or three moves ahead of everyone else. She had to be quick and nimble to survive in the back-stabbing culture of Capitol Hill. She also was a sharper judge of human nature than he was. Add in her scientific reasoning, and one might conclude that she would have made the better investigative reporter.

"I have to get the missing girl angle into the second paragraph, at a minimum, though," said Boundary. Thinking out loud was a quirky habit. At times he blurted out something, as if he had been conversing with Twyla all along. She was used to it.

Twyla propped her head up on hand. Boundary noted firm bicep, a product of weight training and kickboxing. She had won several kickboxing tournaments. She loved the blazing-fast action and the release of anger. It was an antidote to her day job.

"You don't seriously think Cisco kidnapped her, do you Martin? He's in the middle of a tough re-election campaign. Even assuming he's a cold-hearted killer, why would he risk it? Something about this story stinks."

Boundary answered her with a loud snore. Twyla poked him in the ribs with her fist. He did not stir. She laughed and kissed him on the cheek. She adored her big man. She reached over him, switched off the table lamp, and fell back to sleep.

7

Busted

The following morning, Martin Boundary rolled into the newsroom looking like someone who hadn't slept much. In fact, he hadn't slept much. He had logged a mere three hours before the alarm clock roused him from the slumber of the sepulcher.

There had been no time nor any inclination for his five-mile run that morning. He had breakfasted on toast and coffee with Twyla, showered, and dressed himself in the tan poplin suit and white shirt and Kennesaw green tie he had left on the floor at the foot of the bed the night before. He slipped his sockless feet into a pair of penny loafers. Then he had dashed down to the basement garage and roared down the alley on Captain America, his high-handlebar chopper.

Once settled in his cubicle, Boundary began his daily ritual of calling metropolitan area police departments to see if anything big had happened overnight. Most of the news-the murders, assaults, and carjackings—ended up in a briefs column. If he discovered something more heinous, then he'd pitch it as a feature story and gather fresh material—reporters called it "fresh string." His harvest this morning was banal: a bullet-riddled body; a convenience store robbery; some bar fights; and a multi-vehicle beltway crash. He was pleased. He had time to work on the missing girl story.

Boundary looked like a lush. His eyes were bloodshot and his mop of blond hair was uncombed. He had forgotten to shave. Remembering to apply underarm deodorant would have been a nice touch. He was mulling how to pitch the story to City Editor Dan Fogarty, his immediate supervisor, when he was startled by a poke in the back He spun in his chair. Managing editor Kitty Crosse was scowling.

"Rooster wants to see you," she snapped.

"Me? What for?"

"You know damn well," she said.

Editor Rooster Radley's glass-walled office was at the front of the sprawling newsroom. Boundary stood and followed Kitty.

Lola must have complained. Boundary winced. He was in no shape for a tussle. He had a low-grade headache and an addict's craving for coffee. He tried focusing on Kitty's backside, which swung in a metronomic rhythm. She was about 40, he estimated. Hot.

Kitty had a whiskey voice, jet black hair with a single, loose strand of silver, and creamy skin. Sexier than women half her age, Kitty also was a no-nonsense editor. Her job was to ensure that every space in the paper was filled with flawless copy before it went either to the printing plant or online. She was Rooster's strong right hand.

Boundary noticed that Rooster's office blinds were raised. Rooster raised the blinds whenever he wanted to publicly discipline an employee. It was the Observer's equivalent of a flogging at the mast. Everyone in the newsroom would have a

33

bird's eye view of the drama as it unfolded before them like a silent film. Their own fears of dismissal by the famously volatile editor would heighten the tension.

"This is not the best way to start the day," Boundary muttered to himself. He had witnessed more senior employees dressed down by the truncheon-tongued Rooster in previous open-shade ceremonies. Because he was still new, it dawned on him that he might be fired on the spot. To grovel or not to grovel? That was the question.

As he approached the office, Boundary berated himself for having telephoned Lola. He had acted rashly, a bad habit of his.

"Oh, well, you can't un-spill the milk," he muttered as he squared his broad shoulders and stiffened his back and walked through the doorway.

Rooster was sitting behind his desk, gnawing on an unlit cigar. His face flushed crimson with the rust-colored hair that was the source of his nickname. Fogarty, who was half Irish and half Korean, and the epicene Malcolm Truitt were sitting side-by-side on a stuffed leather sofa. They were as stone-faced as a hanging jury.

Cross leaned against the back wall to the right of Rooster's desk and folded her arms across her chest.

"Did you want to see me, Chief?" Boundary asked with a boyish grin. Rooster was not charmed.

"Close the door, Boundary," he snapped.

Martin pushed the door shut and then took a seat in an armchair off to the right of Rooster's desk. He crossed his legs club-man style and nodded defiantly at Truitt.

Rooster scowled. He did not appreciate the young reporter's cockiness. He took a deep breath and was about to roar at

Boundary when Truitt suddenly jumped to his feet and began pacing back and forth like a prosecutor.

"Kitty and I each received a wake-up call this morning from a very angry Lola Gutierrez," said Truitt. "Now, how did you get Lola's unlisted home phone number, I wonder, since I am the only reporter in this organization who has it? There are size 12-and-a-half footprints in the talcum that I sprinkled on the floor by my desk last night before I left; but they could not belong to you, now could they? You wouldn't rifle a colleague's desk, would you?"

"I wear size 13.5," Boundary said.

The bottom of his exposed tan loafer showed traces of white powder. Fogarty laughed out loud when he saw it, quickly followed by an expletive. Boundary's cheeks turned pink when he realized he had a marked sole, and he quickly uncrossed his leg and lowered his foot.

Rooster spit his chewed-up cigar into a trash can, took a fresh one from a desktop humidor, and began violently chomping on it. He told Truitt to sit down and button up. Truitt dropped back down onto the couch like an obedient schoolboy. Then, Rooster snapped, "What's this crap about a missing college girl? Someone in the Democratic Party is playing you like a fiddle, Boundary. You ought to be more damned skeptical. Anyway, your beat is cops and robbers, not Capitol Hill. You should not have called that nasty bitc...Lola."

Boundary replied calmly that the missing girl had in fact been trailing Cisco. He told the editor in anthropological detail about the hazing ritual, adding that it would make a great story.

"Lola suggested it," he added.

It was an unfortunate coincidence that Cynthia Rootewerke

happened to be tailing Cisco, Boundary said, given the Senator's tragic history; but it didn't mean that the girl was any less missing.

"Save the bull, Boundary. I wasn't born yesterday," said Rooster.

Boundary went on offense. He had no choice.

"It's a hell of a feature—college kids enrolled in an elite journalism program tailing senators, like peeping Toms. One of them vanishes into thin air. That's why I called Lola. I was afraid I'd get beaten on this story by the *Times* or the *Journal*. At 3:30 a.m., there are no editors to give me direction, so I took the initiative. I guess I goofed. I thought initiative was a good thing. I'm really sorry. I apologize, Mr. Truitt, for taking liberties with your Rolodex. It's just that I hate getting scooped by the competition."

Rooster's face showed no sign of softening, and Truitt's face had hardened.

"Did this tip come from Carl DeSales?" Rooster asked.

Cross folded her arms more tightly at the sound of the name.

"Listen, Chief, the missing coed is from the Netherlands. Her parents and Professor DeSales are nervous wrecks. Naturally, I wanted to help. You know, a woman in distress."

"DeSales," hissed Truitt, "is a low life with zero credibility."

Rooster pointed a finger at the older journalist and commanded, "Zip it. I'm running this show."

The editor then turned his explicative-rich anger on Boundary and lectured him not to confuse the newspaper work with policing.

"We are neither effin cops nor an effin search and rescue team, nor are we the effin Knights of the Round Table! That creep DeSales stands to gain from accusing Cisco of another

36

murder, in the middle of an election campaign. Those stories DeSales wrote about the Hastings case during Cisco's last campaign were a disgrace. He gave journalism a big, black eye. How he ended up as a professor at a major university is a bigger mystery than the disappearance of one of his school girls if you ask me. You may be too young to know any of this, but DeSales tried and convicted Cisco in print with no hard evidence. It was a low point for him and the profession."

Boundary trotted out Twyla's argument.

"This disappearance is a legitimate part of a larger human-interest story, don't you see? A college kid from Holland disappears on her first full day in the U.S. Capitol, while trailing a Senator as part of a weird Peeping-Tom ritual. These are journalism students and they are being instructed to act like stalkers."

"We don't write a human-interest story every time someone doesn't show up for a meeting somewhere," said Rooster. "Pretty soon every publicity hound in town would be reporting himself missing. As for the J-school angle, it's lame."

"She could be on a drinking binge for all we know," said Cross. "She might have set off to see the Grand Canyon."

Truitt piped up that Cisco had an alibi.

"He was playing golf Sunday afternoon. He has witnesses. In fact, I'm one of them."

"Look, I made a preliminary call to Lola. It's what any reporter would have done."

Rooster shook his head. He wasn't buying any of it.

Boundary hunched his shoulders and lowered his head. Time to show remorse.

"Sorry, Chief. I was exhausted from that other murder story, and I had a lapse in judgement. It sounded like a great story at 2:30 a.m. DeSales threatened to take it to Dwiggens at Bugler.com. I didn't want us to be scooped."

"Stop calling me chief, Boundary! This is not the effin Daily Planet and you are not Jimmy Olsen. As for Dwiggens—his stuff is pure garbage. We compete with credible news organizations. Now, you are to drop this story, understand?" Rooster spit the mangled carcass of his new cigar into his trash can to underscore his point.

Boundary submissively showed the palms of his hands.

"If that's what you want."

Kitty cross leaned forward.

"You were fatigued and suffered a lapse in judgment because you wanted a scoop, Martin. I can appreciate that. I applaud your aggressiveness. But you have to learn to exercise good judgment under pressure. This missing girl story smells like unadulterated bullshit. Take my advice: Steer clear of DeSales."

Truitt smirked triumphantly and added, "Congress is my beat anyway, so keep your nose in the gutter where it belongs. And stay out of my cubicle."

Rooster shot Truitt another murderous glance. Truitt was a valuable reporter, but it didn't diminish Rooster's view that he basically was a snide, conniving, and possibly unethical son-of-a-bitch. Too many politicians leaked him too many stories too often for him to be 100 percent kosher. Members of Congress, in Rooster's estimation, were shakedown artists who always expected their favors to be repaid.

The smirk disappeared from Truitt's face.

Boundary shrugged. He was angry but didn't want to show it. Anyway, he had won. He had stuck his neck out and hadn't had his head lopped off. Rooster told him to go. He stood up, made a slight bow, and exited. He was greeted by a sea of curious eyes.

Boundary returned to his cubicle and immediately dialed DeSales to break the news.

"They'll regret this," DeSales groused. "Dwiggens will end up breaking the story and your paper will look damn silly when the girl is officially declared missing."

8

Golf Corpse

B oundary strode angrily into to the newsroom's galley-size kitchen and bought a cup of muddy coffee from the vending machine. Then, cup in hand, he returned to his cubicle to fume.

Some newsroom gossips stopped by, citing one pretense or another, hoping for a blow-by-blow account of Boundary's run-in with Rooster. They already knew that Boundary had violated Truitt's sacred space. One wondered if Boundary might have a pencil sharpener. "Saw you with Rooster. What was that about?"

Another asked Boundary if he had lunch plans. "I'd love to hear about your meeting."

There were half-a-dozen such inquiries within an hour.

Boundary gave all of the inquirers short shrift. The Observer newsroom was as fierce a jungle as you could find, with reporters competing unceasingly against one another, fang and claw, for prestige and power. There wasn't a trace of the Outward Bound-collegiality common at information-age companies. The reporters would turn his gossip against him, Martin thought to himself.

Boundary had promised to fill Twyla in. He picked up the handset on his desk phone. But before he could dial her number, it began to trill. He picked up the receiver.

"Boundary."

"Martin, it's Joe."

Joe lived in the row home next to the Boundarys. The former newspaperman had created a highly successful business specializing in taking crime-scene photos for the federal law enforcement agencies like the FBI, the ATF, and the DEA. Joe was forever jetting off to Chicago or New York or some other city to visually catalogue the aftermath of a gruesome murder or a mysterious burglary. He had the latest photographic equipment, including infrared and ultraviolet cameras and super-powerful lenses that could make a dust mite look as big as a Chihuahua.

Joe sounded out of breath.

"I have an important tip for you, Martin. The usual ground rules apply."

The rules were simple: Boundary had to confirm the tip using other sources; and Joe never would be mentioned or even alluded to in any story.

Boundary would never burn Joe—not in a million years. Not only was he a good friend, he was Boundary's most trusted source.

"OK, shoot," said Boundary.

"This morning, a groundskeeper at the U.S. Congress Golf Club found a female corpse buried in a sand trap. There's FBI crawling all over the place. No one is allowed through the main gate. If I were you, I'd check out the section of chain-link fence by the 7th tee off on Seminary Ridge Road. There's a utility gate with no razor wire. Neighborhood boys— including one of my nephews— sneak over it to play a sunrise round.

'Rootewerke!' thought Boundary. He took a deep breath. He wanted to hide his excitement. "What did she look like, Joe?"

"I don't know, Martin. I'm not on this— not yet anyway. An FBI buddy tipped me off. He said I might be needed later. I've loaded up my van just in case."

"Was she killed there?"

"Too soon to tell."

"Cause of death?" asked Boundary.

"I have no idea. I know this much: They found a golf club next to the body—an Ogden Titanium. That's a $5,600 Scottish-made club. Get over there as fast as you can. Better put on some pointy shoes. The fence is seven-feet high."

9

Scoop

Boundary left the office without a word to anyone and raced on his motorcycle to the country club, which was across the Potomac River in Virginia off the leafy George Washington Parkway between historic Old Town Alexandria and the Mount Vernon estate. Boundary covered the eight miles in just under 20 minutes, which was impressive, given the volume of traffic. He weaved the cycle through crawling automobiles with the precision of a downhill skier.

Boundary wanted to be the first journalist at the scene. A murder at a congressional playground was huge. Beyond huge. The story would attract a global audience. It could boost his career into high orbit. If the victim turned out to be Cynthia Rootewerke, then he'd have the added pleasure of watching his editors eat crow.

Boundary planned to sneak onto the course, take pictures, and text the scoop to Fogarty. He was pumped full of adrenaline. Few things excited Boundary more than the prospect of breaking a big story.

The front gate of the club was blocked by black Secret Service and FBI SUVs, just as Joe said it would be. Boundary counted 12 of them, plus an ambulance and an FBI crime scene van. There were some local police as well. The feds would lay claim to the crime scene because the club operated under a congressional charter. There were no television news vans there-at least not yet. For all Boundary knew, a convoy of them was on the way. He had to act quickly.

Boundary revved up his chopper and raced to the south side of the course, searching for the utility gate. The east side of the course was protected by a deep, muck-bottomed tidal pool.

He found the gate midway down Fort Haunt Boulevard, a heavily traveled two-lane road with townhouses opposite the golf course.

Boundary parked his bike on a strip of weeds between the roadway and fence, hanging his star-spangled helmet on the roll bar. When there were no cars in sight, he ran to the fence and climbed over it with the agility of a squirrel.

Boundary was attired in his linen suit and a blue, button-down shirt. He had loafers on his feet. He smoothed his necktie and sprinted across the course, using his smart phone's GPS to guide him to the 13th hole. It was a long hike, because the gap in the fence was close to the 7th tee.

No one was in sight, but he heard the murmur of voices over a rise that hid the 13th hole. He approached the hole like a commando, using trees and bushes to mask his advance. He could catch hell or even end up in jail for sneaking onto a crime scene. Boundary thought his caper well worth the risk. He knew in his gut that Cynthia Rootewerke lay buried in the sand trap and that Senator Kent Cisco was her killer.

A helicopter droned toward the course. Police or news? He had no way of telling. Boundary sprinted into a small copse of pine trees and crouched until it flew by. The letters FBI were stenciled on the copter's underbelly. On the other side of the trees, three men and a woman in business attire—probably FBI—buzzed past him in a golf cart. Boundary fully flattened himself on the ground cover of dried pine needles and avoided being seen.

He watched warily as the cart headed toward a sand trap, about 300 yards away. He carried a pair of opera-sized Zeiss binoculars for crime-scene situations like this. He trained the glasses on the trap and focused in. Yellow plastic tape hung on white plastic pickets around the kidney-shaped trap, which lay about 15 yards in front of the hole. The hole itself was at the top of an elevated, treacherously angled green that famously stymied many of the nation's best golfers. A player had to drive or chip his ball within inches of the hole to keep it from rolling into the sand hazard, which was dubbed "The Venus Fly Trap."

Investigators in contamination suits crawled on all fours, methodically uncovering the victim with paint brushes and trowels, treating her like a rare archaeological find. A gaggle of onlookers stood to one side. Many of them wore green coveralls. Boundary concluded that they were groundsmen.

Boundary's best option for getting close to the crime scene was to join that gaggle. It was a long shot. He'd have to traverse some fairway. His one advantage was his suit. From a distance, he might look like an investigator. He heard another golf cart whirring down the fairway, and he hit the deck again. This one had two agents wearing buzz cuts and dark glasses. They were thin and sinister looking. He followed them down the course with his spy glasses noticing that they passed the crime scene. They were on patrol. Would they continue to the 14th fairway or come back up the 12th? He couldn't lie there all day. He took a chance and exited the copse to the 12th fairway, which lay parallel to the 13th. He ran as fast as he could towards the 12th tee, which was across from the 13th hole.

Two hundred yards down the fairway, he heard that whirring again. In a panic, he ran into a row of tall pines that served as barrier between the 12th and 13th fairways and climbed up the branches of one of the bigger trees to hide himself from view. The cart with the two, male agents zoomed by, their eyes looking forward. He clamored back to the ground, discovering that hands and his suit were gummed with pine tar. He swore. It was his only suit. He'd need a miracle from his local dry cleaner to save it.

Once the cart was gone, he sprinted back down the 12th fairway. When he was catty corner to the scrum, he strolled across the fairway and eased into it.

Boundary slowly moved through the workers until he had a clear view of the trap. The FBI's forensics team was photographing the victim's uncovered face. He took some snaps of the scene with his cell phone. He was too far away to capture any details, like Rootewerke's henna-colored spiked hair or her nose ring.

The scrum included caddies, groundsmen, and clubhouse employees. Boundary, who was trying to blend in, stuck out because was the only one in a suit and a tie. Realizing this, he reversed into the thick of them so he would not be noticed by the agents. After a few minutes, an agent with a trowel stood up in the trap to stretch, Boundary caught a glimpse of a newly exposed section of the victim's head. Her hair was long —and blond.

10

Back Story

Boundary stealthily raised his phone to take another picture. This time, he attached a zoom lens about the size of an aspirin.

An FBI agent had warned the scrum against social media postings, threatening violators with jail, one of the workers told Boundary. Boundary appreciated their sheepishness because he'd be the first one to get news of the murder to the outside world. It wasn't every day that a body turned up buried in a golf course sand trap, let alone in a sand trap at the world- famous U.S. Congress Golf Club. Presidents played there with foreign heads of state. One president had spent more time on this course than inside the Oval Office.

A tall, broad-shouldered man in oil-stained coveralls and a tool belt was telling a youthful looking caddie that the greens-keeper, Jose, had discovered the body while raking the trap at 7 a.m. Jose had uncovered her hand and ran away to the club house screaming "Asesinato!"

"That's Mexican for murder," he said.

"Knew that," said the caddy.

"His voice was pitched high as a girl's and I thought he

was saying something about a scary tomato," guffawed the mechanic. "Bobby the bartender over there had to tranquilize him with tequila." He nodded towards a muscular man with a bare pate and a large handlebar mustache.

"Bobby would have a had to give me one too if I found that dead body," said the caddie. "Bodies creep me out."

"Like you ever found one," said the mechanic.

"I been to more than a couple wakes. They freak me, man, laying there liked wax dummies in pressed suits and shiny shoes."

Boundary noticed a team of investigators scouring the grass immediately surrounding the trap. They formed a semicircle that widened slowly as they walked further from the makeshift grave. Boundary took a video of the search and sent it to Fogarty, along with a text message about the killing. Boundary urged his editor to post the story on the web before any other news organizations got wind of it. Then, he turned on the phone's voice recorder and slipped it back into his jacket. He began chatting up the people in the scrum to learn more about the victim.

"Do you know who she is?" Boundary directed this question at a deeply tanned man in evergreen-colored overalls who was standing at his right. The man was middle aged, of average height, and very muscular, with large forearms. He looked up at Boundary suspiciously.

"You a Fed?"

"I'm Martin Boundary, from the Observer." He held out his hand. The man took it cautiously.

"You the boxer? That Martin Boundary?"

Boundary nodded affirmatively.

"I seen you fight once. In Richmond."

"The Colosseum, six years ago, against Stevie Dedalus."

"They let you in here?" he asked. His teeth were stained with tobacco and he had whiskey breath. Boundary didn't want to tell a lie, so he obfuscated.

"I got a high-level call. I help the Feds to crack cases by getting the facts out to the public. Someone reads about it puts two and two together, leading to an arrest."

The man nodded. He relaxed his shoulders became as chatty as an old lady at the head of a grocery market check-out line.

"One of them agents found a small black purse by the tee— a clutch is what the ladies call it. I heard one agent figuring that it might be the spot where the woman was killed."

"How did she die? Do you know?"

"The side of her head was smashed in."

"How do you know?" asked Boundary.

"Because a bunch of us came running out here after Jose discovered her. We didn't know she was dead, so we got down on our knees and started digging with our hands, like a pack of rat terriers. Wasn't a pretty sight. No sir! Someone clocked her pretty good. Her hair was all clotted with blood. When we saw that, we figured she was gone, so we called the cops."

"So, you disturbed the crime scene?"

"Like I said, we didn't know for sure that the lady was dead. We stopped when we saw that she dead was because we all watch them crime shows."

The man nodded towards the agents. "They gave each one of us the third degree, like one of us done kilt her. We told them we were all about saving her. They told us to wait here so they can question us. I'm still shook up —thinking they might try to railroad me because I'm an ex-con."

Anticipating Boundary's next question, the man quickly

added, "I'm nonviolent—I was a heroin addict who got caught swiping stuff from cars to finance my habit. I got five-to-seven and was paroled at the end of two. I came out of jail clean, and I'm still clean. Ask my parole officer. I never hurt a fly my whole life. But you know cops—how they be looking for an open-and-shut case. So, I'm thinking they might try to pin this here girl on me."

A caddie named Mike had been eavesdropping on the conversation and volunteered that the groundskeeper, Jose, who had found the victim, was an illegal immigrant from El Salvador who now feared deportation.

"What's Jose's last name?" asked Boundary.

"Jose something or other; I can't remember. One of them Mexican sounding names, you know?"

He pointed out Jose. The groundskeeper, a short, pudgy man, was behind the tape with the FBI. He was dressed in a dirty white tee shirt, washed-out blue jeans, and thick brown work boots. He had black curly hair flecked with gray and a cherubic face. Big beads of sweat covered his forehead. Boundary snapped Jose's photo.

"He can't speak no English neither," said Mike, a white man in his thirties with red hair, rust-red stubble, and some missing front teeth. "Just a dozen words at most, or twenty. Something like that."

Mike said he never had suspected that Jose was illegal, or else he would have reported him so they could "kick his foreign ass out of the country where it belongs."

"They check you really good before you can come to work here because of all the government VIPs and shit who come here to murder the lawn. Jose has a Virginia driver's license and he owns a little ranch house out in Woodbridge, across from that big shopping mall. I drove him home once when his pickup wouldn't start. How they figured him for an illegal is a mystery to me. He's been working here 15 years at least."

Boundary asked Mike if he had seen the woman's face.

"I didn't see it," Mike said apologetically. "I came up after the other fellers said she was dead."

"Did the cops mention how she was killed?"

"Nope. One agent asked if I knowed any members who an Ogden. He asked everybody here about that."

"She was killed with an Ogden Titanium?"

"Why else would they ask us if we knowed who owned one?" He eyed Boundary as if the reporter was an imbecile.

"They must have found the club," said Boundary.

"Wouldn't know. That's official police business."

"So, then, you didn't see the club?"

"I didn't see much of anything."

"Can I get your last name," asked Boundary, removing a notebook from his inside pocket.

"What you want that for?"

"For a quote."

"In the paper? No way, man," he said. He sidled away. The ex-con moved away too.

Boundary made his way to the bartender, who was as tall and muscular as he was.

"Bobby?"

"That's me. Who's asking? he said good naturedly.

By the looks of Bobby, he had a body-building fetish. His shaved head was teed up on a mound of trapezius muscle. His biceps and tattooed forearms were the size of jack hammers. One forearm bore the eagle, anchor, and globe of the U.S. Marine Corps. He had massive pecs, a boyishly slim waist, and thick thighs that bulged beneath his tight blue jeans.

Bobby also had an unforgettable face. A brown handlebar mustache, which was waxed at the tips, bloomed under his Roman nose the look of a circus performer.

Bobby was large enough to intimidate but his demeanor was jovial. He had a puckish twinkle in his blue eyes and a wry smile. Boundary had a feeling he had struck pay dirt, a source with plenty of knowledge and no reluctance to share it. There was one at every crime scene if you were lucky enough to find him or her. Sometimes, it was a cop; sometimes, a witness; sometimes, a victim; and in rare instances the perpetrator.

"I'm Martin Boundary, from the Observer."

"The college boxer– that Boundary?"

Boundary nodded.

Bobby reached over and shook Boundary's hand. The bartender had an iron grip.

"I boxed a little. I'd never take you on, though. Your hands are too quick."

"I've slowed down quite a bit. So, I'm relieved to hear that you don't want to tangle with me, Bobby, because I'd feel like I was throwing punches at a freight train."

The bartender laughed.

"I've been called lots of things, but never a 'freight train.' What's up, buddy?"

"I'm writing a story about this killing. Can you give me anything?"

"Let me think a minute." He scratched his chin. "I was on duty last night after six. During the day, I'm a weight trainer. There weren't many people in the bar, this being August and most the members down at the beach. I had no women customers, so, obviously, I did not see the victim. The

52

final foursome finished up at nine. I turn off the spigots at ten."

"Did you know them?"

"Sure. I've been here 10 years. I know everybody. Two were members of the Congress and one of them was shit-faced. The others were a billionaire and a semi-shit-faced journalist."

"Can you give me their names? "

"I don't want to be quoted Boundary. What happens at the club stays at the club, know what I mean? They'd fire me in a second for gossiping about the members with a newspaper reporter. I like it here a lot. I get to hobnob with the rich and the powerful. The tips are fantastic. Sometimes, movie directors play golf here. I served Spielberg once. He ordered water, straight up. One of those health nuts, you know? Anyway, my dream is to be in a movie. Move over, Arnold!" He flexed his arm muscles and grinned ear-to-ear.

"I get it, Bobby, and I won't quote you. I'll confirm anything you tell me independently with other sources. Have the FBI guys spoken to you yet? "

"Nope. But they want us all to hang around. They called me in to work this morning. I'm supposed to be at the gym now. I had to take a personal day."

"Anything you tell me, Bobby, I can wheedle the same information out of somebody else. You'd just be providing me with a road map.''

"Really, Boundary? Like I said, I don't want to lose my job."

"Cross my heart. I never burn sources."

"They'd know it was me."

"Was anyone else in the bar?"

"A caddie."

"Could anyone else have seen them leave?"

"There's a guard at the gate."

"See. You are not the only possible source. I swear: I will not put anything in print that could jeopardize your job."

Bobby wrinkled his brow. He liked Boundary. The guy had been a champ, and there were benefits to being on good terms with an Observer reporter. Big Barney had Malcolm Truitt. Big Barney was a mighty smart man. Bobby looked up to him.

"Okay then. Big Barney Magnus was here; you know, the House Speaker?"

Boundary nodded.

"Big Barney was drinking Laphroaig Lore like it was water. We charge $25-per-shot. He was getting an earful from Jimmy Johnson, who, by the way, was running the tab. Johnson spends a fortune here. We give him the star treatment."

"The king of sausage—that Jimmy Johnson?"

"Yep. He and Barney are buddies. They are in here a lot. They've got some kind of a business arrangement. I heard them laughing one time about Barney's 40 pocket votes. So last night, Johnson was going on and on about the Senate's version of an immigration bill reducing the flow of cheap labor from south of the border. He also whined about an ethanol law that would raise the price feed corn. His pigs eat that stuff. Barney claimed he'd fix everything in a House–Senate conference committee because he owned a majority of the conferees. Jimmy was mighty pleased to hear that. There was something said about a tax package too that would exempt certain consumer staples. Johnson left at 9:30 p.m. Said he had to fly back to his ranch in North Carolina. He gave Barney a big pat on the back. He ignored the senator. I gathered they were pissed at one another."

"Which senator," asked Boundary.

"Kent Cisco."

"Who was the reporter?" asked Boundary.

"Your paper's political reporter-the skinny guy with the light hair."

"Truitt? Malcolm Truitt?"

"Yeah. That's the guy."

"Truitt is a member?" Boundary knew that Truitt's paycheck was large relative to his fellow journalists. Nevertheless, he found it hard to believe that Truitt could have come up with the club's $1 million initiation.

"Nah, he doesn't belong. Barney invites him sometimes. I heard him say once that he has Truitt on a tight leash."

"Is that all that Barney and Johnson talked about?"

"Look, understand, I don't hear everything, as a professional courtesy. When somebody is conducting business, I wander down to the opposite end of the bar and polish glasses. On the other hand, if people get loud, I don't plug my ears. I pretend I'm not listening. Last night, those guys got loud, especially after Johnson left. Barney tried to get Cisco to back the changes Jimmy wanted in the tax bill. He wasn't having much luck. Cisco was hopping mad and in no mood to kowtow. Johnson had cleaned Cisco's clock out on the course. The game cost him $3,200.

Boundary looked puzzled.

"They were gambling, Boundary. They played for a pot of $600-per-hole. That's $200 each. Truitt doesn't bet because of 'newspaper ethics.' Johnson won every hole. Cisco was fit to be tied."

"I don't understand why Cisco was pissed off," said Boundary. "You win some, you lose some."

Bobby laughed. "You don't know much about politics, do

55

you?"

"What's politics have to do with golf?"

"At this club? Everything! See, when bets are placed between business guys like Johnson and politicians like Barney and Cisco then the politicians are supposed to win. It's an unwritten rule—a way to exchange *donations* without having to file reports with the Federal Election Commission. But this time around Johnson won every round. He won because he used an Ogden Titanium driver, which adds 50-yards to your drive. Johnson golfs like a pro to start with, so, he really had an unfair advantage."

"You're sure he used an Ogden?"

"That's what Cisco said. He was really fuming about it, which is hypocritical, because Cisco, himself, used one until it was stolen from the locker. He needs every dime he can get for advertising because he's in a tight re-election campaign against a guy named Bob Anthony, a billionaire home builder from Greensboro."

Boundary knew about the race because Truitt had run a feature story on the subject the previous week. Anthony was handsome, bombastic, and had a mop of black, curly hair. The Wharton School grad owned a construction company that was building a planned community on 1,000 acres of farmland. His drop-dead beautiful wife had a Ph.D. in clinical psychology and his twin three-year-old boys were cuter than puppies. He featured them in his television ads. The kids chanted, "Our Dad is amazing! He's a multimillionaire at age 32. Just think of the great things that will happen in Washington, D.C., if he uses his smarts for you!"

The narcissism was working. Anthony had a double-digit lead in the polls.

56

"Big Barney advised Cisco to cool off and make nice to Jimmy," Bobby said. "He reminded Cisco that Johnson had been generous in the past. Big Barney threw his arm over Cisco's shoulder, gave him a bear hug, and told him, 'Jimmy just wants us to know that we shouldn't take him for granted. He's pretty pissed off at you, Kent. You didn't deliver on your promise to push for more guest workers when the immigration bill came up for a floor vote last week. From his perspective, he put you in office and you owe him something in return. Talk to him and make amends. Otherwise, you risk losing his backing.

"Cisco would have none of it," said Bobby. "He was red-faced. He looked like his head would explode. He pushed Big Barney away and said the immigration bill was bigger than Jimmy Johnson—that the voters of North Carolina felt like they were being overrun with immigrants. If he were to go soft on the issue, that would piss them off."

Boundary understood where Cisco was coming from. Several months earlier, a drunken Mexican in the country illegally had crashed his pickup truck head-on into a Baptist school bus near Chapel Hill, killing a teacher and six kids. Somehow, the Mexican survived the wreck, fled the scene, and escaped back over the border. North Carolinians were infuriated, believing that a network of illegals had abetted the man's flight. Most citizens wanted guest workers sent packing.

"Big Barney told Cisco that Johnson felt betrayed. And Cisco said, 'I've done Johnson lots of favors, like when I killed that bill written by you damn House Democrats to curb the pig-shit smells at hog farms!' Then Cisco says, 'Johnson gave to me freely. There was no quid pro quo. I work for all of the taxpayers —not just for Jimmy Johnson.' And Barney shoots back, 'You don't own Johnson either, Kent. That's why he just

57

took your betting money. So, get over it.' Cisco said, 'Jimmy can stick his Ogden up his ass' and stormed out of the bar."

"What time was that?" asked Boundary

"Close to ten."

"Did Cisco drive himself?"

"I suppose so. I don't really know how any of them got here."

"Did you hear or see anything out of the ordinary when you closed up and left?"

"Nope. All I heard was the trilling of tree frogs. We must have a million of them."

Boundary thanked Bobby. For all of his jabbering, he hadn't told Boundary much that he could use in a story about the killing. The fact that Cisco had been at the golf club was interesting, given Boundary's suspicions about the man. But there was no good reason to mention him or Big Barney or even Truitt, because it would amount to guilt by proximity to the scene of the crime.

Boundary took out his phone and pecked a text message on the tiny keyboard updating his old report with some new, minor details about the FBI's methodical excavation of the corpse and the fact that the club had closed the previous night at 10 p.m. He sent it to Fogarty and immediately received an out-of-office reply. He forwarded his update to Kitty Cross, Dan's boss. Almost immediately, she texted Boundary a laundry list of questions to ask the investigators, most of them fairly obvious ones.

"Can't talk to them," he replied. "Sneaked in over the fence. Will kick me out if they see me." He took a snap of the sand trap. The investigators were still on all fours, meticulously brushing sand from the corpse. He sent that to Cross too.

Her answer was "LOL. Good work! Don't get caught!"

Boundary was unsure what to do next: Wait at the sand trap for several hours or make his way over to the clubhouse to buttonhole some of the club officials for comments? He decided to head for the club house. This turned out to be a monumental blunder.

11

Ejected

Boundary hadn't walked more than twenty paces when he was spotted by the two FBI agents who had been endlessly patrolling the course in a golf cart. They scooted up to him and demanded to see his ID. He handed them his press pass. The agent in the passenger seat studied it for a moment and then flashed Boundary a "gotcha" smile.

"You know that you are not supposed to be here, Mr. Boundary," said the agent handing back the plastic badge. "The entire club is a crime scene."

"No one told me."

"You didn't see the tape at the entrance?"

"Nope."

"How did you get in, then?"

Never lie to a cop, he told himself.

"Walked, from over there." He inclined his head towards the distant fence.

"So, you climbed over the back gate," said the square-jawed agent sitting behind the wheel of the cart. "How did you know about it?"

"All the neighborhood kids know about it," he said.

60

"You know the neighborhood kids. Is that your story?"

Boundary shrugged his big shoulders.

"Hop in and we'll give you a lift to the front entrance," said the agent riding shotgun. He was a rail thin, round-faced fellow in a clean and meticulously ironed version of the tarred and rumpled suit that Boundary was wearing.

"Please, let me stay," Boundary begged. "I'm not in the way, just looking around."

Neither one blinked.

"Who is the blond in the trap?"

"How do you know she's blond?" asked the round-faced agent.

Boundary showed him the photo on his phone. The agent's faced betrayed that he was considering seizing it. But Boundary had posted the picture on the internet. His supervisor had alerted him about the news report and the presence of a reporter on the course. Nothing would be gained by confiscating the phone and reading about the seizure later in the Observer. He handed the phone back.

"You'll have to wait for the news briefing, just like everyone else, Mr. Boundary," said the agent. "Now hop in."

Boundary tried to make the most of the trip to the front gate by firing questions at the agents. All he got in return was stony silence.

When they dumped Boundary off at the front gate, the agent behind the wheel warned Boundary that he'd be arrested if he tried to sneak back onto the course.

Boundary immediately phoned Cross and told her about his ejection. She swore.

"Have they identified the victim yet?" she asked.

"Some employees told me that the FBI recovered a purse."

"Do you think the victim is the missing student?" Her voice quavered slightly.

"I don't think so. The dead woman is blond and Rootewerke's hair is henna-colored. By the way, it appears that the victim was killed with an Ogden Titanium."

"What's that?" asked Cross.

"The most expensive golf club in the world. A driver."

"How many members of the country club own them?"

"I'm working on that," said Boundary.

"Did you get a picture of the club?"

"No. We'll have to use a file photo. I'm deducing that it was an Ogden because the FBI asked the groundskeepers which members own them."

"OK, we can use that—about the FBI questioning the workers about the Ogden. Is that OK?"

"Sure. It's solid information."

"Do you have any direct quotes, Martin?"

"None of the guys wanted me to use their names. They're afraid of losing their jobs. There's a club ethos along the lines of what goes on in Vegas stays in Vegas, know what I mean?"

"Got it."

"I talked to multiple people. I'll share the name—your eyes only—when I get back. I'm not manufacturing anything."

"I'll trust you on this. I'll get this into print—with your by-line. Stick by the front gate for a while and see who goes in and who comes out," said Cross. "I want you to write another update in an hour. This is red hot. We've gotten over 70,000-page views already."

"Don't you want me to come in now to write up the main story? I have lots of color."

"Just text me the details and we'll write it up here."

He frowned. He did not want to share the credit for a story after he had done all of the legwork. Reading his mind, Cross added, "You'll get star billing."

Boundary stood outside the gate for over three hours. Nothing came of it. About three dozen reporters from other outlets arrived after his story hit the internet, including television news crews from six television networks, a French video news team, and 10 major newspapers.

His friend Joe drove through the entrance in his crime scene van. They saw one another but betrayed no sign of mutual recognition. Then a medical examiner's van left the club lot. Boundary assuming it contained the victim's body, took some pictures and sent them to Cross.

In hour four of the stakeout, a stocky female agent with short hair and a no-nonsense face came out to front gate and distributed a flyer to reporters which contained the barest information about the crime. At 7 a.m. Wednesday, it related, a groundskeeper had discovered the duct-tape-bound body of a female buried in a sand trap near the seventh hole. The cause of death had not yet been determined. The agent refused to identify the victim, pending notification of next of kin; and she ignored shouts from the raucous gaggle of reporters for additional details.

Boundary took a picture of the press release and sent it to Fogarty, who was back on the job. Fogarty told him to come back to the office to begin working on a story for the following day. He was excited. The murder was hot news. He had already gotten over Rootewerke. The identity of the blond would be the next big development in the story. When you had a victim, then you had a list of possible suspects.

12

Star Struck

Boundary attempted to bum a ride from the newsmen gathered at the front gate to his motorcycle, which was parked a mile away. Everyone was in far too much of a hurry to get back to their offices to give him a lift. Besides, they were irked that the brash, young journalist had scooped them. This was their way of getting back at him for highlighting their inadequacies.

Boundary began walking briskly down the club's rose bush-lined driveway towards the main road. The heat was unbearable and his tree-grimed suit jacket showed a big sweat stain on the back. A classic, cranberry colored Cadillac SRX convertible heading toward the club's front gate pulled up and stopped beside him. Behind the wheel of the fantastically lovely open-topped two-seater was Preston Ferguson, the most popular television news host of the day. Boundary recognized him immediately

The car's air conditioner was on full blast. Preston was attired for a day on the links: pink cotton sports shirt, white linen slacks, gold-rimmed aviator glasses. His signature diamond pinky ring, an item of jewelry which he claimed once belonged to mobster Al Capone, shone on his right hand. His dark hair, which was swept back from his forehead, glistened with hair gel.

"What's the amazing fuss?" he asked Boundary. He had not a clue who Boundary was. He assumed the owner of the rumpled, stained suit must be a journalist.

"Preston Ferguson!" said Boundary. Ferguson was the very sort of household name that Boundary wished to become.

"The one and only. And to whom do I have the pleasure of speaking?"

"I'm Martin Boundary of the Observer."

"Never heard of you, Boundary," he said, shaking hands. "You must be a new man."

"Relatively new. Are you a member here, Preston?"

"Too rich by far for my modest budget. I belong to the club in Bethesda—the one where the chairman of the Federal Reserve Board plays every other day and where the President plays twice a month. I was invited here by a congressman for a fast nine."

"No fast nine today, I'm afraid. They found a woman's body buried in a sand trap by the 13th hole."

The television star whistled. "Was she a congresswoman?"

Boundary shrugged. "That's a good question. It's a woman, with long blond hair. They haven't identified her yet."

Ferguson's jaw dropped. "She was murdered on this golf course? A woman with long, blond hair?"

"Looks like it."

"My goodness. Clearly a federal offense. This course is congressionally chartered! Have they arrested someone?"

"No. But it looks like she was clobbered with an Ogden Titanium."

Ferguson's jaw dropped again. "My goodness. The cops must have a suspect," he said. "There's a guard at the front gate 24/7."

"If they know who the killer is then they are not saying," said Boundary.

"Do any of your golfing partners have Ogdens?" asked Boundary.

"Lots and lots." Ferguson glanced at his gold Rolex.

"Thanks for filling me in, Old Man. I am beholden to you for the thorough briefing. If you ever need a favor, let me know."

"Actually, I do need a small favor," said Boundary. He handed Ferguson his iPhone, which was displaying a digital photo of Rootewerke.

"Is this kid the victim?"

"No. But she's a missing person. You were taping a segment in the Capitol Rotunda yesterday with Senator Cisco. Did you happen to see her?"

He studied the photo carefully.

"Yes, I did, as a matter of fact, I did notice this woman. You can't forget a freak show like that. Those weird body piercings—nails and big screws and bolts. She looked like she had crashed face-first into a hardware store." He handed the phone back to Boundary.

"Did you see her leave?"

"Afraid not, Boundary."

"Cisco play here?" Boundary asked.

"All the time," said Ferguson. "He loves the game. He's pretty good too. He always beats the pants off of me! That's a good thing because he is a sore loser with quite the temper. Say, you don't think Cisco is involved in this killing, do you?"

Boundary shrugged.

"Cisco owned an Ogden, but it was stolen over a year ago, right out of his bag while we were drinking in the club house."

Boundary showed Ferguson the story that had been posted on the Observer's web site. Ferguson scrutinized every word.

"Good work, Boundary. Very good work indeed. You are a young man who obviously is going places."

Boundary leaned his arms on Preston's window sill. "As a matter of fact, I do need to go someplace, in a hurry. Since you won't be golfing, then maybe could I catch a ride with you to the south side of the course? My bike is parked outside the fence there."

Preston smiled warmly and said, "Sorry, Old Man, but I just remembered another urgent appointment. Why don't you call yourself an Uber? Rooster is paying you print grunts enough for the occasional car fare, isn't he?"

"Yeah, great idea Preston," he said. "Thanks."

Ferguson shrugged. "Don't be cross. Be happy!" He looked up at the clear blue sky. "In fact, it's a beautiful afternoon for a stroll, if you don't mind the god awful heat." He laughed. He put the car in reverse, turned around, and sped back toward Washington, D.C. This was big news and he had to let the most important people in his life know about it right away. He had no idea who the victim was, but he had a strong hunch. And the weapon of choice had given him a pretty good idea about the identity of the killer. Stupid twisted brute! He had to warn his colleagues.

13

Ethical Quandary

The murder victim was Bernadette Kathleen Malone, an aide to Senator Kent Cisco of North Carolina—and Boundary's one-night stand.

The FBI press release identifying her came more than 24 hours after Jose had stumbled upon her body. The release noted Malone's powder blue BMW was missing. The press release had popped up on Boundary's cell phone while he was brewing a pot of coffee. It was 8 a.m. Thursday morning and an exhausted Twyla was still sleeping. The news release at first had knocked Boundary's legs out from under him. Malone was dead. Then he felt elated. She no longer threatened him. She could not reach out from beyond the grave.

It was a cloudless summer morning with temperatures already in the mid-80s. Boundary and Twyla both had taken vacation time to spend four days at a beach cottage loaned to them by one of Twyla's co-workers. Boundary had a sinking feeling that his vacation was not to be.

He read and re-read the FBI's press release. He wondered if he might be a suspect. He had a motive. He was one of the last persons to see Malone alive.

'Thank goodness I don't own an Ogden Titanium,' he thought.

Boundary wrote a story based on the release on his cell phone and forwarded it to the news desk. He mulled telling Fogarty about his involvement with the dead woman. He even considering contacting the FBI about it, since he could place her in her apartment early the day before her corpse was found. He agonized over the pros and cons of being cooperative and keeping his mouth shut. He could offer the FBI no really useful information about Malone. He could not even tell them how she performed in the sack. He had been blitzed. Furthermore, he knew first-hand how incredibly lazy cops could be. They always sought an easy lay-up, especially in headline grabbing cases. If he told the FBI about his fling, then they would pin the murder on him, interpreting his cooperation as a sign of guilt. They'd leak his name to the media to give the public the impression that they were on top of things. Twyla would dump him. Rooster would fire him. And despite his innocence, he would always be remembered as a murder suspect.

Fogarty would give the story to someone else if he knew about Boundary's Malone connection, because of the obvious conflict of interest. Boundary did not want to give up the story.

But silence also had its risks: Someone may have seen him and Malone together and report this to the FBI. In this case, his failure to come forward would be damning, since he had been the first reporter at the crime scene. How could he explain his remarkable presence without giving up Joe? After much debate, he decided that the optimum strategy was to hold back. What if someone had seen him with Malone? Chances were, they'd never remember. He passed hundreds of persons on the streets each day and could not dredge up a decent description of any one of them.

Boundary poured himself a glass of milk. His stomach was churning. The fear of losing Twyla was unbearable. He cursed. Why had he argued with her? Why had he stormed from the house? Why did he allow himself to get blind drunk! How the hell had he ended up in the sack with Malone?

He felt light-headed. He opened the first-floor windows of their row house to let in some air. A gentle, westerly breeze drifted through the screens, and he could hear the trumpeting of elephants and the roar of lions at the National Zoo, a quarter mile away. A hint of animal dung hung in the air. One got used to it.

At 8:15 a.m., a white-robed Twyla leisurely entered the kitchen and gave her man a big hug and kiss. She sat down at the small kitchen table and asked Martin for a cup of coffee. She was content as a house cat at the thought of a beach holiday.

Boundary was wearing boxer shorts and a tee shirt. He poured Twyla a cup of Brazilian blend and sat down in the chair at across from her. They had planned to leave at 9 a.m., after the worst of the rush hour. Their packed bags already were in the back of the jeep, which was parked in their basement garage.

"What a glorious day," Twyla said, peering out the window. She was looking forward to some carefree playtime with her husband, a workaholic who was always chasing a story.

Boundary cleared his throat. "Do you know Bernadette Malone, Twyla?"

"What did you say, Martin? I was daydreaming about the beach."

"That murder at the golf course—the one I told you about

yesterday. The FBI identified the victim as Bernadette Kathleen Malone."

"Oh, my God, I do know her!" Twyla said, leaning forward. "Who did it? Do they know?"

Boundary's smart phone started playing "La Cucaracha." He looked at the number on the display.

"It's Rooster."

"Don't answer," pleaded Twyla. She knew what was coming—an abrupt end to their beautiful plans.

"I've got to take it."

"He'll want you to work on Malone's murder. We need this time together, honey. We haven't had a break in months."

He answered the phone.

Twyla's eyes watered. Their holiday was shot even before it had begun.

"I need you in the newsroom right away," barked Rooster without waiting for his young reporter to say hello. "I need a front-page feature on Malone for tomorrow, with some quotes from Cisco. Ask him if he thinks Malone's murder during his re-election campaign is a tragic coincidence or the work of some crackpot who is trying to sabotage him."

"I was about to leave for a short vacation, Rooster." Boundary looked at Twyla when he said this.

"Leave for vacation? You're joking, right? This is front-page news, Boundary. You can't walk away from a huge front-page splash. Where are you off to? Europe? I'll pay the cancellation fees."

"We were headed to Bethany Beach."

"The beach? You're kidding me. You'd rather be at the beach than writing the story of a lifetime?"

"I never said that."

"Then, damn it, get in here! We've got work to do." Rooster slam-dunked the phone before Boundary could respond.

Boundary's heart sank as the dam restraining Twyla's tears suddenly burst. But Rooster was right. This was his story—the story of a lifetime.

The Friday paper was the second most prominent edition of the week, behind Sunday. Nearly a million persons read it. Many of them blogged and Tweeted about the top stories, creating an echo effect that touched an audience of hundreds of thousands more readers around the globe. You could become an overnight sensation if you wrote a compelling story for Friday's edition. Boundary certainly had the material for a compelling story. Cisco's gorgeous aide found murdered on a golf course that boasted most of the members of the United States Congress as its members. This was sensational. He might even be able to work Rootewerke's disappearance into the very same piece.

By now, Twyla was crying hard. Boundary wiped her cheeks with his hand.

"Take the Jeep and go on ahead to the beach, Twyla. I'll join you tonight, after deadline."

"Can't you let someone else cover for you?" she sobbed. "Any old reporter can write a profile. I really was looking forward to having some alone time with you, Martin. It's been too long."

Boundary walked to her side of the table, stooped beside her, and took her hand in his. He kissed it.

"This story is international news, and Rooster wants it to lead tomorrow's paper. I doubt that I'll ever get shot at another story this big. And if I walk away from this one, then I'll have no future at the Observer; none at all. Rooster said as much."

"What about me, Martin? Do you love your job more than you love me?" She bit her lip.

"Come on, Twyla, that's unfair." She had upset him. "I didn't put the body in the sand trap. And we do need my job if we're going to buy a house. Look at all the times you've stood me up because of some floor debate or some last-minute demand from Big Barney. It's the call of duty. Surely, you understand."

In a pique, Twyla turned her head away from him. He stood and stiffened his back.

"I swear, I'll be down at the beach tonight."

"What makes you think Rooster won't want a follow up for Saturday and another one for Sunday?"

"There won't be anything more to write about, unless the FBI makes an arrest," Boundary said. "I don't think an arrest is imminent. These investigations take time. And the killer is twisted. This whole sand-trap burial is a taunt and a tease. He's not going to surrender, because he's having too much fun and thinks he can't be caught. I doubt he's left any incriminating evidence at the crime scene."

Twyla sniffed. She gulped. Her tears continued to flow. Martin put his hand on her shoulder.

"Martin, I know it isn't fair for me to ask you to give up a big story. But, I can't help it. I was dreaming about getting away with you. I should not have pinned my hopes on it."

He knelt down and hugged her. She buried her head in his shoulder. When after several minutes she stopped weeping, she decided to share some things about Malone with Martin to give him a head start on the reporting process.

"Bernadette was a piece of work, I can tell you that. She wore $1,000 outfits to the office—and she wore a new one every single day! She had dozens of expensive designer shoes and bags. There is no way she paid for that wardrobe from her own checking account. Everyone thought so."

"Any idea who the sugar daddy was?" asked Boundary.

"Sugar daddies, plural, is more likely. We assumed she was dating a third of the Senate. Barney used to laugh that the senators hung around her like dogs in heat. Barney ogled her too. I watched him, the old lecher. She won some big beauty pageant once. You should check into that."

"I will. She's from North Carolina, right?"

"Yes. She had a sugary southern accent to make sure you knew it. She dropped by our office at least once a week for a meeting with Barney. She always carried the same leather briefcase, an Italian design. I've seen them advertised on sale for $4,000! Barney always seemed to know exactly when she was coming and would show up at the front door to greet her with a big smile and a bear hug."

"Can I use that detail, Twyla?"

"Not unless you get it on the record from someone else. He knows my husband."

Boundary laughed. "Good point. Why all those meetings with Barney?"

"I don't know. I assumed she was a back channel between Big Barney and Cisco. After he met with her, Barney always had a meeting with about 40 of the members—the ones that always vote with him. We call them "Barney's Trained Monkeys.""

"Any idea what they talk about?"

"I have no clue. Barney keeps the meetings hush-hush. Tim White, our chief-of- staff fumes about being kept in the dark. I asked Barney once about his agenda. He got huffy and told me to mind my knitting."

"He sounds like a sexist."

"That's Big Barney being Big Barney. He laughs when I call him out on it. Blames it on his age."

"Can I have a list of the Monkeys?"

"No. I can't do that, darling. Call around. I'm sure someone else will talk about it."

"Is there anything else you remember about Bernadette? Did she have an affair with Cisco?"

Twyla shrugged. "I never heard any gossip. Some of my office friends saw her at a few fundraising events with Senator Horst of Rhode Island; and in April she attended the White House Correspondents' Association dinner with that gay senator from Wyoming—Dandy Pruitt."

"Maybe she wanted to marry Big Barney."

Twyla laughed. "Big, old, fat, ass-pinching, purple-nosed Barney? She wasn't that desperate!"

"Sometimes it's better to be loved than to love," Boundary said, quoting an old song lyric.

"I wonder if Cisco killed her?" said Boundary.

"Martin, you have no reason to think that."

"Hastings; Rootewerke; now Malone. That's quite a coincidence."

"Don't be ridiculous, Martin. Now kiss me goodbye because I'm heading out."

Boundary lifted her from the chair to her feet and kissed her hard on the lips. She playfully pushed him away. "Whoa there, horsey."

"You look so sexy," he pleaded.

"Save your energy. You're in great demand at work. Remember?"

He kissed her again.

"If you want some, then make sure you make an appearance at the beach house tomorrow," Twyla said coyly.

He tightened his embrace. She tried to squirm free, but he would not let go. She stopped squirming. She loved her man, even though he could be as clueless and stubborn as an ox. He leaned her slowly down across the kitchen table. He opened her robe and dropped his shorts. At the zoo, a lion roared.

14

Miracle Man

The most recent ratings for Preston Ferguson's television program, The Big Event, were as limp as canned spaghetti. Consequently, ad revenues were off by a whopping 65 percent. The Millennials had switched from cable television to streaming the programs they liked directly from the internet; and their elders, were beginning to follow suit. No one in the television industry had figured out how to bring them back. Ferguson trotted out a succession of young, busty co-hosts. The ratings needle hardly had budged.

Ferguson was desperate and depressed. Cancellation of his show was in the cards. Ferguson could not countenance off-camera life. He already had taken a painful salary cut to keep the show afloat. Even so, without a miraculous increase in viewership and ad revenues over the next few weeks, he'd be forced to pull the plug. The once powerful king of the Washington talk-show circuit would be a great, big nothing, going from the social A-list to the D-List, which is to say that he would be delisted from the A-List.

Obscurity. The very word frightened him. He had witnessed the travails of colleagues who had washed out of the business.

They might as well have been swallowed by quicksand.

Ferguson had confided in Big Barney about his plight. Barney was a mentor, a frequent guest, and the source of the cocaine which, next to celebrity, was Preston's favorite addiction. They were bound up by a business requiring discretion, loyalty, and, trust. In return for the cocaine, Ferguson let Barney use his television program's "Green Room" to distribute the drug to the 40 congressional members of his "Cocaine Caucus," who voted any way Big Barney wanted them to vote in return for their nose candy. The value of their votes far outweighed the cost of the drug, which was purchased by Jimmy Johnson, the sausage billionaire. Johnson was the beneficiary of legislative favors that more than made up for his drug outlays. For Johnson, the setup was a virtuous circle.

The Green Room—which was painted green, of course—was a large space adjoining the studio where guests hung out until summoned by the producer for their on-camera appearances with Ferguson. The room was stocked with drinks and snacks and contained a makeup room, where two professionals prepared the guests for the camera.

Half the attraction of appearing on a show like "The Big Event" was the prospect of encountering a fellow Green Room notable waiting for his "hit." A congress of congressmen in a green room was fairly normal. No one would ever suspect they were there for their drug fixes.

Ferguson begged Barney for cash in addition to cocaine. Without money, he'd have to go off the air in a month. Why risk losing a venue that worked as well as the Green Room? Yet, Barney would not commit to propping up the show. Ferguson had put the price tag at $50,000-per-week, which added up to $2.6 million-per year. That was nuts. Barney hemmed and hawed and said he would get back to him.

The meeting unhinged Ferguson. He fretted that Big Barney would move his distribution elsewhere. If this were the case, then Ferguson saw that he would amount to a disgruntled loose end in the chain of business. How could he keep from being silenced? He could threaten to spill the beans to the cops; but then again, they owned some the cops, paying bribes to keep their heads turned the other way. He could run to the newspapers, but they could not protect him either.

"I need a miracle," he muttered. "And I don't believe in miracles."

But, the fact is, miracles do happen.

A few hours after news of Malone's murder appeared in the Observer, Big Barney called Ferguson and asked if he'd like to make an "easy 25 grand." Malone, Barney explained, had a secret love nest off of Connecticut Avenue near Woodley Park. Incriminating items had to be retrieved from the pad before the cops learned of its existence.

Ferguson agreed to take the job because he needed the cash and because he felt that Big Barney still valued his services.

"What items?" he asked.

Malone, Barney revealed, had hidden a video recording system inside her boudoir. Blackmail had cemented her relationship with a large number of congressmen who went on to become members of Big Barney's cocaine caucus. Big Barney asked Ferguson to retrieve the system's hard drive.

"If the cops ever should get hold of this stuff...it's a nuclear shit bomb, Preston."

Ferguson was elated, forgetting for the moment his self-pity. He had a genetic proclivity for grand theft. Ferguson's father had been a London locksmith running a highly profitable burglary enterprise on the side; and he had taken on a nine-year-old Preston as an apprentice, assuming that his son would one day assume his mantel. Together, they boosted luxury goods and jewelry from some of the finest houses in the city. The Russian oligarchs who inhabited the city's swanky Belgrave neighborhood were particularly dependable sources of finery, despite intimidating arrays of electronic security and sanguinary guard dogs. Preston's father often lowered his compact son down into a bedroom through a chimney to disarm the alarm systems and to squirt any dogs with a profoundly effective knockout concoction. His father's eventual arrest by Scotland Yard investigators—who had squeezed a pawn shop owner—freed 12-year-old Preston to pursue a more sensible career path in journalism, at which he excelled. Throughout his career, he nicked notes and papers from the locked offices and houses of bureaucrats and politicians to advance a story or to snatch a souvenir for his secret collection of memorabilia; and, in doing so, maintained his considerable skills. Once many years ago, he had regaled Big Barney with stories of his childhood exploits. Big Barney had remembered, which touched him.

Wearing a slouch hat, sunglasses, and a phony beard, Ferguson entered Malone's apartment building through the locked front door on the heels of a mailman, who had a key to the lobby. To allay the letter carrier's suspicions, he acted as though he lived there.

"Have you a letter for me? Mr. Simmons? Apartment 303?" he asked. Ferguson had done his homework. The mailman handed him a cable TV bill.

Malone lived in the third floor, in Apartment 301. Since Ferguson had no electronic key fob for the elevator, he used the emergency stairwell, deftly picking a lock on the landing so quickly that it appeared to the mailman that the door had not been locked at all.

"Good for the heart, taking the steps," Ferguson called out to the letter carrier.

When he arrived on the third floor, he jimmied open the landing door, and then easily picked the deadbolt and door lock to Malone's apartment. The place looked as neat as a luxury hotel room. Nothing was out of place. There was no sign that anyone ever had lived there. He walked through a living room decorated with Scandinavian-style furniture to the spotless, galley kitchen. The quartz countertops were empty. He opened some drawers and some cabinets. All of them were empty. There were no utensils, glasses, plates. The steel sink showed no trace of water stains.

The kitchen lead to a dining area. The glass-top dining tabled sparkled. A mini bar stood against the wall. He opened it.

"Ah, we are getting somewhere."

The cabinet was fully stocked. Some of the liquor bottles never had even been opened. He helped himself to the contents of the Jameson bottle, drinking right from the neck.

Off the dining room was Bernie's bed room, home of the secret taping system. The chamber was huge, with a wall of windows to the outside. Like the rest of the apartment, the bedroom looked as though no one ever had lived in it. Ferguson rubbed his index finger on the sill over the door and found no dust.

'I must get the name of her housemaid,' he noted to himself.

Ferguson found the recording system's hidden pinhole camera in minutes — in the wooden fame of a mirror hanging

81

opposite the king-sized bed. But it was nearly an hour before he found her hiding spot for the hard drive containing her recordings. Her cunning positioning of the device surprised him. He had dismissed her as a bimbo. He had searched for it under the bed, in all of her empty dresser drawers, and in the empty closets, without success. Then, he began all over again, scrutinizing everything even more methodically. Nothing. He was deeply frustrated. He had looked everywhere but in the bed itself! He removed the pillows, blankets, and sheets, which were crisp and clean. He removed the mattress. Bingo! He found a neat cutout in the box spring's center. The cavity contained a 16-terabyte drive, paired with a powerful antenna. The setup was ingenious.

Ferguson could have left then and there. He had what he had come for. Yet, the lengths to which Bernadette had gone to conceal the hard drive made him wonder if there were other secrets in store. Ferguson thought it logical that she had set up hidden other recording devices in the apartment. Perhaps if he found them, he could wheedle a bonus payment from Big Barney.

He hadn't searched her bathroom. There was booze, so perhaps she had a stash of drugs. The prospect of finding cocaine was incentive enough for him to put in the additional time.

The bathroom was large and deluxe, with gold-plated faucets and handles. Her tiled shower stall large was large enough for two. He examined the sand-colored tile on its walls but found no lens. He removed his hat and scratched his head. His burglar's sixth sense told him that the room contained hidden treasure. He went to the medicine cabinet and opened the door, expecting to find a bag of cocaine. There was a single bottle with a prescription for a drug he had never heard of—ketamine. He left it.

He opened and closed the drawers in the bathroom vanity that held the sink and discovered nothing but makeup and some extra rolls of toilet tissue.

"This is a waste of time," he muttered. Yet he kept looking. He trusted his instincts more than the evidence.

Ferguson once read a spy novel about a clever bathroom concealment for messages, and the book came back to him now. He lifted the heavy porcelain lid of the toilet tank and gently lay it on the floor. He looked into the tank and immediately noticed a strip of clear packing tape around the equator of the black–plastic float ball.

'Now what have we here?' he wondered. He removed the ball and shook it. He felt a slight rattle. Something light was inside. He removed the tape, and the float ball divided into perfect halves. Inside the upper half, Ferguson found a plastic sandwich bag containing a folded legal envelope.

He put the toilet back together and carried the envelope into the kitchen, where he steamed it opened with Malone's red teapot. Inside were two sheets of paper, covered with writing in violet ink. He read and reread them several times with a broadening smile and then carefully replaced the leaves back into the envelope. Hallelujah. He had his miracle. Malone had provided him with the solution to his monetary woes.

15

Suspicion

Following her three-mile trek on the beach, Twyla settled into a white, wooden chair underneath a blue umbrella on the elevated deck of the vacation house. Atop the table was a pitcher of iced tea and her laptop. She poured herself a tall glass of the tea and drank half of it down. Then she flipped open her laptop to study some proposed legislative changes in a tax bill. Twyla had not intended to bring her work to the seashore; but then again, she hadn't intended to spend her time alone. Something about the behavior of her boss, Big Barney, had been nagging at her. He had become more furtive than usual, to the point of lashing out at her when she asked questions about the language in the bill.

The high-speed flow of legislation shepherded by Big Barney troubled her too. The language of bills unfairly advantaged specific constituencies. In itself, there was nothing strange about special interests with deep pockets obtaining favorable legislation. Crony capitalism was as old as the republic. But in the past, this sort of bill seldom made it beyond a subcommittee. Competing special interests with equally deep pockets usually bought off just enough congressmen to block the legislation. Recently, however, the bills had flown through subcommittees and the full committees and had been passed by the full House, without debate. Beyond a doubt, Big Barney was a highly effective speaker—perhaps the most productive one since the legendary Sam Rayburn occupied the revered office. But even Rayburn had to contend with a "loyal opposition." Twyla fretted that there was a strange dynamic at work—possibly an illegal dynamic. She felt compelled to follow her suspicions because she would be guilty by default of corruption if her hunch were true and she failed to act.

She didn't want to jump to false conclusions, however. There were plenty of possible explanations. Barney worked exceptionally hard at wooing members of the House and at forging long-term relations. Every week, he met with the same core group of 40 House members, often one on one. He met with Republicans as well as Democrats. The meetings were brief—five or 10 minutes. But even so, no other leader had been so intimate with his colleagues.

Twyla wondered what Barney said in these meetings. Had he some magic words or some warmth and charm she hadn't detected? The meetings were locked-door, with no record of what transpired. Twyla was bothered by this. She smelled payoffs. She wondered if any of her colleagues harbored similar suspicions?

Twyla was relatively new on the staff, however, and had forged a close relationship with just one colleague, Policy Director Sadie Ramsey, the owner of the beach house. Ramsey knew Big Barney better than her own father. The 45-year-old lawyer had been part of his team since graduating from law school. She considered Sadie to be a straight shooter.

Twyla picked up her cell phone to speed dial Sadie. She paused. How could she phrase a question without sounding disloyal or overly cynical? Could she trust Sadie to maintain her confidence? She decided to take the risk. She did not want to be blindsided by scandal. She wanted reassurance that Big Barney was kosher.

Sadie answered on the first ring.

"Please don't tell me there's a plumbing problem, Twyla," she laughed.

"The only problem, Sadie, is that Martin isn't here yet. Rooster made him work again today."

"Malone?"

"You got it."

"I'm still in shock. And the coincidence of Cisco losing another aide in an election year makes me wonder if some mad man is trying to destroy him. So, anyway, why did you call if there's no plumbing problem?"

"I feel silly asking you this."

"You can ask me anything, Twyla."

"Sadie, I find it strange the way tax bills are flying through the House with no debate. I'm missing some underlying dynamic—and it makes me feel really stupid. How does Big Barney do it?"

"Twyla, you are supposed to be relaxing. There's no mystery about Big Barney's mastery. He's been working the chamber 24/7, cutting deals, making promises. This is a mid-term election year. If the members scratch his back then he'll scratch theirs. He's been moving their pet projects so they can boast to the locals, and in return, they vote for Barney's pet projects."

"Why all of the secrecy. Nothing illegal is going on, is it

86

Sadie?"

"Aren't we paranoid this morning! Listen, child, Barney is shielding his members from the jackals in the press. He acts like a father confessor to these boys and girls. Members can spill their guts and nothing ever gets out. Not even Malcolm Truitt knows what goes on in one of Barney's tete-a-tetes. There's nothing nefarious. It's all about bonding."

"I can understand that. I feel silly for asking, Sadie."

"There's nothing wrong with keeping your eyes and ears open, Twyla. That's what good lawyers do. What exactly unsettled you, if you don't mind my asking? Did someone say something to you? I'm thinking maybe it was Bernadette Kathleen Malone. Big Barney liked her, but in my opinion, she was a real trouble maker. She enjoyed creating conflict."

"I didn't know her," said Twyla, "except to say 'hello' whenever she passed by my desk."

"Forgive me for speaking ill of the dead," said Sadie. "It was terrible what happened to her, murdered out there on the golf course in her pretty white party dress. Now, as for you, enjoy yourself. This is a direct order. There's wine in the fridge. Chill. You don't need that man of yours to enjoy the ocean."

"Amen to that Sadie. It's so beautiful out on the deck. I don't ever want to leave here."

"I know the feeling. Listen, I've got to run. Forget about the office. I don't want to hear from you again—unless it's about the plumbing."

"Thanks, Sadie," said Twyla.

When Twyla hung up the phone, she reopened the newspaper she had been reading earlier. Strange. Martin's story hadn't mentioned a white party dress. The story didn't mention anything at all about Malone's clothing. She lifted her smart phone from the deck table where it rested and searched news stories about the murder from other sources. No one mentioned Bernadette's attire. Strange that she should be wearing a party dress unless she had been at a party. Twyla made a mental note to mention the tidbit to Martin, assuming he made it to down the beach.

16

Brass Ones

Preston Ferguson parked his car in the multi-story garage lot next to Union Station. He entered the station to use one of the few remaining phone booths in the city. He was preparing to blackmail Big Barney, and the booth was the safest way. Barney could not throttle him, and no one legally could eavesdrop electronically on the call.

Ferguson planned to demand a substantial amount from Big Barney. He wanted enough to save his show and pay off the last two years of his son's prep-school tuition. Malone's tell-all letter was his leverage. He knew everything about the drug racket now, and details about several murders, information that could put Barney behind bars for life. He had all the ingredients for a successful negotiation save one—and that was backbone. Fright and apprehension kept him in the phone booth for a good 20 minutes working up the courage to dial.

Barney himself didn't scare Ferguson. However, Jimmy Johnson, the sausage billionaire, the man who had dreamed up the cocaine caucus to further his business interests, frightened him to the core. Johnson, according to Malone's letter, was a homicidal maniac who fed his victims to his pigs. Malone had never seen Johnson kill anyone; but she claimed in her letter that Johnson boasted to her and Big Barney on one drunken occasion about dispatching Cisco's missing aide Susan Hastings in this fashion.

"I can do this. I can be ruthless. I can make this call," Ferguson repeated to himself over and over inside the phone booth, which smelled of stale urine. This was an emboldening exercise. He had read about "emboldening" in a self-help magazine. He repeatedly visualized himself making the call and demanding the payoff. He rehearsed his major talking points over and over again—and then he snorted a line of cocaine through a rolled-up dollar bill.

"Do this, Preston, or you are washed up," he said to himself. Big Barney owed him. He had given Big Barney millions of dollars in free air time, well in excess of what Barney was paying him for the Green Room.

Ferguson dialed Big Barney's private line. Barney picked up after three rings.

"Who is this?" he growled.

"It's Preston, Barney. Mission accomplished."

"Your number didn't show up on my screen."

"I'm calling from a phone booth. It's safer that way."

"Then you have it, the disc drive?"

"Yes. I have it. Took some real brain power to find it. I found something else too. Something meant to destroy you."

"What is it?"

Preston suddenly was feeling cocky, an effect of the cocaine.

"It turns out that we were dealing with an extremely clever and treacherous girl," he said. "I could have left the apartment after I found the drive. My contractual obligation would have been fulfilled. Instead, I took some initiative. I searched the joint all over again from top to bottom. Just to be safe."

"That's great, Preston. What the hell did you find?"

"I looked behind her paintings, under her rugs. I even tossed her dirty laundry. Her cup size was a D, if you're curious. I found the disc drive under her mattress, in a box spring carve-out. She was very clever. James Bond clever. I went back over every square inch of the place. I am not exaggerating: I even plumbed her plumbing. There was an envelope inside the float ball of her toilet tank. It was addressed to an interesting party. Can you believe that? Her hiding things in the toilet tank?"

"Cut the two-bit suspense, Preston" snarled Barney. "Who was the letter addressed to?"

Preston clucked. "You mean to say, 'To whom was it addressed'."

"Whatever, damn you!"

"But are you not first curious as the contents?" teased Ferguson. "I'll give you a hint: a most amazing list."

"List of what?" Big Barney was irked. He did not like being toyed with.

Ferguson cleared his throat. "All of the principal actors and participants of our amazing enterprise, myself included. And a list of each player's recompense. I was low man on the totem pole, it seems. And a roll call of the dead, including Hastings. Bernie, it turns out, was prepared to sell everyone out in the event she was murdered. Fortunately, I found the letter."

"Who was it addressed to?"

"Martin Boundary. He's a reporter at the Observer. The big blond brute who looks like a cross between Robert Redford and an NFL fullback."

"I know Boundary. His wife Twyla works for me."

"Were Malone and Mrs. Boundary friendly? Is that why she

picked Martin Boundary out of all of the reporters in the city?"

Barney grunted. Johnson had told him that Malone had consorted with the reporter. He was now wondering if Malone had shot her mouth off to Twyla. He didn't think so. She hadn't dumped her man for adultery.

Ferguson interrupted the Speaker's train of thought.

"I had no idea of the scope of your business. You must be rolling in dough. And I had no idea that Johnson had done in Hastings. Bernie says in her letter that he boasted of feeding Hastings to his pigs, and warned that the same thing could happen to her if she wasn't careful."

"Did anyone see you?" asked Barney testily. He could tell that Ferguson was high.

Ferguson chuckled. "I wore a hat and a false beard. Inside the apartment, I wore latex gloves and paper slippers over my shoes. No one will ever know that I was there."

"OK, Preston, I admit it, you did good. Get the drive and the letter to me as soon as you can."

Look, the drive is still yours for the $25,000, as we agreed. But the letter, as it was not part of the original deal, will cost you extra."

Barney swallowed.

"How much extra, Preston?"

"A song, really, when you consider what would happen to you if the letter fell into the wrong hands. It's yours for the bargain price of $500,000."

"You're joking," said Barney.

"I'm not. I really could use $1 million; but I don't want to be a prick."

"Preston, I'm more than happy to pay you another $25,000 for that letter. How about it? Fifty grand is a pretty nice rate for a few hours of work."

Ferguson laughed. "A tenth of what I want? Not good enough, my friend. I've done lots for the organization; and I've been woefully underpaid."

"You never once complained," said Big Barney.

"I didn't realize that you were screwing me."

"Your TV show's ratings are not my fault, Preston."

"You need me on the team. You need my Green Room."

"Not for $500,000," said Barney. He added, "You are making a big mistake."

"I'll give you one day to think it over, Barney. You try to burn me, then I'll burn you. I'll take this letter public. You'll go to jail for life."

"You are crazy," Barney sputtered. "You're acting like a two-bit blackmailer."

"I admit I'm a blackmailer. And you, sir, are a drug pusher. So, don't act morally superior."

"How do I know you are not jacking me off? How do I know that the letter isn't something that you wrote yourself?"

Ferguson read him the contents, and Barney could tell from the details from the details that it was real. Barney was shocked that Bernadette had learned so much. Johnson must have shot off his mouth while trying to impress her.

"How about $100,000 per year for five years, plus free coke? That is a generous retainer," said Big Barney.

"Look, I actually could use $1 million, but I am restraining myself because I really like you. Bill collectors are wolfing at my door. I have a kid in an expensive New England prep school. Anyway, you should be grateful for my discovering this letter before the cops did and saving you from prison."

"We can't just write a check for $500,000," Big Barney

said angrily. "The organization doesn't keep that much money in any one account. Besides, Preston, there are money laundering laws. Bankers have to report any deposits and withdrawals of over $15,000 to the Feds. I would have to make small withdrawals at several institutions on different days for us to stay under the radar."

"Get the money from a non-banking source. Take out a mortgage."

"Don't be a dick. You have no idea how complicated the organization's finances are."

Barney's voice had weakened slightly, and Ferguson interpreted this as a sign of acquiescence. He was winning. He was emboldened.

"You certainly are not paying your suppliers with bank checks. You must have a suitcase full of money somewhere."

In fact, Big Barney had several big suitcases stuffed with $100 bills hidden in a false wall of his five-car garage—at the ready if he had to flee on short notice.

"I have enough ready cash to buy coke from the Mexican cartel. I can't stiff those guys. They'd kill me—and you too. The Gutierrez boys are not to be trifled with. Even Jimmy says so."

"You shouldn't trifle with me, either," said Ferguson

"How do I know there isn't a duplicate letter. How do I know you won't come back for more money?"

"You don't. But I won't. Mother Ferguson may have raised a thief, but she didn't raise a liar."

"I need a few days to think about this, Preston," said Barney.

Ferguson suddenly felt irritable. It was an effect of the cocaine.

"It would be unwise to fuck with me, Big Barney. I am a

desperate man capable of desperate actions."

Barney grunted and said promised get back within 24 hours.

Ferguson laughed. He exited the busy train station and lit up a cigar on the sidewalk. He thought , 'You have big, brass ones, my friend. Great big, brass ones.'

17

Cradle to Grave

Boundary dragged himself into his gray cubicle, plopped himself into his coffee-stained swivel chair, and pounded the numerical pad of his hard-line telephone with his thick fingers. He was attired in loud beachwear: a green and yellow, floral shirt, cargo shorts, and cherry-red flip-flops. An animated Rooster had just told him to dig deep into Malone's life and turn it inside out.

"Go back as far as you can, even to her infancy. Where was she born? How much did she weigh?"

"Cradle to grave—except she hasn't been buried yet, Rooster."

"Just do it. I'll give you 1,000 words."

"You want her detailed life story in 1,000 words?" Boundary was incredulous.

"A seasoned journalist could do it in 700. But you're still wet behind the ears, so you get an extra 300. Now quit complaining and get to work."

Boundary had been tempted to tell Rooster about his Malone connection. But Rooster hadn't let Boundary get a word in edge wise. The editor intimidated him, and Boundary also feared that news of his marital infidelity would race like wildfire through the newsroom and end up reaching Twyla. So, he had kept mum. And then, when Truitt suddenly burst in on them to argue that the murder should be his story, owing to its nexus with the political world, Boundary argued that Truitt had conflicts of interest. He had played golf at the club the day of the murder and was therefore an assumed suspect. Boundary knew he was acting like a hypocrite—but he would not let go of the story. He had climbed out too far on the limb to countenance full retreat.

Truitt, stung by Boundary's broadside, had countered that Twyla worked for Big Barney.

"If I have a conflict, then you have one too."

"This is police-beat stuff," growled Rooster.

"So was Watergate, initially," Truitt snapped.

"If this story ever rises to the level of Watergate, then you'll get a piece. But for now, the story belongs to Boundary."

Truitt had stormed out of the office muttering about the 'presumptuous' upstart Boundary and the 'unpardonable' intrusion onto his turf.

"Truitt is too cozy with those guys on the Hill," Rooster had muttered when the older journalist was out of earshot. He closed his office door and told Boundary, "I don't trust him to ask tough questions. I want you to dig up every piece of dirt you can about Malone, no matter whose feathers you ruffle. Call Big Barney, Cisco. Call them all. You got that?"

Boundary had nodded.

He picked up a ballpoint and held it suspended over a yellow legal pad. Where to start? He composed a list of people to call, starting with Malone's Hill colleagues, her family, Cisco, her neighbors. And Joe, his neighbor. He dialed Joe immediately and got an out-of-office reply. He left a message.

Twyla had mentioned that Malone won a beauty contest, so Boundary ran a search. He found a Wikipedia entry for her, which he had not expected. Malone briefly had been a television weather girl in Raleigh, North Carolina, for WGIT. He wondered if Twyla knew this and had forgotten to tell him.

Malone had made quite an impression on the local television audience, according to the short entry. She had been a star for all the wrong reasons and had been fired by the station owner, her own father. There was no elaboration nor footnote reference.

Boundary copied down the name of the television station, visited its website, and took down the contact information.

His phone rang. It was his neighbor, Joe.

"I'm in Chicago, Martin, giving a lecture to the local constabulary about the preservation of crime scenes."

Boundary told him about the Sunday feature. "I could use a news peg at the top of the feature—something that advances the murder story," he said.

"You haven't heard about the car?" asked Joe.

"What car?"

"They found Malone's car in a student parking lot at John Adams University. The FBI is swarming all over it. You should call Ray Cordovan, the campus police chief. He's a publicity hound. Promise to put his name in the paper, and he'll tell you everything."

Joe gave Boundary the chief's cell number. Boundary thanked him profusely for the tip.

Joe had sized up Chief Cordovan accurately. The chief gave Boundary every detail of the discovery, including that there wasn't a single fingerprint on the car. Someone had wiped it clean.

"We got a fuzzy image of the driver. The security cams at that lot are 10 years old. The perp was black or Hispanic, and he was wearing gloves, jeans, basketball shoes with the laces undone, and a hoodie."

"Sounds like one of a million. Do you have any idea who he is, Chief?"

"Nope. We couldn't get as decent enhancement."

"Was there any blood in the car?"

"No blood."

"Was there anything unusual at all?"

"We found an Ogden Titanium driver in the trunk. The FBI took it away for analysis."

"Can I quote you, Chief?' Boundary was excited. This was a big development.

"Sure, as long as you spell my name right."

"Who found the car?"

"A journalism professor named DeSales. He called me directly, and I ran the plate and, bingo, it came back to Malone."

"Carl DeSales?"

"That's the guy. You know him?"

"Yes. I know him darn well. Can I send a photographer around to take a shot of the car?"

"By the time he gets here, it will be gone," said the chief. The FBI is hooking the vehicle to a tow truck as we speak."

"Do any other reporters know about this?"

"A guy named Dwiggens from Daily Bugler.com called earlier."

Boundary swore under his breath. His exclusive news hook for the feature had just gone up in smoke.

He thanked the chief and hung up the phone. DeSales must have tipped off Dwiggens as payback for running the story of Rootewerke's disappearance. Boundary went to the Bugler website. The discovery of Malone's car and the Ogden was the lead story. Boundary swore again. He hated being scooped. He wrote up a news brief and sent it to the copy desk.

Then, he got back to work searching the web for information on Malone. He found the name of her college and then found a list of her classmates.

A finger tapped his left shoulder. When he looked up, Kitty Cross was there with a cup of coffee for him. She was wearing white slacks and a blue top.

"You look like you could use this, Boundary," she said, handing him the cup and tossing her shoulder-length brown hair.

"Thanks, Kitty. I'm seeing double."

The older woman made Boundary feel like a silly schoolboy with a teacher's crush. She had a lovely face. Her father was Danish, her mother Spanish. The blend was striking, with an aquiline nose, large brown eyes, high cheekbones and a broad forehead punctuated by a widow's peak. A few, fine crow's feet in the corner of her eyes hinted she was in her 40s.

"You did good work on the golf course yesterday. This feature you're working on is a big story with national implications; yet, Rooster tells me you seem less than enthusiastic about it."

"Domestic problems, Kitty. I'm supposed to be at the beach with Twyla. She's brokenhearted, and I feel terrible about it."

"Journalism is tough on love. Ask my two ex-husbands." She laughed.

Cross had a sultry voice and a wry smile. She could have

100

been in pictures, Boundary thought.

"I'll let you get back to work so you can get out of here and on your way to the beach." She had deduced from the look on his face that she was a distraction.

The offices at Malone's high school and university were closed. Boundary would have to track down the home number of officials from both schools. This chore would be time consuming. He moved it to the back of his to-do list. He despaired of ever getting to the beach.

Boundary retrieved an electronic copy of a congressional directory and sent emails to aides who might have known Malone. Congressional staff often came in on Saturday mornings to catch up with their work. Twyla was no exception. He might get lucky and get a response. When he finished this chore, he opened his middle desk drawer. He had hung onto the slip of paper with the pilfered private number of Lola Gutierrez, Cisco's explosive spokeswoman. Malone had been Cisco's aide. He needed a quote. He held the slip between his index finger and weighed the pros and the cons of phoning the virago. He wondered if Malone had spilled the beans to Lola about their fling. A call to Lola might invite blackmail or a vengeful phone call to Twyla. He drummed the fingers of his left hand on the desktop and decided after much agonizing that he had to make the call.

Lola picked up on the sixth ring. Boundary had been about to hang up. He didn't expect she'd tell him anything useful.

"Gutierrez. Who is this, and what do you want?"

"Hello, Lola, this is Martin Boundary of the Observer," he said with all the charm he could muster. "Sorry to bother you. I'm calling for Senator Cisco's official reaction to the murder of Bernadette Malone."

He braced himself for an obscene response. But Lola surprised him. She dropped the sharp edge from her voice.

"I suppose you are writing a profile of Bernadette."

"How did you guess?"

"I've been fielding calls about her all day," Lola said. "You think you're the only reporter working on a story? I've heard from the New York Times, the Los Angeles Times, the Wall Street Journal, Bloomberg, and all the rest."

"No. I didn't. I assumed that you would be very busy."

Truth was, he hadn't given the competition much thought at all.

"Did you know Malone, Mr. Boundary?"

That was a loaded question; or was it?

"I met her once." he said. "She seemed nice. She was a looker, that's for sure."

"She was an angel who was easily flattered and manipulated into spreading her legs like a butterfly spreads its wings," said Lola. "But you can't report this. Bernadette has parents and siblings. They are grieving. Why should I trash her? It would do no good and plenty of harm. But it was no secret that she was promiscuous. You can attribute that to a knowledgeable source on Capitol Hill."

"Was she sleeping with anyone regularly?" Boundary wanted to add, "like Senator Cisco," but restrained himself.

Lola hesitated. "Regularly? A steady? I don't think so. She enjoyed variety. She boasted openly about some of her conquests."

Boundary waited for the hammer to drop, but Lola did not elaborate.

"Can you give me some names? I'd like to call them."

"I can't do that to them."

"Did she sleep with Senator Cisco? Was he one of them?" He braced for her outburst.

"I don't know," said Lola. "Kent said nothing about it, but he clearly liked Bernadette. What real man would not like her?

"Do you think someone may have killed her to derail his reelection?"

"Sure. Why not? Some sick slime ball like your pal DeSales could have done it. Where was he on the night of the murder?"

"Next time I see him, I'll ask him," said Boundary.

"Kent is being crushed in the polls because of this. It's unfair. There's not a shred of evidence."

Boundary moved on. "How about some fonder reminiscences of Bernadette?"

"We didn't have much day-to-day contact," said Lola. "She was an administrative secretary, and I run the communications shop. We were in different offices. Down different hallways Always running in different directions."

"She often carried a large briefcase into Big Barney's office," said Boundary. "Do you know what that was about?"

"Did your wife tell you that?"

"A source told me."

"Kent used Bernadette as a courier. He is paranoid about using the internet or fax machines. Says it's an invitation to have stuff end up on WikiLeaks."

"How did Bernadette end up on Cisco's staff?"

"Her father was a friend of Kent's. He owns a television station."

"WGIT?"

"That's the one."

"She was a weather girl there, right?"

"A presenter, not a girl."

"Sorry. No sexism intended. May I have a copy of her original resume and cover letter?"

"I can't give you a copy because of privacy laws. But I can tell you, off the record, what I know."

"Great," he said. It surprised him that the legendary Dragon Lady was so cooperative. But he wasn't about to look the proverbial gift horse in the mouth. He was in a rush to compose a story.

Lola rattled off employment information about Malone and the names of the persons who had provided job references. She sounded as though she were reading from the very job resume she had declined to share.

Then, she abruptly terminated the call.

Boundary laughed out loud. Lola was about as predictable as a stray dog. At least she had been helpful.

Boundary called WGIT and asked for the producer of the news broadcast. The producer was friendly but pressed for time. She told Boundary she had not known Malone, having arrived after the weather girl's abrupt departure.

"Her dad owns the station. He's devastated. He's a sweet guy."

"Is there anyone there now who knew her?"

"They're in management and they will not speak to any outside reporters. Why don't you try her former talent agent?"

"She had an agent? I thought her dad owned the station?"

"All the on-air talent has the same agent—Janice Craight. I don't have a number, but she has a website. Good luck."

Boundary found a website for "The Janice Craight Agency" without difficulty. The site's banner boasted that the agency represented actors, newscasters, authors, voice-over artists, public speakers, and politicians. Craight's picture was in the

104

top right corner. She had raven hair, pale skin, pink pillowed lips, and violet eyes. She was handsome, not beautiful. Boundary judged her to be about 60. When he dialed the agency's main number, a robot instructed him to type in the first three letters of the surname of the employee he wanted to reach. He entered CRA. The robot connected him directly to Craight.

The woman had a deep, sexy, southern accent, the kind that turns grown men into silly putty.

Boundary introduced himself and told her about his Malone profile. He asked about the murdered woman's stint as a weather presenter. Craight said she'd be happy to help.

"Bernadette, God love her, was an on-air disaster," Craight laughed. "The poor thing had the most terrible stage fright I've ever seen—and a very limited memory. She continually forgot details of the forecasts, like the current temperature. The producer, Charlie Raines, tried cue cards, but it was too obvious that she was reading them. She read r...e...a...l...s...l...o...w. Bernadette was on her way to becoming a lovable, successful laughing stock. Everyone tuned in to see her mangle the forecasts. Advertising spiked. I got her a pay boost. I didn't deal with her Daddy. He was hands off on hiring and firing. He delegated all that nasty stuff to Mike Fisher, the station manager. Mike's moved on to one of the big networks.

"Anyway, Bernadette had a bad case of on-air anxiety and she never lost it, but she tried to tackle it head on one night. The rumor was she snorted cocaine. Whatever she did, it made her eyes shine like headlights and bent her smile into a cockeyed grin. The live shots were rolling. She stood in front of the weather map and pointed to it. Then her happy face morphed into a look of profound befuddlement. She blurted, 'What the fuck, there's snow in the forecast!' I never laughed so hard in my life. But the remark didn't go over so well with the viewers. This is the Bible belt, and preachers and their congregations sent in thousands of emails protesting Bernadette's 'vile tongue.' Local advertisers withdrew from her time slot. She might have survived if they had given her the opportunity to apologize. But the rest of the news team said they'd quit if Malone wasn't let go, because she was turning the broadcast into a clown show. I represent all of them, so I could not jump to poor Bernie's defense, although I would have preferred to. The storm would have passed. But Fisher, who had once been a newscaster himself, agreed with them. So out the door she went."

"Wikipedia says she lasted a year," said Boundary.

"No, it was a little longer than a year. She lasted, let me see, fourteen and a half months. They let her go in March, right in the middle of a fucking snow storm."

Boundary roared with laughter.

"Malone's father got in the phone to Cisco and begged him to give Bernadette a staff job so she could save face. Cisco jumped at the offer, Mr. Boundary, because he'd have a contributor with a broadcasting station by his balls. Cisco named Bernadette his personal assistant. She was allowed to announce her career change on the air, which she did, triumphantly. It was like she was saying, 'I'm leaving this shitburg, ya'll, and you're not!' God love her, that was a precious moment. People here still bring it up at parties when they want to have a hoot."

Craight also said Malone had dated Cisco for a time, but stopped because he had what she had described to the older woman as 'the Senator's dark side'."

"What dark side?"

106

"I should not have said that. She never confided in me what she meant. Violence, kink, depression? Who knows what lurks in the heart of a politician? His wife had died of cancer. He never had a happy look after she died. Maybe he was a depressive."

Following the call, Boundary called Lola back and pressed her for more information about Malone's relationship with Cisco. He told her what Malone had told Craight about the Senator's dark side. Lola calmly told him that if he was recording the call to shut down the device. In Washington, D.C., a reporter or anyone else has the legal right to tape a phone call without alerting the other party. Boundary turned off his phone recording system. He was a boy scout. Most other D.C. reporters merely would have assented and left the recorder running.

"Probably he was fucking her," said Lola, after he told her he had shut his taping system down. "We all thought so. But I have no evidence. In the office, he treated Bernadette like he treated every other employee, with cool professionalism. The two of them never made goo-goo eyes at one another. The Senator registered no emotion when his colleagues hit on her—and all the straight ones did. Bernadette occasionally went around town with Cisco at restaurants, the Kennedy Center, and—once when he was on vacation in a very expensive resort hotel in Cabos, Mexico—on the Baja peninsula. A Daily Mail paparazzi caught them hand-in-hand on the beach."

"When was that?"

"Six years ago, maybe? I don't know. There's a photo on some busybody's Facebook page someplace. Try a Google search."

"Could Senator Cisco have murdered her?" asked Boundary,

knowing he might be pushing the limits of Lola's cordiality.

She surprised him again when she answered, "I doubt it, but who knows? I mean, I had a thing with him once. Initially, he was as charming and sophisticated as a Frenchman. And attractive also because he is so powerful. He has muscles. He's very athletic. He played college football at UNC and he works out for a couple of hours every day. I would have done anything for him. Then one night he became angry at me—intensely angry. I never had had a clue he had such a temper. He frightened me."

"He hit you?"

"No. He never laid a hand on me. But in his eyes I suddenly saw a ferocious beast. You know, rage without a trace of the light of reason? I panicked. I fled outside barefoot in 30-degree weather. He apologized in the office the next day and handed me back my shoes— but I told him it was over between us. I gave him my two-week notice. He refused my resignation, which was a relief because I needed this job. After that, he acted as if our thing never happened. So, did I. But it got me wondering about Hastings and her disappearance."

"You think he killed her?"

"I don't know. Once I believed he never could have hurt a fly. That night, I was trembling. This is all off the record. You use it, and I'll call you a liar."

"I won't use any of it," promised Boundary.

The young reporter was excited because Lola was confirming his darkest suspicions about Cisco. He never asked himself the obvious question: Why was Lola abruptly throwing her boss under the bus?

"Did Bernadette use cocaine?" Boundary asked. He remembered what Craight had said. Drugs might figure in the murder.

"I don't think so. How would I know? I mean, at work, she seemed normal. I never noticed any drugs around here."

"Can you think of anyone who might have had a reason to kill her?" asked Boundary. "Anyone at all?"

"A jilted lover, maybe? I don't know. The FBI interviewed me. I told them that Bernadette didn't have an enemy in the world—none I ever heard of."

"How did Senator Cisco act when he learned she was dead?"

"The FBI told him. When I saw him afterwards, it was business as usual. Now, let me ask you something: Was Bernadette one of your sources?"

"I had a brief encounter with her once. I really did not know her." His voice sounded strained.

"You would protect a source. Isn't that, right?"

"Yes, of course," he said. "I would never burn a source. No decent journalist would. But she wasn't a source. I cover crime, not politics. And besides, she's dead. I mean, who is there to protect?"

"I guess your wife tells you everything anyhow."

"We have our firewalls. Whenever we..."

Lola hung up.

"God damn, it is Cisco," Boundary said. "I knew it was Cisco."

18

Pay Back

Ferguson walked carefully down a hard dirt trail in Rock Creek Park, just behind the National Zoo's parking lot, where he had left his car. It was Saturday at dusk, and he was the only person on the trail.

Cicadas were buzzing loudly in the humid air and the water of the fast-flowing creek gurgled musically as it rushed over the gneiss and schist of its bed. Elephants in the zoo sounded an occasional trumpet blast. Swarms of bats were flying low overhead, which made Ferguson squeamish. He never had enjoyed the wilderness. He almost screamed out when some bats came within inches of his head.

The park was an unexpected wild place, given its location in the middle of Washington, D.C. Outdoorsman Teddy Roosevelt used to hike it often during his time in the capital. Ferguson would have preferred to be anywhere else. However, Big Barney had demanded this place for a rendezvous to exchange the disc drive and the letter he had recovered from Malone's love nest, for a suitcase filled with cash. Barney was paranoid about cameras, and they were ubiquitous on the street of the city. Traffic cameras stood on every corner and security cameras had become regular fixtures on the front porches of local homes. Then there were the tourists, forever recording anyone and everything. Ferguson pleaded for a more civilized setting; but Barney was adamant that the exchange take place here in the park.

Ferguson was both frightened and exhilarated as he made his way along the trail with the cautious tread of a blind man. His criminal career was advancing to a higher level. His dad, God love him, would have been proud.

He heard a branch snap ahead. He stopped dead in his tracks and listened. Darkness was closing in.

"Big Barney, is that you?" he said nervously. There was no answer. He wondered if he was walking into a trap.

Ferguson took an LCD penlight from his pocket to guide him. It cast a narrow, bluish beam. He nervously swept the trail with the light as he inched towards his rendezvous. The mosquitoes were becoming obnoxious. He was constantly swatting them away from his face. The sooner the exchange took place, and he was out of there, the better.

Ferguson heard the snapping of another branch, followed by a panicked squawk and the beating of feathers. He fingered a small Sig Sauer.22 in his right pants pocket. The gun was no bigger than a starter pistol. The maker had designed it for women's purses. This diminutive firearm was his insurance. One could not be too careful when large sums of money were in play.

He rounded a spot where big trees on both sides narrowed the footpath and tripped on a thick tree root, landing flat on his face. He got back up, swearing. He had torn the right knee out of his new trousers—$100 down the drain.

"Have a nice trip?"

Startled, Ferguson shone a shaky beam in the direction of the voice. The beam fell on Jimmy Johnson leaning casually against the fat, gnarled trunk of an ancient tree. Johnson wore a crisply ironed safari jacket, meticulously creased khaki pants, and a pair of alligator boots. A brown leather suitcase was on the ground beside him. He took a reefer from his pocket, lit it, and puffed away. The tip glowed bright red in the darkness.

"Want a drag?" he asked Ferguson.

"Jimmy? What are you doing here? Where's Big Barney?"

"Barney had unexpected business. Now let me see the goods."

Ferguson told himself to be cool, that this was payday, that there was nothing to worry about; yet he was nervous. Jimmy Johnson had come all the way from Murfreesboro, North Carolina. He wondered if he should flash the gun, just to make it clear to Johnson that they were in a no-nonsense zone? He decided to keep it snug in his pocket. Why elevate the meeting into a crisis? He had to maintain his cool.

Johnson was growing impatient.

"Hand over the goddamned disc drive and the letter," he said.

Ferguson produced both the envelope with the letter and the drive from the right hip pocket of his pants and handed them to Johnson. Johnson pulled out a flashlight of his own and took the letter out of the envelope. It was Bernadette's handwriting, all right. All loops and flourishes. And, she religiously used violet ink. He hated violet ink. As for the contents of the letter, she had known far more about the enterprise than he realized. Shockingly more. She had been a minor cog purposely kept in the dark. Either he had underestimated her cleverness or someone in the operation had a big mouth. Ferguson's discovery of the letter was fortunate. Security breaches were among his gravest concerns. He eliminated them with extreme prejudice as Bernadette had discovered. He hadn't expected a breach from beyond the grave.

Johnson looked at the address on the envelope: Martin Boundary, the Observer. He wondered if she had leaked information to the reporter. And what about Boundary's wife, Twyla? She had known Bernadette. Now she was getting nosy, asking questions about Big Barney.

Johnson grunted like one of the seven savage, 300-pound, feral hogs caged at his North Carolina hunting estate that could make a body or two disappear overnight. The voracious saw-toothed creatures left nothing to waste. And the hulking animals possessed an incredibly efficient digestive system. They turned human flesh and bones into pig shit in only 10 hours. Human beings, in contrast, required 30 hours to turn their food into compost.

Johnson looked at the drug-addled man standing in front of him and saw more hog feed. How dare the maggot try to blackmail one of the most successful businessmen on the face of the planet? Ferguson's cheek enraged him. Ferguson's wife Betsy already was in the trunk of Johnson's black Cadillac Escalade.

As if he could read Johnson's mind, Ferguson said nervously, "I have insurance, in a safe place—copies of the letter. If anything happens, the pictures will go straight to the police. I guarantee it." Johnson considered this a bluff. Ferguson's wife likely was the agent of his fail-safe system, and she no longer constituted a threat.

"No need to be nervous, Preston. You saved my ass. I am eternally grateful. Don't spoil our beautiful relationship with your paranoia."

Ferguson shrugged. "Where's my money?"

Johnson pointed to the briefcase.

"It's there," Johnson said. "Half-a-million in 100-dollar bills. Open the case and look."

"Slide it over."

Johnson pushed the briefcase across the ground to Ferguson with the pointed toe of his alligator-skin boots. Preston reached down for it with his left hand and pulled the pistol from his right pocket. Johnson laughed when he saw the tiny gun.

"You need not brandish that awesome fire power, Preston. I am not packing. Guns are so low class. Wouldn't you agree that's we'd all be better off wielding the honorable weapons of more ancient times when men were men and cold steel clashed with cold steel?"

"Tell that to Malone."

"Bernadette's end was a tragic; but I have no clue who did her in. I suspect it was Kent Cisco. He's bitter and psychotic and short-tempered—and he was dating Bernadette. And it's just too neat, isn't it, his losing his Ogden Titanium? Then it turns up as the murder weapon! Too clever by half."

Ferguson kept his pistol pointed at Johnson. He laid the briefcase on the hard, bare ground of the trail, undid the lid fasteners, and lifted it open slowly, obviously wary of an explosive. But there was no bang, no cloud of tear gas. Johnson had filled the case with neat rows of crisp new currency. Ferguson experienced a surge of ecstasy. He said to Johnson with a broad smile, "You never, ever will have anything to fear from me. Once I'm bought, I stay bought."

"I want you to count it before you leave, partner. I don't

want you claiming tomorrow I shortchanged you."

"Here? In the woods? It's much too dark."

"Yes, here and now. Count it. I want a signed receipt. Take my light. It's brighter than yours." Johnson lobbed a foot-long flashlight at Ferguson who dropped it and then scrambled to pick it up, moving the light and the pistol together wildly.

"No more sudden moves like that," he warned. A laughing Johnson raised his arms in mock surrender and took two steps backwards.

"My goodness, aren't we jumpy? How about a snort of coke?"

"No, thanks."

Ferguson got down on his knees, lay the gun beside him, stuck the small light in his mouth and the big light on the ground pointing at the case, and counted slowly, with one eye on Johnson. The working conditions were less than ideal for detailed accountancy. Ferguson came up $3,000 short. Johnson told him that all the money was all there, to count it again. He did. This time he came up $1,500 short. Johnson had shorted the case by $5,000.

"Heaven above, Ferguson, did you take arithmetic in elementary school?"

"You make me nervous, Jimmy."

"I'll turn my back on you, if you think it will help," Johnson said sarcastically. "Count again, out loud this time. I'll bet you an extra $10,000 that it is all there, to the penny."

Ferguson considered a purposeful under count. Johnson would have to pay up. He could use an extra $10,000.

Jimmy had his back turned, so Ferguson stuck two wads of cash into the inner pockets of his jacket.

'It will serve the smug bastard right,' he said to himself.

115

He became so immersed in his petty plotting that he never heard the footsteps behind him, nor did he register the whoosh of the Ogden Titanium driver that took him from this life to the next.

19

Shown Up

Rooster cleared Boundary's story just after 10 p.m. Boundary was both physically and mentally exhausted. Twyla was waiting for him. At least he'd have Sunday with her. They'd go to early mass, grab pancakes at a diner, and lounge on the beach. He grabbed his cell phone, crash helmet, and the keys to his motorcycle from atop his desk. His trip to the seashore would take three hours, assuming no traffic and a slap of cool night air to keep him awake on the 129-mile ride.

As he exited his cubicle, Boundary glanced up at one of the dozen TV monitors scattered around the newsroom on ceiling mounts.

"What the...!"

Staring back at him were side-by-side mug shots of Cisco and Rootewerke. At 6-foot-five, Boundary could reach up to the TV's panel and un-mute the speaker. The anchor, a sexy woman who wore her long blond hair over one eye like the 40s film star Veronica Lake, reported that the city police suddenly were interested with the missing Dutch student, in light of the brutal murder of Bernadette Kathleen Malone. The nexus was Cisco. The police, she said, had officially declared Rootewerke a missing person and had questioned Cisco about his whereabouts the day Rootewerke had disappeared.

The report included security camera footage of Rootewerke leaving the Capitol grounds, trailing behind Cisco. This was followed by a clip of Carl DeSales, identified in a screen caption as Rootewerke's college professor, complaining that Cisco had not cooperated with search the day the girl had disappeared.

Boundary swore loudly.

"Your little friend DeSales is playing the police and the television crowd like a violin," crowed a voice from behind him. "He's a virtuoso at media manipulation."

Boundary jumped because he had assumed he was the only reporter left in the newsroom. He spun around and instinctively raised his fists. He faced a grinning Truitt.

"You think that's funny, Truitt, sneaking up on someone?"

"It's no funnier than sneaking into someone's office and stealing phone numbers. But I wasn't sneaking about. I'm here to write a blockbuster for the front page of our Sunday paper."

Boundary pointed at the TV.

"That should have been our story. Thanks to your playing mother hen to your favorite senator, we've been scooped," said Boundary.

"It's equally possible that Cisco is blameless, and that DeSales is the killer. Has that thought ever enter your thick skull?" He tapped his head with his forefinger for emphasis.

"DeSales? A murderer? Don't make me laugh. He's practically a midget."

Truitt removed his eyeglasses and twirled them. "I have a fascinating tale to tell my readers," he said. "Coincidentally, it's about DeSales. Eight years ago, in the early days of Cisco's last Senate campaign, the professor wrote a check for $2,000 made out to challenger Godfrey Teal."

Truitt handed Boundary a photocopy of the check. The young reporter studied it. DeSales' signature with his fancy "S" was unmistakable.

"DeSales also solicited other donations for Teal totaling over $10,000. I have those records from the Federal Election Commission. They have a marvelous database, you know. You should check it out sometime. DeSales, you will recall, was a working political journalist covering the campaign, and he savaged Cisco in a series of stories about the Hastings disappearance. Now we know why he was so eager to hang Cisco. He was backing the other horse in that race. It turns out that Teal had promised him a job as his press secretary. I have this from Teal himself. One wonders why DeSales' is trying to hang Cisco this time around?"

The news dumbfounded Boundary—and his face showed it. Truitt's smirked. He enjoyed the young reporter's agony.

Boundary realized that if Truitt was telling the truth, then DeSales' credibility as a source on the Rootewerke disappearance was zero. But then, what about Lola Gutierrez? Hadn't she intimated that Cisco had a dark side?

"Rooster has set aside some space for my piece," said Truitt, his face glowing triumphantly. "A word of advice, Boundary, from a more seasoned reporter: You should have looked deeper at DeSales and his motive for trying to drag Senator Cisco into this foreign girl's disappearance. He may have killed her himself. He may have killed Hastings too. A good investigative reporter follows every lead to its end."

Boundary pushed angrily past Truitt into Rooster's office.

The editor had just hung up the phone to the printing plant. He was making last-minute changes to Sunday's front page to accommodate Truitt's story.

"Chief, did you see the TV report on Rootewerke?" Rooster was chewing on an unlit cigar. Boundary pointed to TV monitor on a ceiling bracket on the left side of the editor's office.

"It's grade-A bullshit, Boundary. We don't run bullshit even if it's reported every place else. Now get out of here — go to your wife. You did a good job today."

"What about Truitt's story on DeSales?" Boundary asked.

"It's running alongside yours, on page one," said Rooster. "I told you to stay away from DeSales. He's no damn good!"

"Are you going to ignore the missing Dutch girl?"

"There's no corpse, Boundary. There is no evidence of foul play. That TV footage shows her walking about 50-feet behind Cisco, who was walking with an aide. We are a fact-based institution, not a hunch-based one. Now go down to the seashore and chill. Take Monday off too if you feel like it. You've earned the comp time."

Boundary hesitated. He was searching for a response.

"Get out of here, like I told you. Scram!"

He turned and left with his tail between its legs.

20

Deceit

Truitt's expose was the lead story on Sunday. Boundary's story had three inches in a single column on the bottom of page one and then jumped to a half-page on the inside. Though it was years since DeSales had committed his ethical sin of making a political donation while practicing journalism, there was no statute of limitations for outrage.

Online, Truitt's story was the most commented upon and the most-emailed. Boundary's story ranked 16th in views and 50th in comments. The public, it seemed, was not overly interested in the biography of the murdered Senate aide.

Boundary felt chastened. Though he hated to admit it, Truitt was right—he had blown it big time. He hadn't been neutral in his reporting. He had leapt to conclusions. He had acted like a third-rate private detective rather than a seasoned journalist. He'd have to reboot his brain and take a fresh look at the facts. He'd have to work hard to unearth more evidence if he hoped to link Rootewerke's disappearance and Malone's murder.

"Stop reading the paper, Martin," said Twyla. "Come out here on the deck with me and enjoy the ocean. It's lovely today. I've never seen the Atlantic looking so blue." Twyla was leaning over the deck's wooden rail. A screen door separated the deck from the seafront home's sprawling kitchen, where Boundary sat at a table with the old-fashioned, no-battery-required newspaper spread out before him like a tablecloth.

"Why don't you come in and read with me, Twyla?"

They did that some mornings, Twyla reading the story aloud and Martin voicing questions and critiques that the two of them then debated.

"Because I can't take my eyes off of the sea," she said. "And this is a vacation."

Boundary's motorcycle ride to the seashore had been appallingly miserable. An unexpected squall moved in. He had endured 60 minutes of drenching rains and wicked wind blasts that pushed his bike onto the highway's shoulder. By journey's end, he was a shivering wet mop. He had stripped off his sopping jeans and sweatshirt and showered in hot water until the expanse of purple goosebumps covering his body disappeared. Then he slept like an anesthetized patient until Twyla stirred beside him and roused him for morning Mass where he slept soundly during the sermon.

Boundary still felt fatigued. He lifted himself slowly from the kitchen chair, opened the sliding screen door, and stood with Twyla by the rail. She was wearing a red bikini. A few young men playing beach volleyball with their girlfriends below looked up at her with carnal desire evident in their eyes. Boundary heard the girlfriends say something sharp to them and all but one man—a hairy, sumo-sized fellow with long hair and elaborate tattooing—stopped staring. A woman in the group who had purple-dyed hair bounced the volleyball off of the disobedient man's head. His buddies laughed raucously, and the game resumed.

"You look very sexy, Twyla," said Boundary.

"I know. I stopped the volleyball game." She laughed. Boundary laughed too. He squeezed her hand, then kissed it. He loved her. He feared losing her. But he was confident he had dodged a marriage-wrecking catastrophe.

After silently gazing at the sea for a while, they left the rail and sat side by side in white Adirondack deck chairs. Twyla looked at her husband. She spied tension in his jaw. Martin was stewing about Truitt's story; and she sympathized. Martin was losing his bitter, intense competition with the smug veteran. He hated to lose. The competitive drive was part of his DNA. But it had been Martin's own fault for rushing to judgement. She knew that he that he was beating himself for his lapses. She patted Martin on the forearm, rose, went into the kitchen and made two, tall ice teas. She returned, handed him one and sat back down beside him. They gazed silently at the surf and sipped their cold drinks. The sun, unimpeded by any clouds, toasted them with its strong rays. Although it was daytime, a full moon was visible in the cloudless sky.

The moon fascinated Twyla. As a young girl, she had studied it for hours through her father Ned's backyard telescope. She still remembered the names of almost every major crater on the near side: Aristoteles; Copernicus; Maginus; Picard; Tycho. She wondered if Martin was looking at this great white disk in the azure sky.

"Penny for your thoughts." Twyla looked at him search-ingly.

Boundary was not thinking about the moon. His mind was far away from it, 238,900 miles, to be exact. He was replaying the desperate cell phone call from DeSales he had taken during his motorcycle ride to the shore. The call had disturbed him. He told Twyla about it. DeSales had begged him for some show of support by the Observer. He had said, "Listen Martin, my esteemed colleagues at the university have their fangs bared. I am being forced to resign. I was stupid and wrong to have made that political contribution. I did it because Cisco was a killer. I felt strongly that he had to go. But what I did is ancient history! Do you think it's a coincidence that Truitt suddenly dug up this information? He's no super sleuth. He's Cisco's whore. The Senator is a ruthless killer, and a clever one, too. He wanted me off his tail, and it looks like he has succeeded."

Boundary had been too angry to be sympathetic.

"You should have told me about the contributions, Carl," he had seethed. "I look like an ass for trying to get the Rootewerke story into the paper, all because I trusted you as the primary source. My editors think I'm an idiot."

"I hadn't thought about that contribution in years, Martin."

"Truitt says I'm gullible."

"Fuck Truitt. I need you to stay on the scent, Martin."

"What scent, Carl?" Boundary had responded angrily. "No one has seen or heard from Rootewerke since she left the grounds of the Capitol. You have no credible evidence that links her to the Senator. And besides, I'm not Sherlock Holmes. I report on murders; I don't solve them."

"I think that Rootewerke is dead, Martin," DeSales had said with a quaking voice. "And I think the guy that killed Cynthia killed Bernadette Malone too. I think the guy is Cisco. So, don't go telling me that there's no scent. This smells to high heaven."

"The thing is, Twyla, I agree with DeSales," said Boundary. "This whole thing stinks to high heaven. Truitt has tossed out classic red herring to take the heat off of his friend Cisco. DeSales wasn't anywhere near the Hill the day of Rootewerke's disappearance. He was on campus. He was making phone calls. He met with his students that night at the Eagle and the Lark."

Twyla listened to her husband carefully, weighing his every word. She was the logical partner; the careful thinker.

"Please, don't get angry at me for saying this, Martin, but I think Rooster is right. You can't trust DeSales. He may not be a killer, but he is deceptive. He's not beyond bending the facts so they fit his narrative. Truitt proved DeSales' lack of trustworthiness. Those donations were inexcusable."

"I don't have blind faith, in the guy, Twyla. I have other sources on this."

It irked Martin that she had questioned his professionalism. "Such as...?"

"Lola Gutierrez confided in me that Cisco has a dark side," he said. "He scared the shit out of her when they were having an affair. She said he became like a madman. She thought he would harm her physically. She bolted from his house half naked on a winter's night."

"Lola told you that?"

"Her comments were off-the-record."

"After she cursed you out the other day? Doesn't that seem a bit strange, Martin? Why would she suddenly turn on Cisco and confide in you after aggressively defending him earlier?"

"She's having second thoughts, I guess, because of Malone."

"But then, why would she talk to you instead of the FBI? Something does not compute."

"Maybe she's already talked to the cops," he said.

"Did she want you to use what she said."

"No. She said it was off-the-record, for my personal

guidance. She said she'd deny ever talking to me if I printed anything."

Twyla took a long, pensive sip of her iced tea.

"Lola may be trying to set you up, Martin, by goading you into writing a Cisco story so she can yell 'fake news'."

"I'd never rely on her comments for a story."

"Good. Because there are way too many loose ends. If Rootewerke is dead by the same hand as Malone, then why hasn't her corpse turned up? Bernadette's killer is an exhibitionist. You said so yourself."

Boundary said, "There was no trace of Hastings."

"There could be two killers, Martin."

"Rootewerke was stalking Cisco. She took this picture of him under the Capitol rotunda."

He produced a copy of the photo from his wallet and handed it to her. She examined it closely. Cisco and a bunch of journalists were in a scrum. Some journos were jabbing tape recorders in Cisco's face.

There were half a dozen men in the photo, including Truitt and Preston Ferguson. Another senator, Troy Fisk of Montana, was just off to Cisco's right. Twyla handed the photo back and said, "She might have tailed any of them, Martin. She is a foreigner. She knows little about our political system. She might have thought any of them was a lawmaker."

"She was supposed to follow Cisco for the day and report on his activities. That was the point of the hazing game. Anyway, there's security cam footage of her following Cisco." There was pique in his voice.

"I saw the footage on the news. Cisco left the rotunda and then Rootewerke came out walking in the same direction about 30 seconds later."

"Thirty seconds is a large gap. I'm playing devil's advocate here, Martin, to help you think this through. There are multiple, credible theories."

Boundary stiffened and said, "She was less than 50 yards behind him."

Still, Twyla was right. A million things could have happened to Rootewerke. She might have given up the chase or been abducted or gone off to buy drugs. He knew little more than what DeSales had told him about this student. He had been sloppy. He ought to be open to multiple theories, not just assume that Cisco was responsible.

Twyla knew from Boundary's wrinkled brow that she had scored a point and changed the topic. Her husband not only had thin skin but, like her, he had a very a short fuse.

"Martin, something strange happened at the office on Friday, and it was right after Lola showed up to have a meeting with Big Barney—the 11 a.m. one Malone used to have. Lola was lugging a super-sized purse, and I made a crack about her bringing Barney some treats. She gave me the blackest look! She hurried into Barney's office and then like two seconds later, she came out and walked over without saying hello or anything and asked if I was a friend of Bernadette Malone. The malice in her voice unnerved me. I told her I hardly knew Malone. And then she asked me, 'What about your husband? How well did he know her?' I said you had not known her at all. Is that right, Martin? You didn't know her, did you?"

Twyla had caught him off guard. He didn't want to lie; but he could not tell the truth. He wondered if Lola knew?

He turned and gazed out at the ocean before answering. A surfer was catching a small, pathetic wave. Gulls were diving into a thick school of silvery bait just beyond the breakers.

"I ran into Malone at a bar. She chatted me up. She was friendly; asked what I did; stuff like that. I told her and she said she knew you because she worked for Cisco. She called you 'One of Big Barney's girls'."

His momentary hesitation and his glance at the sea struck the sharp-eyed Twyla as an evasion. She pressed him.

"You never told me about this! When was it?"

"That night when I lost my temper. I went out and had a drink to cool down."

Twyla wrinkled her brow. "That was the night before someone killed her! You should go to the police. You may have been one of the last persons to see her alive."

He fidgeted with his hands. "If I do that, then I might have to recuse myself from the story. I'd be a witness. That would be silly. I have nothing that useful to tell the cops. I hardly remember the conversation. It would be a big waste of time for them and for me."

"Don't you remember what she was wearing? Was there anyone else around? Anyone who looked suspicious?" Twyla was in her lawyer mode. "Details matter, Martin. The smallest clue can make a case. You have a moral obligation to go to the police."

"The bar was a zoo, I remember that. It's that new sports bar on Connecticut Avenue—the one with $3 beer during NFL games. The place was, loud, crowded. I was there for a drink, not to socialize. I never looked around. I mean, lots of people must have seen her that day. I'm sure someone there must have talked to the cops already."

"Do you know when she left the bar? Was she with anyone? There may be security cameras."

"She left around midnight."

"You... you stayed out until early morning. I remember. Where did you go, Martin?"

She was reading his face. Twyla was nobody's fool.

"I ordered a Templeton Rye. I was furious with you, to the boiling point. The weird thing is, I can't remember why I was angry. I can't recall our argument."

"It was about your obsession with your work."

"I needed time to settled down. I had this drink. Malone came along and talked to me. The booze went straight to my head. I recall little after that."

"Did you leave with her?" She looked into his eyes. He fought the urge to avert them.

"I left. She may have come out the door with me. Like I said, I was plastered, and I wanted to walk it off."

"I think you should tell the cops first thing tomorrow, Martin," she scolded. "Run it by Joe first and see what he says. You trust Joe's judgement, right?"

"That's a good idea," he said. "I'll talk to Joe. But I want to stay on the Malone story. This story could make me, Twyla. It could be the basis of a best-selling book. If I'm some kind of witness, then Rooster will hand it off to that bastard Truitt."

"Why? You could write about the encounter?"

"That wouldn't be much of a story. Look how little interest there was today in Malone's profile. But if killer turns out to be a congressman, then it's as big as the moon up there. My gut tells me that there's a political element in this story. Malone had the goods on someone. She probably had threatened to squeal. They assassinated her."

He rubbed his face. "I'm getting hot. We should ride some waves." He stood. Stretched his back muscles. "Let's go."

Twyla looked up at him with her big green eyes.

"Martin, you are not lying are you?"

"Lying?"

"About Malone." Twyla knew the other woman's reputation.

"I didn't even remember who she was until she turned up dead," he said. "She spoke to me in a bar. It was no big deal. Let's go swimming."

21

Disgrace

Boundary's phone chimed. He looked at the display: 5:00 a.m. He swore. Was it a telemarketing call? He had recently been pestered by calls from fraudsters steered through all-American exchanges like Ellsworth, Maine, and Pigeon Forge, Tennessee. Blocking their numbers did not seem to bring relief. The fraudsters had an endless supply of numbers. He fantasized about bursting in on a call center and beating the telemarketers to a pulp.

Twyla opened a groggy eye. "What's that?"

"Junk call, I think."

He looked at the incoming caller's number. It was the Observer's number. Strange, this early hour on a Monday. They both would drive back from the shore to Washington, D.C., starting at 8 a.m. to arrive by noon, assuming minimal tie ups along the route. Twyla was to lead in the Jeep, with Boundary behind her on Captain America.

"Work," he groaned. "Go back to sleep, my sweet."

He rose from bed and descended the stairs for the kitchen. "Hello?"

"Martin, this is Dan Fogarty. You had better get in here right away. Rooster wants to see you."

"Are you kidding me? It's 5 a.m., Dan. I'm still at the beach. What's the rush? Has World War III broken out?"

"Something like that."

Boundary went upstairs to the bedroom and threw on his cargo shorts, sandals, and Hawaiian shirt, his only apparel, since he had been in such a rush to get to the seashore to join Twyla that he had forgotten to pack. Twyla rolled over and opened her eyes.

"What's up?"

"That was Fogarty. Rooster wants me in the office ASAP. Something big is breaking, but he won't tell me what it is. This sounds like an all-hands-on-deck crisis."

"You've got to be kidding, Martin? It can't wait?"

"Fogarty said it was urgent, on a par with World War III."

Boundary checked the Observer news site. Nothing jumped out at him. He checked other news sites. Again, he saw nothing. He bent over and kissed Twyla on the lips, passionately.

"I better get going. Be safe, Twyla."

"You too. Don't speed. And don't forget to call Joe today—to get his advice about Bernadette."

"OK." He did not intend to drag Joe into his personal problem. He kissed her again. She smiled and then rolled back over to sleep.

As he raced on his motorcycle towards Washington, away from the salt air and through the farmlands of Delaware and Maryland, he wondered what the hell could be going on? Perhaps Rooster had gotten a tip about Malone's killer. Perhaps the FBI had taken Cisco into custody. Thought after thought raced through his mind.

When he entered Rooster's office at 8:30 a.m., his face

was spotted with road grime. He found Si Greenberger, the newspaper's lawyer, pacing nervously in front of the editor's desk. This was odd. Rooster sat in his high-backed, swivel chair, chewing angrily on an unlit cigar. Two suits were seated on a sofa. They were thin guys with close-cropped hair. Military cuts. They looked like the two Feds from the golf club who had given Boundary a cart ride to the front entrance the day Malone's body turned up. They were glaring at him. Boundary suddenly felt cornered.

"Chief?"

"Don't call me Chief," snapped Rooster. He got up and slammed his office door. He closed the blinds. "These two gentlemen are from the FBI—and they say you're a murder suspect!"

Boundary's jaw dropped. Then he turned to the agents and said, "I didn't kill Malone. You're barking up the wrong tree. This is ridiculous." He turned to Rooster. "I can explain this."

"You knew Bernadette Kathleen Malone," said one of the Feds. He wore blue pinstripes and brown shoes. He had watery blue eyes. "You drank with her at a bar, and you left with her about 24 hours before someone murdered her."

"I met her for the first time in my life at that bar: Zooaloo. I was plastered. She helped me walk out. I had nothing to do with her murder."

The second Fed, who was dressed in a gray suit, handed Boundary a photo. Boundary and Malone sat together at the crowded bar. The print was a grainy black and white. Boundary assumed they had copied it from the bar's security camera footage.

Malone was leaning on his shoulder, and he had a stupid, drunken grin that stretched from ear to ear. They were standing beside a powder-blue BMW parked at the curb. The passenger door was open.

"A bartender remembered Bernadette and let us pull pictures from the bar's security cam. You two left in her car." He handed Boundary another photo.

Boundary felt sick. He sat down in one of the chairs along Rooster's glass wall. He stared at the photo. He had taken a gamble in not going to the FBI. He had lost. He looked the two agents directly in the eyes.

"She came up and sat on the stool next to mine. She asked me if I was Martin Boundary. I had never seen her before. We chatted. She said she knew Twyla, my wife. I bought her a drink. I bought myself one. It knocked me for a loop. I mean, I was drunk—and I hardly ever get that way. Not on a single drink. Look at the picture. You can tell that I was drunk out of my skull."

"Then what happened?" asked the gray suit.

"You shouldn't be cooperating without a lawyer," said Greenberger.

"I did nothing, Si," said Boundary. He looked back at the agents.

"I left with her. I told her I could not walk. I felt like sitting on the sidewalk, but she kept me propped up. Next thing I remembered, I was at her place and it was like 4 a.m. I remember nothing in between. I have no recollection of getting inside her car. I woke up at her place at 4 p.m. and had no idea where I was until I saw her in the bed beside me. That was the first time and the last time I ever saw her; and she was alive. I swear to God!"

"Did you have sex with her?" asked the blue suit.

"If I did, then I don't remember."

"You don't remember?" Eyebrows rose.

"Come on, Mr. Boundary. She was a knockout," said the gray suit.

"I woke up in bed next to her. I have no recollection of getting into bed. In fact, I have no recollection of going to her apartment. It's like the entire period between leaving the bar and waking up is wiped clean."

"Maybe you don't remember killing her, either," said the blue suit.

"She was alive."

"Yet, you knew where her body was. You just happened to be the first journo on the scene," blue suit said.

"Someone had tipped me they found a body."

"Who?" said the gray suit.

"A source. And no, I'm not giving up a name."

"You should have told them about Malone right away," said Rooster. His face was crimson. "You are a material witness in a murder investigation, and a suspect." He slammed his fist onto his desk. "You should have told me!" he shouted. "You had a conflict!"

"I knew I wasn't the killer; and I also knew what I had to offer would not shed any light on the murder. Look, I did not want to wreck my marriage. I love my wife. This will crush her if it gets out."

Rooster jumped in. "Didn't it enter that brain of yours that there might be a conflict of interest in your covering the murder story? You have every reason in the world to place suspicion on someone else, like a senator, to deflect guilt from yourself. You've jeopardized our newspaper's reputation, Boundary." Greenberger nodded in assent.

Boundary squared his shoulders, took a deep breath, exhaled.

Then he said, "I didn't know it was Malone buried in the sand trap. My tipster merely told me there was a body, I presumed it was Rootewerke. After I found out it was Malone... well, so what if I had met her? Lots of people knew Bernadette Kathleen Malone. I didn't kill her. So, no, I didn't see a conflict. I did not consider myself to be a suspect."

"But you must have had sex with her," said the agent in the blue suit. He was a head taller than his partner. Otherwise, they had the same buzz cuts, the same brown brogues. To Boundary, they looked like twins.

"I have no recollection of anything that happened after I left the bar. I woke up beside her. I was naked. She was naked too. So, one might assume that we had sex. I am telling the truth when I say I don't remember."

The two agents looked at him skeptically. So too did Rooster and Greenberger.

"Where did Bernadette park?" asked agent gray suit.

Boundary shrugged. "When I walked home, the next morning, around 4 a.m., I didn't notice a powder blue BMW."

Both agents looked at one another with puzzlement.

"You walked?" asked the blue suit.

"Yeah, in about 25 minutes. That would make it about two miles from my house."

"What was her place like?"

"Hip, contemporary. Modern art. Abstract stuff. Lots of tall windows. One bedroom about the size of my dining room. It was a swanky place."

"Do you remember the address?" asked the gray suit.

"No. But it was just over the Calvert Street bridge, somewhere on 20th Street. It's a newer building. Her place was on the top floor, somewhere in the middle."

The two agents looked at one another again. This was not Bernadette Malone's residence, which they had searched top-to-bottom the previous morning, finding no evidence that Boundary ever had been there. That one was a three-story, Victorian-era townhouse tucked away on a tiny side street near Capitol Hill that she rented for $6,000 per month. The tall agent asked, "Can you take us to this place, Mr. Boundary?"

Boundary ignored the question. He looked at Rooster.

"I made a mistake, Chief. I'm sorry. But I am not a criminal."

Rooster scowled. "You're fired, Boundary. You had a conflict of interest and should have recused yourself from the story. Even a dumb-ass rookie should have known that much. Clean out your desk."

"Rooster, please don't do this." Boundary's voice cracked. Rooster's face remained hardened.

"Don't blame me, Boundary. You did this to yourself."

22

Ruin

Boundary stood outside the Observer's downtown offices holding a cardboard box overflowing with his belongings, including old notebooks, key drives, pens, a recorder, and a framed photo of Twyla in her wedding gown. The two FBI agents stood on either side of him, like mismatched bookends. Starkey, in the blue suit, was six feet tall and his partner, Agent Smee, in the gray suit, was five-feet-eight. They were escorting Boundary downtown to their regional office near Judiciary Square for an interview before going to search Bernadette's pad. Their large, black Ford SUV stood by the curb.

"You sure you don't want a lawyer?" asked Smee, as they strolled towards the vehicle.

"I'm innocent. Get that through your head! I've got nothing to hide."

The agents might try to incriminate him with trick questions. Boundary wondered, with a jolt, whether he should, in fact, get a lawyer. He had never been interrogated by the police before. He knew cops always wanted a slam dunk and that they often bent legal ethics to get one.

"I'm rethinking the lawyer," Boundary said, as Smee opened the back door of the SUV. "I want to ask someone for legal advice."

Smee nodded. Boundary walked across the sidewalk and leaned against the brick wall of the Observer. He phoned Joe on a toss-away phone, and in embarrassed, guilt-choked sentences let his old neighbor what he had done and what he had failed to do, as the Catholic liturgy puts it.

Joe was silent a good, long minute. Then he said, "You'd better tell Twyla; and you'd better get a damn good lawyer. Don't trust those G-men, Boundary. They're likely looking for an open-and-shut case."

"That's what I thought."

Boundary phoned the best lawyer he knew: Twyla. She was in the office. He didn't have the courage to talk to her face-to-face. He was sobbing.

"Martin? Are you crying? Oh my God, has someone died?"

He told Twyla what had happened, leaving out no detail. It devastated Twyla. She wept too; and then she screamed at him not to bother coming home, ever again. He felt numb, sick. He vomited in the gutter after they hung up, enveloped by despair. Now, he did not care what happened to him.

"OK. Let's go. No lawyer," he said. He climbed into the back seat of the sedan.

Down at the FBI's sandstone seven-story regional office building, the two agents placed Boundary at a Formica table in a windowless, eight-by-ten, interrogation room. There was an audio-video recorder staring down at him from the opposite wall. He looked numbly into its cold, glassy, indifferent eye and wondered desperately if God would intervene and get him out of his fix.

He was distraught. The towering Martin Boundary was being crushed by the colossal weight of his woes. He had lost his wife and his job, had no place to stay, and had little cash. He had nothing to hide, either. At least, that's what he believed. He wondered if the FBI had recovered his semen from Bernadette's body. They had not asked him for a sample and he would refuse to give them one if they did. If he had had sex with Malone, then that would change everything. He'd be toast.

Boundary sat on one side of the table and the two agents sat opposite him. They read him his rights and told him that their conversation was being recorded. They confirmed that he had waived his right to a legal counsel.

Starkey flipped open a notebook, took out a ballpoint and wrote something down.

"Tell us about your date with Malone," he said.

"There was no date," Boundary said. He folded his hands on the table. "I told you before, it was a chance meeting at the Zooaloo bar. Malone knew who I was. I'd never set eyes on her before. I would have remembered if I did. She was gorgeous."

They kept asking repeatedly what he and Malone had talked about.

"Small talk. I asked who she was. She offered to buy me a drink. I don't turn down free drinks. I had a rye—and the drink hit me unexpectedly hard."

"Then what?" asked Smee.

"I stood up to go home and nearly fell over. I was ripped. She offered to take me home. She guided me out the door. I think I fell onto the sidewalk. I remember some guys helping me up. Bernadette was watching them, apologizing for me."

"Then what?"

"My mind is a blank after that. I've tried to remember. I can't."

"What was she wearing?"

"A dress, maybe? White slacks? I can't remember."

"Ever black out before, Mr. Boundary?" asked Starkey.

"No. Never."

Starkey asked Boundary if Malone had threatened to blackmail him after they had had sex.

"No. I got up, dressed, left." He would not volunteer she hinted she might tell Twyla. That would provide them with a motive for murder.

"You said you left the bar with her. Did you go directly to her place or did you stop somewhere else first?" asked Smee.

"I told you guys, my mind is blank. I remember standing on the sidewalk. My head was spinning. She was trying to keep me on my feet. I sort of remember collapsing and being hoisted to my feet by a couple of good Samaritans. Then, I woke up in her apartment. I remember nothing in between. It's like I was under an anesthetic."

"On Saturday morning, how did you learn about the murder so fast?" asked Starkey.

"From a source."

"Who? We need to corroborate your story."

"No way, guys." said Boundary, "My source is confidential."

"You're not a newsman anymore, Boundary" said Smee. "We were there when Rooster fired you. You have no legal right to protect a source."

"I was when a newsman got the information. I'm not giving up my source."

There was a long pause. Boundary stood up and stretched. Smee asked him to sit back down.

141

"You love your wife, right Mr. Boundary?" asked Starkey.

"With all my heart."

"That sounds like a motive for murder."

"What? You're joking, right? I love my wife, therefore I'm a deranged killer?"

"You had sex with Malone and she threatened to tell your wife. So, then you killed her. End of your problem." Starkey clicked his ball point in rapid succession.

"Is that what you guys really think? You are both unbelievable! Look, while you are in here jerking my chain, the real killer remains on the loose. He's probably brained the Rootewerke girl too. And, anyway, what you are accusing me of is a crime of passion. Look at the facts: Malone's murder was carefully crafted. She was wrapped in duct tape, hauled onto the most exclusive golf course in the country, and then buried in a sand trap. That's hardly a spur-of-the-moment thing."

The two agents stared at him wearily. Boundary sighed. He threw up his hands.

"We will get nowhere with this murder, agents, unless you open your minds."

They grilled Boundary for another hour and 30 minutes. They asked him about his golf game. He told them he was struggling. They asked about his drinking. He said he had no problem. They asked him if he had ever cheated on his wife before. He told them, "Never." They kept asking the same questions over and over, in subtly different ways.

"Never cheated, damn it. And I'm fairly certain I did not have sex with Malone. I don't remember having sex with her. How could I forget something like that?"

"It defies credibility," said Starkey. "You were naked in bed with a bombshell."

"Was there DNA evidence?" asked Boundary.

The agents ignored the question.

"I doubt it," said Boundary.

"Who was sitting next to you at the bar, besides Malone?"

"I don't recall. Ask the bartender. He had a ponytail and huge forearms with a Bugs Bunny tattoo on one."

"Have you ever lost your temper and punched anyone," asked Smee.

"Only inside the boxing ring. Look, this is ridiculous! I didn't kill Malone. How would I get onto that golf course with her? I'm not a member. I ride around on a motorcycle. Let's say she rode out there on my motorcycle with me. Do you then think she'd voluntarily climb over the fence with me so I could murder her? And, I don't own any duct tape, let alone a $30,000 golf club."

"You could have stolen one," said Smee.

"Are you serious, agent? I've stolen nothing my entire life. I have no police record. Check it out. I'm as clean and buttoned down as a brand new shirt."

"You sure you don't own duct tape, Boundary?" asked Starkey.

"I know that sounds silly, a guy with no duct tape. I don't even own any tools. I use a butter knife for a screwdriver. Do you know what I use for a hammer?"

"Why don't you tell us," said Smee.

"Not a golf club. Sorry to disappoint you guys. I use a 15-pound barbell."

"We'd like you to take a urine test and give us a DNA sample," said Starkey.

"Path of least resistance," muttered Boundary.

"What's that supposed to mean?" asked Smee.

"It's something journalists say about police: that you are lazy and pursue the easiest route whether it is the correct route. In any event, I turn down your request, pending advice of counsel. I want a phone, right now. I tried to be nice and to cooperate, but you two guys persist in being pricks."

"You had sex with Bernadette Kathleen Malone. She threatened to tell your wife," said Smee.

Boundary sat stiffly upright.

"I said, I changed my mind. I want a lawyer."

23

Breakup

Boundary had to see Twyla. He was anxious and panicky at the thought of losing her. He had to save his marriage.

He cobbled together a plausible explanation: Malone had drugged and raped him. He could imagine no other scenario. He was pink with embarrassment. Men did not get raped by women. But, it had to be.

Bernadette Malone must have doused his drink with a Mickey Finn. This would explain his uncharacteristic immobility and memory loss in the wake of the drink.

No one would believe him. He was Martin Boundary, boxing champion, the ultimate alpha male, who had powered estimable opponents about the ring before decisively laying them flat on the canvas. How could he have allowed some strange woman to rape him? He had to admit, his theory sounded fantastic. He had no evidence or witnesses. Twyla, a trained lawyer, would be, at a minimum, highly skeptical. She'd probably tear his defense to shreds. Yet, they were man and wife, not opponents in a court of law. Their marriage had to count for something.

"She drugged and assaulted me." He rehearsed his plea aloud as he left the FBI's regional office towards Twyla's office on Capitol Hill, a distance of less than a mile. He entered the Rayburn office building through the visitor's entrance, since he no longer had a press pass. He passed through the metal detectors and veered toward a long, underground pedestrian tunnel that linked Rayburn to the Capitol, where Big Barney had his Speaker's office. In this way, he avoided the long lines of gawking tourists at the Capitol Visitor's Center.

He texted Twyla that he was on his way. She met him in the corridor outside the huge oak double doors that led to Big Barney's throne room. Martin's little redhead was furious. Her balled fists hung at her side. Her eyes were red from crying. Her grim lips advertised her agony.

"How could you betray me, Martin? We haven't even been married two years yet! What is wrong with me? Tell me!" She was sobbing.

Grief also etched Boundary's face.

"There is nothing wrong with you, Twyla. I love you with my whole heart and soul. You've got to believe me. Malone drugged me."

"You expect me to believe that?"

"I met Malone at the bar, just like I told you on the phone. I got drunk, really drunk, on just one drink! I could hardly stand. She had to have put something in my drink. There's no other explanation. I barely remember leaving with her. The next thing I knew, I was waking up in her bed. It mystified me. I had no idea where I was. I had no recollection of going there. She probably was planning to blackmail me to make me back away from Cisco."

"That's preposterous," Twyla sputtered. "If you expect me

146

to believe that cock and bull story then you take me for one, gigantic idiot."

She slapped him hard across the face. The report turned the heads of persons examining the statuary lining the wing's ornate hallway. She punched him. She landed a staggering blow to his right cheek. Twyla was tiny, but she was no porcelain doll. She was a trained kick boxer. Each of her punches packed a wallop. Boundary covered his face with his huge forearms and backpedaled. A Capitol Hill police officer on duty outside the speaker's door pinned Twyla from behind. She kicked out towards Boundary and narrowly missed his groin, connecting instead with his huge right thigh. Then she slumped in the cop's arms like a rag doll and bawled. A crowd of curious tourists encircled them. Some of them were making video recordings of the event on their cell phone cameras. The officer told them to move away. Twyla retched. That sent most out of the area. Another officer maneuvered Boundary into a corner away from Twyla. The cop who had pinned her let radioed for medical help.

She looked up. Her eyes were glassy and her skin was sickly white.

"You bastard!" Her shout echoed down the corridor. "You dirty, no-good bastard!" She did not tell him she was one-month pregnant.

24

Break In

The young city police detective, a tall, lithe man with ebony-colored skin and a cheerful demeanor, dusted the house extensively for prints and found nothing. He went meticulously about his job like an exterminator looking for the minuscule fecal droppings of an elusive deer mouse, despite being dressed in an expensive, silver-colored suit. He dusted door knobs and drawer handles and light switches and even the toilet handles—places where he might find the prints of an intruder, especially one that was sloppy. He found nothing.

"These guys wore gloves," he said.

The intruders had thoroughly defiled the interior of the home. Hardly a piece of property remained unbroken. They had smashed appliances. They had slashed chairs. In the bedroom, they had busted an antique bed frame and headboard. They had yanked a toilet from its mounting and thrown it through the glass shower door. One had urinated on the carpet.

"Someone must be angry at you, Mr. Boundary," said the detective. "Have you any idea who that might be?" He was cutting out a sample of the urine-soaked carpet for DNA analysis.

Lots of folks. I'm a journalist. It's my job to piss people off."

"Have you received any threats recently?"

"No, but Senator Kent Cisco might have it in for me. You ought to check him out."

"Why would Senator Cisco have it in for you?"

"Because I asked him about the disappearance of a John Adams student named Cynthia Rootewerke. I also think he may have murdered the woman in the sand trap at the Congressional Golf Club."

The detective raised his eyebrows and scribbled in his notepad. "I'll look into it," he said without conviction. "Anybody else come to mind?"

"In an average week, I piss off more people than I can keep track of, including your chief."

"I doubt that the chief had anything to do with this," said the detective. He closed his pad and placed it in the interior pocket of his suit jacket.

"It looks like your visitors were after something very specific, because all your drawers were dumped out. If I had to guess, they did the drawers first, then went to the closets, and then got frustrated and angry, because they didn't find what they were after, and trashed the place."

Boundary nodded. The cop's deduction made sense. The derangement of the house could very well have begun as a detailed search. But for what, exactly?

Twyla had discovered the ransacking when she returned from her job. She immediately had run to Joe, their neighbor, who called Boundary after first reporting the crime to the District of Columbia police. Boundary, who was hanging out at a nearby coffee bar after a night sleeping in the woods, came right over. He smelled of BO and needed a shave. He looked like a homeless person which, in fact, he was.

Joe photographed the destruction at the crime scene in case the couple needed the pictures for their insurer. One of his most powerful cameras hung on a strap from his neck. He walked over to Boundary after the young detective had finished talking to him.

"How you feeling?" Joe asked.

"Not so good, Joe. Hey, you think those two goons from the FBI tossed my place?"

"No way, Martin. This mess definitely is not the Bureau's handiwork. They would have been thorough, but invisible. That's their M.O. If you ask me, they meant this wreckage to be a warning. You've stepped on someone's toes and they want you to back off. You have any files or anything that would cause anyone to sweat?"

"Not here. My thumb drives are in the saddlebags of my motorcycle, and I don't have any strong leads about Malone or Rootewerke, just a few hunches."

"The people who did this think you have something. I heard you talking to the cop. Are you sure you can't think of someone other than Cisco? I can't see a Senator risking his career by tossing someone's house."

"I don't have a clue."

"Give me one other name, Martin. Give me someone you pissed off, no matter how far-fetched the connection might appear."

"A colleague named Malcolm Truitt. I copied a phone number from his Rolodex. He went bat shit."

"Who else?"

"I can't focus Joe. Between the burglary and Twyla, I feel

like I've taken an uppercut. Who knows, maybe Senator Kent Cisco hired thugs."

Joe patted Boundary on the back. Then he roamed the premises taking more pictures. He planned to run the images through his company's mainframe computer to see if he could turn up any helpful clues.

"But, frankly, the urine is the best thing going for you," Joe told Boundary who tagged along like a dog. "If the intruder has an arrest record, this piss will be his undoing. Urinating was a dumb thing to do—a pecker-dillo, so to speak." Joe smiled. Boundary was too upset to enjoy the pun.

Boundary's landlord, Hilda Chesterton, arrived right after Joe left, almost literally on his heels. The police were clearing out. The wreckage inside Martin's and Twyla's home deeply upset the spry, elderly woman. The row house was special to her. She and her late husband, Frank, raised three girls and two boys there. Frank, who had been a master carpenter, died from a heart attack in his basement wood shop at age 46. After retiring from the Internal Revenue Service, Hilda had moved to a retirement community near the beach in Delaware. She drove three hours to see firsthand what had happened to the place after Boundary informed her about the break-in. Being an astute businesswoman, Hilda also scheduled an on-site meeting with an insurance adjuster.

Hilda held onto the house more out of affection than as an investment although its value had at least quadrupled over the years. She had been overjoyed to rent to newlyweds, thinking they might start a family. Hilda had many happy memories of her own kids frolicking through the house, and she became deeply sentimental at the prospect of more children's laughter echoing through its hallways

Insurance adjusters for both Hilda and the Boundarys arrived almost simultaneously. The rental insurance adjuster gave Boundary checks on the spot for a temporary hotel stay and for his damaged furniture and possessions. Hilda's claims adjuster gave her money to repair broken windows, smashed interior doors, and the bathroom. She would need a small army of plumbers, tilers, carpenters, and painters to set the house right again.

Hilda, in retirement, had purchased other rental properties in the D.C. metro area. She offered the Boundaries a fully furnished townhouse across the Potomac River in Old Town Alexandria, Virginia, on St. Asaph Street. A member of the French embassy staff recently vacated the Alexandria property.

"It's a nice place. You can stay there for good if you're afraid to move back here," she said. Hilda added, "We never had a crime problem when I lived here. I don't know what's happening to this city!"

The Old Town property seemed like a good idea to Martin. He and Twyla did not have time to search for a new apartment; and both were familiar with the locale which boasted more colonial-era properties than any neighborhood in the country. In happier days, they had strolled through its picturesque riverfront parks and dined on King Street, the town's thriving commercial and entertainment venue.

Hilda showed them some pictures of the property she stored on her phone. The unit was in an old, 19th century brick brewery that had been transformed into trendy residential housing. Standing across the street were commercial buildings that housed Trader Joe's, a Vietnamese restaurant, a liquor store, dry cleaner, and picture framer. Boundary told Hilda, without consulting Twyla, that they gladly would take it. He handed her the check from the insurance adjuster for hotel stays for the first month's rent, took the keys from Hilda and handed them to Joe to pass to Twyla, who was sitting outside in their jeep.

She did not protest when Joe told her what Martin had done.

Martin stopped at the Jeep when he left the wrecked row home to hand her the other check, for their ruined possessions. Twyla had brought most of them to the marriage.

"You'll be safe across the river in Old Town," he said. "Whoever did this won't think to look there."

"You don't have a key to the new place, do you, Martin? You are not welcome there." Her voice was harsh.

"No. I don't have a key." He was choking up. His eyes misted. "I love you. I want you to be safe."

She eyed him coldly. She did not how he would get along without a job, without a roof over his head. She didn't care. She wasn't about to offer him some money. He had betrayed her. He had created the mess, so let him live with it.

Boundary turned with drooping shoulders and walked next door to Joe's place. Joe broke out two bottles of coffee-flavored beer.

"Help me keep an eye on her, Joe, won't you?"

Joe put his hand on Boundary's shoulder.

"I'll do whatever I can, Martin. Where in the heck will you stay? If I put you up, my relationship as a source would be kaput. You can stay if you don't mind that."

"I do mind, Joe. A journalist is only as good as his sources. Frankly, you're the best one I've got."

"Do you need some money?"

Boundary was too proud to admit that he did.

153

"I can get by, for now. I will look for a place somewhere near Twyla so I can look out for her. The guys who did this might try again."

"You might get a gym membership so you'd have a place to shower," said Joe.

"Not a bad suggestion. I guess I smell pretty bad."

"You do, as a matter of fact. What about work? What are you going to do?"

"I will clear my name by exposing Malone's killer. So, ideally, I'll get another crime-reporting gig. Plan B is to work as a boxing instructor. Hell, I'll flip burgers at a fast-food joint to scrape by."

Joe took a swig from his bottle of beer. "Finding a reporter's job is going to tough, don't you think? Rooster was quoted in the Observer saying you acted unethically. You're also an uncharged suspect in the Malone murder. That's some resume."

"My notoriety makes me ideal click-bait. Somewhere, an online newspaper editor is dying for me to walk in through his front door."

"I hope so, Martin. I really hope so."

Boundary was trying to sound jaunty, but his eyes betrayed a profound sadness. Joe could sympathize. Ten years earlier, he had lost his own wife to pancreatic cancer. She died within two months of the awful diagnosis. Joe still had vivid dreams of her. These were painful experiences. Joe would see his Monica walking away from him down a country road. He would cry out to her to stop; and she, very slowly, would turn and say, "I'm busy; I've got better things to do." Then, she would vanish and he'd wake up, sad and hurt. Joe told himself they were just dreams, and that Monica had dearly loved him. Nevertheless, the dreams tore him up.

Joe could tell by looking at Boundary's anguished face that he was living this nightmare.

"I've got a buddy who owns a moving company, Martin, and I'll make sure he gives Twyla a square deal, if she wants anything moved. I'll put in a good word for you to Twyla."

"Thanks, Joe. You're a good friend. Well, off to begin the first day of the rest of my life." He gave Joe a bear hug.

Boundary's laptop had survived the massive threat of vandalism—it was still in a saddlebag on his motorcycle. He straddled his machine, kick-started it, and headed to a coffee bistro with free wifi in the nearby Adams Morgan neighborhood. He ordered a tall, iced, vanilla latte from a sullen looking, heavily tattooed barista and sat down at a small oval table by the shop's front window. He opened his laptop and surfed hotel and motel sights in Alexandria. There were no rooms he could afford within 60 miles. The Nats were in the running for the title. Baseball fans had flooded into town for a three-game series against the Phillies. He'd have to go two or three hours away in any direction to find anything for the night, which was out of the question. His calendar would not permit it. At 9 a.m., Boundary and a legal aid society lawyer had to meet with Starkey and Smee. If he skipped the interview, he was liable to end up in jail.

He searched Craig's list for an Air B&B, but they too were dear, and too distant from Twyla's new place. When the sun went down, Boundary chose a clearing in the mosquito-infested woods by the Potomac River, between Ronald Reagan Airport and Old Town and unrolled his sleeping bag. He doubted he'd disturb anyone there—or that anyone would disturb him. Hidden beyond some dense thicket, Boundary and his motorcycle were invisible to passersby on a nearby bike trail. For dinner, Boundary tore into a sandwich wrap he had gotten at a Trader Joe's. Then, he rolled out his sleeping bag and climbed in. Fortunately, the bag had built-in mosquito netting, for otherwise, by dawn, swirling clouds of the voracious insects would have sucked away all of his blood.

Before dozing off on the hard ground, he read the digital-version of the Observer on his cell phone. A prominent story recounted his one-night stand with Malone and his conse-quent dismissal from staff. Underneath the story were over 400, unflattering reader comments. They called Boundary "a scumbag" and "a sick, demented, killer," and "unethical" and "criminal."

This was the online equivalent of a lynching. Most shocking to him, the reporters hadn't reach out to him for a comment. They had judged him guilty without providing him with the opportunity to mount a defense.

Even if Boundary one day were to prove his innocence, his reputation would remain stained. People always would recall the time that Martin Boundary was a murder suspect.

Boundary shut off the phone to preserve its battery and said a short, intense prayer asking God for a break. Then he tried to get comfortable as complete darkness arrived with a symphony of unfamiliar sounds.

At first light, Boundary hopped up, rolled up his sleeping bag, relieved himself in the underbrush, took a quick skinny-dip in the river, and then motored across the Memorial Bridge to the FBI's regional office on 4th Street, N.W. He wore his seashore cloths—shorts, Hawaiian shirt, and red flip-flops. His other clothes were in a closet of the ransacked townhouse. The detectives had prevented him from taking anything the previous day. He intended to pick up his suit, underwear, and a pair of loafers later.

When he arrived at the FBI building they ushered him into an interview room, where his young public defender, Sam Waxlong, was waiting. Waxlong, two months out of the University of Virginia Law School, looked like a skinny teenager. But he was cheery and bright. He had passed the bar exam with flying colors on his first try.

Boundary, under Waxlong's guidance, composed a formal written statement about his night with Malone, detailing his evidence that the woman had heavily drugged him.

Waxlong stayed alongside Boundary when the two agents resumed the interview from where they had left off the day before. The lawyer seemed nervous. He had confided in Boundary he never had represented a defendant during an FBI interrogation. Waxlong also was not comfortable seated by his client. Boundary guessed it was because he smelled like something that had climbed from a frog pond. Bathing in the Potomac River had not been a brilliant idea.

"Are you a golfer?" Smee asked Boundary.

"Ever see an elementary school girls' field hockey game, Agent Smee? They swat the ball around a few yards at a time. That's how I play golf."

Waxlong elbowed his defendant in the ribs and cautioned in a whisper, "Stop being a smartass."

"But you own clubs?" said Smee.

"A second-hand set from Goodwill. Sam Sneads. They're in my garage. Someone trashed my house yesterday. He bent every single club. Before you Fearless Fosdicks try to pin the burglary on me one as well, I have an alibi. I was with you two when it happened."

"No need for insults, Mr. Boundary," said Starkey.

Boundary pounded on the table with his fist, his anger suddenly rising. Waxlong laid a hand on Boundary's forearm. The former boxer angrily shook it off. He stood up. His face was crimson.

"You guys destroyed my life," he shouted. "The real killer is still out there. His trail is growing cold because you two are looking for easy headlines."

An older male agent and a young female agent, rushed into the room, Tasers drawn. Boundary held up his hands and slowly sat back down.

"You have a violent temper," said Smee evenly.

"So, I've heard. But there's one thing about us hot heads that you fail to appreciate: we don't go around plotting elaborately staged murders. Believe it or not—and I'm repeating myself here for the camera—I don't even own a roll of duct tape."

"You had a PC in the house, right?" asked Starkey.

A look of bewilderment showed on Boundary's face. What did that question have to do with the price of eggs? He looked at Waxlong and raised his eyebrows. Waxlong shrugged his shoulders.

"I had a 10-year-old Lenovo until yesterday. The people who trashed our house reduced it to smithereens."

"Did the PC have a hard drive?"

"Of course."

"The local police didn't find one."

"They never mentioned that," said Boundary.

"Was there sensitive information on the drive?"

"Besides all of our financial records? Not really. I had old news clips pertaining to Cisco's missing aide, Susie Hastings. I had news reports on Rootewerke too. She's the Dutch girl who vanished while tailing Cisco."

"Anything else?"

"Not really. I had no concrete leads, just hunches."

The two agents looked at one another.

"What's the relevance of this, agents?"

"Maybe your client removed his own hard drive," said Starkey.

"That's preposterous," said Boundary. He paused and then said, "Oh, I get it! You think I might have been exchanging love notes with Malone. I never e-mailed her in my life. Check out her P.C."

"We'd like you to take us back to Malone's apartment building, Mr. Boundary, so that we can do just that. We can't locate the exact apartment where you claimed to have been. Will you do that for us? Will you help us find her unit?"

He looked at the lawyer.

"You're telling the truth, about not killing her?" Waxlong whispered in his ear.

"I am. I'm innocent."

The lawyer slowly nodded his assent, hoping Boundary was honest, hoping that the agents would not find any incriminating evidence at Malone's apartment

25

Partial Redemption

From the back seat of the Ford sedan where he sat beside Waxlong, Boundary directed Starkey and Smee through the city's congested streets to a contemporary brick and glass condominium building. The eye-catching structure was four stories high, with wide glass double doors in the front. There was no doorman at the entrance, only a small, bronze-colored keypad. Jack Coogan from the building's management company met Boundary and the two FBI agents outside. Starkey showed Coogan their search warrant for an apartment "owned by" Bernadette Kathleen Malone.

"There's no security camera," said Smee, with some surprise after casting his eyes carefully around the door frame.

"Sure, there is," said Coogan with a sly smile. "It's staring you in the face."

Smee looked again, scanning the door frame left to right and back again. He saw nothing.

"So, you're going to make us stand here all day and guess?"

"No, because you'd never would find it, no matter how crafty you might be." Coogan pointed to a flea-sized aperture at the top of the keypad. "The latest technology. Believe it or not, it takes great video."

"We'll need to see some footage," said Starkey.

"In that case, you will need another warrant. The home-owner's association here is a bitch to work with—all lawyers."

Waxlong smiled sheepishly.

"I'll see to that now," said Starkey. He walked down the side, cell phone to his ear.

Smee asked how long the management kept the video recordings and Coogan said, "It automatically recycles when the ten-terabyte, solid state hard drive reaches its capacity."

"We will need everything that's on it," said Smee.

Coogan showed the palms of his hands to show his helplessness.

Smee, Boundary, Waxlong, and Coogan went inside. For all appearances, they looked like a gaggle of housing inspectors. They took a freight elevator to the third floor. Boundary remembered that he had ridden down three floors on an elevator to leave the building almost a week before.

"The apartment was on the street side of the hallway, third floor. But I forget the number on the door."

When the group exited, Boundary notice that there were five apartments on the street side. Boundary said it had to be 301 or 303.

"It was about halfway down the hallway."

Coogan said 303 had married tenants, both members of India's diplomatic corps. The Kurumba Corporation owned unit 301.

Smee showed Coogan a picture of Malone.

"Ever see her?"

"Nope. But I work strictly 9 to 5. There are lots of tenants I've never seen. They are early risers and late returners. Hill people."

"Can you let us into 305?" asked Smee.

Coogan, once more, held out his palms in a show of helpless-ness. "You'll need another warrant, because this warrant is for Malone's place. Like I said, lawyers run the owner's asso-ciation here and they are super-pricks. They want everything by strictly by the book."

Smee called Starkey, who was still outside, waiting for confirmation of the warrant for the security system's hard drive.

"We need another one, my friend, for a unit owned by The Kurumba Corporation. Boundary thinks it's the one used by Malone. No, I have no idea what the Kurumba Corporation is."

Coogan unlocked the door to Unit 301.

"Now, I'm allowed to enter a unit if I suspect a serious maintenance problem. I'm going in, because I think I smell gas. I will leave the door open. If you wander in, then I probably won't notice. I'll have my head inside the oven."

"But this building is all electric," said Boundary. He had seen a plaque by a fire alarm near the front door.

"Might be the smell of a dead dog, then" said Coogan with serious lips and laughing eyes.

Boundary, Waxlong, and Smee followed Coogan inside to a spacious living room with two, eight-feet-tall sliding glass doors leading to a long balcony. The room's furnishings looked like 1960's Danish Modern, now valuable antiques. A 62-inch television covered most of the wall opposite the sliders. An eye-catching stainless steel, galley kitchen at the far end of the open space looked unused.

"Recognize the place," Smee asked Boundary?

He shook his head in the negative.

162

"I only recall the bed. Its headboard was blond wood with LCD reading lamps at each end."

"The bedrooms are through that door by the kitchen," said Coogan. "There are three, each with an en suite bathroom."

The first bedroom was on the left and had balcony doors. A king-sized bed with a frame made of white maple was the centerpiece of the chamber. The head board was tall with LED reading lamps arrayed along the top and built in side tables with drawers on either side. An abstract painting on the wall above the headboard resembled a collage of human eyes and ears. A side doorway to a large bathroom with a ceramic tiled double shower. The wall opposite the bed featured a large mirror.

"This definitely is the place," Boundary said.

The bed chamber was as spanking neat as a five-star hotel room. The blankets and sheets looked fresh and were topped with a neatly folded extra blanket. The bathroom was spotless as an exhibit in a plumbing contractor's showroom.

Smee said to Boundary and Waxlong, "You two can run along, now. Don't touch anything on your way out. I'm bringing in an evidence team. You are 100 percent sure this is the place, right Mr. Boundary?"

"This is definitely the place. I recognize the bed," said Boundary.

"You will keep in mind that Mr. Boundary cooperated with your investigation won't you, Agent Smee?" said Waxlong, pointedly.

"Sure. Look, I should not be telling you this, but we found an Ogden Titanium at the bottom of a pond by the 14th tee out at Congress Country Club. We've lifted a partial print. It wasn't Boundary's."

"Whose print was it?"

"We don't know. A male, based on an analysis of the residual amino acids. The perp isn't in our database."

"Something else," said Smee. "We found footprints from a size 11 golf shoe."

"I wear the size 13," said Boundary. "And I don't own golf shoes."

"So then, my client no longer is a suspect?" asked Waxlong.

"The Department of Justice will issue a press release to that effect, but I can't tell you when they'll get around to it. Now, please leave so we can secure the premises."

26

Heartbreak

Old Town, the picturesque historic district of Alexandria, Virginia, once was a Potomac River port from which George Washington shipped tobacco to England from his Mount Vernon plantation, ten miles to the south. The community was a time capsule. Stately mansions, small, two-story, wooden row homes, churches, and meticulously restored buildings along Old Town's streets had been standing since the 1740s. Gadsby's Tavern on North Royal Street pretty much still served the same fare as in 1796, when Washington dined there. The stately Carlyle House on North Fairfax Street had served in 1751 as headquarters for England's General Braddock at the beginning of the French and Indian War. Other buildings in this historic urban area predated the Civil War. Robert E. Lee's boyhood home, a stately, red-brick mansion with a large garden, graced Oronoco Street. The four-story townhouse that Twyla now occupied was modern, part of a renovation of the Civil War-era Portner Brewing Company building on St. Asaph Street, one of Old Town's busiest business thoroughfares.

The new townhouse came fully furnished, including pots,

165

pans, dishes, and silverware, which was fortunate, owing to the massive vandalism of Twyla and Martin's previous rental. The destruction was so vicious and frightening that Twyla was uncertain she wanted to stay in the Washington area any longer. The breakup of her marriage infused her with a profound sadness. She wanted to run away. Yet, she was carrying their child and the latent excitement of that miracle kept her going.

Twyla was considering hiring a divorce lawyer. Martin was no good. He had told her over and over he loved her, and only her. She had believed him. Then he cheated on her. She could not let go of her anger.

Martin had shown a reckless disregard for her. What if that Malone woman had AIDS? Martin could have transmitted the disease to both her and their unborn child. Apparently, the dumb brute never entertained the possibility. He didn't know about the baby. Even so, she found it impossible to forgive him for putting herself and the baby at grave risk.

Her mother had dared ask her, "Will you at least talk to Martin? Will you at least tell him you're expecting?"

Twyla had slammed down the phone in a rage. She was more receptive to her father, Ned, a retired Navy captain, who said he would drive over from their home in Annapolis and punch Martin in the nose, if Martin ever dared to show up at her front door.

Not only had Boundary betrayed her, he had publicly shamed her. The story was everywhere. Boundary had been the last one to see Bernadette alive. A security camera outside a bar showed them climbing into her BMW. The clip was a YouTube sensation. So many reporters called her at work seeking comments and interviews, she had to take a sick leave.

166

Big Barney, with a fatherly tone, told Twyla that she could take as much time off as needed.

Girlfriends said they were there for her, that the worst thing was for her to be alone. Yet, more than anything, she wanted to be alone, listening to "Stomp on Your Man" music on the country radio station.

"Walk out because he's a dirty cheat. Use him for wiping mud off your feet," Shamela Pittie wailed over the airwaves. The song struck a chord with Twyla. She sobbed uncontrollably. She let the music play on because crying was a purgative.

She went to the bathroom cabinet, took a sleeping pill from a plastic container, and swallowed it with a cup of water. Back in the living room, crowded with unpacked moving cartons containing most of her clothes, Twyla curled up on the couch under a blanket and cried some more. She fell asleep with her hand on her womb. She did not hear it a short time later when a person rattled the knob while trying to open her front door.

27

Al Capone's Ring

T he FBI's forensics team took Malone's bed sheets for DNA analysis. They vacuumed the carpets. They searched for blood. They discovered her bedroom's video recording system and located the empty square cut out in the box spring.

"Look at this," said Starkey, pointing to the cutout and its wiring. "Someone grabbed a disc drive and then left this place looking as though the housemaids had been here."

The agents also found a medicine cabinet containing a prescription drug commonly associated with date rape.

The condo's front-door security camera also yielded crucial evidence. The agents recovered a video showing a groggy look-ing Boundary entering the building with a smirking Malone. Boundary was stumbling, swaying to the left and to the right like a rickety barn in an Oklahoma crosswind. Malone was laughing as she struggled to keep the hulking man on his feet. The video showed Boundary emerging three hours later and captured Malone leaving three hours after that. She was in a white dress and tall, spike heels. She glanced at her watch, which had a diamond-studded band. The camera by the door showed her walking to a powder blue BMW parked by the curb and opening the driver's side door. She died in the same getup, minus the shoes.

The video records ran from a week before Malone's murder to the present. The agents, using the FBI's latest photo-enhancing computers, spent hours looking at the feed to see if other suspects might emerge. Mainly, the video showed residents of the condo leaving for work and returning many hours later. Malone's first appearance was with Boundary. Apparently, she used this apartment infrequently, and pre-ferred her townhouse on Capitol Hill. It turned out that she was behind the corporation that paid the mortgage. The agents wondered why Malone hid her ownership interest and where she had gotten over half a million dollars for a down payment.

The video footage covered five days. Coogan watched with the agents, identifying the residents entering and exiting the building.

There was one pronounced oddity. A bearded man wearing sunglasses and a slouch hat entered the building with the mailman two days after the discovery of Malone's body. The same man left 75 minutes later carrying a paper shopping bag. Smee ran the footage of the man seven or eight times, stopping it and restarting it, blowing up parts of the image for closer examination. Unfortunately, the picture was dark.

"I think I know who that is," Smee told Starkey.

"You know that guy? How can you tell? The image stinks."

"By his right hand."

"His right hand? Are you kidding me?" Starkey looked at a still frame. He focused on the hand. He saw nothing but fuzz.

"I'll magnify the image for you." Smee used the zoom function. Starkey looked again.

"Are you looking at that pinky ring?" Starkey asked.

"Yes. Preston Ferguson, the television journalist has one exactly like it."

"Are you sure?" asked Starkey. "There isn't much detail." The ring had a square setting holding what appeared to be a large, round diamond. But the details were grainy.

Smee, a celebrity junky, said, "Ferguson bought himself a four-carat diamond from the Al Capone collection to celebrate his first ten years on television. He insured it for $1 million. I have the news article on file at home. That's got to be Al Capone's ring."

"How did Ferguson get that?" Starkey sounded skeptical.

"Al had a brother, Ralph, who kept all Al's stuff at a lodge in Wisconsin while he was in a federal penitentiary for tax evasion. When Al got out, he never asked for it back. He had brain rot from syphilis. In the 1950s, Ralph's heirs cleared out the lodge and sold Al's valuables to a dealer. A private collector bought the ring for $25,000, and Ferguson claimed to have bought it from the private collector for $250,000. He flashes it around. It's his trademark."

Smee was an amateur paparazzo in his spare time, with a wall of framed photos of professional athletes and movie stars whom he had spotted in Washington.

"Lots of men in this town wear pinky rings," said Starkey. "You can't conclude that the guy in the picture is Ferguson based on this photo."

"Ferguson's father was a cat burglar," said Smee. "When Ferguson was a tyke, his dad used to let him down a chimney on a clothesline so he could unlock doors from the inside. He wrote a book about it. The craft is in his blood."

"Are you sure?" Starkey was reluctant to pester a big star like

Ferguson without stronger grounds. If Ferguson squawked, a supervisor might come down on them, leaving a blemish on his spotless record.

"I'm certain enough to want to chat with him, Starkey."

"You had better be right about the pinky ring, Smee. That's all I've got to say. The shit will hit the fan if we drag in this guy and he's not the man in the picture."

"It's him," said Smee, tapping the photo with his index finger.

Ferguson lived in a 100-year-old, limestone, slate roofed mansion on a swank side street near the National Cathedral. Starkey looked the address up on Zillow, which estimated its value at $8 million. The agents didn't phone ahead, wanting to surprise him. Suspects, in their experience often blurted out the most incriminating details when shocked by a surprise visit from the FBI.

Ferguson's cranberry colored Cadillac XLR was in the circular driveway. The car looked as if it had just rolled off a showroom floor. The top was down. Tall locust trees on the spacious front lawn protected both the driveway and the front of the two-story home from the hot sun, now at its zenith overhead. The agents found the front door of Ferguson's house slightly ajar. This was strange. In a wealthy enclave, residents lived behind heavily locked doors.

Smee pushed the door open and inquired in a booming baritone if anyone was home. There was no answer. He inquired again, this time even more loudly.

"FBI! Is anyone home?"

Again, there was no response. He looked quizzically at Starkey. This was a scene right out of a second-rate detective movie. They'd probably find a gruesome crime scene on the other side of the door, Smee thought. He had a small radio clipped onto his belt, and he used it to call for a police back-up. Then, the agents drew their Glock Nines and entered.

Smee went first into the large, marble-floored foyer, sweeping the gun left to right. Starkey, just behind his partner, kept his gun pointed at the floor. He didn't want to shoot Smee in the back if all hell suddenly broke loose.

There were winding staircases on either side of the foyer. Smee bounded up the one on the left, to scout out the upstairs. Starkey went through the foyer into a vast living room. He found no sign of life as he looked around. But when he glanced down, there was ample evidence of death. Two huge spots of blood stained the white Berber carpet. Starkey got on his radio to Smee.

"There's a bloodbath in the living room," he said breathlessly.

28

Down and Dirty

Boundary sat stiffly on a tan metal folding chair in a cramped office on the second floor of a run-down brick Victorian house on Q Street, North West, interviewing for a job with the notorious Jeff Dwiggens of Bugler.com. Dwiggens' office had the charm of a rat's nest. Random piles of yellowing newspapers, some four-feet high, stood along all four walls. A sooty window looked out over a litter-strewn alleyway, its top half accommodating a rusty air-conditioning unit that rattled loudly.

Other "offices" on this floor advertised a guitar teacher, a medicinal pot dealer, and a body piercing shop.

Dwiggens sat in a squeaky roller chair behind an ancient and grizzled oak desk. He had contacted Boundary out of the blue a day earlier and had quipped he supposed Boundary desperately needed a job. Boundary swallowed his pride. Dwiggens was a journalistic pustule, operating a site whose major hallmarks were sensationalism and a careless disregard of the facts. Despite its sordid reputation—or, perhaps, owing to it—the site attracted millions of daily readers from around the world. Boundary needed the exposure.

Dwiggens' brand of reckless journalism was a career killer for persons yearning to belong to a distinguished news organization. Boundary had little to lose. He had no future—and he was desperate for a press credential and for money.

Dwiggens offered Boundary $1,000 for a detailed article about his affair with Malone—a low ball price for what Boundary could offer. Boundary was in a dire financial strait, but too proud to allow a snake like Dwiggens to exploit his predicament.

"The Daily Mail called me too," Boundary lied. "They offered me $5,000."

Dwiggens, a practiced prevaricator, said, "That's bullshit."

The editor was short, bone thin, and a bloodless pale. He had a vulpine face, black eyebrows as bushy as woolly buggers, and a matching black mane, which he wore slicked back like a Wall Street sharpie.

Dwiggens' eyes were a gold-flecked brown, and they darted about like tetras in a fish tank. His voice was raspy, and he spoke with a heavy New York City accent.

Dwiggens reminded Boundary of a 1930s movie hoodlum. Despite the summer heat, he wore a black suit with thin, chalk-white stripes. He wore a starched white shirt and a narrow black necktie.

Dwiggens leaned back as far as he could in his chair and asked with a trace of sarcasm, "So what would you offer me if I were to offer you 5,000 clams?"

"I can tell my side of the story," said Boundary, crossing his legs club-man style. "Nobody but the FBI has heard it. I also have details of the Malone investigation that no one else has."

"Yeah, that's good. But I really want you to focus on the sex. For example, how did you two love birds meet? How soon did you end up together in the sack? I assume this Malone gal was a red-hot tamale under the sheets. Elaborate. Ours is not a PG publication indisposed towards salacious detail. We aim to please our readers. Capisce?"

"I don't recall having sex with her," said Boundary.

Dwiggens lurched forward. "You're pulling my chain, right?"

"There's circumstantial evidence indicating someone drugged me."

"Wait a minute, you were in bed, naked, I assume. Am I right about you being naked?"

Boundary shook his head in assent.

"And you claim you don't remember screwing possibly the most gorgeous woman who ever walked the halls of Congress? You claim she drugged you? You expect $5,000 for that?" He threw back his head and laughed.

"I got that reaction from the FBI, too" said Boundary. "It's the truth."

Dwiggens shook his head in disbelief.

"Listen, Boundary, I'm not looking for 'I know nothing!' I'm looking for 50 shades of titillation. I want the men to get woodies and the women to pant. If you can write a story like that, then I'll pay you five grand, no problem. Use your imagination. I mean, the broad is dead. Who will challenge you?"

Boundary sighed audibly. Dwiggens wanted pornography, not the truth. He stood up to leave. The movement of his leg muscles caused the metal chair to scrape loudly against the dirty white linoleum floor.

"Now hold on a minute, Boundary," said Dwiggens, trying to win the big man's confidence. "We're merely having a negotiation. Don't be rash. I have investors and a fiduciary responsibility to look out for them. I have to pinch every penny to ensure a profit." He picked up a ballpoint from his desktop. "See this? I took it from a hotel. My investors budgeted zero for paper and pens. They are thrifty, so I have to be thrifty too."

"I will not manufacture smut," said Boundary.

Dwiggens leaned forward and grasped Boundary's left arm.

"You have integrity. I get that. Maybe I'll take your story—but not for $5,000, or even $1,000. Look, how about instead of you writing a first-person reminisce, you let me interview you? This will give anything you say much more credibility."

"You pay for interviews?"

"No. But you will get your side of the story out there. You'd like that, wouldn't you? I mean, if someone drugged you, then you've gotten a bum deal from old Rooster."

"I can give free interviews to anyone," said Boundary. "I'm sure that one of the television networks would jump at the opportunity."

"OK. I'll give you $200. How does that sound?"

Boundary stared at him blankly.

Dwiggens tapped his fingers on his desktop. He had a high forehead. When he furrowed it, it resembled a line of Atlantic breakers. He needed a hot story, known as 'click bait' in tabloid parlance, to attract online advertisements. Boundary was a hot commodity at the moment, the nexus of sex, murder, and politics. Dwiggens figured that he could sensationalize the headline, no matter what Boundary wrote. "Naked Woman" would be part of the banner. The public would click on any story referencing a naked human being. He could also hype

Boundary's assertion about being drugged.

"Naked Woman Raped Me: Ex-Boxing Champ Says a Big-Bosomed, Capitol Hill Sex Queen Knocked Him Silly."

Dwiggens' wolfish eyes narrowed. He sucked pensively on his ballpoint. He might go as high as $3,000. He'd try to get the story for under $1,000.

"Listen up, Boundary, how about I bring you onto staff?"

"For how much?" asked Boundary. He hadn't expected the offer of a full-time job. He was interested. He wanted a credential.

"I will pay you $200 for a six-day week to start. If you work out, then I'll bump it up."

"Are you serious?" Boundary did a quick calculation on his cell phone's calculator app. "That's $10,400 a year. Hamburger flippers make more than that."

"So, go flip burgers." Dwiggens leaned back in his chair and grinned. "I'm giving you the opportunity to be a newsman again. You get a credential that is worth a bundle in this town. The doors of officialdom magically will open to you."

"No way, Mr. Dwiggens." Boundary got up again and turned to leave.

"Wait, wait! What's with you, Boundary? Didn't anyone ever teach you how to make a deal? Sheesh. We're just talking here. Banter. You do know what banter is? I say something and then you say something. You know, the old give and take, the back and forth. If you leave, then there's no negotiating. Leaving is crazy. You're leaving money on the table."

Boundary stared coldly at Dwiggens. The editor squirmed.

"How about a cup of coffee, Boundary? You and I can go down to the corner to Starbucks, and I'll buy you whatever you want. Do you feel like having a latte with me?"

Boundary sat back down, steaming. "I don't want a latte or a Frappuccino or anything but a minimum salary of 75 thousand."

Dwiggens' twisted his mouth into a tortured frown. He wrinkled his brow, scratched his head, and tapped his fingers on the table.

"I don't pay myself that much, Boundary. You can see from my surroundings that we're barely profitable. I got this broken-down desk at a thrift store." He slapped the desktop with the flat of his hand. Boundary noticed that the outer edges of his fingernails were crusted with dirt. "Like I said, frugality rules. What you see before you is a young web startup—a 'unicorn.' If we work hard and we work smart and we build up the publication, then the riches will follow."

He twisted his lips into an ingratiating smile.

Boundary leaned forward and smiled. "Think of me as a good return on investment. I will bring you scoops. Lots of them. Advertising will follow."

"Like what? Give me an example."

"I'm not giving away the store, Mr. Dwiggens."

Dwiggens paused, tapped his fingers again, re-wrinkled his brow. He sorely wanted Boundary's story. As for the promised scoops—he could use credibility. Boundary had a track record for producing hard-hitting stories. And the Malone killing had the makings of a political scandal. Local television stations intimated that Senator Kent Cisco was behind Malone's disappearance and the disappearance of a Dutch exchange student, as well.

Selling news was like selling ice in the hot sun. If you didn't unload it quickly, it evaporated. The Boundary story had legs, for now. If Dwiggens waited too long to get it, then he'd

178

miss the opportunity to generate public excitement. The daily deluge of outrageous news, both real and fabricated would bury Malone's murder.

"I'll tell you what I'll do, Boundary—and I wouldn't do this for anyone else, so you can't bloody advertise it: I will pay fifteen- cents-per-word for the first 750 words. Anything above that in a day and I pay you five-cents-per-word. Our longest features run 2,500 words, tops. So, if you produce a 2,500-word story every day of the week then, that's $73,000, which is not bad considering our perilous economic position, here. But let me warn you, Boundary, I have very high standards. I won't publish any piece of garbage. Your journalism has to be top-grade or I'll toss it back in your face. We got a deal?" Dwiggens figured that he could fire Boundary as soon as he submitted the Malone piece.

"Are you joking? No serious journalist can crank out a quality 2,500-word feature every day, seven days a week. I want $5,000 for the Malone feature. Take it or leave it." Boundary crossed his arms across his chest.

Dwiggens picked up his pilfered pen and tapped the butt end on his desk a couple dozen times. His eyes narrowed. His thin lips were taut. He turned the pen over and scratched calculations on a piece of paper laying atop his desk. Then after looking intensely for over a minute at whatever he had written he looked up at Boundary.

"Where are you going to go if I don't yield? What's your Plan B? You know what I think? I think you are trying to bluff me. I think you are desperate for cash. They bounced you from the Observer for unethical behavior. None of the traditional news guys will touch you. So where are you going to go? What are you going to do?"

"A college in the Midwest wants me to coach its boxing team." Boundary told this outright lie without blinking. He figured that Dwiggens was lying to him so why not lie right back? They were negotiating.

Dwiggens stared at him, looked back at the paper.

"You are a stubborn son of a bitch, Boundary," he said. "A genuine son of a bitch."

"Deal or no deal?" asked Boundary.

"I'll give you $700-per-week. That's my final offer. That's around $36,000. I know it sounds small potatoes but look around this place. This ain't the big leagues, at least not yet. If revenues grow, then your salary will grow with the revenues."

"I'll take it," said Boundary, "along with a $1,000 signing bonus."

Dwiggens frowned. He could do $1,700. He would drive Boundary to write four or five stories and then dump him.

"You're a prick, Boundary, you know it?" He stuck out his hand.

"I want a signed contract."

"A contract? You don't trust me?"

Boundary got the contract that promised him $700 at the end of every week and a $1,000 bonus when he delivered his account of his night with Malone.

He asked Dwiggens for a $1,000 advance. Dwiggens laughed at him.

"You got balls, Boundary. No advance. Deliver and get paid. I want the story tomorrow."

Boundary had $100 in his pocket. He needed a place to stay, preferably indoors. He needed to eat. He needed a post office box for his mail. The State of Virginia wanted $50 bucks for the renewal of his motorcycle registration.

When Boundary left the shabby headquarters of Bugler.com, he went straight to St. Matthew's Cathedral, which was about eight blocks away, and rang the bell of the imposing brick rectory. He figured that if he could not get help from a church, then nobody would help him. He wanted a loan, not a handout.

A portly Spanish housekeeper answered the door. She looked him over. He looked like a bum. She said curtly, "It's after 5 p.m. The office is closed. You can come back tomorrow."

Boundary put his foot behind the door before she could pull it shut. He was wearing flip-flops, so he was leaving himself open to injury. He asked for Father Francis, the elderly priest who had heard his confession. He told her it was important.

"He will be furious if you do not tell him I'm here."

Worry crept into the corners of housekeeper's eyes. She slowly opened the door and waived him inside to a cramped waiting room off the rectory's vestibule. He sat in an old red-leather armchair to wait thumbing through old copies of the Catholic Reporter. After about 10 minutes, the elderly priest stuck his head through the doorway. He showed no sign of recognizing Boundary and asked what he wanted. Boundary blurted out the details his marital and economic situation. He asked the priest for a loan.

"I will pay you back the moment I get my fee," said Boundary earnestly.

"Can you trust this Dwiggens to pay up?" Father Francis asked him. The priest was familiar with the editor's dubious reputation.

Boundary pulled his contract from the back pocket of his shorts. The priest unfolded the document and studied it carefully.

"I've never seen a contract handwritten on a sheet from a

yellow legal pad. I suppose you could make it stand up in court if he shafts you. Now how much do you need, young man?"

"A thousand, to carry me through until my first paycheck."

The priest rubbed his chin. "That's a lot of money. We're not accustomed to handing that kind of cash out to petitioners."

"I have a job. I will pay you back," said Boundary earnestly.

"How about if I write a personal check?" asked the Priest. "Would you able to cash it at your bank?"

"No. I mean, I have a joint account with my wife. I guess I could open a new one in my name with the check."

"Then you'd have to wait days for the check to clear," said the priest.

"Look, I am ashamed, coming here, begging for money. But I'm desperate. I slept in the woods last night," said Boundary. My motorcycle is low on gas. I need a permanent address to renew its registration, and I've got $100 in my pocket, which would buy me a night in a fleabag motel."

"What about your parents?"

"They live in Philadelphia. My wife lives down here. I have to stay near her."

"Would it help if we both drove over to see your wife and talked to her?"

"I don't know," said Boundary. "She's pretty upset with me. She says she never wants to see me again."

"You never know. The human heart is a complex organ. Let's give it a try. I'll get my car from the garage and meet you out in front. Think you can cram yourself into the front seat of a Beetle?"

29

Porky

J immy Johnson looked out of a huge window of his hilltop mansion down the lawn, and over to the pens where he kept two prized boars, Goliath, 500 pounds, and Isadore, 400 pounds. Workman were sweeping the pens with metal detectors. They wore masks because of the stench.

To Jimmy, pig excrement represented the sweet smell of success. His pork business had elevated him into the ranks of the world's billionaires. Tables overflowing with orchids, amaryllis, roses, lilies, and carnations perfumed the air inside his house, all paid for from pork sales.

Residents of a subdivision built near Jimmy's estate sued him a few years earlier for more than $20 million, arguing that the stench from his animals and pens prevented them from enjoying their backyards. He had bribed lawmakers into passing a law protecting hog farmers from air-pollution claims. He smiled as he recalled his ingenious subterfuge. Hell, he had been there first. Had the homeowners learned that he was a silent partner in the development and had minimized the odors emanating from his lands for a couple of years then they would have risen to greater outrage. But they did not understand and would never discover his role, the suckers.

Jimmy sat behind an immense mahogany desk and reviewed the daily paperwork for his estate. His golf course needed sand for the traps. Fifteen acres of sunflowers needed an irrigation system. His workmen had released two, 300-pound boars into his hunting preserve that morning for the 40-member "Cocaine Caucus," who would be spending a weekend of excitement and camaraderie with him in advance of a vote on a tax change that would save him millions of dollars. "Hostesses" were being bussed in from Miami to care for the congressmen after the arduous and dangerous hunt. Jimmy would show the lawmakers how to run down and spear the bear-sized beasts. His chef would roast it on a spit over his gigantic backyard barbecue pit for their evening banquet.

Jimmy wondered if any of the lawmakers would disgrace himself. It required extreme courage to take down a charging boar with one of the steel-tipped oak-shaft lances Jimmy had manufactured to Medieval specifications. He loved reading about that period. His mansion had a 2000-square-foot post and beam dining room built to resemble King Edmund Iron Side's Wessex mead hall. Crossed spears and boar heads decorated the oak-paneled walls and the mouths of the hearths at either end of the room were 10 feet high.

The congressmen would be lead into the estate's dense pine forest by handlers with 10 Mountain curs and two ferocious looking Dogo Argentino mastiffs. The snarling curs would track and surround the pig, and then the mastiffs would rush in and latch onto one of the boar's ears with their iron jaws and hold it until the hunters caught up. When the mastiff's released a boar, the fear-crazed, razor-tusked animal inadvertently would charge one hunter with murderous intent.

Stopping the lunging beast with a spear required nerve, daring, and a keen eye. The trick was to plant one's feet on the ground and drive the shaft deep into the boar's throat, holding on to the shaft after the tremendous impact while the other hunters swarmed in and bludgeoned the boar insensible with wooden mallets. If the spear man missed the sweet spot with the lance, then he was liable to gored by the animal. Not only could a boar's tusks slice a man to ribbons, they could infect the terrible wounds with an array of deadly bacteria.

No boar had ever gored one of Jimmy's guests. Whenever a spear man missed the mark, then Jimmy jumped in like a battle-crazed warrior and slew the beast with a blow to its crown with a heavy iron hammer.

Jimmy checked the paperwork for the hunt. He was short a spear and immediately phoned his blacksmith to make a new one. When he looked up, there was a workman in his doorway with something in his palm. The workman had been sweeping the metal detector down at the pens.

Johnson got up and walked over to the man rather than invite him into his office. The workman handed Johnson a piece of jewelry. Johnson recognized Preston Ferguson's distinctive platinum pinky ring with a 3.65 carat diamond, the one once owned by gangster Al Capone.

Jimmy laughed as slipped it onto his left little finger. The ring was a size 9 and fit perfectly. He showed it to the workman and asked, "What do you think?"

"I think you should be careful about wearing it," he said. "Someone might recognize it."

Jimmy continued to admire the ring.

"Took the boar a long time to pass this thing!" he guffawed. "Find anything else?"

185

The workman shook his head in the negative.

"Betsy was wearing a big wedding rock and matching ear-rings. "Look around some more. Give the boars some coffee! Finders, keepers."

The man smiled. The wife's wedding ring had a four-carat diamond. Each earring had a two-carat stone.

30

The Basement

Father Francis, with the help of a friendly pastor at a Virginia parish, found Boundary a room in an African American quadrant of Alexandria for $500 a month, an absolute steal in a city known for its exorbitant rents.

The pair's surprise visit to Twyla's had not gone well. She had opened the door, taken a cursory look at Boundary and the priest, and then slammed it in their faces. Boundary had never seen her so angry.

Father Francis, who had seen the ups and downs of thousands of marriages, was philosophical about the mission's failure.

"Marital wounds can take a long time to heal," he said.

The priest treated Boundary to meatloaf at the Royal Diner, a few blocks from Twyla's townhouse, and then took him to look over his newly rented room. The chamber was in the cinder block basement of a small, brick row home owed by a frail African American named Patsy Quander. Though far from perfect, the spare room was considerably better than Mother Nature's hard earth.

The room was windowless, which meant that it did not

conform to the city's stringent fire code and therefore was an outlaw rental. Light came from a pair of ceiling mounted florescent bulbs turned on and off by pulling on a thin chain. The floor was bare concrete, but it was clean, like every other square inch of the home; and it boasted of an adjoining bathroom with a fiberglass shower stall barely large enough to accommodate the big man.

"If I wash my face, then I can step out, turn around and go back in to wash the back of my head," he joked to Father Francis.

"Don't let Mrs. Quander hear you say that. She's a proud woman. She'll throw you back out in the street," whispered the priest.

Most important for Boundary, the room put him six blocks from Twyla's townhouse, enabling him to keep a protective eye on her. The sacking of their former home was not a random criminal event.

Mrs. Quander was from New Orleans and spoke with a sunny, Creole lilt. She boasted to Boundary she had spent most of her life as a chef in a fancy French restaurant on Lake Ponchartrain. The sweet odor wafting from her small kitchen attested to the truth of her claim. He smelled shrimp, sausage, and spicy tomato sauce. Although he had just lunched with Father Francis, the enticing aroma made his mouth water, and he did not turn down the plate she offered him.

As Boundary wolfed down her delectable gumbo, Mrs. Quander laid down for him her unbreakable commandments. If Boundary used the kitchen, then he must leave it as spotless as he had found it. He was to wear paper booties over his shoes inside the house. She had baskets of the teal coverings just inside the front and back doors. No smoking, loud music, snoring, or drunkenness, she said sternly.

"And no girlfriends! I'm a God-fearing woman and will not countenance adultery, premarital sex, or homosexuality under my roof," she said. Boundary nodded.

"My nephew Brutus will eject you if you break any of the rules. There will be no appeal, no refunds. You may be a big man, Mr. Boundary, but Brutus is even bigger. He's six-feet eight and weighs over 300 pounds."

"Sounds like a football player."

"Tackle at LSU. One year with the Saints before he blew out his knee. He now works in accounting," she added with no small amount of pride.

Boundary assured the tiny woman he would be a saintly tenant.

"I don't smoke. I can't afford to drink. I've given up women—or, rather, women have given up on me. I live like a monk."

"Well, that's good," she said.

"If you say so."

Although the mattress on his new bed was so thin that Boundary could feel the hard steel springs underneath, he was so dog tired that as soon as he paid the rent with money that Father Francis had given him, he fell asleep on it like a comatose patient.

He may have broken the rule against loud snoring, but Miss Quander would not have been able to tell, having removed her hearing aids.

Boundary awoke suddenly at 5:30 a.m., stirred by the sound of a trash truck. He left the house quietly, so as not to disturb his landlord, and ate a $6 breakfast at a spot called Extra Perks on Royal Street half-a-mile away; and then walked to the

Trader Joe's supermarket on St. Asaph Street, across from Twyla's town house. The usually bustling thoroughfare was quiet at that hour. A man in a small sedan who was tossing newspapers over his roof and onto doorsteps drove past him. A trim, elderly woman in sweat pants rounded the corner, walking her small dog—both using rapid, mincing steps. She spoke to the animal as if it were a human infant, cooing about the size of its poo, which she dutifully picked up from the sidewalk with a scooping device.

A white panel truck crawled down the street and parked in back of Twyla's jeep. The driver who looked like an Aztec, was chatting on his cell phone. Boundary assumed he was a contractor.

Boundary hung out near the bottom of a winding, white concrete staircase set back from St. Asaph's on a plaza between the Trader Joe's market and a Vietnamese restaurant that had an outdoor patio crowded with umbrella-covered tables. The staircase led up to another plaza on Washington Street, a six-lane highway that ran through the heart of Old Town. Offices and shops filled the upper plaza. After about an hour, Boundary climbed the stairs, bought himself a cup of iced coffee from Starbucks, and replanted himself on the bottom step where he could watch Twyla drive off to work.

Boundary felt as invisible as a deer hunter in a tree stand. Set back the way he was, persons walking on the sidewalks on either side of St. Asaph's did not notice him. He was a piece of furniture, like the Vietnamese restaurant's outdoor tables.

Boundary glanced frequently at his wristwatch. Seeing Twyla on the previous evening had aroused his heart. He wondered if she had felt anything for him other than anger.

Boundary wanted to tell her how empty his life had become

and that he was profoundly sorry, and then plead her forgiveness. He debated standing directly outside her front door, but decided it would be too rash a move.

"Absence makes the heart grow fonder," he muttered. He hoped there was solid wisdom underlying that 17th-century adage.

Her forest green front door opened precisely at 7 o'clock and Twyla exited, locked up, and then hurried to her Jeep, which was parked snugly against the curb, between the white cargo van and a black Mercedes Benz sedan. She was wearing a teal jacket, white blouse, white slacks with matching sandals, and her wedding band, a hopeful sign.

At the sight of his wife, Boundary buried his face in his hands and sobbed. When he looked up, the Jeep was gone, as were the van and the sedan.

Boundary pulled himself together rose swiftly and climbed the steps to Washington Street. He had a story to write and a check to collect. Despite the hot weather, he hustled to the Metro station a mile away and grabbed a Yellow Line to downtown Washington. He exited the train at the Dupont Circle station, jogging up a 188-foot-long escalator to the street. From there, it was a short walk Dwiggens' Q-Street office, where Boundary could use a PC and a phone.

Dwiggens greeted him coldly, which Boundary found surprising. The editor had been as saccharine as a car salesman during their previous meeting. Boundary wondered if Dwiggens was having second thoughts about their arrangement.

"You said I could have a place to work," Boundary said, looking around the office. The only desk belonged to Dwiggens.

"There's an empty office down the hall," Dwiggens said,

rising from his chair. He was half the size of Boundary. Boundary could see dandruff on top of the editor's head.

Dwiggens led Boundary to an ancient oak door with a glass doorknob. He inserted an old, Victorian shop key into the keyhole and yanked hard. The door opened with a loud shudder, exposing a closet-sized space illuminated by a bare light bulb and furnished with a small computer work station holding a 1990s era PC. There was no telephone and the battery of Boundary's cell phone was down to 15 percent of capacity. The sole outlet in the room was powering the PC and its monitor. Dwiggens read the look of consternation on Boundary's face.

"There's an electrical outlet in the hallway where you can charge your phone. Make sure that keep the door open to monitor the foot traffic. The marijuana pharmacy attracts some rum-looking customers." He added, "Save the story to the hard drive when you're done, and then I'll show you how to forward it. OK? In the meantime, I've got a website to update, so please try not to disturb me."

He turned and hurried back to his office.

Before writing his story, Boundary wanted touch base with Joe and with either Smee or Starkey to learn if there had been any new developments in the Malone murder investigation. He hoped for on-the-record evidence that would establish his innocence. The public, grown cynical of press reports in the wake of Donald Trump's election, would label as "fake news" any claim of innocence attributed to anonymous sources by the prime suspect.

Joe answered on the first ring and he sounded excited.

"Martin, you'll never guess what happened: Preston Ferguson is missing. Someone my have murdered him. I'm told that his living room is a bloody mess. But you can't report this yet because if you do then the cops will know someone has tipped you off. I can't deal with a leak investigation—so protect your source! Get over to Ferguson's place in Cathedral Mews." Joe gave Boundary the street address. Boundary knew it, having once driven through the posh, four-block area while joy riding on his motorcycle. The neighborhood was an enclave of stone mansions from the "Roaring 20s," with wide green lawns, towering trees, and semicircular driveways. The steeple of the National Cathedral towered over the neighborhood. Several U.S. senators lived in the area, as did a partner of the Crystal Group, one of the world's largest hedge funds.

"The homicide detectives are stymied. They found buckets of blood, but no other evidence—no prints, no hairs, no fibers."

"Any sign of Preston's wife, Betsy?"

"She's missing too. The blood on the carpet might belong to one or both; or it might belong to someone else. We're waiting on the lab boys for answers. Cops are collecting DNA samples from the son to see if there's a match. He was away at boarding school. Both of their cars are on the property. Preston drove a Cadillac, and it's parked in the circular drive. His wife's Lexus is inside a detached garage."

"How long before you see a lab report?"

"At least 24 hours. This could be the first murder in the history of Cathedral Mews."

Boundary thanked Joe profusely, ended the call, and went down the hall to announce to Dwiggens, "I have another juicy story."

He filled Dwiggens in and told the editor not publish any-thing until he had time to visit the scene and speak with the investigators. Otherwise, Dwiggens would alert the city's entire press corps destroying Boundary's time advantage.

Dwiggens offered him $200, assuming a scoop. Boundary accepted. It was easy money.

"I'll send you a video of the crime scene as soon as I get there. Then I'll dictate a story."

Boundary ran outside and hailed a cab. Dwiggens immediately put a short news alert out on his website to generate traffic and advertising buys: "Talking Head Preston Ferguson Murdered in His Living Room." He used his own byline. Within seconds, he had $10,000 in ad bookings.

Boundary fully charged up his phone in the cab's USB port during the five-minute ride to Cathedral Mews. He planned to take a lot of videos. When he arrived, he found the property crawling with police. Evidence teams dressed in their white jump suits were exiting and entering the premises. Police cadets were combing the home's large yard, which was fenced off by yellow crime-scene tape. Police vehicles lined both sides of the street.

A TV news satellite truck rolled onto the block just as Boundary disembarked from his cab, which meant that had to act fast, before a public affairs officer took over the show. He wondered how the TV crew had found out about the crime so quickly.

Boundary walked up to a uniformed police officer at the driveway on the other side of the tape and asked, "What happened, officer? Preston Ferguson invited me over for coffee. Is he OK?"

"What's your name?"

"Martin Boundary. "

"Wait here," the policeman said. He spoke into a radio and

announced there was a visitor for Ferguson. A few minutes later, Smee came through the home's polished oak double doors. He frowned when he saw Boundary.

"What's this bullshit about a coffee date, Boundary?"

"Is it true? Was Ferguson bumped off?"

"Who said he was bumped off? He's unavailable for comment. Now what's this about an invitation?"

"The day Malone turned up in the sand trap, he told me to call on him if ever I needed a favor."

"And you picked this morning?"

"Yes. Why don't you confirm it with him?"

"He's indisposed."

"How about Betsy?"

"Unavailable," Smee said.

"A double-homicide."

"I never said that, Boundary."

"Come on, Smee, toss me a bone. It doesn't have to be a femur. I'm flat broke, and I'm trying to make a little scratch."

Smee turned and walked back towards the mansion.

"I helped you, Smee. I voluntarily led you Malone's love pad. That was a major break in your case. Come on, throw me a crumb."

"OK, I'll give you this, but off-the-record. We've linked Bernadette to a stash of a date-rape drug."

"I need something on-the-record."

"Not from me."

"Nobody will believe an unsourced story like that from me. I'm the one person with the most to gain from the revelation."

"Try the campus police chief at John Adams, where they found Bernadette's Beemer. A huge bottle of the drug was in her glove compartment. At first, we thought someone had

195

drugged her, but the toxicology came back negative. Her prints were all over the medicine bottle."

"How about something about Ferguson? He's disappeared, right?"

"There's red stuff on the carpet in the house and no Fergusons. For all we know, it's barbecue sauce. End of story. Now beat it."

"Are you ruling out blood?"

"We're not ruling anything out, nor are we jumping to conclusions."

"Why is this an FBI investigation?"

"Our mouthpiece will brief the press later. Stay on that side of the tape. I won't be as forgiving as I was at the golf course if you try to sneak in here." The agent turned and walked back into the house.

Boundary quickly dictated a story to his phone's stenographer app and sent it to Dwiggens for publication. The lead was, "A celebrated talk show host and his wife appear to have been murdered in their Cathedral Mews home. Detectives are surveying a bloody crime scene in the mansion of Preston Ferguson, host of the Big Event talk show, and his wife, Betsy, a celebrity real estate agent. The Fergusons are missing, but their cars remain on the property. The FBI is investigating and will release a statement later this morning."

Boundary also sent Dwiggens some video, and some "color," like the number of police vehicles parked on Ferguson's block and some comments from neighbors who were gawking at the activity from their manicured front lawns. When he pushed the send button, he cursed himself for not holding out for more money. Dwiggens would make a mint on this one. But he had no time to dwell on it. He was in a hurry to call Chief

Cordovan at John Adams and get something on the record about the date-rape drug—a revelation that might win back Twyla.

31

Discovery

The drug in Malone's car was ketamine, a powerful anesthetic for animals often used by rapist to dose a woman's drink. Ketamine acts in the memory like an anesthetic. The victims can't recall anything that happened to them while drugged.

Malone had had enough ketamine in her glove box to sedate a stable of dray horses. The FBI traced the pills to a York, Pennsylvania, veterinarian named Vincent Boyd, who had retired to the Cape Verde Islands the previous year. The island's parliament had never approved an extradition treaty with the U.S., and consequently, the tropical paradise off the coast of Senegal had become the domicile of several high-profile American fugitives. Yet, Boyd wasn't a fugitive, so it was highly curious that he had moved there.

"I've volunteered to fly out first class to Cape Verde tomorrow to ask Boyd why he gave Malone so much ketamine," Chief Cordovan boasted to Boundary.

"Sounds like a wonderful boondoggle," said Martin. He was standing on the sidewalk in front of Ferguson's house, his cell phone plastered to his ear. An army of journalists had assembled outside the crime scene, waiting for the FBI's press spokesman to tell them what was going on.

"Damn straight it's a boondoggle, Boundary; but you can't quote me on that. I have an official excuse for making the trip: Transporting ketamine to our campus is illegal."

"Boyd couldn't have driven the car into your campus."

"Doesn't matter, Boundary. If he wrote the pill prescription and Malone didn't have any horses, then he becomes an accessory to every crime involving those pills, including illegal transportation to John Adams University. If she used the pills on you, then Boyd might be an accessory."

"Did Bernadette own any horses?"

"That's something I aim to find out."

"Can I phone you after you interview him?"

"Sure, if you promise to spell my name correctly."

A scrum of journalists had gathered on the sidewalk around Boundary. A cop with a megaphone said an FBI spokesperson would brief them in 30 minutes.

"What's all the noise, Boundary?" Cordovan asked, as the crowd noise increased.

"Preston Ferguson is missing and may be dead. I'm across the street from his house in the middle of a great, big media circus."

"Ferguson, dead? That's rich. He's the FBI's leading suspect in Malone's killing."

"Ferguson? Are you kidding me?"

"The Bureau has video surveillance of Ferguson entering Malone's apartment building and later exiting it with a grocery bag. He may have grabbed videos of Malone behaving badly with congressmen. Hell, maybe there are pictures of you, Boundary," Cordovan laughed. "Anyway, the theory is that

199

Malone was blackmailing Ferguson too, so he killed her."

"How do you know all of this stuff, Chief?" asked Boundary.

"The Ferguson case is a multi-jurisdictional effort, and I know several of the investigators. Girls will talk."

"Is Ferguson the sole murder suspect?" asked Boundary.

"They've lost interest in you because of something in the autopsy findings."

"Have you seen them?"

"They're sealed. I gather that they didn't find the killer's physical evidence on her body."

"So, I didn't have sex with her."

"Your loss, buddy."

"Who killed Ferguson?"

"The FBI theorizes that Ferguson used the videos to black-mail someone else and that that person killed him."

"That sounds far out. Do they have a suspect?"

"No, just the theory. Except for blood on the rug, Ferguson's place is clean. If there was a hit, then it was a professional."

"A hit?"

"The neighbor across the street noticed a white panel truck in the driveway the night before. He assumed it was a contractor."

Boundary's gut told him that Ferguson was not cunning enough to be Malone's killer. The fact that security camera had caught him at Malone's love nest established that he was sloppy. Malone's killer had been meticulous.

"Ferguson might have retrieved the videos from Malone's apartment for somebody else and then they double-crossed him," said Boundary.

"Maybe, and maybe not," said the chief. "Maybe he tried to play Malone's bribery game with the same person who killed her. At this stage with so few clues, there are dozens of explanations. Checking them all out will take months."

Boundary thanked the Chief and ended the call. It elated him because the Chief's on-the-record comments about Malone's stash of ketamine supported his own contention that she had drugged him silly. Twyla might forgive him now.

Boundary waited another 30 minutes for the FBI's crime scene briefing. The spokeswoman was Agent Janet Cleary, and all that she would say was that the bureau was investigating a "possible homicide."

"Why is the FBI involved?" asked a reporter from a local TV station.

"We're not at liberty to discuss this at the present time," Cleary said. But Boundary knew the answer, thanks to Chief Cordovan. He hurried back to the closet-sized Bugler.com office to write his story.

Dwiggens was thrilled and stuck his head into Boundary's closet to congratulate him.

"You've really put Bugler.com on the map, Boundary. You've earned your extra cash." Dwiggens handed Boundary two, crisp, $100 bills and then reached into his pocket and peeled an extra $20 from a folded wad.

"Here's a bonus for a job well done."

"I'm overwhelmed," Boundary said dryly as he pocketed the money. He might have become homicidal if he'd known Dwiggens had already made $11,000 from the story.

Boundary spent two hours writing and re-writing his first-person account about his encounter with Malone. Seldom had he been more focused while crafting a story. The difference this time was that his entire future would rest on his words.

His first version of the story was 5,000 words—the length of a major magazine piece. Dwiggens had forewarned Boundary that the publication's readership could digest nothing more than half that length. So, after an intensive, line-by-line edit, Boundary cut it down to 1,500 words.

Boundary's story emphasized the suspicion of the cops that Malone had been slipping congressmen Mickey Finns, taking them into her bed, and videoing them as part of a blackmail racket. He took the readers into her love nest, describing the luxury apartment in detail, and revealing that the FBI had found evidence that television star Preston Ferguson had removed a video-taping system from the apartment. These sensational revelations, he felt, would electrify the public.

Boundary's lead sentence was, "Police believe the Congressional Golf Club murder victim Bernadette Kathleen Malone may have been drugging lawmakers and other Washington notables, dragging them into bed to photograph them during sex. She may have been blackmailing them to finance a lavish lifestyle. I was one of her unsuspecting victims."

Boundary described his sudden wooziness and disorientation and his waking up in bed beside her hours later with no recollection of the events in between. He related the discovery of ketamine in her car and he quoted Chief Cordovan about Malone's fingerprints being found on the bottles. And he reported on the Chief's pending trip to Cape Verde to visit Dr. Boyd.

Boundary discretely omitted that, as he got out of bed to leave, Malone had turned over and sat up, looking like a naked goddess, instantly causing a rigidity that caused him to redden; nor did he mention Bernadette's allusion to Twyla or his threat to kill Malone.

But he reported that sources claimed an autopsy found no

traces of semen in Malone's body.

It filled him with satisfaction as he transmitted the story electronically to Dwiggens. A lot of persons would be ashamed for judging him so harshly. Twyla, Rooster, his colleagues, his in-laws. Longing for vindication, he was impatient to see the story posted online.

Dwiggens read through the story once, as Boundary hovered over his shoulder, but didn't comment beyond a grunt. He pulled a battered checkbook from a drawer and wrote one out to Boundary for $1,000.

"As per our written contract," he said, handing it to Boundary

"When will you post my story?"

"Give me an hour. I want to proofread it. Then, I'll tease the headline. Nice job, Boundary. Now go home and get some sleep. You look beat."

Boundary tucked the check into his wallet. Though he was, in fact, exhausted, he planned to open a checking account. He wanted to repay Father Francis.

When Boundary left, Dwiggens rose from his desk and locked the door. He read through Boundary's story again. What a mess! It was as boring as Leviticus. Boundary made such a big deal about being drugged; yet, he had no lab report to prove this ever had happened. That kind of unsubstantiated opinion had no place in a news story, so Dwiggens cut it.

After reading through the story two more times, Dwiggens decided to make it appealing. This was his prerogative as an editor. He began by changing Boundary's lead.

"I was the last man to go to bed with sex goddess Bernadette Kathleen Malone before someone brutally murdered her and buried her in a sand trap at the Congressional Golf Club. But it turns out I wasn't the only man to bed her. She was Capitol Hill's most prominent sex siren, maintaining a luxurious love pad where she secretly videotaped wild sexploits with congressmen and celebrities. She may have blackmailed them, including TV news commentator Preston Ferguson, her suspected murderer. Ferguson faked his own death and now is on the run."

Dwiggens had made up the last part about Ferguson.

"So, sue me," he laughed to himself, because it was a safe bet that the TV star was dead.

Dwiggens manufactured two paragraphs describing videos of unnamed congressmen in bed with Malone. He had one moaning loudly, "Please don't stop," and another whooping like an Indian chief.

Dwiggens quoted Boundary musing about his tryst with Malone, 'Was it a dream or was it real?' Dwiggens described Boundary rising light-headed from a bed that was a bouncy sex trampoline.

"I was woozy," Dwiggens improvised. "I had never been knocked out in the boxing ring when I was a collegiate champion, yet this blonde bombshell had me seeing stars dancing around in my head."

Dwiggens laughed. 'That was good,' he thought. 'Fantastic.'

He moved Boundary's reporting about the date-rape drug to the bottom of the story. He left out Boundary's quote from the police chief that Malone's fingerprints had been all over the plastic vial containing the drug. He also excised Boundary's detailed description of the symptoms of the date-rape drug, including loss of memory and will power. The stuff about the semen? It was pure hearsay, so he deleted it.

Boundary had hoped the story would engender public sym-

204

pathy for him. When Dwiggens published the salacious re-write under the headline, "I was the Last Man to Sleep with a Busty Senate Aide before Someone Brutally Bludgeoned Her," the story attracted 3,000 views-per-minute. Links to the story went viral on social sites. The hits rose geometrically. Advertisers linked to the story. The story paid for itself within minutes. Dwiggens received invitations to discuss it on a popular news talk shows, exposure guaranteed to drive more traffic to his website. The editor was ecstatic. This was a big payday for him if not for Boundary.

The story outraged members of the U.S. Congress.

"This Boundary is describing videotapes that no one has seen. They likely do not exist. The entire story is preposter-ous." Big Barney had prepared the statement and had ordered the congressman to deliver it to the news media, which had been deluging his office with requests for a comment about the Bugler's explosive story.

In fact, Big Barney had seen some of the videos. In one, Mal-one had him moaning like an old, barnyard bull. Fortunately, Jimmy had the hard drive locked up in an underground vault.

"That sneaky Bernadette literally had me by the balls, and I didn't even know it," said Barney. "Now we have a bunch of members by the balls. We have to let them know we have the videos lest any of them try to break away from us, you know what I mean?"

"Maybe you can host a film festival some weekend," said Jimmy.

"No, it's better if we bring them in one at a time for a personal airing," said Barney. "My farmstead in Pennsylvania would be the perfect venue."

Boundary's hoped-for groundswell of sympathy never materialized. Instead, the story generated an avalanche of snarky tweets and Facebook posts, with male readers asserting with wicked glee that Boundary had been lucky to have been dragged into bed by the bombshell. Women readers jumped to Malone's defense, accusing Boundary of blaming the dead woman for his own promiscuity. Not one of them could imagine Boundary going to a bar in the middle of the night after a tiff with his wife solely to have a shot of whiskey. He wanted 'revenge sex,' said one woman, whose comment appeared on social networks hundreds of times.

Boundary was apoplectic. Dwiggens had depicted him as a braggart, proud of bedding a murdered woman. The story was nauseating. Dwiggens had treated the ketamine discovery as incidental.

"Son of a bitch," he shouted, while hurling Boundary his Chrome book across his tiny room into the cinder-block wall. The device's plastic case exploded into hundreds of pieces.

Boundary climbed the basement stairs two at a time and blew by Ms. Quander who was sipping coffee in the kitchen, heading outside to a gravel driveway to his Captain America motorcycle.

He kick-started the bike and roared out of the driveway onto Wythe Street. He had the light a block away on Washington Street and hung a left towards the District. He hurtled down road, blowing past four yellow traffic signals and reaching 95 mph by the time he entered the George Washington Parkway. The speed limit was 40 mph.

Boundary, weaving recklessly in and out of traffic, made the trip from Alexandria to the Bugler in slightly over ten minutes. He hopped off the bike with his Stars & Stripes helmet and goggles still on his head and bounded up the stairs to Dwiggens' second-floor office. He turned the knob. The door was locked. He could see Dwiggens' outline through the frosted glass. He pounded on the door, called for Dwiggens to open it, and then rattled it again. Dwiggens did not move.

"I'm warning you, Dwiggens, open up or I'll kick down your door." There was silence.

Boundary lifted his right leg and kicked the door just below the knob. He heard the jamb splinter as the door swung open and banked into the wall, shattering the glass. A cowering Dwiggens peaked over his oak desk.

"Are you crazy, Boundary?"

Boundary reached over the desk and yanked Dwiggens to his feet by his shirt collar.

"You're a scummy, rat-faced, piece-of-shit. You twisted my story like a hair braid. You made me sound like Hugh Hefner boasting about screwing his centerfold models. How do you think my wife will react when she sees your crap?"

He shoved Dwiggens back into his chair, which was on rollers. The editor and his chair careened across the floor and thudded against the plaster wall.

"You lay another hand on me, Boundary, and I'll file charges." The editor's voice quaked with fear. "Walk out of here now, and I'll only charge you for damage to the door."

"What about the damage you've caused to my marriage, you son of a bitch?" Boundary shoved him and the chair again.

"As the editor, I had the right to change the story. Everything in the story was factual."

"The silk sheets, the trampoline bed, me seeing stars? It's all fiction."

"Poetic license. The spirit of the story was truthful."

Boundary grabbed Dwiggens by the collar again.

"Listen Boundary, what you did was try to use me and the Bugler as a marriage counselor and then charge me for the privilege. Well, I am not a marriage counselor. I don't give two cents about how your relationship with the missus stands. That's between you and her. You know what my job is? It's selling paying ads by attracting eyeballs to the website, not dispensing a soppy, self-serving apologia that makes you out to be a rape victim. Now get your gorilla paws off of me or I will call the cops!"

Dwiggens pulled out his cell phone from a back pocket and waived it at Boundary. Boundary tore it from his spidery hand and smashed it against the wall. Technology was not faring well with Boundary this day.

"That's the latest iPhone," Dwiggens screeched. "It cost me 1,000 bucks!"

Boundary swept Dwiggens' computer monitor onto the floor.

Dwiggens covered his face with his arms and pleaded, "Don't hit me!" just as Boundary gave the rat-faced editor a hard slap across his left cheek.

"Not my face! I'm on TV tonight."

Boundary turned to leave. Then, he changed his mind. He turned just as Dwiggens was dropping his arms and socked him in the eye. The blow was not enough to spill the editor from his chair, but he'd have a terrific shiner at air time.

32

No Mercy

Boundary rang Twyla's cell phone the next morning, and an automated voice instructed him to leave a message after the tone. Upon hearing a beep, he dictated to the machine: "I deeply love you, Twyla. I can't describe how angry and miserable I feel. The story in the Bugler is a total crock. The editor twisted my words and concocted the facts. I'm positive that Malone drugged me with ketamine, and I was so drugged out of my mind, I never had sex with her."

Twyla's father earlier had e-mailed her the shocking story with a note attached: "Dump the cocky son of a bitch." The boastful story had infuriated her to tears. Martin had sounded pathologically narcissistic, proud that he had bedded Malone hours before her murder. The horrid story was generating tens of thousands of comments, virtually all of them negative.

Twyla was so distraught, she called in sick to work. She cried throughout the morning. At noon, she met here friend Sadie Ramsey for lunch on bustling King Street in the heart of Old Town, a five-minute walk from her home. Sadie, a legal counsel for the House Financial Services Committee, was definitely Twyla's most trusted friend on the Hill. She knew Martin had confessed at the beachfront house she, Sadie, owned, to his affair with Malone. Sadie too had seen Boundary's story in the Bugler; and its flip tone had sickened her as well.

"We both should have a stiff shot of something," said Sadie, patting the Twyla on the forearm. "I'm buying. Name your poison."

Twyla declined. "Alcohol is a depressant, and I'm already overly depressed. I'll have a Diet Coke."

"A little Merlot won't hurt, will it?"

"I'm abstaining from booze, Sadie"

"How unlike you, Twyla. Say, you're not..."

Twyla twisted uncomfortably in her chair.

"Never mind. I'll have a whiskey sour."

When the waiter bought their drinks, Twyla told Sadie about her consultation with a divorce lawyer. She was planning to file in court by the end of the week.

"I showed the Bugler.com story to my brother, Edgar," said Sadie. "He's a criminal defense attorney, you know. He thinks the ketamine revelation buried at the bottom of the story changes everything, Twyla."

Twyla shook her head in the negative.

"Ketamine is a powerful drug, common in date rapes," said Sadie. "A few grams in a drink would knock anyone cold. And ketamine is deadly if administered in too large a dose, triggering a heart attack. Edgar says you are lucky that Martin is still alive."

"Am I? Read the story again. He sounds like he had the time of his life."

"Don't be so hardhearted, Twyla," said Sadie. "Maybe he's

embarrassed that this gal raped him."

"Nothing in that story suggested embarrassment. And exactly what proof does he have that someone drugged him other than the vial in Malone's medicine cabinet? Did he have a blood test or a urine test? How do we know that she used it on him?"

"Edgar says traces of the drug break down rapidly in the bloodstream, making it nearly impossible to detect after 24 hours."

"How convenient," said Twyla.

"The circumstantial evidence is compelling. The John Adams University police chief said Malone had enough ketamine in her the glove box of her Beemer to knock out a stable of thoroughbreds."

"Martin is a jackass, not a horse."

"Twyla. Be reasonable!"

"If he were innocent, Sadie, then why did he try to cover up the affair? He should have gone directly to the police."

"Obviously, he did not want to lose beautiful you, Twyla. He assumed correctly that with your fiery temper, you'd see red and refuse to believe him."

"It was Martin's temper that caused the whole thing and brought this down on our heads," Twyla seethed. "He walked out of the house in a fury and went straight to that bar, with betrayal on his mind to get back at me."

"Do the police have any idea who trashed your place? That seems strange. There has to be a Malone connection, don't you think?"

Twyla shook her head. "The cops won't tell me anything," she said, "but they've warned me to be careful. There was DNA evidence, you know? One of the perps pissed all over my wedding album."

"How awful! Can the cops say who it is?" Sadie was intensely interested.

"They aren't telling us anything."

"Maybe whoever trashed your house thinks Martin knows something about Malone's murder. Have you ever thought of that?"

"Yes, Sadie, I've thought of that. But Martin knows nothing beyond what he wrote about in the paper."

"Maybe Malone mentioned something important to him," said Sadie. "Maybe, she said something that didn't appear to mean anything."

"That's all conjecture. For all I know, Martin might have killed Malone to shut her up!"

"What a horrid thing to say, Twyla! You can't believe that! Are you sure you won't have a glass of wine?" She looked Twyla squarely in the eyes. Sadie suspected her friend was pregnant because Twyla never, ever had turned down a glass of wine before.

"I'm sure," Twyla said. She did not feel like telling Sadie her secret even though she suspected Sadie had guessed it.

"We'll, I'm ordering myself half a bottle of chardonnay. You can have some if you change your mind."

Seven miles away, Martin was sitting in the edge of his bed, on his cell phone pleading with Agent Smee to let Twyla view the security video of his drunken entrance into Malone's apartment. The footage showed that he had been seriously impaired. He looked like he had just absorbed a haymaker to the chin. His legs were rubbery. He had a stupid grin on his face. He listed first to the left and then to the right like a ship rocking in a storm. One untainted drink of rye whiskey would not have affected him that way. In the video, Malone, five-feet-eleven, struggled to keep him from toppling over. Twyla would appreciate Malone had drugged him once she saw the footage.

Smee declined, explaining that the FBI's investigation was ongoing. An illegal leak of information to Boundary might taint the evidence and inadvertently benefit the perpetrators.

"Can you at least tell me when the lab will release the results of the tests on Ferguson's carpet, Smee? I need some news to hawk. I'm flat broke."

"A couple of days," the agent said. Then he made an excuse of an office visitor, to end the call.

Boundary swore at the agent. Boundary felt that Smee owed him something substantial in the way of atonement. He stood up. You can't trust the cops, he thought. They were lazy. They lied. They manufactured evidence.

Boundary's white-walled basement room was a block away from a community center that housed a sizable boxing gym for the neighborhood kids, who were mostly black and Latino. Boundary walked over to the gym to take out his frustrations on a body bag.

As he pounded furiously away, Hank Hodges, the gym's manager, approached him. Hank was a former Golden Gloves champion.

"Remember a kid in your class, Sammy Hernandez—ICE deported him, yesterday."

"Sammy! He was my most promising student," said Boundary.

"His parents, his sisters, all of them snuck in from Guatemala. Now they can't come back legally for ten years."

"What did his parents do for a living?" Boundary asked.

"The dad was in construction and the mom worked for a maid service. They were good people," said Hodges.

Boundary gave boxing lessons at the gym in exchange for free gym privileges. Hodges knew Boundary by reputation and it awed him when the former collegiate boxer asked him about making a hard-luck deal. Hodges needed an extra hand for his programs but lacked the budget, so Boundary's arrival had been a godsend.

Boundary's boxing students uniformly were tough and rambunctious kids, ages nine to 12. They all harbored the delusion of becoming the world champion. Based on the physical appearances of their fathers, none of them ever would ascend to that elite circle. However, Boundary would not spoil their youthful fantasies with a lesson in genetics. He was trying to teach them the virtues of discipline, endurance, and sweat equity. Their goal, no matter how unrealistic, rendered them more pliable to his good-natured prodding.

After hitting the bags for over an hour, Boundary showered, dressed, and boarded the Metro at a nearby station for a ride to the Library of Congress, where he could surf the web for free on one of about a dozen PCs, looking for web publications that might buy his future stories. Boundary desperately needed cash again. So, he was frantically writing crime stories for various web sites for what amounted to pocket change. A mugging or car theft or holdup story that would have been passed over by most DC news sites sometimes was saleable to an out-of-town site simply because the crime had occurred in the Nation's Capital. The public was as fixated on Washington, D.C. because cable networks had transformed politics from a sober profession into a clown show. But the income from this piece work was not steady. Multiple editors had rejected

Boundary's last three pitches—a night club shooting; a report on a serial cat burglar absconding with women's shoes in upscale Chevy Chase; and the trial of a cab driver who had left a demanding customer off on a shoulder of the Washington Beltway.

"Everybody has or will have this crap," one crusty editor complained. "It's blotter fodder. Dig up something original."

Boundary had plenty of great ideas for original stories. He could get a fresh lead on Malone's murder or be the first journalist to break the news of the lab findings on the evidence from Ferguson's home. The outlook for developing those ideas quickly, however, wasn't promising. Boundary was only as good as his sources. Joe, his primary source had clammed up.

"I'm sorry Martin, but the Bureau has hired me to photograph the Ferguson house and to shoot infrared at the golf course, to see if there are any foot impressions beneath the turf. I am now bound by the rules of secrecy."

"I am desperate, Joe."

"Why don't you see if the Fergusons' son knows anything," suggested his friend. But the son was in seclusion with some relatives in Connecticut, and Boundary had no clue how to reach him. Besides, the kid was 15. Boundary doubted that the son's relatives would permit him to speak with a reporter.

Then Boundary got an idea. If Cisco were in fact a serial killer, then he might have been killing for decades. If he had, in fact, killed Malone, then he might have bludgeoned other women with golf clubs.

Chances were that the inquiry would lead to a dead end. The biographies of U.S. senators were thorough. On the other hand, when Cisco first ran for office, the internet wasn't as nearly has informative as it was now. They scattered newspaper databases from that period and held most of their information on rolls of microfiche. A search seven or eight years ago on the scale contemplated by Boundary would have taken months. Now, however, Boundary had access to databases like ProQuest, which had digitized hundreds of newspaper stories going back to the 19th Century, allowing for a massive search in a few hours.

Most likely, he would find he was on a wild goose chase. But he had learned early in his journalism not to dismiss any lead out of hand. Occasionally, dogged digging would yield a story that was pure gold.

Boundary looked at his watch. It was 5 p.m. He'd follow his hunch the following day. There was a place where he wanted to be—on Twyla's door step.

33

The Plea

September provided no respite from the hellish summer heat. Hot, thick humid air clung to the flesh, making life outdoors miserable. It quickly transformed the clothing of those compelled to venture outdoors into sweat-soaked rags. Pedestrians largely kept to the shady side of the street.

Boundary sat on a two-foot high wall in front of a Vietnamese restaurant on the opposite side of St. Asaph Street from Twyla's townhouse, almost directly opposite her front door. He fanned himself with a bus schedule. He was waiting for Twyla return from work so he could explain the disgusting story in Bugler.com.

A handful of dogs had forced their owners into nature's furnace. There was a tall, thin elderly woman patiently walked her arthritic Golden Retriever, frequently using a handkerchief to wipe perspiration from her forehead and a fanatical runner, drinking from a water bottle as he went along with his greyhound. A hard-looking Latino with red and blue Aztec warriors tattooed on each of his forearms sat on another low wall in front of the Trader Joe's, about 30 yards away to

Boundary's right, drinking beer from a container hidden in a brown paper bag. Boundary assumed he was a construction worker.

Boundary sipped tap water in an old, plastic soda bottle. He poured some water over his head for relief.

A little past eight, Twyla parked their Jeep in front of the townhouse, slipping it expertly between an Audi SUV and a Volvo, with only inches to spare. Boundary hopped up from his perch, briskly crossed the street, and called out to her.

"Twyla, it's me, Martin. Please, stop and talk."

She glared at him.

"I'm not ready for this, Martin," she said.

"Twyla, I didn't write that news story. It was a crock. The editor mangled it. The real story is that Malone drugged me out of my mind!"

"You should not have been at that bar, Martin."

"I love you, Twyla. I would never betray you."

"You slept with that woman and then you slept with me. I feel dirty, Martin. What if she had had a venereal disease like herpes or even AIDS? We're you going to pass it on? Were you drugged out of your mind when you put me at risk?"

"I didn't have sex with her, Twyla."

"That's not the impression I got from your story."

"The editor re-wrote that piece without my permission, Twyla. He made up half the stuff because he said my original story was boring. The FBI says there was no semen in Malone's body. You've got to believe me."

"You went to a bar; you sat next to a beautiful woman; and chatted her up. Then, you left with her. Am I right?"

"She chatted me up!"

"You should have ignored her."

"Be reasonable, Twyla."

"You were a married man. You should never have flirted with her. But you flirted and ended up on her 'love trampoline.' She was a damn whore, Martin. You slept with a goddamn whore, and then you came home and you slept with me."

"I still am a married man," Boundary said. "I'm begging my wife for forgiveness. You ought to see the video from her apartment's security camera, Twyla. There's no doubt she drugged me. I hardly could stand up!"

Twyla did not answer.

"Look, I am not diseased; and this wasn't my fault, Twyla. I was sitting on a bar stool minding my business and Malone sat down next to me and talked. Hell, how was I to know she was a predator?"

"I find it hard to believe a supposedly intelligent man let a woman drug him out of his mind, Martin. There had to be a part of you that willingly went along with her."

"What about Bill Cosby?" he said. Cosby was a famous comedian who multiple women claimed had raped them after slipping them a mickey. He had admitted as much in legal depositions, according to the newspapers. Cosby supporters had tried to depict the women as willing partners who just had gotten high. Women's groups were outraged by the charge. Twyla had been too.

"You said those women were innocent victims. Well, I was Cosby-ed by Malone."

Twyla glared at him.

"I did not have sex with that woman," repeated Boundary.

"You sound just like Bill Clinton."

"I was ashamed when I found myself next to her and was afraid of losing you. That's why I said nothing. Listen, what if you got drugged at a party and someone raped you and later claimed you consented? Would you run home and tell me about it? How would you feel if I found out, and I treated you like a leper?"

"You should have told me, Martin. You should have come straight out and told me."

Martin looked down at his feet.

"I should have. I know that now. I made a mistake, Twyla."

"What if I had been pregnant, Martin, and you gave the baby and me a disease just because you were ashamed to confide in your wife? What if you damaged our child?"

"Are you pregnant, Twyla?" His voice cracked. She stared at him. She did not reply.

"Can I come in, Twyla? Can we please sit down and talk this out?"

His eyes looked soulful. Twyla scowled.

"Just leave me alone, Martin. I'm sorry, but I can't stand the sight of you. You're a selfish bastard, you know that? You only of yourself."

Twyla scurried into the townhouse, closed the door and rammed home the deadbolt. Then she ran upstairs to the second floor and threw herself on her bed and wept bitterly.

34

An Old Case

The following morning, Boundary grabbed a red rent-a-bike from a rack in Old Town and pedaled nine miles to Capitol Hill and the Library of Congress to search newspapers over a 20-year period for murders involving golf clubs. He had sold his beloved, rare Captain America motorcycle that morning to his landlord's son for $20,000.

The transaction had made him moody. After losing both his motorcycle and his wife, he wondered if life was worth living. He pedaled the bicycle hard and took crazy chances in heavy traffic, giving the finger to motorists who dared to honk their horns in protest.

The route was long and indirect. He had to take the Mount Vernon Trail north to the Memorial Bridge over the Potomac River to the Thomas Jefferson Memorial; and then he had to turn south and navigate the Capital's congested streets. Motorists detested the city's bicyclists, who thought themselves immune from vehicular traffic laws. Bicyclists deplored the motorists, who seemed to disregard their right to share the road.

Although new to bicycle commuting, Boundary quickly embraced the violent partisanship. He soundly kicked the passenger door of a taxi that wandered into the bike lane, denting it. The enraged cabbie sped up and swerved at him, forcing him onto the sidewalk where he nearly took out an elderly pedestrian. When Boundary recovered and caught up to the cab at the next light, he kicked it again, this time cratering a rear fender. Then he sped through a red light, leaving the cab behind, and detoured up a side street, pumping his fist in the air.

Because of the heat and humidity, Boundary rode shirtless and in flip-flops. He sported knee-length swimming trunks and carried his "office" attire in a bright orange backpack.

When Boundary arrived at the library's Jefferson Building—a 19th-century palace fronted by Italianate fountains—he dried himself with a terry-cloth towel, put on a Hawaiian shirt, pulled a pair of cargo shorts over his swimming trunks, and combed back his sweat-soaked hair.

Inside the library, the air was refreshingly cool. Boundary climbed a white marble staircase to a room filled with the computer terminals. The room was crowded with researchers. He plopped himself in the first open chair he came across and examined the keyboard. The lettering of multiple keys had been worn away. Boundary had no training as a touch typist. Rather, he was a self-taught five-fingered, visually referenced, keyboard pounder. His hands moved across a keyboard with the gracelessness of a crippled crab. For a typist of his level, the terminal was useless. Boundary hadn't a clue whether any blank key was a W or an E.

He searched the crowded room until he located a keyboard whose white lettering was reasonably legible. Small wonder it was empty. A 300-pounder occupied the chair to the right, spilling belly flesh into Boundary's comfort zone; and a man on the left smelled like he hadn't showered in days. Boundary swallowed focused laser-like on his task.

The idea of researching murder by golf club came from a college text on criminal pathologies called "The Mind of a Mass Murderer" that Boundary had found in a used bookstore. According to the chapter on homicide by psychiatrist Morris Brinker, who was world-renowned expert on the criminally insane, serial killings were highly ritualistic. A psychopath selected and killed all of his victims in much the same way, for a myriad of twisted reasons. For some, the repetitiveness made them feel good. A perverse pursuit of perfection drove other demented killers. In their minds, their previous murders had been flawed, and they had a compulsion to repeat their action to get it right.

Boundary's quest was to discover if there had been any unsolved murders similar to Malone's and if Cisco had been in the vicinity when any of the other crimes had occurred. He appreciated that this line of inquiry was a long shot, but he had nothing else to go on. And, well, one never could never foretell the outcome.

Boundary spent two hours searching databases until he finally hit pay dirt. He discovered a 22-year-old series of stories in the Baltimore Sun about the golf-course slaying of a 15-year-old girl named Lucille Shank. The pretty, brown-eyed teenager had been bludgeoned with a putter and buried in a sand trap on a public course a block from her home in an unincorporated Baltimore suburb called Arbutus. Lucille was the only daughter of plumber Robert Shank and his wife Anne. Her parents reported her missing the previous evening after she was late from choir practice. The next day, a golfer named Art Smith drove his ball into the trap and discovered the girl's body. A day after that grisly discovery, Maryland State Police arrested 18-year-old John Surratt, the girl's next-door neighbor. According to the final story in the series, Surrat pleaded insanity, and the judge sentenced him to a psychiatric prison in Cumberland, Maryland, a small, down-on-the-heels city in Maryland's western panhandle.

Surratt had not bound Shank in duct tape. He had bludgeoned her with a golf club after having sex with her on a fairway. Stanley maintained that the sex had been consensual and that he panicked when Lucille accused him of rape. He claimed he swung the club merely to frighten her, inadvertently striking her head. The police said deep scratches on Surratt and flakes of his flesh under the dead girl's nails suggested a violent struggle.

The murder case was controversial because the police and the girl's parents were convinced that Surratt faked mental illness to avoid a death sentence.

The story was intriguing, but there was no Cisco connection. The Senator had been a member of Durham's city council at the time. Still, the case intrigued Boundary, and he had invested a lot of time digging it up. He saw an opportunity to write a crime feature about "another famous golf course murder." Though it was ancient history, the murder had all the elements of "click bait"—it would be a sensational, salacious story that would appeal to the public's baser instincts, driving a high volume of traffic to the publisher's website.

Boundary realized that a great deal of legwork would have to be done before he could pitch the piece to publications like the Daily Beast or the Huffington Post. The standards of journalism required him to discover what had become of Surratt. Was the killer still a patient in the psychiatric hospital or living in some unsuspecting community? Boundary also would have to reach out to Lucille Shank's father and any siblings; the prosecutor; Surratt's defense attorney; and the investigating detectives. He'd also have to peruse the original court record. The to-do list added up to weeks of work.

Boundary downloaded the stories to his laptop. He had to find contact information for the main characters and then hit the phone. For this, he had to work elsewhere. The Library of Congress strictly enforced its code of silence.

Boundary's bike ride across the river to Alexandria was uneventful. He took his time on the Mount Vernon bike trail bike, which paralleled Virginia's Potomac River shoreline, absorbing the beautiful views of the capital's skyline and monuments. When he reached Old Town, he swung by Twyla's place to deposit a love note in her mail slot. Then, he dropped the bike off at the rack where he had picked it up, bought a sandwich wrap at a corner grocery for his dinner, and walked back to his basement apartment where he scarfed down the wrap and then fell asleep a little after 7 p.m. He slept until 5 a.m. the following morning.

Wide awake, he went for a 10-mile run along the Potomac to Roosevelt Island and back, hit the bags at the for an hour at the gym, and then trained some kids from the boxing program. He showered and changed and then knocked on manager Hank Hodges' door.

"Any chance I can use a phone, Hank? My cell is out of juice."

"Sure, there's an empty office down the hall. But if anyone asks, you are conducting boxing club business, understand?"

Boundary nodded and thanked him.

225

The office was small and windowless. Boundary shut the door and sat behind the steel desk which had a heavy black-plastic phone on top. His first call was to the Cumberland, Maryland, psychiatric hospital. No one named Surratt was a patient, he quickly discovered from the operator.

When he pressed the operator for more information, she transferred him to the line of Dr. Hugo Brinker, the facilities director. The avuncular man was oddly happy that Boundary was inquiring about the decades-old case.

"The doctors on our board at the time declared Surratt sane and released him when he turned 21," said Brinker.

"You wouldn't be related to Morris Brinker, would you?" asked Boundary.

"Morrie was my older brother. He passed away last year."

"I'm sorry to hear that," said Boundary. Boundary explained how "The Mind of a Mass Murderer" inspired him to look for killers who used golf clubs as their weapon of choice.

"I'll help you all that I can. Frankly, we could use publicity. The state government has slashed funding and we may be forced to release some of the population prematurely."

He invited Boundary to visit and see for himself how precarious conditions had become for the high-security hospital's 200 patients, and Boundary accepted. A report about the possible release of criminal maniacs would be an easy sell, providing him with some ready cash.

"What we do here is crucial for reclaiming the lives of very sick people, Mr. Boundary," said Brinker. "With the proper medications, we can perform miracles on patients who in the past would have been declared insane and locked away. But our existing drug supplies are running low and we can't afford any of the newer, better medicines."

"I'm very interested in what you have to say about the budget crunch, Dr. Brinker," said Boundary. "I am also interested in the Shank case. I read in an old news clip that Surratt was committed for life," said Boundary. "How could he not be there? How could he only serve three years? This sounds preposterous."

"Stanley Surratt was sent here by reason of insanity, not for his crime. Also, he was a juvenile. A board of psychiatrists released him because they judged they had cured him. We are prohibited by law from imprisoning sane persons. Beyond that, I really have no information I can disclose, Mr. Boundary, due to the state's patient privacy act."

Brinker added, "I hope you understand that mental illness is a disease—a chemical imbalance. The drugs are getting better all the time, and people who would have been locked in padded cells in the past now function normally. Unfortunately, the public thinks like persons from the Dark Ages and many educated folks equate psychiatry with Freud and Jung. Come see the progress we've made for yourself."

"I will. I promise, Doctor."

Boundary scheduled a visit for two days later. He had no idea how he'd get there.

The drive to Cumberland was a good three hours on a superhighway that cut through the beautiful, green mountains of the Western Maryland. Boundary was behind the wheel of Hank Hodges' 45-horsepower Volkswagen "Thing," which crawled up the steep hills like a golf cart and was knocked sideways bypassing trucks, so the journey took him an extra hour and a half. Top speed on the flats was 65 mph, and on the inclines, he had to keep the car floored in third gear to maintain 40 mph.

The price was right. Boundary only had to spring for gas, plus the cost of any breakdowns. Hodges kept the car in showroom condition. The fact he loaned it to Boundary was a testament to his deep respect for the former boxing legend.

Cumberland in Colonial days had been a major gateway to the West. George Washington had linked up here with the ill-fated British General William Braddock during the French and Indian War. Now the city had a doughty, run-down look. No new homes appeared to have been built there since the early 1900s. The city's major industry these days was serving as was a highway rest-stop for Washington metro area motorists headed to Deep Creek Lake, a resort an hour further on. Every major restaurant chain had a franchise just off the city's interstate exits.

The air in Cumberland was 10 degrees cooler than in D.C. The leaves on the surrounding mountains already were turning bright yellow and deep red. In another two months, skiers would pass through Cumberland on their way to Wisp, the Deep Creek area's ski resort, which received 100 inches of snow every winter. Boundary drove with The Thing's convertible top down so he could luxuriate in the mountain air. By the time he arrived, he was nearly deaf from the roar of the wind and the angry traffic that had swarmed past him at 70 miles per hour.

The psychiatric hospital looked like something Andrew Carnegie might have designed—a brick castle, complete with ornamental battlements and observation towers. Its 19th Century builders had perched it on a rocky outcrop high above the town where it afforded its patients a sweeping vista of the city and the Potomac River. The lofty location made any contemplated escape less likely.

228

From hospital's small parking lot, Boundary saw a flotilla of kayaks wending its way downstream towards the Nation's Capital, 184 river-miles to the east. A coal-fired, 19th Century train engine blew its shrill whistle as it hauled three open cars full of tourists to Frostburg, a college town about 15 miles away.

An unarmed guard in a navy-blue uniform escorted Boundary from the hospital's reception area to Dr. Brinker's oak-paneled waiting room. Boundary sat down on a green-leather, claw-foot sofa. He examined the only painting on the wall—an ancient-looking portrait of a Canada Goose grazing in a pasture filled with cows.

After just a few minutes, Dr. Brinker burst happily into the room. He eagerly had been awaiting Boundary's arrival. He ushered Boundary through double doors to his palatial office where he had a pitcher of iced tea and scones set out on a coffee table. One side of the office had two eight-foot-high windows looking out over the river. The wall opposite it had a floor-to-ceiling bookcase. The wall behind Brinker's desk was dark oak and had a six-foot fireplace. A portrait of a youthful George Washington shaking hands with British General Braddock hung over the mantle.

Boundary was famished and, when Brinker invited him to help himself to the repast, he quickly dug in.

"Yes, yes. Eat up. No doubt, you're starved," said Brinker, who watched Boundary with amusement. "The endless truck traffic makes the ride in from Washington exhausting."

The doctor wore a light blue suit and a yellow silk tie speckled with tiny violet polka dots. Boundary guessed that Brinker was about 60 years old, but he actually was 10 years older. He had a head of thick salt and pepper hair and a matching mustache and goatee. He wore black-rimmed glasses with thick lenses. He could have been a Viennese colleague of Sigmund Freud, thought Boundary; either that or a 19th Century band master.

Boundary washed his first scone down with a healthy gulp of the iced tea. He bit into a second. When he had cleared his mouth, he asked, "Where did Surratt go, Doctor Brinker? What's he doing now?" Boundary took a notebook from the inside his linen jacket.

"I have no idea. John's been gone for decades. In any event, I would not be permitted to disclose his current whereabouts, even if I knew where that was. His release occurred long before my time here. Dr. Jake Tepper, my predecessor, handled the case, and he passed away five years ago."

Boundary looked glum. He felt the story slipping away. Brinker saw his disappointment and tried to be helpful.

"Off the top of my head, I can recall some names of the psychiatrists who evaluated John, if that helps. I have no idea where any of them are, however."

"Any lead, no matter how minor, would be a great help," said Boundary. He pulled out a pen and a notebook.

Brinker gave him four names. They jointly had written an article about this case for a psychiatric review that no longer existed. Brinker had no copy of the society's archives. "Usually, the papers end up on a back shelf of a university library. Three were professors. I'd try Yale or Penn or Pitt."

Boundary scribbled the names in a notebook and thanked the administrator. Then Brinker gave him a tour of the facility, which reeked of antiseptic.

"We have to guard against bacterial infections, the scourge of hospitals everywhere," explained Brinker.

Boundary interviewed nurses and physicians about the

hospital's inadequate budget. He could interview none of the patients, most of whom were sunning in the castle's expansive courtyard. Some sat on benches and chatted or read. Four of younger men played basketball. One middle-aged patient was either talking to himself or using a blue-tooth device for a cell phone call. Boundary couldn't tell.

When the tour ended, Brinker handed Boundary some anonymous case histories for his story on the hospital's budget cuts. In each case, a patient who had been improving because of a cocktail of pharmaceuticals regressed when some of the drugs had to be discontinued.

"Many of our patients are professionals. There's a lawyer here, and an engineer. They could contribute to society and pay taxes. The state legislature's budget math is nonsensical. The way to reduce costs is to cure the patients and send them back into the world where they will work and pay taxes—not deny them crucial medications."

Boundary he taped a brief interview with Brinker outside of the front door. The visit had lasted two hours. Brinker easily could have given him most of the information over the phone. On the plus side, Boundary, made a new friend, an expert who might prove valuable. He had gotten leads to pursue regarding on Surratt; and the budget cut story would be red meat for liberal-leaning news organizations and bring him some quick cash. So, he was philosophical when he squeezed his six-foot-five frame into the uncomfortably small car. He turned the key and the only sound was a loud buzz.

Boundary found a mechanic in Cumberland who was old enough to remember how to rebuild a starter. Boundary arrived home well after midnight. He went straight to bed. Mrs. Quander woke him the next morning with a loud knock on the cellar door. She demanded his $500 rent, due the previous day. Boundary had $250 in his wallet. The mechanic in Cumberland had gotten the other $250. He handed all of his cash to Mrs. Quander and promised to pay her the balance after he visited an ATM.

"I don't like installments," she said. "I have overhead."

Boundary spent the morning on a new laptop he had purchased with some of his motorcycle proceeds, pounding out the Brinker interview. He fleshed out the story with quotes from a Maryland senator who had voted reluctantly for the cuts.

"We can't raise taxes any higher. The citizens are screaming, and businesses say they'll transplant to Virginia, if we do raise them. We can't cut education, because the teachers' unions are too powerful. And the law prohibits us from running a budget deficit. This hits those persons without voices, groups like the mentally ill and people on welfare. If the public demands we restore the services, then maybe next year, we can work something out," the lawmaker said.

"What if the cuts force Dr. Brinker to release mentally ill patients into the general population," asked Boundary.

"He'd better not," said the lawmaker.

Boundary sold the story to the "Donkey Post," a Democratic news organization. The editor paid him $600, which was about $200 more than he had expected. He fist-pumped the air. This was his first payday in weeks.

That afternoon, Boundary bicycled back over to the Library of Congress. Traffic was light and there was no sign of the cabbie who had run him off the road two days earlier.

Boundary went to the library's microfiche department. Not all of the Baltimore area newspapers were digitized.

Trolling for stories on microfiche was grunt work. Microfiche is an analog technology, with no search function. One's eyeballs do the scanning. Boundary had to scour almost every page of three different newspapers—a daily and two weeklies—to make certain he did not miss any information. The Baltimore Sun's archives were digitized, and he had recovered half a dozen stories about the case from that paper alone.

The Surratt case had gotten lots of play because the golf course where Shank died was a popular destination for local duffers. The News-American, which no longer existed, was particularly aggressive in its coverage. A reporter named Vince Keller had been dogged in his coverage of the case, blowing rings around the Sun.

Keller had written a detailed story about the victim's parents—Robert and Anne Shank. According to the piece, Surratt was arrested by Maryland State Police Detective Sergeant Rick Joyce and confessed to killing Shank. Another Keller story was about Surratt's controversial commitment to the mental institution by Circuit Court Judge Clarence Murphy. Joyce had testified that Surratt was rational and should face life in prison.

"He's faking mental illness," the detective asserted.

Boundary spent hours going through the microfiche. When his eyes began to burn, he took a lunch break in the library canteen. Between bites of a tuna salad sandwich, he struck up a conversation with a good-looking long-legged brunette that had been sitting at the bistro table next to his. She was scribbling in a reporter's notebook.

"Who do you report for?" he asked. "I rarely see a fellow journalist in the Library of Congress."

She smiled and extended her hand.

233

"I'm Carmen Klouse. I work for the Observer."

"I'm Martin Boundary."

"I know who you are," she said.

Boundary looked at her quizzically. She told him she was Rooster Redburn's newest hire.

"Have we ever met?"

"No."

"Then how did you know me."

"It's just that you're kind of famous."

"You mean infamous."

"We looked up your profile on the net, because of what happened. The newsroom still talks about you. We saw the story in the Donkey. It was good."

"Thanks."

Klouse looked uncomfortable. She re-crossed her chorus-girl legs, which were sheathed in tight-fitting, stretch blue jeans. Boundary had trouble keeping his eyes off of them.

"Rooster describes you as being 'ethically challenged'."

"Because I didn't admit to a murder I didn't commit?"

"Come on, you know it's more complex than that. I agree with Rooster. You should have told him up front about your conflict of interest. The cover-up can be worse than the crime."

"So, Rooster is still talking about me?"

"He gives an ethics spiel to all the new hires. You are the centerpiece of the program."

"I will find the killer," said Boundary.

"Is that what you're doing here?"

Boundary shrugged. "How about you, Carmen? What are you doing here?"

She frowned. "Tax reform. It's a total snooze. I have

to compare Reagan's 1986 deal with the administration's proposal. I wasn't even born in 1986."

"When were you born?" She looked like a grown woman to Boundary. She was thick and thin in all the right places. She had big blue eyes, high, apple-shaped cheekbones, and pillowed lips. Boundary imagined she would devastate in a bikini. He wondered why she was wasting her time in print. One of the cable channels would add her to their babe line-up in half-a-second.

"Twenty-five years ago."

"You look younger."

"Are you flirting with me?"

He was lonely, forlorn. He was also hornier than the brass section of the National Symphony Orchestra.

"I'm married," he said.

"I know. I read the story in the Bugler. You were, like, drugged?"

"Someone drugged me—but the Bugler story was a load of crap. I didn't write it. The editor did."

"There's news," she said.

"This isn't an interview."

"Well, murder suspects are public figures," she said, curling some of her long, amber-shaded hair around an index finger. Her long nails were red.

"I'm no longer a suspect," he said curtly. "The FBI plans to issue a press release. In fact, it was due out yesterday. I'll have to call over there and see what the holdup is."

"I look forward to seeing it," Carmen said.

"Maybe Rooster will run the announcement in the paper," he said sarcastically.

"Maybe."

235

Boundary wished Carmen well on her tax story and headed back up to the computer stations to hunt down contact information for his list of persons connected to the Shank case, including the three psychiatrists that Brinker had mentioned. Carmen was pleasant enough, but dangerous. She struck him as ruthlessly ambitious, and he was afraid that if he lingered any longer, she'd try to twist something he said into a sensational story.

Boundary began his search by trolling online telephone directories and social media sites for mentions of the names. He started with the sentencing judge, Clarence Murphy, and immediately found the man's obituary in the Baltimore Sun. The jurist had died one month earlier in a car crash. In an ironic twist, a drunken driver he had sentenced to house arrest was behind the wheel of the other vehicle—and the drunk survived the crash with minor injuries.

The News-American reporter, Keller, was dead too, at age 50 from pancreatic cancer. When he passed, he had no wife, no kids, and no living parents or siblings. All that remained of him was on the microfiche.

Boundary had better luck with Detective Joyce, who had retired 10 years earlier to run a fishing camp in Maine, according to an archived State Police newsletter. A short search yielded a link to the camp's website and reservation line. Boundary went outside, sat on a bench, and dialed the 800-number. The former cop picked up the phone on the ninth ring. He was cross when Boundary identified himself as a reporter and said he wanted to ask some questions about Stanley Surratt. Joyce groused that he didn't have time to talk because he was paddling a 15-foot canoe in the middle of a lake with two customers who had hired him to take them to smallmouth

236

bass hot spots.

"I'll call you back later," he said.

Boundary returned to the workstation to discover the where-abouts of Mr. and Mrs. Shank. He wondered how they react when he told them about Surratt's release. He would have to handle the elderly couple gingerly. The interview would be central to his story.

He knew from old news clips that the Shanks had owned a brick cape cod house on Maple Avenue, which ran perpen-dicular their town's quaint shopping district. The current occupant of the house, according to a reverse directory, was Paolo Suarez, a master electrician.

Boundary accessed a street view of the home using Google Maps. The houses, all wooden structures, dated to the 1940s. They appeared roomy, solid, and remained attractive over 75 years later.

Mrs. Suarez answered the telephone. When Boundary inquired about the Shanks, she told him she and her husband purchased the house from them "a very long time ago," but never met the couple. A lawyer had handled the closing, she said. Mrs. Suarez could not recall the lawyer's name. Boundary fretted might have to visit the Baltimore courthouse to unearth the transaction's records, which would take the better part of a day.

With data from an online street directory, Boundary phoned everyone on the block, hoping that one of them had remained in touch with the couple over the years. He reached five residents, all of whom purchased their homes long after the Shanks had left. None of them knew of any old-timers still living in the area.

Investigations can be pure drudgery. Boundary made a list

of Baltimore-area residents of the same last name, hoping for a relative. There were 300 Shanks. He picked 25 of them at random, reached 11 of them, and came up empty. There had to be an easier way.

They had buried Lucille Shank from St. Katherine Tekakwitha Church, the local Roman Catholic Parish. Boundary reached out to the pastor. The priest never had heard the murder story. The pastor in place at the time of the funeral had been dead for over a decade, he said.

"Are there any old timers left from that era—maybe a member of the Knights of Columbus," asked Boundary.

"They've mostly all moved on to lower-tax jurisdictions with warmer weather," said the priest. "When people retire, they cash out of their houses and move somewhere else. Can't say I blame them. We're a little island bounded by major superhighways like Route 95, Route 395, and US 1. You get claustrophobic here."

Boundary ruefully wondered if he should consult a Ouija board to find the Shanks. He was growing frustrated. He had not expected the story to be a slam dunk. But without the victim's parents, his story was looking less and less certain. He felt like he was spinning his wheels. Deep doubts about the story's worth nagged at him. Would a 40-year-old murder really interest anyone? He considered dropping it and moving on to some other story; and yet his gut would not allow him to let go of the story. He swore at himself for being impractical and then kept on digging.

Boundary took a break about 3 p.m. and stretched his legs by walking around the library. Former detective Joyce phoned Boundary as he was about to re-enter the building.

"How was the fishing?" Boundary asked.

"We got 15. Not a great day, but not a bad one, either. Now why are you digging into Surratt? That was a very long time ago. Did he escape and commit another murder? If he did, then it wouldn't surprise me."

Boundary told him about Malone and about Surratt's release.

"You're kidding me? They let that psycho go? God help us all!"

Boundary described Malone's murder.

"That sounds like a psychopath. Surratt killed Shank because she would not submit to him. He's likely to have grown into a wife and child beater."

"The doctors at the hospital said they cured him."

"That's a laugh, because Surratt never was insane," said Joyce. "He was pure evil—a ruthless, conniving bastard who took a sadistic pleasure in hurting women. He never fooled me. We had three unsolved rapes of young women within a 10-mile radius of his home. That's within bicycle range. Every one of those rape victims had been hit on the noggin and knocked unconscious. Did you know that?"

Boundary said he had no idea.

"Stanley hit one with a rock and the other two with a baseball bat. All three survived, but two suffered severe head traumas that left them mentally disabled. He approached all three from behind, so none of them got a look at him. And there were no prints or fibers."

"Didn't you have his semen?" asked Boundary.

"Back then, we didn't have the DNA know-how to link those three cases to Surratt. There were no more knock-on-the-head rapes after we locked him up, though. So, it didn't take Albert Einstein to put two and two together."

"But you never prosecuted him for those three rapes?"

"We tried. I went at him for hours in the interrogation room. So did my partner. We roughed him up good. You could get away with that back in the day. He was a hard nut. We couldn't break him. And he was cunning. He immediately admitted to killing Shank, because he knew we had him cold. We found the murder weapon in a pond and his fingerprints were all over the shaft. Then, he pulled that insanity bullshit and the goddamn judge fell for it."

"Psychiatrists testified he was insane," said Boundary.

"Those doctors were a bunch of quacks. Surratt was a first-rate actor, and he knew how to play to that audience. He talked of nightmares and alien abduction, his remorse, and his desire to make amends to mankind. They swallowed his malarkey hook, line, and sinker."

"I will find him," said Boundary.

"Good luck with that. He's a crafty son of a bitch. He must be in his early 50s now. I expect that he's still raping and killing. Deviants never change, Boundary, unless you cut off their balls."

"Have you ever performed the operation?"

"I would have loved to have had the opportunity."

Boundary was glad that Joyce was no longer a cop.

"Could Surratt have been telling the truth about the other women? There are lots of evil people in the world. You know this better than I do."

"Like I said, Boundary, the rapes stopped after we locked him up. Could it have been sheer coincidence? Sure. But I don't think so."

"Are his parents still around?"

"Surratt's dad had a massive heart attack and died a week after his son's arrest. His mother, as far as I know, is still around."

"What happened to the Shanks?"

"They moved. California, I think. They had at least one other kid—a son. I think his name was Paul. But I'm not sure."

"Where in California?"

"I couldn't tell you. Sorry. I know it's a big place."

35

Leg Work

The FBI's press release absolving Boundary came out later that day. The text stated that Boundary no longer was a person of interest owing to new evidence in the murder investigation. The FBI noted that it had been the lack of DNA evidence and the security tapes of Ferguson entering and exiting Malone's building that led to the FBI's decision. Boundary would have granted an interview to any journalist who called him. But no one did. They had treated his arrest as the front-page news. They buried his exoneration in the briefs column.

Boundary sent copies of the press release to all of his professional contacts, including Rooster. He received no replies. He was certain it was because the Bugler.com story had made him out to be a loathsome narcissist. He was, in the patois of the capital, "highly radioactive." Boundary mulled getting a lawyer to sue Dwiggens. The probable expense gave him pause—as did the realization that Dwiggens could counter-sue him for assault. He tried to focus on his pursuit of Surratt.

Boundary got a significant break in the Surratt story several days later while he was performing online searches at a Starbucks on a used laptop. He found a reference to a Dr. Rudolph Kensington, one name he had gotten from Brinker. It was in a three-year-old news item in an online copy of Midwest College's alumni newsletter—about a reunion for its graduates over 80. There were three. The story mentioned that Kensington, now of Ormond Beach, Florida, at age 95 was the oldest member of the group. Boundary laughed ruefully. He imagined the good doctor was dead by now. How many persons lived to age 98? He dialed a number he had discovered in an online phone directory.

Kensington picked up the receiver on the second ring. He was pleasant and cooperative and sounded spry and alert for someone approaching the century mark. He struck Boundary right off as a lonely codger with a sharp mind who welcomed conversation.

"John was 100 percent cured and I'm the one who cured him," he boasted. "He wasn't a mad killer, just an angry kid with a massive inferiority complex and a twisted libido, which I untwisted with therapy and drugs. He swung that club at the girl in a blind rage. It was dark. He did not know where she was standing. He didn't care. He swung the club without weighing the consequences. You know how dumb kids are. We all know, because we all were young and stupid once. I put him on one of the latest wonder drugs available, and he became gentle as a lamb—and remorseful too. He probably is protective of women now. It would not surprise me if he were an active feminist."

"What about the other victims?" asked Boundary.

"There were no other victims," said the doctor. "The police tried to manufacture some, dragging in every woman with

100 miles who had been hit on the head. John didn't have a driver's license. He had a bicycle. Unless he knew how to fly, there was no way he could have attacked those other women."

"Do you think Surratt might have gone on to college?" asked Boundary.

"I assume so although I don't know. He was bright enough. But he lacked funds. I don't know how he fared. He never contacted me once he'd left the hospital."

"Did that surprise you?"

"It happens a lot in psychiatry. I was part of a past he wanted to forget."

"Do you know if he lives in California?"

"No, I don't. I imagine that wherever he is, he's leading a very productive life. He very well might have a wife and children and be a highly respected member of some upper-middle class community. You really ought to have the human decency to leave him alone."

Boundary told Kensington about Bernadette's murder, his hunch that it was a serial killer, and the computer search that had led him to John.

The psychiatrist said, "That's original, using the world's most expensive golf club to kill someone; but the killer is not John. John did not premeditate his crime. He has no sick imagination like the killer you describe. His parents were strict and beat him constantly. They conditioned him to lash out physically. As I explained, his temper subsided when I placed him on medication and gave him counselling. A practiced killer who is cool, cruel, and methodical committed the murder you describe. He's also a publicity hound."

Boundary mentioned the Shank girl's parents.

"Those wacko people should have been locked up and

treated too. They sold their home when they learned of John's release and moved to California to find him. The father was intent on killing him for revenge and nearly succeeded once. John told me this! I remember now. He wrote me once because he needed me to share prescription information with psychiatrists out there. That was the only time I heard from him."

"Maybe the Shanks killed him?"

"No, I doubt it. They kept sending me threatening letters for years. Their rage persisted."

"Do you know where the Shanks live now?"

"I doubt the parents are alive. Few geezers make it as far as I have."

"Where was John when he wrote that final letter, Doctor Kensington? It had to have a return address"

"I supposed it won't hurt to tell you—Benicia, a bay side town about 20 miles outside of San Francisco. I remember because I had a sister living there . She's passed away. Cancer."

"I'm sorry," said Boundary.

The old man rattled on for 30 more minutes about his sister and her treatments.

Finally, Boundary thanked him, hung up, and immediately and logged onto the Internet to search the listings in Benicia and its surroundings for anyone named Shank. He had a gut feeling he would strike pay dirt.

36

Spy vs Spy

T wyla positioned her new pen-sized DVD camera in the green-leather cylindrical holder she kept at eye level on a bookshelf standing against the wall in front of her desk. From that vantage, the wide-eye lens of the spy pen captured images of her entire office. Although the pen was sleek and inconspicuous, it housed a powerful memory chip capable of 60 hours of continuous recording. She had returned Martin's recording pen to the pen holder by her desk phone, allowing it to record her day's conversations.

Twyla had been busy reviewing legislation. Big Barney was on a tear. A dozen of his bills had flown through various committees. Barney's 40 special House members—the ones he described as being "up to snuff"—moved the legislation with Prussian efficiency. Twyla wondered what secret incentive Barney had up his sleeve. Lock-step loyalty in the House of Representatives was highly unusual. An editorial writer for Barron's magazine had once described the House as "a collection of 435 mayors trying to advance narrow, local interests." Cooperation usually had a shelf life because a Speaker had a limited number of favors to trade. Twyla wondered if everything Big Barney was doing was on the up and up. For her, the thought of being even innocently associated with a political scandal was frightening. She had a good reputation, and she wanted to protect it.

Twyla left work early—and made a point of letting everyone know it, in case the infiltrator was a colleague. She was impatient to discover who was spying on her.

Twyla drove her mustard-colored Jeep from her designated parking space in a House parking lot towards Annapolis to spend the night with her parents in their cozy water-front cottage. She had called ahead without hinting at her big news. She was bursting to tell them about her baby.

Twyla blurted out the news as soon as she was inside her parents' door, delighting both of them.

"I'm going to be a grandfather—at last," said Captain Ned. "I was counting on you! I don't think your brother will ever settle down."

"Dave's only 30, Dad," laughed Twyla.

Her mother gave her a tearful bear hug.

"I have to knit booties," she said.

"Is it a boy or a girl?" asked. "I want to make sure your mother buys the right color yarn. No grandson of mine will be wearing pink booties!"

"I honestly don't know. I told the doctor I wanted to be surprised."

"Well, Captain, I'll knit a pair of each. Twyla will have more children, won't you darling?"

"I met with a lawyer about a divorce," said Twyla.

"Oh no," said Agnes. She cried.

"I know your husband is a bum, but aren't you rushing things?" asked Captain Ned.

Old-fashioned Catholics, Twyla's parents felt that whatever God had joined together should remain as one. Captain Ned, who retired from the Navy, and his handsome wife Agnes, herself once a redhead, had many bitter clashes over the years; but they not once entertained a divorce.

Both parents strongly urged Twyla to consider a reconciliation, which nearly caused her to storm out of the cottage and return to Alexandria, 50 miles away.

"Please, don't be angry with us," said the Captain. "Over the years, we've seen friends devastated by divorces. And a child needs a father and a mother."

"My child doesn't need a father like him," said Twyla. "He's a rover boy."

"Martin might be telling the truth. I heard on the news that the Bernadette woman had date-rape drugs," said Agnes.

"Please, let's not talk about this! If you don't drop the subject, then I'm leaving. I can't take it! I came here to share my good news, not for a lecture."

"We're sorry, dear," said Agnes. "Aren't we, Captain?"

"I've said my piece," said the 60-year-old, square-faced sailor.

Dinner conversation was restrained. Her father asked Twyla about her job, yet another sore topic. She said, "Everything is going great." Then she looked out the dining room's sliding glass doors, commenting on the lovely view of Back Creek.

Agnes asked about the burglary investigation.

"No arrests. Have any burglars struck your neighborhood , Mom?"

Things lightened up after dessert, with a game of Scrabble before bedtime. Twyla was victorious, but wondered if her parents, both expert players, had let her win.

Afterward while lying in bed, Twyla felt guilty for being so terse with her folks. They were trying to protect her. They were so irritatingly old fashioned, but could not help being from a different era.

The next morning at breakfast, she engaged in some fence-mending, inviting them to stay with her in Old Town close to her due date, so they could conduct her safely to the hospital.

"We'll be there. I'll chart the shortest course from your place to the front door of admissions," said Captain Ned.

"Be sure to remind us, Twyla," said Agnes.

Twyla left the cottage at 6:30 a.m. Even at that hour, traffic along Route 50 into Washington was bumper-to-bumper. Her speedometer read 25 mph. At least she had an audio book to listen to as she endured her interminable stop-and-go journey. Captain Ned had recommended it: "The Cruel Sea", a taut, dramatic telling of the lives of the crew of the "Compass Rose," a British Corvette assigned during World War II to protect convoys in the North Atlantic from prowling German submarines.

Twyla reached the office at 8 a.m. She greeted her colleagues, made routine phone calls, and, when she was certain of no interruptions, removed her spy pen from the bookcase and attached it by cable to one of her computer's USB port. This was a moment of high suspense: Had the pen's video captured anything?

For an agonizing minute, the replay showed nothing but a gray blur, causing her to wonder if she had set it up properly. Then, suddenly, the picture became crisp and clear. Her desk appeared in full color. She typed a fast-forward command into her computer and watched as the minutes sped by. When the video feed showed 10 p.m., it showed someone suddenly

249

walking into her office and standing by her desk. Twyla reversed the video and played it back in real time.

The intruder was a woman dressed like a member of the cleaning crew, in a gray smock. She was dragging an upright vacuum cleaner. She plugged the vacuum into the wall and switched it on. Then she sat down behind Twyla's desk and removed Martin's pen from the pen holder. She clicked it to "play" and held it to her ear. Twyla used a computer function to zoom in on the woman's face.

"Oh my God!" she said. "I don't believe this! Oh my God!"

37

Chairman of the Board

Big Barney convened the emergency meeting of the leadership of the Cocaine Caucus in a portable office beside Jimmy's refrigerated warehouse in Lanham, Maryland, 10 interstate-highway miles from the Capitol. His face was fevered. His heart was pounding against his rib cage like a jackhammer. Events were spinning out of control, and Barney was a control freak. Too many bodies were dropping, inviting a larger police response. Big Barney's chest tightened. This was a crisis. He felt as if he were inside one of those old Sergio Leone "spaghetti" westerns, with a killing about every three minutes. Malone's former veterinarian was dead, and it was clear to Big Barney from the news reports who the killer was. According to the Washington Observer, when officials on Cape Verde Island took John Adams University Police Chief Ray Cordovan to visit Dr. Boyd at his condominium, they found the veterinarian trussed with duct tape. The killer had bludgeoned him with a golf club found at the scene of the crime.

Barney yanked at his hair. Jimmy Johnson had a private jet, Air Pork One. Jimmy Johnson was impulsive. Jimmy Johnson was violent. Jimmy Johnson was not circumspect.

Jimmy Johnson liked to bludgeon his enemies with golf clubs. Eventually, some Sherlock at the FBI would put two and two together and link Johnson to the crimes—and then the jig would be up for all of them. The Capitol Hill cops on Big Barney's generous pad were getting nervous, extremely so; as were some of his cocaine congressmen. Several of the lawmakers told Barney that if push came to shove, then they would do the shoving. They'd turn on their Leader to save their own skins. There was talk among the more crooked of Barney's cops of putting Jimmy in the ground. That might have been a problem solver. However, Barney's greatest weakness as the CEO of a criminal enterprise was an aversion to pulling the trigger on anyone. If he could reach accommodations in Congress with those despicable Republicans then, he could iron out problems with anyone without resorting to a "final solution." Barney had all kinds of muck on his hands, but he was determined never to have blood on his hands. Scandal was a pervasive feature of Congress. Assassination was not. Barney was a respecter of Congress's hallowed traditions.

"Jimmy, Jimmy, Jimmy, your hubris outweighs your brains," mumbled Barney. The last thing he needed was a task force assigned to the Malone case. The FBI already added additional manpower after the Ferguson's disappearance—so many, in fact, that they were tripping over one another. Three different agents interviewed Big Barney about Malone and he gathered by their questions they were not coordinating their efforts. He had given them all same, bland answer:

"She was the dearest, sweetest kid in the world. Those reports about blackmail and drugs shocked me. Frankly, I find them difficult to believe. One never would have guessed Bernadette was capable of such skullduggery—not in a million years."

Not everyone in his gang was sufficiently disciplined to stick to a perfectly scripted, innocuous answer in the face of repeated interrogations. If the FBI increased its pressure, then the chances were that someone would get cold feet and crack. The jig would be up for all of them.

Jimmy's sloppy housekeeping had created another grave dilemma for Big Barney: The network has shuttered Ferguson's green room, and he desperately needed a new venue for the weekly distribution of cocaine to the members. Disaster would ensue if the drug-addled congressmen missed their fixes, even for a day.

Every Sunday for many years, Lola had passed out baggies of cocaine in the Green Room of Ferguson's television studio, three blocks from the U.S. Capitol Building. Congressmen filing into a green room raise no suspicion. In the cable news era, the need for an endless supply of political show horses and talking heads was a fact of life. But now that Jimmy had erased Ferguson from the face of the earth, there was no easy way to distribute the drugs to so many users. Finding a Ferguson replacement would be risky and time-consuming. Barney needed a quick fix.

Jimmy had screwed things up royally. If Barney had been like Jimmy, then he would have clobbered Jimmy with a golf club. However, Big Barney was not a violent man. In all of his 66 years, Big Barney never once had raised a hand in anger. Physical violence made him queasy. He would call on Karumba Corporation's board of directors for an elegant solution.

The board's membership was small: Big Barney, chairman; Lola Gutierrez, treasurer; Jimmy Johnson, an inside director; and Capt. Bryce St. John of the Capitol Police Force, an outside director. The agenda always was in Barney's head. When he sat at the head of the cheap, folding conference table, he cited the two items for discussion: the distribution problem and the publicity problem. Jimmy had guffawed on hearing item two. Lola raised her hand.

"I have a solution to the distribution dilemma, but it will cost us $2.2 million up front."

"That's some solution," said Jimmy, caustically. "What is it, a yacht?" Jimmy was obsessive about minimizing expenses to maximize profits. He ran his pork empire in the same crusty tight-fisted manner. He paid his factory workers the minimum wage. He ran off union organizers. He limited his employees to two, three-minute bathroom breaks every eight-hour shift and 20 minutes for lunch.

"Are you a religious man, Jimmy?" asked Lola.

"I worship the almighty dollar," he said.

"I will turn you into a church-every-Sunday man," she said. He laughed.

"Me? Never happen."

He looked her up and down. Dark, curvy, full-lipped Lola was more beautiful than any woman he had ever seen on a Spanish-language Telenovela, and those women were dyna-mite.

Lola turned toward Big Barney.

"There's an abandoned church for sale on H Street, in northeast D.C."

"Carver-Langston?" asked Capt. Smart. His voice dripped with skepticism. Carver-Langston was the city's most violent section, a place where someone was more likely to be pricked by a bullet than by a mosquito.

"The Mount Calvary Temple of Salvation is on the market.

254

It's a red-brick building with a small bell tower and 10 rows of pews that can accommodate 100 persons."

"Off-street parking, I hope," said Chief Smart. "Those people strip anything that isn't moving, so if your car ever breaks down on the street there then get out and run."

Jimmy roared with laughter. "That's one of your better lines, Smart!"

The chief smiled. Lola stamped her foot and said, "Pay attention. This is important. There's a 30-car lot surrounded by a seven-foot-high, barbed-wire-topped chain-link fence. Besides the fence, there are iron burglar bars on all the church's windows, including the stained-glass."

"So, Lola, are you proposing that we buy this church and start a new religion?" asked Jimmy. He had a smart-ass grin on his face, seemingly dismissing the idea out of hand. Lola was nonplussed. She was accustomed to dealing assholes who dismissed her ideas solely because she was a woman. There were nearly 100 of them in the Senate.

Lola looked Jimmy in the eye and said, "We will set up a dummy corporation to buy the church property: Gospel Prosper LLC. I've drawn up the papers. Our rep is in Las Vegas. We are untraceable and non-taxable. I also have a pastor lined up, a former inmate with a clean record since his last release four years ago. He's an assistant pastor at a church in Temple Hills that runs a $1 million-per-year bingo operation. He has a team of ex-inmates who can serve as security, janitors, parishioners, whatever we need. My idea is that our congressmen claim to be members of a ministry serving the poor and that they visit once a week."

"Brilliant! I like it," said Capt. Smart. "The local cops won't pay attention to a church."

255

"How do you know this ex-con minister is dependable?" asked Barney.

"My cousins know him. They say he's OK."

"Why pay so much for a building in the middle of a slum that no person in his right mind would buy?" asked Jimmy. "Are you taking a finder's fee, Lola?"

"There are multiple bidders. A local funeral director who specializes in send offs for shooting victims wants the place. Some billionaire from mainland China is interested too."

"The advertised price is $1.2 million. The other buyers are trying to knock it down. I've offered the full price in cash to the owner. I need another $500,000 essential improvements, like a video surveillance system on the bell tower to cover the church grounds and the adjoining streets; and for shoring up an old, Prohibition-era tunnel that leads from the church basement to the basement of a residence a block away."

"The church was a speakeasy?" asked Jimmy.

"No, the house was the speakeasy. Whenever the cops raided it, everyone grabbed the booze bottles sneaked over to the church," said Lola.

Jimmy wrinkled his brow and drummed his fingers on the table.

"Smart. Sounds like you've thought this through, Lola. I move we adopt the motion to purchase the properties."

"I second the motion," said Capt. Smart.

"OK, it passes," said Barney. He slapped the table with the palm of his right hand.

"I'll set up a bank account in the name of the new corporation and hire a local lawyer to consummate the deal," said Lola. "We should be up and running within 30 days. In the meantime, I will take care of business with the caucus one-

CHAIRMAN OF THE BOARD

on-one, at their homes, at restaurants, in their cars. This is risky, but can't be avoided."

Barney pointed at Jimmy and grumbled, "This complication is your goddamn fault. Where do you get off killing people without the board's sanction? Can't you see the predicament you've gotten us into? The FBI has the equivalent of a task force looking at Malone and Ferguson, and now this veterinarian. You've endangered everything with your Charlie Bronson antics."

"Ah, come on, Barney. Malone was a loose cannon who had to go. You know it. I know it. When she took that reporter Boundary home it was way beyond the pale. And then there was that letter that Ferguson found. She was a little traitor and putting her down was the right thing to do. A debate would have delayed the inevitable."

"Why did the murder have to be so melodramatic, Jimmy? Why the hell did you leave her in the goddamn sand trap, wrapped up like an Egyptian mummy? You could have made her disappear, couldn't you, like Hastings?"

"My back was acting up, Barney. I couldn't carry her body out of there. Gosh, she was a big-boned girl."

"Why bring her to the golf club in the first place?" said Barney, whipping himself into a storm. "Of all the crackpot ideas that..."

Johnson's eyes narrowed. A dark cloud of contempt passed over his face, transforming it into a stark portrait of malevolence that cowed Big Barney into a fearful silence.

"I did it for the sake of convenience. Bernadette was in the trunk of my car, making a racket. I was feeling high after our stop at the clubhouse and was afraid of getting stopped for drunk driving on my way back home. So, I took care of her.

257

End of story."

They were opposite one another. Johnson leaned his elbows on the long, rectangular table and stared into Big Barney's milky brown eyes.

"Do you think you would have had the guts to kill her, Barney? Do you think you could have made a clean getaway like me? Let's hear it from the expert."

"You said you would make her appreciate that silence was golden, Jimmy."

"Well, Barney, I couldn't reason with the woman. So, what was I to do? Anyway, you have no cause to niggle and nag like an old lady. I didn't leave a single shred of personal evidence at the golf course. The Feds are stymied. I'm running circles around those flat feet."

"He's right," said Capt. Smart. "At first, they thought Martin Boundary did it. Now they suspect Ferguson. They think he killed his wife, too, and took off. I read that in the paper."

"Is Ferguson's blood on the carpet, Jimmy?" asked Big Barney.

Johnson shrugged. "What if it is?"

"The case will become a double murder as soon as the FBI's lab rats figure it out."

"Interpol is working the Cape Verde killing," said Smart.

"I had nothing to do with that," said Johnson.

"The duct tape? The bludgeon? Come on, Jimmy. That's your M.O.," said Big Barney.

"Could be a copycat. Cripes, Malone's killing was international news."

"Were you in Cape Verde, recently?"

"Me? I was in Mauritania. That's 1,000 miles to the east.

I'm starting a sheep-slaughtering operation there. The people are mostly Moslem. Moslem's are reproducing at the fastest rate pf any group on earth. Sheep is the new pig."

"And you didn't slip away to Cape Verde?"

"Slip away to Cape Verde? Don't be absurd, Barney. How does someone on a highly publicized, highly visible visit to Nouakchott sneak away to Praia? That's like trying to slip away from Chicago to Miami."

"A thousand miles is nothing nowadays, Jimmy, especially for someone with a private jet. Your escapades are putting our little gold mine in extreme jeopardy. Perhaps it's time to close up shop."

"Close up shop? Before you move my tax bill? Don't be silly. We're talking $1 billion in savings for me over ten years. I won't be screwed out of a major tax break; not after the time energy, and kickbacks spent to build my operation."

"That's the problem, Jimmy," said Barney. "It's not your operation, it's our operation. I whip the members. Lola imports the product. The captain keeps the cops from getting nosy. This is not a one-man operation, amigo, and you've got to stop acting like it is."

Johnson turned beet red.

"You're a goddamn pushover, Barney. That little prick Ferguson was blackmailing us. He had to go. The vet was an unpredictable liability as well. Malone was consorting with the Observer's crime reporter. Were you going to give her a pass? Each of you will end up living like a king because of me. One tax bill and we're out of this, off to our personal paradises."

"If we don't get caught, Jimmy. If the cops don't connect the dots," said Barney. "Otherwise, *paradise* will be a federal prison."

"There are no dots for the cops to connect. End of story." Jimmy leaned back in his chair.

Barney sputtered angrily, "This is idiocy. Get control of yourself. You can't keep killing people willy-nilly. We have 40 liabilities in the U.S. House. You can't kill all of them! Can't you get it into your head that there has to be an end to the murders?"

"What about Boundary?" said Jimmy. "Can we be sure Malone didn't spill the beans to him?"

"He never got the letter," said Smart.

"How do we know she didn't tell him something?"

"He doesn't have a clue," said Lola. "I had his house searched."

Big Barney turned even redder. He looked like a cartoon character whose head was about to explode.

"That was your brilliant idea to trash Boundary's place?" said Big Barney, glaring at Lola. He threw up his hands. "Jesus Christ, people, we can't be a collection of one-man bands."

"I thought you'd want to find out about Boundary, that's all," said Lola defiantly.

"It was a cock-up, said Smart. You cousins pissed their DNA all over the place."

"They have no police records," she said coolly. "And we had to learn if Malone had given Boundary anything."

"And you learned fuck all," said Smart.

Lola shrugged. She decided it might be best to keep the bugging of Twyla Boundary's office to herself.

"Boundary was the leading murder suspect. If he had known anything, he would have spilled the beans to get himself off the hook," said Smart. "If that had happened, then we would not be here having this conversation."

Big Barney pulled off his left shoe and struck the table with its rubber heel.

"No more freelancing," he yelled. "From now on, I want every action vetted by this board. What else have you been up too? Anybody?"

Lola bit her lower lip.

"Good. Keep your eyes open, people. We are in a precarious situation."

On the drive back to the Capitol, Barney took a swig of gin from a pocket flask to help to settle his stomach. Everything might unravel. Early on, he had anticipated this possibility, and prepared. He had foreign bank accounts with $14 million in kickbacks from Jimmy. He owned a beach villa on Jimbaran Bay in Bali because Indonesia had no extradition treaty with the United States. But he hadn't planned on things unraveling so soon. This was a bitter inconvenience because passage of the tax bill would earn him $50 million. He already had greased the palms of over 200 congressmen, including his caucus members. He agonized over running or staying in place. He decided he'd wait on tenterhooks, prepared to flee in an instant. He would order a standing ticket with Emirates airline to fly directly to Bali from Dulles International Airport. He'd keep rolling the dice until things got dicey. Then he'd vanish.

Had Big Barney been more observant, he would have noticed that Johnson was wearing Preston Ferguson's giant diamond pinky ring, displaying his trophy in plain sight. Had he seen it, he would have driven straight to Dulles.

38

Unexpected

Twyla gasped. Lola! Lola had bugged her desk. Twyla had frozen a frame of the cleaning woman captured by her own spy pen and zoomed. The image was crystal clear and in full color.

Why? Twyla was at a loss to explain the espionage. Was the spying related to Cisco and the missing college student? Perhaps Cisco really was the serial killer that Martin had imagined him to be and Lola was trying to determine just how much Martin knew, assuming that he would share everything with his wife. Twyla entertained various other explanations but was unable to puzzle out a cause for Lola's subterfuge. She desperately wanted to talk to someone about it and get some sound advice; but she was not at all certain whom she could trust. Lola was cozy with a great many coworkers in Big Barney's office—including Big Barney.

Discussing this with Martin was out of the question because she detested him. She could not trust the Capitol Police because one of them had let Lola into the office after hours.

She considered calling her former neighbor Joe, the photographer, who had contacts within the FBI. But Joe might blab what she said to Martin, who, in turn, would feel duty bound to guard her day and night.

She pressed the speed-dial number for her friend Sadie and asked her if she could break away to discuss something important. Sadie could tell that Twyla was upset.

"Sure, I can lunch with you, girlfriend," said Sadie. She was bubbly, having received her cocaine ration from Lola minutes earlier. "Meet me for lunch."

Boundary found a listing for Shank's Marina in a telephone directory for the San Francisco Bay area. He dialed the number and a brittle male voice answered "Mack here."

Boundary asked to speak to Mr. Shank, the marina's owner.

"This is Mack Shank. If you want a slip, you're out of luck."

Boundary identified himself as a reporter and asked Mack if he knew Robert and Anne Shank from Baltimore.

"They were my folks. Why are you interested in them?"

"Because I'm trying to discover whatever happened to John Surratt. The cop who arrested him says he belongs back in jail. I heard your dad ran into Surratt in Benicia."

"I was eight so I remember little. Rumor was he moved down to Mexico. My Dad was going to kill him for what he did to Sis and the grief it caused all of us. Dad somehow had tracked Surratt to Sonoma County, but he had no definite address. Even so, he moved us out here and opened a garage. Dad and Surratt walked right smack into one another at the Second Street Café one morning. Dad threw a punch and missed as John flew out the door. He vanished. That's the last time anyone saw that bastard."

"What year was that, Mack?"

"I think it was 1971."

"Did your father ever try to find him again?"

"Dad gave up the chase after that. We had a good life here. Dad's business was booming. The night of the run-in, he told me that Surratt was a ragged, pathetic, frightened piece of shit who'd always be on the run. After that day, Dad never talked about revenge anymore."

"Where are your parents now? I'd like to talk to them."

"Dad died of a heart attack a few months after the Surratt sighting. Mom passed away last year."

"I'm sorry. Do you have other siblings?

"I had an older brother. He died in the First Gulf War."

"Can you describe what he looked like—Surratt, I mean," said Boundary.

"The Baltimore cops had a mug shot. Surratt was a short kid with a big nose. You might try to get ahold of the photo. It might give you some idea of how he would look now."

Boundary thanked him. Mack had a given him a good idea. He spoke to a clerk at Baltimore's Police records division who said the picture was in an old warehouse. He gave Boundary a reference number and a caveat: a fire at the storage facility 14 years ago had destroyed thousands of records, but the reference numbers did not reflect the disaster. In other words, Boundary's search might be fruitless. He laughed ruefully. There was nothing easy about this story, nothing at all.

39

Betrayal

Twyla and Sadie each grabbed a salad and sat at a small table in the Senate's underground cafeteria. Sadie, who at 35 was 10 years older than Twyla, was a top-notch lawyer. Early in her career, before taking a committee post on Capitol Hill, she had been a criminal prosecutor in the Department of Justice, specializing in narcotics cases. She had gotten so many convictions that a Mexican cartel had put a bounty on her head.

"What's up, Twyla? You look troubled," said Sadie.

"First off, I am pregnant," said Twyla

"That's lovely, Twyla," said Sadie. "Of course, I guessed as much the other night. You were showing the classic signs, like avoiding booze. When are you due!"

"Eight months from now."

"How exciting. How're things with Martin?"

Twyla grew somber again. "No change. But that's not what's troubling me."

She told Sadie about Lola Gutierrez bugging her desk with a pen recorder stolen from her house during the break-in.

Sadie sat bolt upright. "Are you sure it was Lola? How did

she get in? Isn't there a guard?"

"She slipped in with the janitorial crew. She was even wearing a smock and pushing a vacuum cleaner. I have photos."

"Does anyone else know about this?"

"You're the first one. I need your advice."

Sadie stirred her coffee, looking thoughtful.

"Cisco might have put her up to it," said Sadie.

"Why?"

"I don't know. Maybe he killed Malone and wanted to see if you and Martin talked about it to see how much you two know."

"That makes little sense, though. I mean, I've thought this through. If Martin had anything other than a theory, he'd have written a story weeks ago. I thought maybe Lola was looking for something else—maybe inside information on legislation?"

"Why would she do that?" said Sadie.

"To sell it, maybe. To lobbyists."

"That's far-fetched. I mean, I thought Big Barney had a backdoor channel to Cisco and that they shared everything. Lola would be in the loop."

"How did Lola get ahold of Martin's recording pen? She had to know the persons who trashed my house, Sadie. The pen was in our kitchen junk drawer."

"Are you sure?"

"Pretty sure."

"Maybe you should ask Martin," said Sadie. "If he cheated on you once, he may have cheated on you twice. Maybe he gave the pen to Lola as a gift. Look, I am sorry that I said that. It's completely off the wall."

"I could run this by the city police detective who investigated the burglary," said Twyla.

"I don't know, Twyla. Barney might get upset if you accuse Lola of burglary."

"I could show him the video."

"That's an idea. Can I see it?"

"I hid it in my new place, just in case the burglars track me down and come back. I wonder what Lola could have been looking for at my old house?"

"If you ask me, it sounds increasingly like Cisco had something to do with Malone's killing," said Sadie. "Would you like me to poke around?"

"No. Please, Sadie, you can't tell anyone about this. Maybe I will talk to Martin. I don't know. I am really confused."

"How wonderful! You and Martin should get back together." Sadie looked down at her wristwatch. "Listen, dear, I have to run. Please, stay in touch; and don't do anything rash, like running to the police, until you know more. I mean, it might be a cleaning woman who is Lola's doppelgänger. Have you considered that?"

"No. I hadn't, and I should have. Thanks, Sadie. You're right."

After leaving Twyla, Sadie returned to her office and immediately telephoned Lola Gutierrez. She made the phone call without the slightest pang of conscience. Her drug dependency had eroded her self-control and her sense of human decency. Twyla had just become an easy means for an extra fix.

"I have some important information, Lola, regarding your moonlighting career as a janitor. I would like to be rewarded for bringing it to your attention."

"Sure, no problem" said Lola. Sadie repeated Twyla's tale

of the recording pens.

"She has my picture?"

"She might show it to the cops."

"Don't breathe a word of this to anyone else. You got that Sadie?"

"Cross my heart. What about my reward?"

"Two extra bags."

"Wonderful."

Lola Gutierrez hung up and immediately and called her older cousin, a thick-set man named Luiz.

"We've got a serious problem," she said. "I need people to disappear." She told them about the new threat posed by to her and the drug operation by Twyla Boundary and her husband.

"We can handle it," her cousin assured her. "They're as good as gone."

40

A Challenge

Martin Boundary was punching a cracked, leather speed bag at the boxing gym. He loved the thumpa-da-thumpa-da sound marking the viper-quick speed of his fists. The strenuous workout was an attempt to clear his mind of negative thoughts. He was feeling more the lonely outcast than ever because of his failure to reconcile with Twyla. He took solace in the musical rhythm of boxing. His Zen-like concentration on the teardrop-shaped bag left no room for his worries and concerns.

The doors of the gym were open to the street, and a cool breeze freshened the sweat-laced atmosphere of the warehouse-sized facility. He hit the bag nonstop until his cantaloupe-sized biceps and muscular shoulders began to burn and perspiration from his brow dripped into his eyes, blinding him. Then he picked up a white towel from a bench and wiped his face. There was a folded copy of the Observer on the same bench and his journalistic nemesis Malcolm Truitt had a front-page story from North Carolina about the sinking campaign fortunes of Senator Kent Cisco because of scandalous news reports linking him to Malone's murder and the disappearance of Dutch student Cynthia Rootewerke. Boundary seethed. Truitt had sabotaged him when he pitched a very similar story to Rooster. Now, the bastard was stealing his idea.

Cisco was alleged in speeches that his political opposition was behind the slander in the tabloid press. He threatened lawsuits for libel and slander and vowed to apply the same smear tactics against Bob Anthony, the young challenger who was leading Cisco by double digits in the polls. His protestation was that of a guilty man, thought Boundary.

Anthony, similarly dismissed Cisco's comments as "the rants of a desperate man" and focused instead on the hot-button issue of illegal immigration. He promised to rid North Carolina of "those criminals who have entered our country illegally."

Boundary smashed a body bag. He was furious—and jealous. Truitt was basking in glory, and he was stuck in Palookaville. He was certain that had Rooster let him follow his hunches, he would have found evidence linking Cisco to the murder.

It was all so obvious. Malone had been blackmailing Cisco. She had threatened to release damaging information during the campaign, and Cisco had killed her. Ferguson had some-thing on Cisco, too—and likely was beside Rootewerke and Hastings. Boundary was certain he had figured everything out and that if he doggedly pursued his hunches, then he would uncover the crucial facts. If, if, if! He struck the body bag with increasing fury. He wanted to burst back onto the journalistic playing field with a big story, but he wasn't making progress on anything. His John Surratt feature was stalled because he could not track the man down. Boundary pitched it to Meg Sloan, the editor of a D.C. city magazine, anyway, and she tossed it right back into his face.

"A story about a killer being released 30 years ago is not news, Boundary. But if that murderer is now a teacher or a cop or, better yet, still killing people, then it's a human-interest story," Sloan said firmly. "The sinner makes the story, not the sin."

Surratt's trail was colder than Sioux Falls in January. He had no clue of where he went to after fleeing Benicia, and he had no idea of what the man might look like. The killer's mug shots had gone up in flames at a Baltimore evidence warehouse the previous decade.

Boundary saw Truitt's face on the bag and struck it angrily. Boundary was so utterly focused on obliterating the imaginary face he did not notice the loud entrance of an aspiring heavyweight with perfect musculature and oversized vocal chords. He did not hear the boisterous boxer's imitation of Muhammad Ali's "I-am-the-greatest" shtick.

Hank Hodges had warned about this kid. The youth had an abundance of talent but was too proud and know-it-all to be teachable. After three easy fights, the young boxer had developed a bloated ego. He was impatient to become heavyweight champion of the world and he let everyone know this—constantly.

The young man called himself 'Fist-O-Cane.' He blustered that he was the storm of the century, a category six boxer in a world of category ones and twos. He bragged that he had the punching power of Hurricane Katrina, the powerful storm that had flattened New Orleans. he decked anyone who responded to his claims with derision. Fisty was a thug at heart.

Hodges hoped that Fisty would be his pathway to the upper rank of fight managers. But if the kid did not correct some bad habits, then he'd lose when he eventually met an equal. Hodges complained to Boundary that Fisty had the fatal habit of dropping his right just before he was about to launch a haymaker, exposing himself to a jab to the jaw from an alert opponent.

"He refuses to correct it because he says he is too quick," said Hodges, shaking his head ruefully. "That boy will get his head handed to him one day. Maybe that's the only thing that'll teach him," said the silver-haired coach. However, Hodges could not foresee this comeuppance occurring in the immediate future, due to a dearth of boxing talent in the pro ranks.

"It's the drugs, Boundary, see? Drugs are everywhere. Pot, heroin, crack. It's an epidemic. Our very own bubonic plague, and the rats and fleas spreading the disease are us! The dopers are getting younger and younger. I have to get six-year-olds in training to build up a stable because all the 14-year-olds are on drugs. It breaks my heart because this is a great sport. Now Fist-O-Cane, he's no doper—but he's one big dope, which creates another set of problems. I wish you could help me think of some way of getting through his thick skull. He has a chance to be someone, and I need a good fighter to help pay for my retirement."

Four, wisecracking, young friends dressed in the long tee shirts, knee-length shorts, and oversized baseball caps at skewed angles accompanied Fisty. Each one wore a gold chain necklace. Hodges called them the Blingateers.

"Look what we got here, bros: it's the great white hope," Fisty spouted while looking Boundary up and down.

Boundary ignored him.

"Hodges says you were real special once upon a time, back

when you was a college boy. Is that right?"

Boundary continued pounding the body bag.

"You lost the big one though. Ain't that the truth?"

Boundary stopped the body bag between his gloved hands and walked past Fisty and his retinue, back to the speed bag. Fisty and the group followed like a flock of malevolent sheep. Boundary wondered what was going on. Was Fisty merely having fun; or was he trying to pick a fight? Boundary studied their faces. He could not tell. These guys were hard cases.

"I ain't never lost a fight to anyone," said Fisty, puffing out his chest. "I ain't never had to stay in the ring for over one round to win. I am overpowering—a force of nature." He beamed and his friends laughed and clapped.

Boundary stopped flicking the speed bag and said, "That record won't last. Coach Hodges says you have a hearing problem."

"A hearing problem? Me? Coach Hodges be pulling your legs, Old Timer. There ain't a thing wrong with my ears. I've got 20/20 hearing, see what I'm saying?" His friends laughed raucously.

"Coach Hodges tells me you don't pay attention to solid advice."

"That old fool! He says to do this and do that and adjust this and adjust that. But I got my own style, man, and it's effective. Just ask those three chumps I dropped to the canvass with these 200-mile-an-hour fists. You can visit them in intensive care."

Fisty's groupies howled again. Boundary smiled. He enjoyed the young man's humorous bravado. Fisty definitely had charisma.

"Coach Hodges was a decent boxer in his day," said Boundary softly. "You ought to take his advice. He can make you even better than you are now. That's what coaches are for. Coaches helped me, back in the day when I was like you and thought I knew everything. If Coach Hodges spots a weakness in your technique, then watch out: Some other sharp-eyed trainer will see it too; and some young fighter with a more open mind will listen to that trainer and exploit it and reduce Fist-O-Cane from category five to a drizzle." He smiled. Fisty did not appreciate the lecture. He liked to talk, not listen.

"You don't know nothing man," Fisty snapped angrily. He pointed an index finger at Boundary. "You are old and washed up, Martin Bound-fairy. Look how you slap that bag—like some senior citizen escaped from the nursing home."

Boundary laughed. He felt like a senior citizen. His biceps were sore, and he had a pain in his lower back.

"Yeah, I am old. I'm out of shape. It happens to the best of us. You win some big ones and you lose some big ones. Now if you'll excuse me, I've got to take a shower."

"You get in shape, Old Timer. I want to spar with you. I want to see what an 'Old Limpy' champion can do."

"I don't fight anymore, Fisty. I don't even spar. The fight has gone out of me."

"Afraid?"

"I'm afraid I might accidentally hurt you."

"You killed a guy once, right? Caused him a hemorrhage of something like that."

"Something like that."

"Well, I ain't got no hemorrhage. I will spar with you, old timer. You think you can teach me, but I will teach you!"

41

Brilliant!

E very morning and evening, Martin Boundary played guardian angel. Partially hidden behind an electric pole on North St. Asaph Street, he watched to make sure that Twyla made it safely to and from her Jeep.

Boundary had memorized the physical details of Twyla's block, much like a secret agent would, including the faces of the people he passed and the colors and makes of the cars parked along on the curbside. There was a comforting regularity to the block's daily activity. The same persons walked the same dogs at the same time; and the same persons parked similar cars along the curb to dash into Trader Joe's for shopping or into a nearby restaurant for a meal. Boundary was vigilant in noting even the slightest alterations in the pattern because they might signal danger.

In the late morning, after Twyla was safely away, Boundary returned to the gym and helped Coach Hodges with the sweeping, the towel washing, and the instruction of young boxers, some of them so small and skinny they hardly could keep the big, leather gloves lifted in front of their eager faces. When the afternoon rolled around, Boundary retreated to the public library on Columbus Street where there was free internet access. The reporter spent some time looking for clues about Surratt and part of the time reading up on the life of Senator Cisco.

Once a week he met with Joe and Joe's basset hound, Beasley, in the Cleveland Park section of Washington to review his findings. They met in a cafe that specialized in baking rich, French pastries, which were Joe's particular weakness, and cheesecake, which was Boundary's Achilles heel. Boundary had never met a cheesecake he didn't like.

One morning, Joe zeroed in on the digital photo that Rootewerke had taken of Senator Cisco on the day she had vanished.

"This bothers me, Martin," he said, tapping it with a porky index finger. Joe took a bite from a Gateau Basque pastry and chased it down with a generous gulp of coffee. Beasley made a whimpering sound, and Joe gave the dog a hunk of the pastry, which he chewed on contentedly. Then Beasley lay back down on the sidewalk and closed his perpetually sad eyes.

"Why is that, Joe?"

"Cisco isn't front and center. He is on the right. A bunch of reporters are in the center, including Preston Ferguson and your buddy Truitt. What if Rootewerke mistook Truitt or one of the other reporters for the Senator and followed one of them? She was a foreigner after all. What would she know of American politics? I mean, if you or I landed in Holland and visited their parliament, how would we distinguish between the tour guides and the politicians?"

"That's an interesting observation, Joe." said Boundary. "Twyla made the same point. But Rootewerke had an upper-classman with her. He would have pointed out the Senator. And her fellow students saw her following Cisco out of the building, so that theory doesn't wash."

"It's best not rule out other possibilities. Let's say she was following Cisco. Was anyone following her?"

"I don't know."

"There's a danger in latching on religiously to a theory, Martin. You always complain about cops taking the path of least resistance. Maybe you're doing the same thing."

Boundary reddened with embarrassment—Joe was correct.

Joe moved on to John Surratt. Boundary complained that there was no way to track him down.

"He could have changed his name, Joe. And he could be anywhere—or dead. I might have to scrap the project. I hate to do it because I invested so much time."

"Are his parents alive?" asked Joe.

"No," said Boundary. "His father died of a heart attack while John was in the hospital. His mother died three years ago in a nursing home in Arbutus."

"Three years ago? You might have a good lead right there."

Joe's comment perplexed Boundary. This was obvious to Joe from the puzzled expression on Boundary's face. Joe told him to look up the mother's obituary.

"The obit writers always make a list of the survivors. Perhaps Surratt's new name will show up. I can't imagine that he didn't go to his mother's funeral."

"That's brilliant," said Boundary.

"Maybe. Maybe not. It depends if he volunteered the information to the funeral director. Chances are that he didn't."

"Even so, Joe, it's a lead. I was all out of leads."

After the meal, Boundary, filled with hope, grabbed a cab to the Library of Congress.

42

Blockbuster

Boundary's story about John Surratt was the lead story at the PufferFishPost.com, a hot, new web-based news site. Boundary was ecstatic. He was back in the game. He had hit a home run. Joe's hunch had been spot-on. The son had showed up at his mother's funeral. The obituary had identified him as Carl DeSales.

The revelation that Surratt was DeSales had prompted Boundary to swear loudly in the Library of Congress, bringing the silence police to his carrell almost immediately. He could barely contain himself. It changed his entire view of the murders and disappearances—and of Cisco. He berated himself for relying on his gut rather than on a ratiocination. Everything seemed so clear to him now: Carl DeSales was a clever psychopath.

Boundary confronted DeSales with his discovery, and the professor gave him a face-to-face interview, protesting his innocence in the Malone killing and in the mysterious disappearances of Hastings and Rootewerke. He was amazed that Boundary had discovered so much about his old self, John Surratt, an identity he had buried decades ago.

"I killed Shank purely by accident. I swung the club to frighten her, not to strike her. I was a stupid, hormone-addled kid. We had been making out on the putting green behind the clubhouse. It was dark. She resisted after I tried to feel her up, and then she jumped up and accused me of rape. I went nuts. She would ruin my life with a lie. My parents would have killed me! Dad would have whipped me with his belt. Then she screamed, like in a horror movie. It unnerved me. I told her to shut up or she would be sorry, and instead she screamed louder. I picked up my putter and waived it.

" 'Shut up,' I said. 'Shut up or I'll knock you out.' I swung the club to scare her. I really didn't intend to strike her. It happened so fast. The end of the club struck her and she fell. At first, I thought she was faking. I told her to get up, but she didn't move. I tickled her. I shook her shoulder. Then I thought I had knocked her out. I got a handful of water from a bucket someone had left out in the rain and threw it on her face. She didn't stir. She wasn't breathing. I put my ear to her heart, and it wasn't beating. It was unbelievable. I shook uncontrollably. I ran home like a coward and hid in my room. I should have run for help. I never thought of that. I ran to my room and stood in the dark, quaking. I wondered if I had dreamed the entire episode—until the cops came to the house."

"Then what happened, Carl?"

"I confessed right away. I still agonize about her death, Martin. I erased her life. I was a monster. But I'm not a monster anymore. I've dedicated my life to protecting women from fiends like Cisco."

DeSales related that he had suffered a severe breakdown before trial and ended up in the mental hospital.

"I hallucinated a lot. I had nightmares and saw ghosts. The Shank girl came in my sleep almost every night. I tried to hang myself. I was really out of it. I couldn't distinguish between my dream state and my waking state. They gave me shock treatments. Treatment of mental illness was primitive. Then the doctor prescribed a wonder drug called Lithium, and it did the trick. The hallucinations disappeared. The nightmares disappeared. I still take medication. They've moderated my chemical imbalances. I am a fully functioning, non-criminal human being who has been trying to make amends for a crime by my former, untreated self. I am different today. I am unlike the teenage me. You understand this, don't you?"

Boundary tapped his pen against his notebook three times.

"I talked to the cop who was running the Shank murder investigation. He says you faked your mental illness."

DeSales sadly shook his head. "I wasn't faking. That cop doesn't know jack shit. How did you find me out, anyway, Martin? Who gave up my secret identity?"

"You did."

"What do you mean, 'I did'? Are you playing games with me?"

"I was researching murders by golf club because of Malone, to see if there were links to any past crimes and I came across John Surratt, whereabouts unknown. I tracked you to the hospital in Cumberland, Md. and then to California where you had your dramatic run-in with Mr. Shank; and then, your trail went cold. On the advice of a professional sleuth, I read your mom's obituary in the Baltimore paper. Carl DeSales was listed as a survivor."

"God, I was afraid when that obituary appeared. A stupid, old aunt provided the information to the funeral director. But after a few years, I felt safe."

"Where did you go?"

"After California, I moved to a small, desolate town in North Dakota where I legally changed my name. I became a ranch hand for three years; and then I was a correspondent for the Bismarck newspaper, writing about cowboy stuff. By then, I felt so safe with my new identity I enrolled in the state university and majored in journalism and criminal Justice. I've lived a productive life, Martin. I never injured another human being."

"You've hurt Cisco pretty badly," said Boundary. "Doesn't that count?"

"He's a serial killer."

"Where's the proof?"

"He's clever, Martin. He's a real snake."

Boundary asked DeSales if he had an alibi for the day of Malone's murder.

"I was at the Kennedy Center, at the symphony."

"I need a quote for the story."

"I was at the Kennedy Center, at a symphony."

"Are there witnesses who saw you there?"

"Did I have a date? No. I had a glass of white wine during the intermission. Maybe the ticket counter people will remember me? I also have a credit card receipt."

They talked for 45 minutes more. Afterwards, Boundary poured himself into writing his story, and the end result was vivid and gripping. He evoked the dark, moonless night that Surratt killed the girl, and he chronicled the devastating impact of the crime on the Shank family. His description of the elder Shank's vain pursuit of Surratt to California, his death, and the suicide of their youngest child was particularly powerful, as was his sympathetic description of Surratt's own agony and his sincere but flawed attempts to redeem himself as DeSales by crusading Cisco for his alleged murder of Susie Hastings.

Boundary's feature became an overnight internet sensation, copied on thousands of social media sites around the globe. Even the Observer mentioned the story, though citing the website, not Boundary, as the source. He took it as a mean-spirited snub from editor Rooster Redburn. No other journalist following the Malone murder had thought of looking at homicides committed with golf clubs. No other journalist had been as energetic and dogged as Boundary. The story was as solid, complete, and well-written. Rooster was vindictive and small. Boundary swore he would show up his old boss one day.

The Silicon Valley engineer who had founded Puffer-Fish.Com offered to put Boundary's name on the masthead as its Washington Bureau Chief. Boundary jumped at the offer even though the title was honorary and the bureau was a Potemkin Village. He now could print business cards that proclaimed his exalted title. And because he belonged to a news organization, he could apply for a Capitol Hill press pass, which would increase his access to lawmakers and boost his journalistic credibility. As for pay, Boundary got $1,000, which wasn't much to shout about. But it was better than nothing.

The day after Boundary's story appeared, DeSales phoned Boundary to say goodbye.

"Where are you going, Carl?"

"My life is ruined, Martin. I've lost my job. My friends suspect I'm still a psychopath. I'm so tired. You do not understand. You did a job on me. I have no present and no future. There's one path left and I'm going to take it."

"What are you saying?"

"Don't be naive, Martin."

"Carl, you can't mean..."

DeSales hung up the phone. Boundary immediately dialed 911 and gave the dispatcher DeSale's address. If he was wrong... then he'd deal with it. But he wasn't wrong. When the ambulance crew arrived at DeSales' apartment, the door was open. They found his body on the kitchen floor.

Boundary wrote the suicide story and then went out and got drunk at a corner bar. His moment of glory had turned into horrid remorse. He had killed the man with his keyboard. He'd never entertained the possibility. DeSales was rehabilitated. He had been cooperative and equable during the entire interview. He had not pleaded with Boundary to withhold the story. He had behaved as though he could capably deal with the fallout. There was no sign of trouble until he phoned Boundary to announce he was killing himself.

Boundary felt like giving up the whole dirty, disgusting business of journalism, just as he had given up boxing. But he couldn't give it up, he realized the following morning, when Special Agent Smee rang him out of his drunken slumber with a heads up. Something big was going down. The FBI would make a major announcement at 11 a.m. Boundary had best get over to the Justice Department.

Boundary checked his cell phone for the time. He had three hours to pull himself together.

He drank a quart of milk, threw it up into the toilet took an ice-cold shower. Then he ate some unbuttered toast, drank three cups of coffee and dashed out the door.

At 10 a.m., Boundary called the Department of Justice, where the press briefing was to take place, to reserve a seat. The press spokesman, Veronica Cleary, put him on the list, which she said was a long one.

"Your seat is way in the back."

He took a taxi to the Justice Department's austere looking sandstone headquarters on Pennsylvania Avenue and arrived 30 minutes early. Television camera crews already were in place. He saw Agent Smee, who told him that the FBI director himself would make the announcement.

"It's about your little Dutch girl," he said.

"They found her body?"

Smee smiled and shrugged. "I've already told you too much, Boundary. Don't jump to any conclusions."

FBI Director Tom Fitzgibbons, a former Notre Dame full-back, entered the briefing room at precisely 11 a.m. The cameras of the still photographers clicked rapidly. Fitzgibbons drew himself up behind the podium and cleared his throat. He was tall and broad-shouldered with steel gray hair trimmed high and tight, like a Marine. He had a sharp chin, a hawk nose and small, intense green eyes. He wore a tailored gray suit with a starched white shirt and a bright red tie.

"Today the FBI closed the file on what has become a high-profile missing person because of unfortunate rumors about U.S. Senator Kent Cisco's possible involvement," he said. "Cynthia Rootewerke, the Dutch student who disappeared over two months ago, is alive in Norfolk, Virginia with an AWOL sailor. Both Ms. Rootewerke and the sailor, Taylor T. Grimes, of Nomerci, Georgia, were admitted to a hospital for the treatment of opioid addiction. Grimes is in the custody of the Military Police. Ms. Rootewerke is being deported. I will now take questions."

Every hand in the auditorium shot skyward, including Boundary's. Fitzgibbons took first question from a network television reporter, which was customary. Fitzgibbons wanted to ensure that his would appear on at least one evening news broadcast.

"Did Rootewerke stalk Senator Cisco, as reported? Was he ever a murder suspect? How did the FBI track her down?"

Fitzgibbons answered "no" and "no" to the Cisco questions.

"How did you find her?"

"She was spotted by a local hairdresser who had seen the missing student's photo in a post office," said Fitzgibbons.

"Did Carl DeSales have any idea you had found that his student before he killed himself?" asked a MSNBC reporter.

"I don't know," said Fitzgibbons.

Boundary's heart raced. Perhaps his story hadn't triggered DeSale's self-destruction.

Boundary was recognized by name. Agent Smee smiled.

"Is there anything new you can tell us about the murder of Bernadette Kathleen Malone, Senator Cisco's murdered aide?" he asked nervously.

"I can't get into the nitty gritty because the murder remains under active investigation," said Fitzgibbons.

"Is Preston Ferguson a person of interest?"

Fitzgerald ignored him.

He took a few more questions. How and when had Rootewerke hooked up with the sailor?

"We did not interview her, owing to her current condition. We intend to ask her for details once they discharge her from the hospital."

"Have you interviewed Grimes?"

"We leave that up to the Navy. Good day to you all."

285

Fitzgibbons abruptly walked away from the podium and out a side door of the auditorium, ignoring shouted questions. When he disappeared behind the curtain, the press corps descended on Boundary. It was the moment he had dreamed of.

"Who do you think killed Malone?" asked a tall, lanky television reporter.

"One of her blackmail victims," said Boundary.

"How many were there?"

Boundary shrugged. "This is a big town."

"Did she blackmail you?" asked a female reporter.

"No. I didn't sleep with her. But she drugged me. That story in the Bugler wrongly attributed to me was a complete fabrication by the website's editor."

"Do you feel responsible for DeSale's suicide?"

"I feel terrible about it. Terrible. But the story was relevant, given his crusade against Senator Cisco."

Reporters are like lemmings. The crowd around Boundary grew. Reporters stuck microphones in his face and asked multiple questions about his marriage, his career, and his interview with Cisco.

He had had enough.

"Please guys. I've got to work too," he protested. He thanked them, exited the building, and retreated to an internet café two blocks away. Boundary ordered an espresso and then phoned PufferFish.com to pitch his story on Rootewerke, but got a busy signal. He dialed Lola's number, since she was Cisco's press spokesman, to get a response to the Rootewerke revelation. Her assistant picked up. Boundary asked if he could speak to Lola.

"It's about Rootewerke," he added.

The assistant said they would post there a press release on Senator Cisco's website and that there would be no further comment.

Boundary cursed himself. He deserved the cold shoulder. He had been cocksure for weeks that Cisco had murdered the Dutch student, despite being cautioned by wiser souls about jumping to conclusions. Hadn't Kitty Cross presciently suggested that Rootewerke might have run off with a serviceman? Both Twyla and Joe had raised red flags about his murder theory, and he had ignored them, trusting his gut, instead. Even Truitt accused him of being rash and gullible. He had been wrong, wrong, wrong! Lola had brainwashed him. He felt like an imbecile. Regarding Malone's murder, he had no strong theory. He'd have to return to square one—with a healthy dose of clinical detachment.

43

Fight for Life

At the beginning of a sparring match, boxers agree on a specific level of violence. Coach Hodges set it at 30 percent.

"Slap fight. Nobody gets hurt," said Coach.

"That means a Category 3 storm, Boundary, which is still enough to blow over your tired old bones," sneered Fisty, playing to his fawning followers sitting in the ringside bleachers. There was a tough looking Mexican with them. He had tattoos of Aztec warriors similar to the ones on the arms of the fellow that Boundary had seen sitting on the wall at Trader Joe's a few days earlier. The man handed Fisty a thick envelope prompting a wide smile from the boxer. Fisty stuck it in his ringside duffel bag.

Boundary had agreed to spar Fisty as a favor to Coach Hodges, who had given him work when he most needed it and because he needed to build up a cash reserve for a new motorcycle. His earnings from freelancing stories were unpredictable and often thin. Pufferfish.com hadn't paid the $1,000 it owed him. Late payment was a habit with these web outfits. Boundary spent hours each week like a bill collector, hounding various editors for his back pay.

Despite his financial woes, Boundary was leery about stepping back into the ring, even for sparring. It went against his better judgement. He was old by the standards of boxing, and he knew he was not in the greatest shape. When he boxed in college, he worked out a minimum of four hours daily. He was down to two hours now, and, his once lightning fast hand speed had slackened. He ran 10 miles each day. Fisty probably ran 15. Boundary worked the bags for an hour each morning. Fisty probably worked on them for five, minimum.

He also had killed a man in the ring and had sworn off the sport of boxing because he never wanted to hurt anyone in the ring again. But, he really wasn't going back on his anti-boxing pledge, was he? This merely was a slap fight in protective headgear. Boundary never heard of anyone killing a sparring partner. They would pay him $200 for a little over an hour's work. Easy money. Coach Hodges wanted Boundary to give Fisty a slap on the jaw when he dropped his right, to send the narcissist a message. He would educate the young boxer, not batter him.

Fisty was training for a bout that would be televised on ESPN in three weeks. He would go up against a rising star from San Antonio named Louis Villa. Villa had nicknamed his right hand "Puncho," because he subdued his opponents with a wicked right-handed uppercut. Puncho would put down Fisty for sure if Fisty failed to heed Coach Hodges' warnings.

Coach Hodges rang the bell, and the two opponents sprang from their corners, bouncing on the balls of their feet. The initial sparring was one-part shadow boxing and one part fencing. Fisty backed Boundary up with a lightning fast flurry of grazing punches. Boundary shocked the younger man and himself, with a skin-scraping lightning quick left cross, which would have flattened Fisty if Boundary had tried to connect. He saw a look of surprise cross Fisty's face and he felt good. He had not lost as much of his edge as he had feared. His muscle memory, honed through his youth, returned to him as if someone had thrown a switch.

Fisty's retinue was shouting, "Put him down. Put the old man down."

"I will, I will. There's no hurry," Fisty shouted. He threw a haymaker which Boundary easily ducked. The force of that punch spun Fisty around like a top. Everyone laughed, including Boundary. He assumed that Fisty was clowning, not trying to kill him. The bell sounded, ending the first five-minute round. The minutes had flown by like seconds.

Boundary felt winded and thirsty when he returned to his corner. His upper arms ached. He was in good shape, but to flourish in the ring, even for a sparring match, a boxer has to be in excellent shape. He worried about being able to go the full ten rounds. It would humiliate him if he had to quit early. Fisty would mock him. He might not get the full $200.

When Coach Hodges sounded the bell for round two, Boundary advanced cautiously towards the center of the ring. Fisty came on full force—a Category 6. He staggered a surprised Boundary with a lightning fast roundhouse to his ear pad.that knocked him to the canvas, his head ringing. He felt like he had absorbed a hammer blow. His headgear was askew.

He rose slowly to his feet and tried to signal Hodges to stop the match, so he could adjust his chin strap. But Fisty came in quickly for the kill, and Boundary had to raise his gloves over his face to protect himself.

An appeal to Coach Hodges would have done no good. The

thugs in the stands came down to ringside and pinned the coach's arms as soon as Fisty upped the violence.

Hodges was yelling, "Stop the fight. Stop the fight." One man gagged him with a towel.

Fisty was blazing fast, but so was Boundary, who parried most of Fisty's blows. Boundary's defensive quickness surprised the overconfident Fisty. Boundary landed four stinging rebukes to Fisty's washboard stomach, forcing him to retreat.

"Cool it," said Boundary. "We're sparring."

"You're in trouble now," said Fisty, bounding on his feet. "Big trouble. I'm going to take your head off."

A student boxer at ringside furiously rang the bell to stop the round. Fisty ignored the signal and kept coming. He aimed a punch at Boundary's nose, which Boundary blocked with raised forearms. The blow caused a burning, stinging pain more extreme than anything Boundary ever had experienced. He wondered if Fisty had hidden horseshoes in his gloves.

The student who could not have been older than 14, jumped into the ring and stood courageously between the two boxers, his arms outstretched to keep them apart. And Fisty immediately took the kid down with a short, sharp blow to his kidney.

"You coward," shouted Boundary, as the young writhed on the canvas in pain. "Why did you hit the kid?"

"You hear that?" Fisty shouted to his crew, "He say I'm a coward. I will make him cry like a baby for that."

Boundary squared his big shoulders as Fisty moved in, tossing jabs.

Fisty landed a flurry of punches to Boundary's rock-hard midsection, driving him back several steps, yet failing to deliver a catastrophic blow. These punches also were shockingly painful. Boundary knew he could not absorb more of them. He

291

grabbed Fisty tightly around his rib cage. Fisty responded by head-butting Boundary's chin, drawing blood.

Boundary threw a hard blow to the hard plastic cup protecting Fisty's groin. Fisty screamed out, cursed, and retreated.

"I will get you for that low blow, O-Limp Man," he shouted.

Boundary was dazed from the head butt. His jaw ached, and he felt the blood rolling from his chin down his neck and over his chest.

Fisty lowered his shoulders and ran full speed at Boundary, who, matador style, sidestepped the raging bull at the very last second. Fisty ran hard into the ropes, nearly toppling over them. He quickly regained his composure and laughed.

"That was a cool move, like James Bond. But it's your last good move."

He stalked Boundary with graceful measured steps.

Boundary gasped for air. His arms were heavy as logs. His legs were rubbery. His ribs burned. Fisty landed a smart right jab to Boundary's left eye, which staggered the former champ. His eye puffed up, blurring his vision. Fisty moved in, feigned a jab, and delivered a karate kick to Boundary's right knee, sending him face first to the canvas. Boundary immediately bounced back up, realizing that he had to fight for his life. He had trouble maintaining his balance because his knee cap felt like it was full of ground glass.

Boundary's only hope was for Fisty to throw a left and drop his right—the bad habit that Coach Hodges fretted about. So far, Fisty hadn't made that the mistake. Boundary had to force him to commit it.

As Fisty advanced, Boundary pressed his gloved hands together and raised them to the top of his head, so that his forearms shielded his face. He wanted Fisty to throw a left-handed jab to his unprotected midsection. Fisty took the bait.

The force of Fisty's punch drove Boundary backwards, so that when Fisty dropped the right for a follow up, Boundary was too back to deliver the decisive counterpunch.

Fisty circled to Boundary's left, where his swollen eye restricted his vision.

"Look at you, huffing and puffing like an emphysema patient," taunted Fisty.

Boundary raised his hands again. Fisty unleashed another hammering left to Boundary's midsection, nearly knocking the wind out of him. But this time, Boundary did not yield an inch. Fisty dropped his right to deliver a haymaker to the side of Boundary's head. Swift as a striking cobra, Boundary dropped his own left and brought it up under Fisty's chin, snapping back the flippant boxer's head. Fisty's eyes rolled upward, and he thudded to the canvas, where he lay motionless.

"Oh, no!" said Boundary. He knelt down slowly and felt Fisty's neck for a pulse. It was strong.

Fisty's angry crew climbed into the ring, but stopped and ran out of the gym when they heard an approaching police siren. A student boxer had slipped out of the gym to summon help.

Coach Hodges tore off his gag and jumped into the ring to minister to Fisty. He touched Fisty's jaw. Anguish clouded the coach's face.

"Fisty is my retirement plan. Look what you did to him, Martin. His jaw looks broken. If Fisty can't fight next week—then my life ruined."

"You've got to be kidding Coach? Look what that son of a bitch did to me. He karate-kicked me. He head-butted me. I think he has horseshoes in his gloves. I was fighting for my life!"

"Call an ambulance," Hodges shouted to the first cop to enter the gym. Fisty was still out cold.

Hodge's removed the fighter's gloves. He shook one and a bar of steel fell out.

"I told you, Coach! He was trying to kill me."

Coach Hodges glared at Boundary. "You incited him."

"I did what?"

"You were passive aggressive."

"You're joking?"

"I want you to leave here right now and never come back."

" I'm injured, Coach. I need an ambulance, too."

"Call your own."

44

When It Rains

A police officer in a squad car took Boundary to the hospital emergency room. There, he spent the first 20 minutes filling out forms and then waited in agony for three hours for x-rays. Five hours after entering the hospital, the doctors diagnosed two fractured ribs and cartilage damage in the right knee. They gave him rib wraps, a knee brace, crutches, and painkillers and sent on his way. The bill came to $14,000. He had an insurance policy with a $15,000 deductible, the only one he could afford. Instead of making him an easy $200, the sparring practically wiped his bank account out.

When he explained to Mrs. Quander that he would be late with his rent, she kicked him out.

"No offense, Mr. Boundary, but I'm a businesswoman, not a charity. Try that Homeless Shelter over on Henry Street. They might have a free cot tonight."

Boundary stuffed his belongings into a 33-liter rucksack. He hobbled on the crutches four blocks to the local library where there was a payphone. He phoned Father Francis at St. Martin's and the housekeeper said the elderly priest had died a week earlier.

Boundary hung out at the library until closing. Then, in desperation, he crutched his way to Twyla's doorstep. He had a throbbing headache and horrid looking black eye. His ribs stung when he inhaled. He was sitting on her doorstep grimacing when Twyla turned the corner, on her way back home after a walk along the Potomac River. He raised his head, and she gasped.

"Oh my God, Martin! What happened to you?"

"One of Hodges' boxers," he said. "We were supposed to be sparring, but he tried to take my head off."

Twyla stiffened. Her sympathy vanished.

"You climbed back into in the ring after promising me you'd never fight again? But then, what are promises to you?"

The remark cut him to his heart. He said, "It was a setup. We were sparring. The other boxer had horseshoes inside his gloves. I have broken ribs to prove it. I think someone paid him to kill me."

Twyla crossed her arms.

"You told me you were done with boxing."

"I need a place to stay, Twyla. I used up my bank account to get patched up. My landlady tossed me out onto the street because I can't pay the rent. I am low on pain pills. And, you need me here. Someone paid that boxer—a guy I've seen hanging out across the street."

"You're just trying to scare me. You will say anything and do anything to get your way."

"Look good at my face, Twyla. Did I make this up?"

"You can't stay here. I won't have you."

"I've no one else to turn to."

"You should have thought of that before you had your wild fling with Malone."

"I've told you I didn't sleep with her. It was a setup."

Twyla stared at him angrily.

"It's always a setup when you do something wrong. Martin Boundary never is to blame!"

Boundary shrugged. He felt defeated. He would never change her mind.

"Goodbye, Twyla. Take care, because I'm never coming back."

She glared at him.

Boundary stood unsteadily and painfully slipped his arms into the rucksack. He crutched himself down the sidewalk. Twyla shut the door and threw the deadbolt.

45

Salvation

The following morning, a thud outside the front door jarred Boundary awake at 4 a.m. He rose quickly from the sofa where he had been sleeping and yanked the door open. The landing was empty, except for the morning Washington Observer.

His ribs still ached and his face remained swollen. He made his way to the kitchen, took ice cubes from Kitty Cross's freezer, wrapped them in a towel, and held them against his face for 20 minutes. Then he made himself some toast and coffee.

Cross, his former managing editor, had let him spend the night after he turned up at her front door. He was too pathetic to turn away. Cross fed him dinner, listened as he poured out his woes, but gave him no hope that Rooster ever would rehire him.

"The stubborn, old goat feels you deceived him and tarnished the paper's reputation," she said. "Move on, Martin."

Boundary had been drawn to her door by more than simple desperation. The hardy young man was, from time to time, wholly a creature of his hormones. Since his separation from

298

Twyla, the longing for female affection and sexual relief dulled his reason. Boundary was lonely, forlorn—and at the moment , in need of female affection. When he had knocked on Kitty's door begging for a warm place to sleep he hoped that she would offer to share her bed.

His sexual fantasy evaporated within minutes of entering her snug, designer townhouse. Rooster's neck tie hung from the back of a leather recliner.

"Is Rooster here?" Boundary asked with alarm.

"That man always leaves something behind," said Cross. "It's either his wallet, his glasses, his cigars, or this tie. I'll reunite him with it tomorrow."

Boundary blushed.

"Rooster is a bachelor. I don't carry on with little boys or married men or little boys who are married men," she said with a laugh and a toss of her hair. She was beautiful and self-possessed and had seen right through him—and he felt like a goddamn fool.

Cross fetched a blanket and told him to sleep on the living room couch. She handed him three tens and a twenty and warned him that Rooster would be over for coffee at 6:30 a.m.

"I'd appreciate it if you were gone by then, Martin. He'll throw a tantrum if he thinks you have been here with me."

Boundary set his iPhone alarm for 5 a.m. He closed his eyes and passed out.

It was not an easy night for Boundary. He had to lie on his back. Every time he turned in his sleep, sharp rib pain awoke him.

Boundary was out on the sidewalk by 5:30 a.m., groggy, unbathed, and unshaven. Cross had been running her shower when, without fanfare, he exited her front door.

The city was dark and quiet and the morning air was cold. Boundary, who was wearing a tee shirt, shivered.

Some residents of the block were out walking their dogs and they stared suspiciously at Boundary's black and blue face as he crutched by them. He looked like a bum. He could tell from their dark looks they resented him being in their upscale neighborhood.

He shuffled along on his crutches for 30 minutes until he was within a mile of his old neighbor Joe's place, but his knee was too painful to continue on. His ribs roared with pain. He could spare no money for pain pills.

Boundary hobbled into the Cleveland Park Metro Station, used $10 of the $50 that Cross had lent him to add value to his fare card, and took a Red Line train to Metro Center, where he switched to the Blue Line, back to Alexandria, planning to camp in woods along the riverbank.

Sitting in a train car brought a modicum of relief. The seats were upholstered and comfortable. Boundary nodded off to sleep. He awoke in time to exit the Blue Line at the elevated Braddock Road Station in Alexandria. The sun now was a bright yellow ball, and the air was considerably warmer. Boundary took the AT5 bus from the Braddock Road station to St. Asaph Street; and when he left the bus, he sat on the outdoor staircase near the Vietnamese Restaurant to watch over Twyla's townhouse.

Boundary saw no sign of the Mexican with the Aztec tattoos who had been outside of Trader Joe's the last time he had watched over Twyla. He was certain the tattooed man was the same hombre who had handed Fisty an envelope before the sparring match. Had been a payoff to kill him? Boundary had made up his to call the police if he ever saw the man near there again. He was in no shape to confront the man himself.

After a couple hours, Boundary became intensely hungry. He made his way to the Royal Diner, a block away. Tourists and businessmen packed the booths, so he slid onto a stool at the lunch counter, resting his crutches beside him, and ordered the three-egg omelet with a side of sausage and a cup of coffee. The elderly waitress looked at him sideways. He knew she was wondering about his nasty shiner. He gulped down the glass of ice water she had given him and thought about his immediate future.

He might ask his parents for a loan, but he was loath to do it because they were elderly and living primarily on Social Security. They would gladly give, but it would hurt them financially. Anyway, he was too proud to ask and too ashamed to tell them about his broken marriage.

He could enlist in the Navy. He always romanticized about being onboard a destroyer. But that would take him far away from Twyla. He had given up on abandoning her after Kitty's rebuff brought him back to his senses. They were man and wife, in good times and bad times, whether or not she liked it.

He ate slowly, taking small bites and modest sips of his coffee. The meal with tip would set him back about $14. He intended to make the most of it.

After Boundary finished and paid his bill, he returned to his perch on the wall. To kill time, he checked his phone for texts and email. He had a week's worth of service on the pre-pay plan. After that, he's be off the grid which was a frightening thought for the young man. He felt it was easier to be homeless than to be phone-less because his phone was his major link to the world at large. He would be unable to solicit work, contact sources, or stay in touch with his parents. He'd be a hermit.

As he scrolled through his mail, Boundary did not expect to find anything noteworthy. He scrolled and scrolled, deleting one junk email after another, and then stopped suddenly and stared in utter disbelief. There was a message from Twyla, of all people. The email was time-stamped 7:00 a.m. that morning. He hurriedly tapped the screen to open it. The message read, "Martin, please come home. I forgive you. I have something important to tell you."

He re-read it slowly. He zeroed in on "please come back to home." He re-read it again. He examined the address line to make certain he was not being spoofed. It looked legit. He bawled uncontrollably like a baby.

"You okay, fellow?" An old timer had stopped. "Can I do something for you?"

Boundary wiped away his tears with his hand and grinned. "Good news!" he croaked.

46

Big Barney's Boy

Big Barney had a major misconception about the investigation of Malone's death. He thought the FBI was zeroing in on Preston Ferguson. In fact, the agents were wending their way from Bernadette Kathleen Malone's medicine cabinet to Big Barney's 100-acre horse farm along the Susquehanna River, just south of York, Pennsylvania. Special Agents Smee and Starkey had been pursuing the prescriber of the date-rape drug ketamine found in Malone's medicine cabinet. The veterinarian, Vincent Boyd, a year earlier, had sold his practice in downtown York to a new practitioner, Virginia Sheridan. Boyd's retirement had been abrupt and unexpected because he was just 50 and had built a successful practice. But he had been in a great hurry to sell. Sheridan, a sharp-featured woman with jet black hair and bulimic thinness, told the FBI that Boyd seemed to be in a hurry to exit the business.

"I made a low-ball offer for the practice—you know, the opening gambit—and he accepted it without blinking. It shocked me. But you don't look a gift horse in the mouth."

She allowed the FBI to examine the Boyd's records, which

he had left behind in boxes in a large closet. They showed that the Boyd had prescribed a few ketamine tablets to Malone for her cat. The record matched a pill bottle discovered in the glove compartment of Malone's BMW. The FBI agents were curious. Why would Malone come to Pennsylvania to treat her cat, assuming there was one? And where Malone had gotten the rest of her stock? The agents had discovered 20 plastic pill containers filled with ketamine tablets in Malone's medicine cabinet. There were no prescription labels.

The office records showed that Boyd had prescribed a huge amount of ketamine to a horse trainer named Phil Landsberry who worked on Big Barney's spread. Malone had been to Big Barney's farm two years earlier for a big congressional meeting with Senator Cisco. He had volunteered this during an interview with the agents. So, it was possible she had met Landsberry.

A quick background search by the agents found that Landsberry had a checkered past which made him an unusual hire for the Speaker of the House. He was part of a thoroughbred doping scandal in the early 1990s.

Smee and Starkey wondered why Landsberry needed so much ketamine. According to Boyd's records, Big Barney owned just three horses. He once temporarily had stabled about 40 horses for congressional gathering. Malone, a horsewoman, volunteered to saddle up the congressmen.

Smee and Starkey paid a surprise visit to the farm on a Tuesday, when the U.S. House was in session and, therefore, Big Barney was away. They wanted Landsberry all to themselves.

The two agents found Landsberry sweeping out the horse stalls. He was a portly, red-faced man of 60 with thinning, disheveled silver hair. His face showed both shock and fear when the agents swept into the stable and identified themselves.

Starkey and Smee grilled Landsberry in the tack room about the ketamine prescription for 45 minutes. They didn't get much. Landsberry's vulnerable look was deceptive. Underneath that frightened expression lived a hard-boiled egg. He gave up nothing other than that the drugs were for settling down 10 unruly horses that Barney once kept in the stables—vicious, untrainable animals finally sent to the glue factory, he claimed.

"We have three new horses, now—gentle ones. I don't give them anything."

"Can we see your stock of ketamine?" said Smee.

"I flushed it all down the toilet after we sold those wild ones," said Landsberry. "You can't leave unused medicine lying around."

The two agents followed up the next day with an office visit to Big Barney, who was uncommonly jovial. He did not seem to know much about the drug, other than he had read Malone had used it for date rapes.

"Did you know Dr. Boyd, the veterinarian?"

"Sure, I did. He'd come out when the horses were sick. But he worked mostly with my stable boy. I can have you talk to him if you think it would help you."

"Mr. Speaker, did you know Landsberry was an ex-con?" asked Starkey.

"I did. Would either of you two gentlemen like a drink? No? You don't mind if I have one? Edmund, would you pour me a scotch, please?" Edmund was his deputy legal counsel.

Big Barney told the agents he was a member of an organization that advocated hiring ex-cons to reduce recidivism.

"The program has worked well, too. Say, should I fire him?

Is he pushing pills? Is that what you two are intimating?"

"Was if Bernadette Kathleen Malone a guest at your farm in York County?" asked Smee.

"I'm sure she was a guest of mine at one time or another," he said. "I invite Senate Leader Cisco and some of his members to meet here with House members from time to time. What happened to Bernadette was unspeakable! Gosh, she was a sweet, sweet girl. I hope you find the monster who killed her."

"We are doing our best," said Starkey.

"Do you have a suspect?"

"No comment," said Starkey.

"Did Bernadette ever ride one of your horses, Mr. Speaker?" asked Smee.

"I think so. She grew up around horses. Phil might remember. I don't ride, myself, because I'd need an elephant to support my weight." He patted his extended belly and laughed. "But she helped guide riders around the place a year back at a big meeting. I remember that."

"So, she knew Landsberry."

"He ran the stables. Wait, a minute! Did she get ketamine from Phil? Is that what you are suggesting?"

The agents both shrugged.

"What do you use the drug for, Speaker Magus?" asked Starkey.

"Me. I don't do drugs. I like scotch." He laughed. "Anyway, isn't ketamine a sedative for horses? We had about a dozen wild bastards we had to calm down so we could load them onto trucks for a one-way trip to the glue factory. I had gotten them from a ranch in Wyoming. The seller claimed they were trail horses. But I think they were actually a bunch of unbroken wild ones."

Afterward, the two agents paused outside the Capitol building. Smee asked Starkey for his thoughts on the interview.

"I think the fat bastard is lying," said Starkey, as he lit a cigarette. "He was overly jovial."

"My thoughts, exactly," said Smee. "I think we should hustle back up to York County tomorrow and lean on Phil a lot harder."

"Good idea," said Starkey.

Next day, when they returned to Big Barney's farm, about a three-hour drive from FBI headquarters, there was no sign of Landsberry. His bed in a cozy apartment above the tack room appeared to be undisturbed. There were no clothes in his closets or his chest of drawers.

The two agents called in the local police and told them to treat the room like a crime scene. They put out an all-points bulletin for the missing man. Big Barney, reached at his office, expressed surprise, alarm—and he feigned ignorance.

"I don't know where he is! Why would he run?"

"Did he have a car?"

"An old Chevy. A '65 Belair!"

Maryland State troopers found the car at a rest stop on southbound Route 95 that day. They found dried blood on the asphalt by the left front tire.

47

Lola in Love

L ola felt compelled to consult with Jimmy Johnson about the best way to deal with Twyla Boundary, who now knew of Lola's involvement in the burglary. Lola had little respect the opinions of anyone else on the board. Big Barney was a red-faced, purple-nosed drunk. Captain Smart was a quibbling bureaucrat, and a sexist. Johnson was handsome and resolute—and he spoke fluent Spanish, so they could communicate with none of the misunderstandings that her imperfect English sometimes caused. Johnson also possessed a menacing swagger that she admired. He was matter-of-factly ruthless. He did not hesitate to eliminate a problem "with extreme prejudice." He was untroubled by morality. He was decisive, the absolute monarch of his enterprises. This turned her on.

Lola, whose father ran a Mexican drug cartel, had a similar worldview. So, Jimmy Johnson and Lola had bonded. She had knocked Ferguson cold with the Ogden Titanium in Rock Creek Park and then helped Johnson wrap him in duct tape and put him in the back of Johnson's black Escalade.

Lola first met Johnson many years ago at a Cisco fundraiser.

She flippantly offered him some cocaine, seeing if she could shock him. He surprised her. He said he wanted some, given that the fundraising party was such a boring affair.

Lola was a small-time dealer, supplying a few congressmen and lobbyists with the drug to supplement her meagre Capitol Hill salary. Her high-quality product impressed Johnson. He asked her to partner with him. It was Johnson's brain child to give the cocaine to members of Congress for free, in exchange for political favors. He had previously formed a "Big Barney Super Pac" for corporate clients seeking favors from the Speaker. Barney trusted Jimmy, and he liked the idea of supplying drugs. Drug use among caucus members was rampant. If a Democratic congressman got caught buying drugs on a D.C. street corner, the deal could end up in a major investigation that would disgrace the party. Controlled distribution would keep the members away from the street gangs and give the speaker leverage.

Barney soon had enough subservient legislatures by the nose to deliver on most corporate requests, be it for tax cuts or regulatory roll backs. Cash poured into his campaign coffers, which enabled Big Barney to bankroll the reelection campaigns of the congressmen who were playing ball with him. The combination of cocaine and campaign funds was a fabulous inducement—a veritable choke collar.

Barney, himself, could siphon off a small fortune. He had millions stashed in offshore banks and exotic hedge funds.

Lola too had become exceedingly wealthy, well beyond her dreams, and her family's drug enterprise benefitted handsomely. Lola's two cousins smuggled the dope from family-owned farms in Mexico, hidden in corn shipments to Jimmy Johnson's feed silos in North Carolina. Johnson personally delivered coke to Lola in Washington, D.C., bring the shipments aboard his corporate jet.

Johnson treated Lola and her cousins well, with cash payments regular as clockwork. She had no complaints about the man. That was unusual for Lola, who found fault with almost everyone.

Lola was driving the four hours from the Capital all the way to Murfreesboro, North Carolina to meet with Johnson, because she no longer trusted the telephone. Government agencies monitored cell phones night and day.

Lola always maintained a healthy paranoia. A successful executive in a thriving criminal enterprise must assume that the cops always are just one step behind. She encrypted her emails, used toss-away cell phones, and made certain sno one ever saw her with her cousins.

Lola knew that the FBI had a small task force assigned to the Ferguson murder because this tidbit had been in the Observer. The risk to the organization was high because of all the special agents asking questions. She had done her best to have the FBI follow the leader—her boss, Senator Kent Cisco—by spreading word to certain reporters, including Martin Boundary, that Cisco had a violent temper. That effort had failed. Preston Ferguson, who had tried to blackmail the organization, was now the chief suspect, thanks to quick thinking by Jimmy. Lola could not have hoped for a better outcome.

The board had assumed that Ferguson had shared his knowledge of Malone's letters with his wife. But she went to her death protesting ignorance. The FBI had found no copies of Malone's letters inside the Ferguson home, else Lola would be in jail. It appeared Preston's fail-safe system that would deliver the letters to the police in the event of his death was a lie.

But what if Ferguson had set up a fail-safe? Part of Lola wanted to flee the country right now. She had a healthy stack of cash in a bank in San Juan Del Cabo on the tip of Mexico's lovely Baja Peninsula, a popular resort. But Lola's affection for Johnson prevented her from fleeing.

In fact, Ferguson had set up a fail-safe system, albeit a flawed one. A young, inexperienced Washington estate lawyer named Carter Buscombe Smith had two sealed envelopes locked in his safe. Ferguson had instructed the lawyer in writing to deliver the letters if he ever came to harm. One letter was for Rooster Radley at the Observer and the other for Martin Boundary. Though Ferguson had disappeared, he was not yet officially dead;and there was speculation he faked his death to avoid dealing with the collapse of his television program. It caught Smith in a quandary. Should he open and read the letters, given his client's disappearance? Should he deliver the letters to the recipients? But then, Ferguson might show up.

Smith, a 32-year-old who had a barely profitable practice, decided it best to abide strictly by the bar's ethics and strictly adhere to Ferguson's instructions.

Johnson's plantation-style mansion was in the middle of 300 acres just east of Murfreesboro. The main house crowned a small hill that provided spectacular views of the countryside, including a wide stretch of the Chowan River.

A uniformed guard at a Check Point Charlie-type sentry post checked Lola's driver's license and then opened the gate to Johnson's long, twisting driveway. As Lola motored along it, she marveled at the pork king's manicured domain, including his golf course with a star-shaped, five-acre lake as its centerpiece. Jimmy had told her he stocked the lake with alligators.

Johnson had set aside 100 acres of the estate running down to the river as a forest preserve for wild boar hunting. The remaining property contained a state-of-the-art pig-breeding facility, powered by methane from hog excrement.

The reptiles were Johnson's newest fixation. He contemplated exporting canned gator meat to China.

Lola noticed that clubhouse by the course was still under construction. The building looked like a glass palace. Jimmy told her he wanted to hold a major professional golf tournament on his estate to promote his pork company.

"My course will be more fabulous than Augusta," he had boasted. She had been to the famous Augusta course and could see that he had not been exaggerating.

The first five holes were difficult. On each, golfers had to drive the ball over one of the fingers of the star-shaped lake. Johnson had played three solo rounds on his course, and his scores were in the 70s, which was superb considering difficulty. But he had never driven a ball from between the teeth of an enemy there, which was at the top of his bucket list.

Johnson came down from his veranda and greeted Lola with a perfunctory kiss on her left cheek.

"Welcome to Hog Heaven—that's what I call this place."

She laughed. She wrinkled her nose. Jimmy guided her to a set of wicker chairs on the veranda where a deaf serving woman poured them iced coffee. After some small talk, Lola sheepishly told him about the break-in at the Boundary house and her subsequent blunder with the recording pen that allowed Twyla Boundary to link her to the burglary of her home. Lola expected Jimmy to explode in anger. Instead, he

312

shrugged and agreed with her it would be best if the Boundarys vanished—and the sooner, the better. He dismissed Big Barney's concern about his having committed too many murders. That was mere squeamishness.

"There are dozens of murders each week in Washington. The city's Keystone Kops cops can't keep up with them. The Boundarys will be another statistic."

Jimmy's eyes sparkled with maniacal glee as he fantasized about killing both Boundarys on his new golf course. The boxer was big and brave and would submit to his little obsession with driving golf balls, should he offer to spare Twyla's life. Of course, this would be a false promise.

Johnson instructed Lola to have her cousins bring the couple to his estate.

"It must be a clean snatch. I don't want either one of them physically damaged. Are your cousins capable of that?"

"They have disappeared hundreds of people in Mexico," Lola said proudly. "There is never a trace, only the tears of their loved ones."

"I want each of them trussed in duct tape, shoulder to foot, like Egyptian mummies. This is very important."

"Why not plastic ties?" asked Lola. Ties, she thought, would be simpler and safer.

Jimmy's eyes narrowed and his nostrils flared.

"Do exactly as I say," he snarled.

He chilled Lola to her bones.

"Yeah, Jimmy. Sure Jimmy. Duct tape."

48

Passion Unleashed

Martin Boundary furiously crutched his way down St. Asaph Street and pounded on Twyla's front door, nervously waiting for her to answer. The thought he had been the victim of a cruel internet hoax crossed his mind. But when Twyla opened the door, she was smiling radiantly. Boundary threw his arms around her, allowing his crutches to clatter to the sidewalk, buried his head into her shoulder and wept for joy.

"Oh, God, Twyla, I've missed you! I've never been so miserable in my life."

Twyla cried too. She told him she forgave him and that she believed Malone drugged him. She invited him inside, closed the door and invited him to sit down on her couch, a contemporary piece she had gotten from Ikea. She sat down beside him.

"I have great news, Martin. We're going to have a baby."

His jaw dropped. His eyes lit up. He whooped like a Hollywood Indian. He embraced her again.

"When?"

"In eight months, silly."

"Math was never my forte," he laughed. "This is the greatest news ever. Can I tell my mom and dad?"

"Of course, you can."

Twyla told him she had something else to tell him. Her voice changed. She sounded frightened.

"Lola Gutierrez was behind the break-in. So, there may be a Cisco connection."

"Are you sure? That doesn't add up. She tried to implicate Cisco in Malone's murder."

Twyla told Boundary about his spy pen and how she had purchased one of her own to spy on it. Then she showed him the video footage of Lola retrieving his pen from her desk.

"Maybe DeSales had it right. Lola must have been spying on you for Cisco."

"I am frightened, Martin. I don't know what to do. Should I go to the police or tell Big Barney? What do you think?"

"I think we definitely should report this to Capitol Police. I have a contact—Captain Andy Smart."

"I think I've seen him around. But can we trust him? One of the police must have let her into my office."

"Andy is okay."

Boundary immediately texted the details of what Twyla had told him to Sharp's personal cell phone number. Sharp called back within a minute and told Boundary he was 100 miles away on Virginia's Assateague Island, taking part in a surf-fishing tournament.

"Tell you what, Martin, I'll come over to your house when I get back the day after tomorrow. Are you going to be around?"

"Sure. I'll be here. We live on St. Asaph Street in Old Town, now." Boundary gave Sharp the address.

"You'll be my first stop," said Sharp.

Boundary told Twyla what the cop had said.

"In the meantime, we'd better take precautions. You are not to leave this house alone. Understand me, Twyla? I escort you to the Jeep. When you come home from work, I escort you back inside. I saw a guy sitting across the street the other day — a nasty-looking dude. He left after you drove off. It was the same guy who handed Fisty an envelope before the sparring match."

"You were looking out for me, weren't you, Martin?"

"Yes. I sat on the concrete staircase across the street."

"I'm thrilled that you did that," she said. "It shows that you love me." She threw her arms around his neck and kissed him passionately on the lips. He kissed her back with equal passion. She leaned back into the cushions. He laughed for joy and unbuttoned her blouse. She unbuckled his pants and shoved her hands inside his underwear.

49

Planning

Uncle jumped up from behind his oak desk.

"Paolo! Luiz! What a pleasant surprise. What brings you back to Mexico?'

"We need your help in planning a snatch, Uncle," said Paolo "It's a rush job."

Paolo and Luiz were first cousins of Lola Gutierrez. Though they were a year apart in age, they could have been twins. Both young men had Aztec lineage. They had light brown skin and dark-black eyes. Both were stocky and relatively short at five-foot-six. Each face was broad and featured the ancestral hooked nose and an extra fold of skin on the eyelids, which gave them a sleepy look.

But this pair was not sleepy. They were enterprising. They made certain that Uncle's drugs made the journey undetected from Mexico to Johnson, a complex task that required cunning and ruthless efficiency.

The cousins were bold but not cocky. They operated from detailed plans. Orchestrating the kidnapping of Martin and Twyla Boundary would be a challenge. They had been closely watching the pair. The Boundarys were athletic and wary.

They sensed that they were in danger and took precautions. Every morning, Martin Boundary carefully checked the street before he and his wife walked to her mustard-colored Jeep. Every evening, escorted her from the Jeep to the front door.

Boundary had installed security cameras outside the front and back door of the townhouse. Probably he also had installed window alarms and motion detectors on the inside.

Uncle—Lola's father—examined surveillance photos of the Boundary residence. The paunchy, grey-haired man with the salt-and-pepper goatee looked grandfatherly. One never would have guessed that he had been a cold-blooded hit man in his youth. As a leader of the family cartel, he also had planned several kidnappings and disappearances. Uncle never boasted by leaving severed heads as some of his competitors often did. His victims vanished without a trace. Uncle's greatest feat had been the snatching of 50 police cadets in two school buses. Neither the men nor the vehicles ever were found. Uncle was the only man on earth who knew where the remains were because he had killed the ten men who had helped him conduct that bloody operation.

Paolo and Luiz lived in awe of Uncle. He had been like a father to them after a rival cartel gunned down their own father as he crossed the Sierra Madre mountains with pack horses laden with cash from the family's U.S. operations. Paolo was 12 years old and Luis was 14 years old when that happened. By the time the boys reached 14 and 16, Uncle had identified the six members at the competing cartel who had committed the murders. He had pictures of each hombre, of their homes and families, and detailed street maps of their neighborhoods. He helped his young nephews meticulously plan to snatch the men, one at a time, to avenge the murder of their father.

He trained the cousins to shoot and to stab and to act with emotional detachment in the administration of cruelty.

"They tortured your father. They cut him into tiny pieces while he was alive," Uncle told the boys. "You must repay them in kind." And they did.

The detailed intelligence collected by Paolo and Luiz about the Boundarys impressed Uncle. They had catalogued Martin and Twyla's movements down to the minute. The nephews had photos of the street in front of the townhouse and of the alley behind it. They had studied pedestrian and vehicular traffic along the block to determine times of peak activity. They knew when cop cars would drive past. They knew how many people went in and out of the Trader Joe's market across the street at any hour. They knew the daily routines of neighbors.

After presenting Uncle with their dossier, Paolo and Luiz sat in stony silence while he carefully absorbed the information. When he finished paging through it, he smiled warmly.

"Great work, boys! Martin and Twyla Boundary are both influential people. You can't walk up in public and bump them on the head. You must take them in a quiet place, like their own home."

"Tainted food, Uncle?" asked Paolo. They had subdued tough hombres in the past by inducing them to eat drug-laced desserts.

"Yes, food. That's a good idea."

"But how, Uncle?" asked Paolo.

"Mrs. Boundary is expecting a baby. So, what if Lola's friend Sadie sends the lady a gift of wine?"

"Mrs. Boundary does not drink—because of the baby," said Luiz. "Sadie said so. It is in the report."

Uncle thumbed through the report again and wrinkled his brow. He was thinking.

"The problem here is that both Boundarys must eat or drink the same thing at the same time. If one goes under before the other, then we have a problem. We need two, simultaneously sedated persons."

"Steaks– a gift box of filet mignon," said Luiz. "I got a gift box of steaks once."

"Too complicated. The cooking could break down the drug," said Uncle. "But you are onto something. We will deliver a cake to them. No, make it an apple pie. I am thinking of Snow White. Remember that fairy tale? Imagine a gourmet apple pie—one that two normal Americans cannot resist.

50

Poison Pies

The most popular pies in the Washington, D.C., metro area came from a restaurant called "Sid's Terribly Delicious New York Deli and Dessert Factory," which occupied a large space on the busy corner of 13th and G Streets, N.W., about three blocks from the White House. A grossly obese president had enshrined the restaurant by gorging himself there during his three years in office. He had died of a sudden heart attack before completing year four.

Sid's was always crowded, regardless of the time of day. The deli served breakfast, lunch, and dinner and midnight snacks. The epicurean landmark was a popular hangout for journalists, bureaucrats, and spies. Occasionally, some White House honchos longing to look in touch with the common man dropped in, hoping that someone would snap and Tweet photos of them tearing into a corned beef on rye.

Paolo and Luiz on Friday bought an apple-cinnamon pie, which they gift wrapped after lacing it with ketamine crystals. They attached a gift note, purportedly from Sadie, reading, "Congratulations on the Newest Boundary." They had stolen a Ford van from a dealer's lot in Hybla Valley, just south of

Alexandria, and had a nearby chop shop paint it to look like one of Sid's ubiquitous purple and gold delivery vehicles.

The box contained more than a pie and poison. This was an age of science, not fairy tales. Hidden in one fold of the cardboard box was a tiny listening device, which would to let them eavesdrop on the Boundarys as they reacted to the gift. Although the microphone was as tiny as a pinhead, it was powerful enough to pick up the sound of chewing and the thud of bodies dropping to the floor.

The cousins tested and re-tested the device at various distances. The audio was superb—clear as a bell up to 500 feet, and adequate up to 1,500 feet. The microphone was well worth the $5,500 they had plunked down at a spy shop for the setup which included a receiver and headphones. They'd add it to the bill submitted to Jimmy for "delivery services."

Luiz emailed a letter to the Boundarys on what looked like official Sid e-stationary advising them to expect a Saturday delivery of the pie. He even included a toll-free number to reschedule the shipment. Lola had hired a woman to play the part of customer representative should the Boundarys call; but they never did.

Paolo and Luiz pulled up outside the Boundary house in the van at 10 a.m. sharp, Saturday. They double parked. Paolo carried the box with the pie to the front door and rang the bell. Twyla answered the intercom.

"Who is it?"

"Sid's Deli," he said. "Pie from Miss Sadie for Mr. and Mrs. Martin Boundary."

"Please leave it by the door," she said. Twyla and Martin had agreed on a protocol for deliveries. They would not open the door while the delivery man was present, lest it be a setup for a home invasion.

"Yes, ma'am," Paolo said. "No need to tip if you really don't want to." He placed the pie on the doormat and climbed back into the van. Luiz drove around the block, pulled up to a curb on Wythe Street, put on headphones, and tuned a receiver to the frequency of the hidden microphone.

They heard the front door open and close, followed by the rustling of paper.

"It's a congratulatory gift from Sadie!" they heard Twyla say. "Mmmm, it smells divine. I've heard Sid's apple pie is to die for."

The two kidnappers smiled at one another.

"Would you like a slice, Martin?"

"Maybe we should wait for Captain Sharp." The cop was to stop by that afternoon on his way back from Assateague Island.

"I can't wait. I'm a pregnant woman."

"Give me a minute, Twyla. I have to answer this email. I think I may have a job interview—with a TV station." He sounded upbeat.

"That's great, Martin. I think I'll have a piece. I'm so starved. Martina is hungry too." She laughed. Her nickname for the unborn child was still new.

"You mean that you and Hulk are starving," bellowed Martin Boundary. The child's sex remained a mystery.

Luiz and Paolo looked at one another. They both frowned. Were there four people in the house? Their research had turned up no one named Martina or Hulk. And was Twyla going to eat the first slice alone? If Twyla Boundary conked out before anyone else had a bite, then they'd have to resort to Plan B.

Luiz started the van and pulled into the alley that ran directly behind the row of townhouses where each unit had a rear entrance. Paolo had had the foresight to bring a tactical ram with an air-powered assist that delivered 40,000 pounds of force, enough power to knock a locked door off its hinges. An F-16 fighter jet's engine exerts about 17,000 pounds of force. Paolo and Luiz could burst into the townhouse, regardless of how many deadbolts were on the door, and subdue Martin Boundary with Tasers while he fretted over his unconscious, wife. They would move so quickly that he'd never know what hit him.

The criminals climbed out of the van and stood by the back door, ram in hand. Paolo was wearing headphones, hooked to a portable receiver that was the size of a cell phone. He heard Boundary say, "Okay. Done. Sending my resume. Pie time!"

"Hurry. The baby and I are so famished, we might eat the entire pie," Twyla laughed. He heard Boundary make an "mmm" sound. He heard Twyla setting out some plates and flatware. Boundary said, "Let's dig in!" A few seconds later, the brothers heard a loud thump. Then another.

"Show time," said Luiz.

51

Hog -Tied

Martin Boundary woke up in the back of a van, trussed neck to ankles in duct tape, including a piece covering his mouth.

'Idiots,' he thought. There were videos all over the internet instructing persons how to free themselves from duct tape. You didn't have to be a Houdini because duct tape, although uncommonly sturdy, is far from indestructible. As the videos showed, the tape would rip apart when subjected to directed force.

Boundary moved his jaw up and down in a chewing motion and liberated his mouth from the tape. He whispered Twyla's name. She did not answer. He rolled around in the dark interior of the van until he struck something soft in the front of the cargo space. He poked her with his head and whispered her name again. There was no response. He put his ear against her. He could hear a rhythmic breathing.

"Praise Jesus," he said.

Boundary tried bending his legs to loosen the tape, but he was jolted by the knifelike pain his right knee, which had been injured by Fisty. He then arched his back to loosen the tape around his torso, but he was limited in the force he could exert by his fractured ribs. Twyla's life depended on him getting free of his bond. In one of the videos that Boundary had seen on YouTube, a well-constructed man wrapped in duct tape and placed on his back had been able to turn on his side, bend his knees and then arch his back again and again in rapid succession in order to weaken the material. The man had used time-lapse photography. Boundary estimated that it had taken about 20 minutes of continuous effort for him to shred the tape. Boundary might have to struggle for considerably more time because of his knee and rib injuries.

What Boundary did not realize was that his kidnappers had wrapped him in two layers of duct tape. They only had enough tape then to give Twyla the once-over; but they were confident the single wrap would hold the tiny woman.

The truck had about 10 linear feet of cargo space and a height of about five feet. Boundary estimated the width at four feet. They had put Twyla in the front portion of the cargo space, up against the cab.

Boundary surmised by the hum of the tires they were moving at a fairly high speed down a major highway. He'd have to be careful not to shake the van too much as he slipped his bind.

Boundary slithered to the back of the truck where there was plenty of lateral space. Then, he gritted his teeth and exerted force by rapidly and repeatedly jerking his body, which jolted his injured knee and rib cage with repeated shocks of intense pain. Boundary counted out the seconds to measure the duration of each of his struggles. He reached eight counts on his first attempt. He waited for his pain to subside and tried again, this time wriggling furiously to the count of 10. The tape still held. The only consequence of his struggle was more pain and lots of sweat. He concluded that he would have to push himself to count closer to 20 to weaken his bonds.

"You can do it. Ignore the pain. Your body is strong; and your mind is stronger than your body. You will free yourself and save Twyla and then kick ass!" he said aloud.

Boundary gritted his teeth again and determinedly threw himself into the effort. The strain on his injuries was enormous, but he kept going. He hit five, then 10. He urged himself, 'Keep going. Think of your wife, your child!' On the count of 15, the van crossed a piece of roadway buckled from the hot weather. The impact tossed Boundary into the air and sideways, slamming him into the side of the left wall of the van. His injured ribs took the lion's share of the impact and his pain was so intense that he immediately passed out.

52

Curiosity

Attorney Carter Buscombe Smith was leaving his office early, carrying with him the two letters entrusted to him by Ferguson. He hailed a cab and instructed the driver to take him to his home in Chevy Chase, about a 15-minute ride. Smith had a Sub-Zero freezer at home. He had just read instructions on the internet on secretly opening letters by freezing them, which reduced the adhesion of the glue. The letters could be resealed as the glue thawed. He had Ferguson's two letters in his briefcase because his instincts told him that Ferguson had come to a terrible end. He'd look at the contents of the letters and then decide whether to pretend he had never read them or to alert the authorities.

Smith lived in his childhood home on Nebraska Avenue. He had updated the 150-year-old Dutch Colonial after his parents passed away, leaving him the property. He could have easily sold it, but he had too many cherished memories of the place to let it go. His train platform built when he was eight years old still occupied most of the basement. His childhood room had his Scout honors and academic awards on bookshelves and on the walls.

Smith remodeled the kitchen and the two-and-a-half bath-rooms, refinished the hardwood floors, and converted dining room into a home theater with a 56-inch television with surround sound and an extensive library of old movies. He was in the long process of watching all 65 of the films in which British comedian Peter Sellers ever had appeared.

Smith's furnishings were modern and hip. A maid service kept the place spotless. He occasionally had a house guest—a woman named Priscilla with whom he carried a long-distance love affair via Skype.

The deep freeze method of unsealing an envelope was perfect for Smith because he did not own a teapot with which to steam it open. He had purchased a $5,000 a Sub-Zero refrigerator-freezer because his designer had told him it would enhance the value of the house if ever he should sell.

Smith often mulled a move to Sarasota, Florida where he could press his suit of fair Priscilla. However, his relocation remained highly theoretical because of Smith's strong attach-ment to his two-story house and the lukewarm reaction by Priscilla when he once mentioned the possibility.

Smith placed one of the envelopes next to some salmon steaks He closed the door and waited 20 minutes. The deep freeze was set at 15 degree below zero, the summer tempera-ture of the South Pole. Twenty minutes should be more than enough time for the glue to freeze, he surmised.

Smith retrieved the envelopes and found that the flap re-mained sealed.

He sat down on a white, wooden chair by his kitchen table, wondering what to do. His heart was racing. He was short of breath. He stumbled to the sink and took a glass of water. Ferguson forcefully had instructed him not to open the letters.

That did not mean that someone else could not open the letters. He was certain that something terrible had befallen Ferguson and that the letters might provide a clue.

53

Survival Instinct

Twyla regained consciousness an instant before the truck struck the bump in the highway. Bounced, but not as violently as Martin, owing to her position towards the front of the truck.

Twyla was groggy—but alert enough to remember watching the YouTube video on escapes with Martin. They had joked about it because how many persons were kidnapped and bound with duct tape? Really! They had been amazed that the video had attracted 500,000 views. Twyla made chewing motions, and the tape came loose from the sides of her mouth and fell to the floor, just as had happened on the instructional video.

"Martin," she said. There was no response. The back of the van was pitch black. She wondered if she was alone. She did not want to raise her voice too high. Twyla snaked her way across the deck of the truck toward the back door and bumped into something that felt like a body.

"Martin?"

She could hear heavy breathing.

"Martin?" She spoke directly into his ear. "Can you hear me? I need you to wake up."

She said a Hail Mary and wiggled across the metal floor to a spot with more room, then began to kick her legs and twist her upper body in a titanic struggle with her adhesive bonds. Her exertions stretched her bonds and loosened the tape's grip. A small seam appeared by her hands, which were flat against her thighs. She could wiggle her fingers. After another round of struggling, she could claw away some tape, which weakened the integrity of the entire mummy wrap.

Twyla rested. She was exhausted, hungry and thirsty, and she desperately had to pee.

"Oh God," she uttered. She thought her bladder would burst. She wet herself—and then she cried. She was so tired. She was pregnant. She was in danger and so was her baby and her husband. She felt profoundly helpless.

"God, please help me!"

Twyla snaked and kicked and bent again, with more effort. She could feel that she was making progress. She twisted and kicked and bent her body as rapidly as she could. Then she felt the truck decelerate. The vehicle made a sharp turn that sent her rolling into the wall and then resumed its course at a lower speed. They were off the highway and must probably close to some horrible destination, like a quarry pit. She would not have much more time to escape.

Twyla was sweating, reeking of urine and growing weak. The van rattled and bump as if it were going down a dirt road. And then, suddenly, it stopped. She heard both doors of the truck's cab open and shut. Two men were speaking to one another in Spanish. Then, there was a third voice, also speaking Spanish. And then the third voice broke into Southern-accented English and said, "Bring me Martin Boundary so I can take care of him first."

332

Twyla recognized that voice. She had heard it in Big Barney's office and hundreds of times on the television and the radio and the internet. It was Jimmy Johnson, the king of pork. Johnson wanted them dead? Why would Johnson want to hurt them? What the hell was going on? Johnson was one of Big Barney's biggest contributors. Neither she nor Martin had ever had direct contact with him.

She heard the back door of the van rattle. She could not let her captives see her hands, which now were free. She turned over on her belly. She would fake unconsciousness hoping to buy more time. She might not save Martin, but she damn well would save their baby.

54

Disbelief

Attorney Smith handed the letters Ferguson had entrusted to him to FBI agents Starkey and Smee. The agents thanked him, expecting he was providing them with a lead for their investigation of the television reporter's sudden disappearance. They would need a warrant from a judge to open the letters. This could take a day or more. A faster means would be to deliver the letters to each of the intended recipients and hope that either Boundary or Rooster Radford, or both, would share the contents with them. This was the course they selected.

Starkey took Rooster Radley's letter while Smee headed over to Twyla Boundary's townhouse in Alexandria with the one addressed to Martin Boundary. She might know her estranged husband's current whereabouts.

Starkey arrived at the Observer in just under 10 minutes. He had to cool his heels at the front desk while the rent-a-cop cleared him through and printed him out an identification badge, complete with a blurry color picture. Then he had to wait for a copy boy to come down and escort him to Rooster.

Starkey walked hurriedly through the newsroom behind the

copy boy. Truitt, who was pounding out a story on a budget agreement, immediately recognized Starkey as a Fed. The gray suit, brown belt with matching brown shoes, and military-style haircut were clear giveaways. All Feds dressed alike, with no sense of fashion. Truitt preferred black shoes with gray.

'What's this about?' Truitt wondered, as Rooster ushered the agent into his glass-walled office. The agent was telling Rooster something and Rooster's eyes had widened. The agent reached into the lining pocket of his jacket and produced an envelope which he handed to Rooster. Rooster tore it open and hurriedly read it. Then Rooster, in animated fashion, said something to the agent. Rooster picked up his telephone receiver, pushed a speed-dial button, and shouted something. Kitty Cross came running from the rear of the vast newsroom and into his office. He handed the letter to her, and she scurried out to a utility room that contained a copying machine. About five minutes later, she rushed back into Rooster's office with a stack of paper.

Truitt had gotten up from his desk and moved towards the utility room to ask Kitty what was happening. She waived him off as she ran back towards Rooster. Truitt noticed that Kitty had forgotten to remove the original from the copier. When he picked up the paper, he saw that it was a letter written in violet ink. It was signed "Bernadette Kathleen Malone." He read it and re-read it.

"Jumping Jesus, this can't be true! A dope ring? Forty drug-addled congressmen? Big Barney? Jimmy Johnson killing Hastings! It has to be a scam." But then, based on Rooster's reaction and a Fed, he could not dismiss it as one. This possibly was a huge story, and he'd be a laughingstock if he missed it, because the ring had been operating right under his nose, and

335

he was supposedly the best reporter on Capitol Hill.

Truitt replaced the letter on the copier and hurried back to his desk. He dialed a "hotline" number for Barney and when the Speaker answered, he told him about the letter and asked if it were true

"I need it on the record, Mr. Speaker."

"Come on, Malcolm, the letter is ridiculous on its face. Do you really believe I could be spoon feeding cocaine to 40 congressmen and get away with it? This is a hoax. Don't get suckered by it, my boy. You'll end up looking like a first class ass. Listen, duty calls. I've got to run."

Truitt thought Barney was right. The letter was ridiculous on its face. But then, why would Malone write such a thing? He called congressmen named in the letter to see what each had to say.

Meanwhile, Rooster was re-reading the letter to himself and muttering, and swearing like a carpenter who had nailed his thumb with a hammer.

Starkey grabbed a copy the letter from Cross and quickly scanned it. He could not believe what he was reading. Was it truth or fiction?

"Where's the original?"

"I must have left it on the copier. Wait here. I'll get it."

"No," said Starkey. "It's evidence. I'll get it." He removed a pair of latex gloves from one of his pockets and retrieved the original.

"I ask you not to write about this," he said to Rooster when he returned to the office. "The letter may or may not be real. If it is real, then I would not want to tip off any of the principals of its existence. "

"I'll give you 24 hours," said Rooster. "After that, we will

336

make phone calls."

Over on the south side of the Potomac River, Smee pulled up to the Boundary residence and knocked on the front door. A uniformed policeman opened it, surprising Smee, who showed the cop his FBI identification.

"What happened?" Smee asked.

The policeman said he was investigating a report from an elderly woman who lived in a unit across the alleyway from the Boundary's rear door. She had seen two men in a delivery van smash in the back door.

"Looks like they used an air-powered ram, because the door was off its hinges," the patrolman said. The patrolman walked the agent into the kitchen. Smee saw two forks, two broken dishes, and two slices of half-eaten apple pie strewn on the floor. He stooped down and probed the pie with a pen. He noticed tiny white crystals.

"They drugged them. Did you get a vehicle description?"

"A purple delivery van from a D.C. deli. The deli owner says it could not have been one of his."

Although it was against procedure, Smee opened the letter to Boundary from Malone. His gut told him that Boundary and Twyla were in mortal danger and that the letter might contain relevant information.

Smee read it and then reread it.

"My God. This is unbelievable!"

Malone had laid out the entire history of the Cocaine Caucus and detailed the murder of Hastings and her conversion into pig manure at Jimmy Johnson's estate. She detailed other murders and unsolved cases from other jurisdictions that Malone attributed to the cousins of Lois Gutierrez. Malone also described Jimmy's sick boast one evening about making

337

people disappear. This, she felt, he intended as a warning to her. The threat, she wrote, had occasioned her decision to compose her letters.

"If ever I disappear, it was Jimmy! He's insane," she had written in violet ink.

Smee immediately phoned Starkey.

"The Boundarys have been kidnapped. I think I know where they are—at Johnson's estate in North Carolina. The man is a lunatic," Smee said.

"I've read Malone's letter, too. Do you think the stuff she says is real?"

"Yes, I do, because the Boundarys were kidnapped this morning by two men in a delivery truck. There's a witness—one of their neighbors. I think you ought to request that the North Carolina State Police get to the Johnson estate right away. Fax them a copy of the letter so they can get a warrant."

Starkey said, "The letters could be a hoax. We have lifted no prints or analyzed the handwriting and the ink."

"We can't wait. If the letter is bullshit—well, I'm willing to take the chance."

"How can we be sure it was Johnson who kidnapped them?"

"We can't. All we have to go on is this letter. Look, I may be putting my career in jeopardy, but my gut tells me that the Boundarys are in terrible danger, so I'm willing to take the chance."

"I'm with you all the way," said Smee.

Smee got into his car and used his onboard computer to scan the letter and attach it to an email. In defiance of FBI protocol, he faxed it to the North Carolina State Police and then followed up immediately with a phone call.

338

"Are you sure of this?" asked a State Police detective. "Johnson's a enormous deal down where with lots of political clout."

"Drag your feet, detective, and you will have innocent blood on your hands," said Smee.

Smee started his car and steered it towards the ramp to Route 95 South and the Marine Corps base at Quantico, Virginia, where the bureau had a helicopter. If his superiors cooperated with him and authorized an emergency flight, then he might find the Boundarys' bodies before the pigs got through with them.

He swore. Dealing with his superiors would be a nightmare. He sent them a copy of Malone's letter.

55

The Smell of Death

The back doors of the van opened suddenly. Twyla, her eyes shut, heard a man climb into the cargo compartment.

"Shit, man, it smells like piss in here," he said. He poked Twyla in the ribs with the pointed toe of his cowboy boot. The jab was painfully sharp, but she didn't squeal. The man poked her again, harder this time. Twyla continued to play possum.

"The girl is still out," he said.

She heard Martin moan. The man must have poked his ribs too.

"The big man is awake. Help me lift him."

She heard Martin being dragged across the van's bare metal floor. The two men were breathing heavily as they pushed and pulled him. Then the doors closed again. Twyla waited a minute and then resumed her struggle against the duct tape.

Paolo and Luiz were small, but powerful. They took a few minutes to move Boundary's limp body from back of the van and lay him in the back of a golf cart to drive him down to a lakeside tee, where Johnson was twirling his Ogden Titanium like a baton while waiting impatiently for his victim. Both men were winded and soaked with sweat from the effort.

The sky was blue. The air temperature was a comfortable 78 degrees. The greens and fairways were brilliant emerald. A full moon was visible in the afternoon sky.

Johnson had been knocking balls down the fairway. He sent them long, low, and straight.

When the twins arrived with the mummified Boundary, Johnson had them place him on the tee. He told them to return to get Twyla.

"She's still asleep, Boss," said Paolo.

"Then pour water on her face." He reached into the cart and removed a plastic cup from the drink holder. "Paolo, go to the lake and fill this up."

Paolo ran to the star-shaped lake as Johnson watched with amusement. When he dipped the cup in the water, a giant gator lunged at him. Paolo screamed and fell head-over-heels backwards. He rolled head-over-heels a few more times to get away from the lake, stood, and ran like the devil. Johnson roared with laughter. Luiz scowled. The practical jokes of this madman did not amuse him. His brother could have been killed. He fingered a long switchblade knife in his pocket. He would stick it right through Johnson if ever he hurt Paolo.

Martin Boundary's eyes were closed. Johnson leaned down and smacked the boxer's cheeks until they opened. They were glassy, but fierce. Johnson let out a delighted chuckle.

"Come join us in a game of golf, Mr. Boundary," he said. Boundary struggled with his bonds. Johnson rapped him on the ribs with the driver and the boxer grimaced.

"My, my, aren't we sensitive," laughed Johnson. "I was told that my man Fist-O-Cane bruised you. You're lucky to be alive. I paid him to kill you."

Boundary was wide awake now. Johnson gave him his William Tell spiel and told him to hold the tee high in his teeth, lest the swing accidentally remove his nose. He stopped over and stuck the tee into Boundary's mouth, and Boundary defiantly spit it out.

"This is how you killed Malone, isn't it? You played with her and then bashed in her brains."

"She had no brains, which is why she found herself in such an uncomfortable predicament. She blabbed to you, Mr. Boundary. She had to be put away."

"Blabbed what? She knocked me out. I woke up in her bed. I left. We hardly exchanged two sentences."

"You are pulling my leg, Boundary."

"I am not. Anyway, what could she have told me that justified murder? " He was working his arms, trying to get free.

"Lie still and let me drive my ball. Then, I'll tell you. If you cooperate with my golf game and convince me you were in the dark, then your missus lives."

As Johnson set a new tee in his mouth, Boundary saw Al Capone's pinky ring on Johnson's hand. He knew in that instant that Johnson had killed Ferguson too. The man was a psychopath.

'He's intends to kill me and Twyla. I got to buy time,' he thought.

"Okay, it's a deal, Johnson. Give it your best shot."

Johnson carefully teed up the ball. Boundary closed his eyes. He gambled that Johnson would hit the ball, not his head. He was right. He felt the whoosh of the club. The tee sent shock waves through his teeth, and he yelled out in pain. He spit out some broken pieces of tooth and blood.

342

When he opened his eyes, Johnson delightedly was watching his ball sail down the center of the fairway. Boundary noticed that a huge alligator had come up on land from the nearby lake and that Johnson and he had not seen it. The gator appeared to be at least 10 feet long.

The reptile gave Boundary an idea. Boundary tried to keep Johnson distracted so he would not notice the beast lying behind him.

"You had me going, you know it, Johnson? I thought Cisco was the psycho killer. Now it turns out it's you. You killed the Fergusons, right?"

Johnson looked down at Boundary's blood-spattered face and beamed. He had spoiled the inquisitive young journalist's dental work. Oh well, he wouldn't be eating dinner tonight, anyway.

"You know what your problem is, Martin Boundary? You're not very analytical. You jump to conclusions. Why, for instance, would Cisco kill the daughter of a major contributor? Did that question ever enter your mind?"

"Have you killed many others, Johnson?"

"You really don't know? The girl really did not confide in you? Interesting. I thought she had blown Barney's and my little enterprise and that you had blabbed about it to your wife."

"Barney? Big Barney? What are you talking about? And Twyla and I separated. We never talked."

Johnson leaned against his Ogden Titanium and provided Boundary with the gist of the Cocaine Caucus. He withheld nothing because Boundary shortly would take this knowledge to the grave.

Boundary was astounded. How had they gotten away with it,

right at the seat of the federal government? This was a huge story.

'I'm going to be the one to break it!' he thought, unaware that his old nemesis Malcolm Truitt had a head start.

"Why not spare Twyla?" asked Boundary, when Johnson had finished. "I swear, she doesn't know a thing."

"Ah, there you are wrong, Boundary, very wrong. She knows Lola was spying on her; so, she has a dot she can connect to some other dot. Your pretty wife is a danger to us."

Johnson glanced at his wristwatch. He had a meeting in Raleigh with some supermarket executives in an hour.

"Time marches on. Farewell, Boundary."

The gator had moved within three feet of Johnson and now was still as a log.

"Take another tee shot off of me. Don't torture Twyla. She's pregnant."

Johnson smiled.

"Your self-sacrifice is admirable. Aren't you scared though?"

"I'm wagering that you have at least an ounce of decency," said Boundary.

"Wagering is for fools, Boundary, unless you own the casino. But I will take your offer. That last shot gave me great satisfaction. There's a full moon visible today? Did you notice? If you keep absolutely still, so I don't muff this shot, then I'll make sure that Twyla's passing is painless. Understand?"

"Yes."

Boundary wasn't gambling, however. He had a plan.

56

Wildcat

Twyla used her freed hands to rip at every piece of tape she could reach. This allowed her more movement to weaken her bonds. She freed herself in less than two minutes.

What next? They would come back for her. She was a kickboxer. She took a few practice kicks. When the kidnappers opened the door, she'd have a height advantage, standing in the cargo area. She would take one kidnapper out with a kick to the face and then attack the other one. They would not expect her to be waiting for them like a violent jack-in-the-box when they opened the door.

She heard the golf cart coming across the gravel parking area. The cart stopped. She heard footsteps approach the back of the van. Both doors opened. She was looking directly at Paolo, who uttered a small cry of surprise.

Before he could react, her right leg shot out and delivered a devastating blow to his jaw, breaking it. He went down, screaming and rolling around in pain. Luiz was in the cart. She leapt from the truck and ran up the gravel road leading from the parking lot. Although she had done no road work in several weeks and was a month pregnant, Twyla was still in good shape. Luiz ran after her. He was bow-legged. She was leaving him in the dust.

Johnson, who had looked up towards the parking lot when he heard Paolo scream, yelled to Luiz, "Use the golf cart, you damn ninny." Then Johnson looked down at Boundary and grinned.

"Your wife is a little wildcat! She took off for the woods. She won't get far. I have guards in Jeeps patrolling the perimeter of my property. Now where were we, exactly? Oh, yes, one more tee shot. Do you mind?"

Johnson smiled coldly and bent over to place the tee between Boundary's lips. Boundary, who understood that Johnson would eventually bash his brain, decided to begin the process early. As soon as Johnson's head was within a foot of his own, he jerked himself up with all the force he could muster and head-butted Johnson in the face, breaking the businessman's nose and sending him staggering backwards, screaming in pain. Johnson was blinded by his tears. He never saw the gator. He would have stepped on its snout had the reptile not first latched onto his foot and dragged him screaming into the lake which soon after became a bloody, frothing frenzy of swirling reptiles. Martin ignored his headache and concentrated on freeing himself from the duct tape so he could save Twyla.

Twyla looked over her shoulder and saw the golf cart coming up fast behind her. She veered off the road onto a weed-and-rock-strewn pasture on the north side, which she hoped would be rough going for her pursuer in the small-wheeled vehicle. Twyla made for some woods about 50 yards away.

Luiz followed, bouncing through the field. He was yelling into a hand-held radio with his left hand and steering with his right. He ran over a rock and nearly lost control of the cart.

As Twyla neared the woods, she heard a louder vehicle. A black Jeep was roaring up a rutted dirt track that ran through the trees.

Twyla swerved to avoid it, heading through the woods back in the direction of the golf course. She was winded, with a sharp pain in her right side. The underbrush was thick with thorns. She looked out through the trees into the pasture. Luiz had abandoned the golf cart and was hopping into the passenger side of the Jeep. She ran deeper into the woods, where the trees were bigger and a vehicle could not penetrate. She came upon a rusted metal tube fence about four feet high. She climbed over it, thinking how the fence would delay her pursuers, not the possibility it was an enclosure for dangerous beasts.

The Jeep crashed through the woods, mowing down several yards of saplings, and stopped at the fence. Twyla heard Luiz order the driver, "Stay right here. Leave this to me." That was a break: It would be a fair fight, one against one.

Luiz vaulted the fence and snapped open his switchblade when he landed on the other side. The blade was six inches long, gleaming, and saw-toothed like the mouth of a killer shark. He advanced slowly, yelling, "Bitch, now you will pay for hurting Paolo! I will cut you up good."

He swept the knife back and forth menacingly. Twyla backed up a few steps and assumed a fighter's ready stance. She had never trained against a knife-wielding assailant. She worried that she could not take him down.

"You think you can fight me, woman?" taunted Luiz. He laughed derisively and then charged her. There was blood lust in his eyes.

57

In Pursuit

Boundary freed his arms. His ribs were jolting him with electrifying pain, but his desire to rescue Twyla helped him to endure it. He stripped the tape from his legs and shoulders and then grabbed Johnson's Ogden Titanium and used it to cane his way up the gravel road towards the van.

The van was atop a small rise, and he could not see what was happening to Twyla. When Boundary reached the van, badly winded, he spotted the black Jeep in the woods several hundred yards away and concluded that the occupants were after Twyla. There was no way he could reach her quickly with his bum knee, so he opened the driver's side door of the van and climbed in. The keys were in the ignition. Boundary started the van and backed it up to turn around, almost running over Paolo, who scrambled to his feet to avoid being crushed. Paolo screamed as best he could. Luiz looked over his shoulder out across the field towards the source of the cry and saw the van driven by a man with blond hair racing towards the woods with Paolo staggering after it. When he turned back towards Twyla, he found that she had vanished into the woods. He cursed. He shouted for the armed guard who remained behind to intercept the van's driver. Then he advanced into the woods to find Twyla.

The guard ran towards the edge of the woods and trained his pistol at the windshield of the approaching van. Boundary saw him and, expecting gun fire, swerved sharply away as two of the bullets intended for him burst through the passenger side. He swerved back sharply toward the guard, and the van flipped onto its roof. The force of the crash, together with the exploding airbags, knocked him unconscious.

Twyla realized that her best hope for survival was to elude her pursuer and take him by surprise. She was gasping and out of energy. Her last meal, hours before, had been a bite of drug-laced apple pie.

Twyla searched for a makeshift weapon and found a sturdy oak stick. Then she lay flat on the forest floor and covered herself with the leaves, leaving an opening for her eyes. Her plan was to let Luiz walk past her and then jump up from behind him and club him on the head.

Twyla heard sirens in the distance and they appeared to be coming closer and closer. The sound gave her hope. Then, she saw Luiz approaching. The guard came up behind him and said something to him about a van. She could not make out their words.

"Did someone call the cops?" she heard Luiz ask the guard.

"Not that I know of. Might be a fire down the road."

Luiz told the guard to return to his Jeep and position himself to head off Twyla if she tried to make it to a two-lane road bordering Johnson's estate.

"Use a stun gun. I want to take care of her personally," he said. Then Luiz advanced carefully on foot towards the spot

349

where Twyla lay hidden. Perhaps, she had climbed a tree? He looked up. There were dozens of hiding places in the forest canopy. The sirens were getting even closer, and he swore he would find and kill her before any police arrived.

He called out, "I will find you, Chiquita. I will kill you."

Twyla's heart was pounding against her rib cage. She tightened her hand around the club. The sirens were getting closer. If she could stay hidden, then she could await the cavalry instead of trying to take out her pursuer. The man was vicious looking, and she had doubts she could succeed with her stick against his knife. She had never trained for this.

The first state police car roared into the estate and stopped at the flipped van. The trooper looked into the overturned van's cab and saw Boundary sprawled against the passenger ceiling. He radioed for the local first aid squad. The cop could not tell if Boundary was dead or alive. The doors were bent and would not open. He smashed in the glass, reached in and felt Boundary's pulse. It was strong.

The cop then went to the rear of the van to check the cargo compartment. That's when he saw Paolo staggering towards him. He noticed the tattoos on Paolo's thick forearms. They fit the description of a desperado mentioned in the FBI bulletin that had sent him and six other troopers rushing to the estate. He drew his sidearm and waited for the man to draw nearer.

Paolo raised his hands in surrender and then collapsed to his knees. The pain of his broken jaw was unbearable.

Luiz walked ahead of the spot where Twyla lay buried in the leaves. If Luiz got way ahead of her, then she could go back the way she came in. This was a more prudent option than fighting.

The problem was that Luiz was walking slowly, moving

forward five feet and then pausing minutes at a time to listen. He would move forward five feet and then stop and listen for minutes at a time. He was less than 10 feet from where she lay. Her heart continued to beat wildly. Why would he not move ahead more quickly? Then she heard the distant sound of other people walking through the woods. Maybe it was the police, she thought.

Twyla twisted her head slowly to see what was happening. Luiz was waiving at three of the estate's guards who approaching him in a line, like beaters on a hunt.

"You didn't see her?" shouted Luiz. One guard shrugged.

"Then you are around here," said Luiz. "Did you climb a tree, little bird? Don't worry. We will find you."

Now what? They paralyzed her with fear. She had had a small chance against Luiz alone. But she had no chance against Luiz and a troop of armed guards. She could not outrun them. They might shoot her down if she tried. She had to stay hidden right where she was.

Twyla was a courageous woman, but she not fearless. Since childhood, she had been phobic about roaches, rodents, and snakes. Her selected hiding place under the forest's carpet of crisp, brown leaves had disturbed a four-foot-long copperhead hiding similarly nearby. The snake suddenly slithered in front of her face. Instinctively, she jumped up and screamed at the top of her lungs, causing Luiz to jump out of his socks, to the mirth of the three guards. Luiz laughed too when he saw Twyla furiously brushing the leaves from her hair.

"Bugs, Chiquita? You are afraid of bugs?"

He charged her. Twyla plunged her arms frantically into the leaves searching desperately for her club. When she felt it, Luiz almost was on top of her. Twyla took a fierce whack at him, striking the left side of his head. The sharp sent him scuttling sideways. Twyla readied herself again as he gamely shook off the blow, smiled maliciously, and came back at her with the raised knife.

"It's a good day for you to die," he said. The three guards ran toward him, and he waved at them to stand back.

"This hellcat is all mine. Watch me cut her up into tiny pieces." He lunged at her and slashed at her with the knife. She countered with a kick to his gut that doubled him over.

The tip of Luiz's blade had caught Twyla high in the left thigh. She could feel the sting and the warm blood running down her pant leg.

"I cut you," he crowed, coming towards her again, slashing wildly. Twyla backpedaled and then hopped to one side when he leapt at her. This time, she struck him on the back of the head. Twyla was losing strength. The blow stunned him but did not slow him down. Enraged, Luiz charged once more—but it was a feint. He halted, and she swung early. He charged again, and Twyla turned and ran. Luiz grabbed her hair and pulled hard, snapping back Twyla's head. Her feet went out from under her. She was flat on her back. Luiz stood over her, holding the knife.

"I will tame her first before I kill her." He knelt down, straddling her with his knees, and pressed the serrated blade against her throat.

"You will make love," he said. Twyla sobbed.

Luiz laughed. "I changed my mind. I am just going to kill you." He raised the knife. He heard gunshots. He spun around. His companions were firing wildly into the brush. Then they scattered. A gigantic black shape exploded from the brush. It was an enormous boar with tusks at least four-feet long. Luiz stood up and froze. Twyla quickly shimmied up the trunk of a small tree. She hugged it tightly and watched as the speeding animal speared Luiz with its razor-sharp tucks. His death screams were horrible. Then there was more gunfire, and the boar dropped in its track

58

Enlightened

Boundary emerged from a coma in a Murfreesboro hospital three days later. Twyla was at his bedside when he opened his eyes. She was on crutches.

Boundary was ecstatic to see her. They kissed for a very long time. He was full of questions, like, how did she ever get away?

He was explaining, "I tried to save you, Twyla. I tried—and I failed you-again. There were tears in his eyes."

"Your crash saved me, Martin. A cop saw the overturned van and stopped. Otherwise that trooper would have driven past the golf course's access road and gone to the main house."

"What trooper? What are you talking about?"

" You're the last to know. Some newsman. The story has been in every paper in the country."

"What story?"

Then she related her tale about Luiz and the boar and the state police who shot the animal and rescued her.

"The FBI had nabbed Lola at the Texas border. Big Barney and Jimmy Johnson disappeared. The Feds believe Big Barney is in Bali, which has no extradition treaty with the U.S. They don;t know where Johnson is."

"I know exactly where Johnson is, Twyla," said Boundary.

"Good, because there's a $100,000 reward for information leading to his capture," said Twyla.

Boundary rubbed his tongue along his broken front teeth. The reward money would buy him some cosmetic dentistry.

Special Agents Smee and Starkey visited later that day, and Boundary told them approximately where they could find Johnson.

"There are hundreds of gators in that lake. I guess we'll have to slice open bellies until pieces of Johnson fall out," said Starkey.

"I'd like the hide of that crock for a pair of cowboy boots," said Boundary. "That gator saved my life. If kill the poor fellow, then the least I can do is memorialize him as fine footwear."

The agents told Martin about the discovery of the Ferguson's digested remains in the hog pen. They also told him they suspected Johnson had killed Big Barney's stable boy.

"Is this all on the record?" asked Boundary, who now had a cast around his ribs.

The agents laughed.

"This story is all over the media, 24/7. Sorry, Martin. No scoops for you. But you will be a big celebrity for a day or two when you get out of here. I am sure the world would love to your account of feeding Johnson to the alligators."

In the political realm, the discovery of the Cocaine Caucus wreaked havoc. The Justice Department indicted forty congressmen on bribery and drug charges. A new House Speaker replaced the fallen Big Barney. Several Capitol Police officers were indicted too.

No one was more eager to hear about the Boundary's narrow

escape than Rooster Redburn, the Washington Observer's fiery editor-in-chief. He and Managing Editor Kitty Cross dropped into the Murfreesboro hospital for an afternoon visit. Boundary was both surprised and shocked because Rooster was a control freak who loathed to be out of the newsroom. Boundary knew of no other occasion when Rooster had left the paper during the day, even for lunch. When Rooster was ill, the doctors visited to his office, not the other way around. When Rooster needed a haircut, the barber arrived. When Rooster had a business lunch, it always took place at a corner table in the Observer's cafeteria. During exceptionally busy news cycles, they had known Rooster to spend consecutive days at the office, catching catnaps on his couch. Now, here he was with his number two, hundreds of miles from the Capital, which meant that Dan Fogarty was in command. Boundary should have felt puffed up; but, in fact, it humbled him.

Rooster ignored the pleasantries. He was intent on business.

"Boundary, we have a sudden opening for a Capitol Hill reporter following the abrupt resignation of Malcolm Truitt."

"Truitt resigned?"

"It's a long story. Suffice to say, he tipped off Big Barney that the jig was up."

"And you want me back?"

"Yes, I want you back."

"Thank you, Chief," said Boundary. "I appreciate this more than you can know. I am so sorry that I damaged the reputation of the paper."

"You dented the reputation of the paper. Now, however, the public perceives you as a hero."

"I'd like remain on the police beat, if that's okay with you. Politics bores me to tears."

"How about it if we stretch the police beat to include crime in government?"

Boundary furrowed his brow.

"That's a pretty big assignment. Does that mean I get a raise, Chief?"

"Yes, damn it. And don't call me Chief!"

59

Uncertain Future

Boundary was back working at the Observer in two weeks. A steady stream of colleagues welcomed him back. So many of them wanted to hear his first-person account of his narrow escape from death at the hands of the demented Jimmy Johnson, that he grew weary of repeating it.

Three-thousand emails from fans clogged his inbox, and he had to sort through 30 phone messages, mostly from TV stations reaching out for interviews. He was tired of the publicity. He hated being the story. He laughed to himself ruefully when he recalled that he had wanted to be a media star like Preston Ferguson. Now, he longed for anonymity so that he could go about his work chronicling the capital's crime.

At midday, he phoned Twyla, who had begun working as chief legal counsel for Senator Kent Cisco.

"Guess what, Twyla? Rooster gave me back my old cubicle. And it was pretty much like I left it, as if he expected to rehire me some day."

"That was thoughtful."

"Truitt's cubical was given to a rookie. It's bigger than mine"

"Then you had better watch out," said Twyla. "Say, Martin, is something going on there? I'm hearing rumors."

"What sort of rumors?"

"That the Observer is on the market."

"Really?"

Boundary stood up and looked around the newsroom. Nothing was amiss. Telephones were ringing. Colleagues were working diligently on stories. A board in the front of the newsroom tallied the items that were getting the most internet views. Rooster was bawling out a reporter, blinds up. Kitty Cross was in a glassed-in conference room, conducting an editorial meeting.

"If that were true, Twyla, I would have heard something by now. Gossip spreads hear faster than the flu. And I've talked to just about everyone in the newsroom today."

"I hope it's not true," said Twyla. "There are so few good papers left."

"Yes. The public seems to be opting for sensational crap. We could end up like Dwiggens' rag. Who did you hear the rumor from, anyway?"

"Senator Cisco," she said. "He heard it from Senator Schooner of New York."

Boundary moaned. Schooner was derisively known as Mr. Wall Street. If the rumor came from him, then, perhaps, it was true.

"I'll ask Rooster about it when I can buttonhole him. A sale would be absolutely awful. There would be layoffs, and who knows what else. But I can't see the family giving up on the company—not after a century of ownership. God, I hope

Senator Schooner is wrong."

THE END

About the Author

Jim McTague is a contributing editor to Barron's and a regular guest on several radio programs, where he discusses politics and the economy.

From January 4, 1994 to June 30, 2015, he was the Washington Editor and a columnist for Barron's Business and Financial Magazine. He was also a credentialed White House and Congressional correspondent.

Jim authored "Crapshoot Investing: How Tech Savvy Traders and Clueless Regulators Turned the Stock Market into a Casino" (FT Press: March, 2011). He delivered lectures on his book's findings to financial professionals in Boston, Chicago, and New York; at the University of Iceland in Reykjavik (2014); and at the Haub School of Business of St. Joseph's University in Philadelphia, Pa. (2015).

Before 1994, Jim was the Washington bureau chief and a managing editor at American Banker newspaper; the banking reporter for USA Today; the banking reporter for the Dallas Times Herald; the Pennsylvania State House correspondent for the Philadelphia Daily News; a municipal reporter for the Asbury Park Press in New Jersey; and a line editor at TV Guide.

He earned an M.A. in English from the Pennsylvania State University and a B.S. in English from Saint Joseph's University.

Made in the USA
Middletown, DE
22 September 2018